KU-163-454

FULL MEASURE

T. Jefferson Parker

SANDSTONEPRESS
HIGHLAND | SCOTLAND

This edition published by
Sandstone Press Ltd
Dochcarty Road
Dingwall
Ross-shire
IV15 9UG
Scotland
United Kingdom

www.sandstonepress.com

First published in the USA in 2014 by
Dutton, part of Penguin Group (USA) Inc.

Web site: *www.tjeffersonparker.com*

ISBN: 978-1-908737-80-9
ISBN e: 978-1-908737-81-6

The publisher acknowledges subsidy from
Creative Scotland towards publication of this volume.

Cover design by Stuart Brill, Dorchester
Typeset by Iolaire Typesetting, Newtonmore
Printed and bound by Totem, Poland

Praise for T. Jefferson Parker's *Full Measure*

'A tense and compelling drama of the wars without and the wars within – and of the flame of violence that burns through the American psyche.'

T.C. Boyle, author of *World's End*

'Chekhov once wrote that a pistol put onstage in the first act must go off in the second act. In FULL MEASURE, the characters themselves are the guns – each a weapon defending a different idea of what America is, and all of them fully loaded with human fallibility. Thanks to intricate and excellent plotting, their struggles with one another -- and with their own consciences -- make this book as compelling as it is unpredictable.'

Stephen P. Kiernan, author of
The Curiosity and *Last Rights*

'I have always loved T. Jefferson Parker's thrillers. Now he has done something truly rare for a writer--stepped way out of his comfort zone to create the stunning *Full Measure* ... What a brave and daring writer. What a good and thoughtful-provoking read.'

Lisa See, author of *Shanghai Girls*

'Scorched earth? T. Jefferson Parker *begins* there. Emotionally devastating, tense, moving toward an explosive climax, this is a great American book by a master at the top of his game. Parker is entering *East of Eden* territory here. Family, war, racism, violence and the sometimes painful demands of love fight for air in this charred landscape of the heart. Wow!'

Luis Alberto Urrea, author of *The Devil's Highway*

For those who serve

If America ever ceases to be good, America will cease to be great.

1

The camel spiders of Afghanistan were the size of his hand but they couldn't kill his strong young body. Neither could the little saw-scaled vipers that were almost invisible on the sand and crawled into his bedding at night. The heat of the summer fighting season couldn't kill him, and not the winter cold that barreled down the mountains, heavy as a freight train, straddling them where they slept or did not sleep, on the ground behind the Hesco blocks or on rooftops or hunkered ten-to-a-room at base. The skinnies couldn't kill him with bombs hidden in the rocks or buried along the roads, nor with grenades launched from the hills or mortars fired from behind the ridgelines. Not with their AKs or sniper rifles or aged, wired-together long guns left over from other wars in another century. Not with knives or hatchets or sticks. Nothing could kill him so Patrick Norris did the killing, until they sent him from Sangin back to San Diego in the fall, a free man, twenty-two years old, wounded on the inside only.

He arrived at Lindbergh Field and when he walked into the terminal people set down their bags and clapped. He nodded once and slung his duffel over his shoulder and kept his eyes ahead.

As he washed his hands in the restroom an older man at the next sink looked at him in the mirror. "Afghanistan?"

"Yes, sir."

"Thank you."

1

"You're welcome, sir."

"Headed home?"

"Yes. Fallbrook."

The man passed a gnarled hand over the faucet sensor and the water sprayed out. "I hear the fire was bad there. When the flames hit the groves. You can still see smoke in the north."

"I know."

"I was in Korea, fifty-one and two."

"Maybe I should thank you."

"Now the South Koreans have a better health care system than we do. We're twenty-third in the world. It's all changed for the worse here. The country. The people. The government. Everything's gone bad."

"I hope you're wrong."

"It doesn't matter what you hope."

"Maybe you don't know jack, sir."

"I know it when I see it. Well, thanks again."

Norris rode the outdoor escalator down, the sun at his back and warm on the desert camo, his duffel riding the step behind him. To the south stood the downtown high-rises, and yachts bobbed on a spangled bay. He thought of all the fish under that water. The colors dazzled him. He had not seen anything like this for over a year and he felt the salty breeze on his face and held in a lungful of good American air. It smelled like heaven. Like safety, Patrick thought, finally. He counted blessings: arms and legs still attached, blood contained, brain working. He closed his eyes and thought of Myers and Zane, and they and the many other ghosts in his heart rose and hovered.

When he opened his eyes his older brother, Ted, was standing down on the ground level, smiling up at him from where the steel steps of the escalator slid underground. They hugged and slapped each others' shoulders. Ted was tall and heavy; Patrick short and lean.

2

"I'm glad you came back home," said Ted.

"Where else would I go?"

"I mean not in a box!"

"I got lucky," said Patrick. A hundred times he could have died, he knew – a thousand. You quit counting. God is Luck.

Ted slung his brother's duffel over his shoulder and they walked into the parking lot. It was hard for Ted to carry heavy things, having bad feet since birth, but Patrick let him. Two young women rolled their luggage past and Patrick and his brother looked at them but they didn't look back.

"Mom and Dad are cool that you didn't want them here to meet you," said Ted. "They understand you need some peace and quiet. But just a warning – they've got the house all decorated up for you. We're lucky it survived the fire. Almost all eighty acres of our trees are gone, Pat."

"I wish I could have done something. Command got me here as soon as they could."

Ted's pickup truck had a raised body and big tires so the men sat up high. They rode the interstate north toward Fallbrook, which lay in the hills between two small rivers, twelve miles from the Pacific. Far from town Patrick could see the pall in the sky and when they got closer the smell of fire hit him even through the air conditioning. Along the frontage road a caravan of bulldozers and backhoes clanked back and forth toward town. The air was white like fog and the burned oaks were black skeletons hung within it.

"They're just now letting people come back," said Ted. "It was mandatory to get out, Pat – big government going house to house like the Gestapos, ordering us citizens from our homes. Dad cussed them out good and we stayed. We hosed down the house and outbuildings, and what we could of the trees. Then the water pressure ran out. It took the firemen a while to get here, because of all those other fires that started first. You know how avocado trees burn, like they got gas on them – all that good oil. Dad had to let old Miguel go. *That* was not a happy moment. So now you can run the whole thing, like Dad always wanted."

Patrick felt a chill steal over him. They wound into the hills. A creek bed ran alongside the road, and the oaks that grew there were now just shorn outlines of what they had been. Even with most of the hotspots extinguished days ago, the ground still and reeked and smoked. Patrick had never seen the creek because of the thick foliage but now that it had burned he saw the slender slick of water crawling through the ravine no faster than a snake. "It's good to be home," he said.

Ted looked over at him with solemn admiration on his face. He was twenty six, four years older than his brother. "Did you see some bad things over there?"

The admiration made Patrick uneasy. He'd done little to deserve it but Ted had always adored him, always tried to look out for him. Patrick thought of the cards that life can deal, right from the start, such as bad feet and the fever and seizures that had found Ted in his crib and almost killed him. And how Ted's life had been a series of quiet failures.

"You did good for your country, Pat. I'm proud of you."

"Don't be. I did what everybody else did."

"Heroes always say that."

"There were heroes but I'm not one of them. I'll tell you something, Ted – that war was a waste. It sounds like I'm against my country but I'm not. I would have died for my guys. Some of them died for me. But it was supposed to mean something bigger and it didn't. Just a lot of death for nothing. Just a lot of Marines getting shot and blown up."

"But you helped the people over there."

"No. The villagers are already halfway back to the stone age where we found them. They won't change because they don't want to. So it doesn't mean anything, if they won't even

4

try to hang onto what we accomplished. It just means we were there and then we were gone. Like footprints. There were some good things, too. I had my men and a dog. He smelled out bombs. He saved some lives. I already miss it, but not the things I thought I'd miss."

Patrick looked at his brother. Ted was big and pale. He had shaved his head and gotten a new tattoo – a bracelet of POW barbed-wire – around one wrist. It looked wrong on him, Patrick thought. Ted had never been a prisoner of anything except his own misfortunes. The tattoo should be "Mums" or a heart with a girl's name inside it, thought Patrick. He knew from texts and Skypes that while he was in Sangin, Ted was driving a taxi and taking classes at the state university in San Marcos. And that three weeks ago Ted had broken up with yet another girlfriend. There was always a woman Ted loved but didn't love him. Then another. Maybe a girlfriend tattoo wasn't such a good idea after all.

"The big memorial for the Dark Horses is next week," said Ted. "Third Battalion, Fifth Regiment. I always liked the sound of your unit. *The Three/Five. Get Some!* Pendleton's flying in soldiers and families from all around the country. Speeches, color guard, everything. Mom and Dad already got a written invite signed by a real brigadier general."

"I heard about it."

"Are you going to go?"

"I'll go."

"I wish I could of done what you did. Too bad I always screw up."

"You're off the drugs, aren't you?"

"I'm off the thirties *and* the booze." Patrick knew that thirties were 30-mg oxy-condone, "hillbilly heroin," an addictive prescription painkiller. Ted's addiction had been discovered by his mother a year ago, about the time Patrick was walking his first patrols of the poppy fields in the Sanjin District. The

5

coincidence puzzled Patrick. He had come to see that life was often made of pieces that didn't fit.

"You did your part, Ted. You got clean and you're back in school."

"Was. The college expelled me for some stuff I put on the Internet."

"What stuff?"

"I did a cartoon of Mayor Anders."

"Damn you."

"It's freedom of speech, Pat. I'm really sick of her and the rest of government, collecting all my tax money and spending it on things we don't need. We didn't need the new library. What was wrong with the old one? And how big a pension will she and her friends at City Hall get? How come they didn't spend the money on more firemen? It's government waste of our dollars, Patrick. Why can't I say that? So I drew a cartoon of her as a dealer at a blackjack table. She's leaning over to push big stacks of chips to a homeless family on welfare. I exaggerated her breast size. The college said it was against women, hateful and antigovernment. I'm expelled. But I'm not charged with anything."

"Damn you, Ted. Can't you leave anything alone?"

"I didn't mean anything by it."

"You *want* to mean something by it, Ted! That's the whole point. You piss me off. If you won't control yourself who will?"

Ted frowned grimly and pulled a CD from the door slot. "Listen to this music, Pat. It's Cruzela Storm. She's local and she's . . ."

Patrick snatched the plastic case away from his brother. "If you won't control yourself who will?"

"It's the same old thing, Patrick. Ideas get into me – "

" – I know, and you say you don't know where they come from. Bullshit. You're too old for that excuse now."

6

"I'm sorry I hurt her feelings. But when the ideas get into me I don't know what they're going to look like when they come back out. Does anyone? I don't have anything personal against Mayor Anders. I apologized on her website and never heard back. There's no talk of stalking charges. Nothing like that. But there's good news, too, Pat. I'm spending sixty hours a week in my taxi. *Sixty*. And making some serious money."

Patrick let his head rock back against the rest and watched the scorched earth scroll past his window. He saw Ted lean his head back too. A campaign poster for Mayor Evelyn Anders, apparently running for re-election next month, flashed by. On blackened chain link fence along the road, the families of returning soldiers had already hung new signs and banners welcoming home their Pendleton-based husbands and fathers and daughters. *WE LOVE YOU, JASON! XOXOXO! WELCOME HOME TAMARA!*

"There's yours, Pat! We made it ourselves, soon as the fire got put out."

Patrick looked at the clean white banner hanging on the fence, the red-and-blue lettering and the goofily oversized image of his serious, Marine Corps face under his dress cover. He was surprised how young he looked and how old he felt. He thought of Myers and Zane and the others dead in Sangin, and of Salimony and Messina and Bostik, alive here in California.

You can't dwell on all the times you should have died or it'll drive you crazy. Look at the guys who won't ever get to think back on that war. Look at the guys it ate alive. Then look at yourself and figure the difference between them and you. There isn't any.

Coming into town from the east, Patrick saw that the fire had been capricious, destroying one grove but sparing another, burning one house to the ground and ignoring the next. Like snipers, he thought, or mortar rounds. He saw

7

Valley Pumpkin Patch, with straw Halloween witches on strings hanging from the surrounding sycamores, and acres of big orange pumpkins stretching away. He'd run those fields as a boy. He had always loved the fall here. Now his heart ached in a general way and he sensed there was much more to come.

Downtown looked much as he had left it, but there were many more empty storefronts. He was surprised how many. For Rent. For Lease. Even the Navy recruiter was closed and empty. The east side was mostly Mexican business – markets and the bakery and the shoe and music stores. Here the streets and sidewalks were busy with young mothers pushing strollers and the older women carrying plastic shopping bags in both hands for balance and kids on foot and on bikes. By the number of youngsters out on this afternoon, Norris guessed that Fallbrook schools were not in session because of the fire. It cheered his heart to see people walking around, living their lives without carrying guns or getting shot at or wondering where the IEDs were hidden. They don't know how good they have it, he thought.

Further down Main Street were most of the nice older buildings – City Hall, the community theater and the banks and restaurants, the dance studio and Cultural Center, hair salons and art galleries. A *taqueira* boasted the world's best tacos while a drive-through claimed the world's best burgers. Patrick liked the world-class braggadocio in his small town.

And he also liked that here in Fallbrook, Japanese owned the sushi places, Chinese families ran the Chinese restaurants, Koreans owned the Korean restaurants, Indians ran the smoke shop, Pakis the liquor stores and Mexicans the *carnecerias, zapaterias* and *joyerias*. There were blacks, mostly stationed at nearby Camp Pendleton. There were California Indians – Cahuilla and Rincon and Pala – descended through the centuries, clannish and proud. And Guatemalans, almost all of them males, some very young and their shirts always tucked in tightly, who toiled as field hands and gardeners.

Avocado Capital of the World! Patrick looked up at the smoke-smudged banners on Main Street and smiled. He recalled from fourth grade history that Fallbrook was originally plotted as a town site in 1885, declaring itself dry of alcohol. He had gotten out the local phone book that night, to find that Fallbrook had thirty-one churches, one synagogue, three taverns and four tattoo parlors. He thought of Fallbrook as a shrunk down version of the republic.

2

The Norris house sat on high ground overlooking eighty mostly burned acres. Jack and Spike, both wearing yellow ribbons on their collars, followed the truck up the drive, barking. Patrick got out and touched their spacious Labrador heads and saw the big yellow ribbons fluttering on the oak trees and the porch railing. He hated the ribbons. He pet the dogs. He'd thought of them often and almost longingly in Sangin, but now he felt little for them. Ted was pointing to where he'd cut back the decorative plants and trees just a week ago, pure luck he said – he'd had no idea how important it would be when the fire came. Patrick looked out over the slopes, steep and blackened. The San Luis Rey River trickled far down valley in an untouched cushion of green.

His mother pushed through the door and hurried down the wooden steps and pulled herself into his arms. Caroline's tears were wet and warm on his cheek. She firmly stroked his face and head as if to confirm their wholeness, and Patrick smiled then he felt a great ledge of relief break loose inside him and tumble downslope, breaking into smaller and smaller pieces. They couldn't finish their sentences.

"God, Pat, it's so good . . ."

"I'm really . . ."

"I just can't believe you're . . . look at . . ."

Patrick climbed the steps to the veranda, where his father hugged him heartily. Patrick noted a new lightness in him, though he wondered if it might be his own strength from patrolling with eighty pounds of gear and a twenty-pound machine gun almost every day for a year. Archibald smelled of the same shave cream he'd used for all of Patrick's remembered life. "It is damned good to see you, son."

"You look great, Dad."

Ted limped by them with Patrick's duffel and went into the house. Patrick followed, his father and mother close on either side, and they squeezed through the door awkwardly, each person trying to lead the mission.

"Civilian chain-of-command is always a little inefficient," said Archibald. He'd been Navy, service being a Norris tradition since the Spanish-American War.

"I'll get used to it again," said Patrick.

A few neighbors had gathered, and some of the church people. Patrick appreciated their smiles and hugs and handshakes but felt the discomfort he caused in them, their ignorant but heat-swelled gratitude. There was a table set up with food and soft drinks and more yellow ribbons and he wished he was back at FOB Inkerman eating an MRE, smoking with his battle buddies, just being necessary. Or maybe fishing out on Glorietta Bay.

"You'll want to see the damage immediately," his father said. "I'll make you an authentic drink. I take it you'll be staying with us?"

"Just a night or two, Dad."

"Oh, *Pat*," said Caroline.

"I need my own space, Mom."

"I wish your brother aspired to that," said Archie. "Rather than living in the bunkhouse the rest of his life."

"Don't start in with all that now, Archie," said Caroline.

Ted came down the hallway and into the sharp glance of his father. "I'm working on getting my own place, Dad."

"That's good to know."

Patrick glanced at the awkward and uncertain friends and neighbors, then let his eyes wander the high-ceilinged great room. Nice to see the familiar white walls hung with his mother's treasured paintings, the mullioned windows, the tile floor and stately area carpets woven in Afghanistan decades before he had gone and seen so much death there. The great room of his life. How could any of it seem so new? Sunlight came through the shutters and made crisp white slats on the walls. From the wet bar, beneath the oil portrait of his father and uncle gazing down as if they had foreseen all of this and more, Archibald studied his older son again. Patrick watched him. Then Archie returned with two large tumblers filled with ice and amber liquid and topped with lemon twists.

"To the groves, then. Caroline, Ted, friends and neighbors – I need a few minutes alone with Pat."

Patrick and his father walked a dirt road side-by-side, through the scorched trees. Norris Brothers Growers was a second-generation concern begun by Patrick's grandfather and great uncle in 1953. As a child Patrick had learned that growing avocados was a risky business due to the vagaries of drought, water, wind, consumer demand, tree disease – from borers to lethal root rot – and competition from Mexico and Chile. He also knew that a third-generation Norris hand-off would have to take place if the ranch was to remain in the family. But Patrick had not fallen in love with farming. His dispassion had cost him some portion of his father's respect, which remained lost now. Ted's early interest in growing had gone unremarked by his father.

This was the best avocado country on Earth, Archibald had always maintained. The hills stood almost eight hundred feet above sea level, picking off the river breezes and the rain clouds that watered the fruit. Much of it was steep terrain, the decomposed granite soil draining beautifully. Now the

12

air was pale and rank. Norris's father told him that three Fallbrook citizens had died in the fire – a dad and two young children. What kind of man stays behind in a wildfire with two young ones? he asked.

"You can see where the fire burned through Big Gorge," he said, gesturing with his tumbler. "It was really screaming by then. I watched a pair of coyotes try to outleg it. The gusts were fifty miles an hour, all bone-dry and straight from the desert, so you can guess who won that race. L.A. was burning. Orange County, too. And San Diego – terrible fires south of here. Ours broke out last so it took quite a goddamned while to get help. Fallbrook Fire says it looks like a downed power line way up in Rice Canyon, fanned by the Santa Anas. San Diego Gas and Electric, of course, they're on the hook if that's true, so they're saying it had to be arson. Either way, like a lot of the growers, Norris Brothers doesn't carry crop insurance. As you know."

Patrick looked down at the blackened swath of what they called the Big Gorge. He could see where the fire had jumped the dirt road and taken out ten acres of trees in a rough circle. It looked like a giant IED had exploded. Standing around the edges of the circle like witnesses were trees that had partially burned, portions of their trunks still carrying life and some branches untouched, their ash-dusted leaves fluttering in the breeze.

"Patrick, I don't know if there's anything you can do for your brother. But if there is, please do it. I'm at the end of my tether with him."

"I'll take him fishing. He likes that."

"He became stranger every month you were gone. First the dope. Then Evelyn Anders. Christ. I wonder if he's back on the drugs. He seems either high or low, no functional middle. And he spends almost all his free time alone in the bunkhouse. God knows what he does on the computer. I

13

can't get him to see doctors anymore. They all threw their hands up on him anyway."

Patrick took a long swallow of the bourbon. He felt the same bottomless pull of it that he always felt but only surrendered to on occasion. Still, he felt that such an occasion would be soon at hand and it was something he'd looked forward to in coming home – a good peaceful bender. These people will miss the point of it, he thought: I'll drink to remember the good things, not to forget the bad.

"As you know, I let Miguel go. I just couldn't afford him, after this. Now I need help rebuilding our groves and our business. And of course someone to take it over someday. My first choice is you, as it's always been."

"I don't want it, Dad."

"I'm trying to make you want it."

"But I don't. I know that's an insult to you. I'm just not a farmer and never will be."

"I hear no insult at all. But you're actually a damned good farmer. Ten summers teach a boy a lot. I've got another five years of muscle left in me, if we can make it through this thing. You know, you could help me get this place up and running again, and chase your dreams later. Plenty of time in the future to buy that boat and guide those clients and catch those fish. How much money have you socked away for the boat?"

"Eleven grand."

"That won't buy much."

"If I start off in the bay I won't need that much boat."

"So, you mean a panga like the Mexicans use?"

"I need a center console, good decks for casting, and a trolling motor for stealth."

"And you think there are enough fly-fishermen around San Diego for you to make a living?"

"If I figured right."

14

"There's what, three or four other guys already doing it?"

"Two on the bay and two offshore for the big stuff."

"Eleven grand?"

"A used boat, for sure, Dad."

His father squinted out at the charred hills. "Farming isn't a dream, Pat. It's just a living. Business was bad enough before this. Ag water was cut back thirty percent because of drought, so I had to stump thirty acres back in May. Yield is down but prices are okay. It killed me let Miguel go. I actually cried. You realize he arrived here without even one dollar in his pocket because the smugglers had robbed him? They'd even taken his shoes. But your grandfather liked the look in his eyes and hired him on the spot, got him papers. He was with us for forty years but I had to let him go. My watch. Me. Of course, there's still goddamned Lew Boardman across the valley hiring one hundred percent illegals, so his bottom line doesn't look half bad. He only lost a couple of acres. But even without the drought and the fire, this operation isn't worth near what it was before the recession. And I can't break it up and sell it to a builder, not with the twenty-to-one zoning we've got. I don't think I could sell it for that purpose anyway, in good conscience."

"I don't think you could, either."

"I haven't listed it but I told the realtor six months ago I'd entertain offers in the three million range. We had some interest. Then, three months ago, a two-million dollar offer from a Newport Beach doctor. Of course I told his realtor to go to hell. A day after the fire came through, he dropped the offer to a million-three. It's an insult offer. It would cover our debt and leave us with very little. Our cash flow is down to almost nothing. We lost this last a big part of season's paycheck to the frost. And of course, because of this fire, our spring fruit probably won't develop."

Archibald sighed and shook his head in the closest thing

15

to defeat that Patrick had ever witnessed. In him Patrick saw himself some decades from now. He tried to imagine himself here in Fallbrook as a grower but he could conjure to mind no more than rough sketches of this land and a small town, and the faint silhouettes of what might be a family. They seemed like the drawings of a child.

Suddenly the artillery on Pendleton boomed. Patrick saw a blast of bright light and his ears roared as panic surged through him, then he fell. The roar grew and he was grappling with something, then everything disappeared – the fear and the sound, even the light. He lay on the burnt ground, breathing hard and covering his father. He felt his father's heartbeat and smelled his aftershave as he disentangled from him and helped him stand. Patrick laughed quietly, partly in humor but mostly in embarrassment. His ears were ringing so loud he wondered if his father could hear. Sweat drenched his back and he tried to brush the soot from his uniform while his pulse settled. "Car doors slamming are the worst."

"It'll take a while, Pat. It's hard to come back. But few things in the world will ever mean more to you than what you did over there."

The "meaning" part still escaped Patrick but he knew that he had done his duty. And now it was time to do it again. Maybe this would mean something. "Alright. I'll do what I can here on the farm, Dad. But there's a condition – we bring Ted on board. He'd love to pitch in. It's what he needs."

"He's not fit for it. I don't mean to be judgmental."

"Then don't judge. He knows you don't believe in him, Dad. But it's time to try again anyway."

"He posted hateful things about the mayor. I can't go into Fallbrook without feeling notorious."

"If we work his ass off he'll be too tired for nonsense like that."

"I've tried, Pat. A thousand times I've tried. I don't need

16

to catalogue his failures and utter lack of attention." Patrick considered the double meaning of that last word.

"We're just putting him to work, Dad. It's the right thing."

"Okay. He's your responsibility. It shames me that I can't pay either of you."

"Ted can drive the taxi evenings and weekends. I can probably deliver pizza. Again." Patrick felt constricted, as if by a large snake, and he could see his dreams puff right out of him and vanish into the foul air.

"You were just eighteen when you left. I'm very damned pleased with you, son. Very."

3

Archie retired early, tumbler-in-hand, leading his shadow down the long hallway past the sconces and the family photographs. Patrick sat with his mother, who laid out the dismal ranch finances. In the living room the windows were all open and the acrid smell of a burned world was made heavier by the damp ocean breeze that came almost nightly up the river valleys on either side of Fallbrook.

"I can't distract him from himself any longer," she said. "It's been like this every night for a year. He's obsessed with the idea of loss, which of course creates loss. And he enjoys his gift of prophecy. Complaining. Drinking. He acts as if God sent drought, the frost and the fire to ruin him. Personally."

Caroline was a tall, trim woman with a regal posture and a head of striking black hair. She usually wore expensive jeans and boots and crisp white shirts, and silk scarves with subtle pattern, loosely knotted around her fine neck. Her face and nails were always done. Patrick had never seen her leave the ranch anything less than put together. Even at home she would rarely let herself be seen in work clothes or thoughtless combinations of casual wear, or any garment associated with exercise or sleep. Patrick found her less vain than simply dutiful about presenting the woman who she had chosen to be. Sometimes he wondered what she had given up for this.

"But that may change now," she said. "You've brought

him hope. God bless you for that." She sipped a glass of red wine and the dimmed overhead lights caught her hair and cast sad-clown shadows under her eyes. "Was it bad in Afghanistan? Your emails and calls were cheerful enough though few and far between."

Patrick nodded contritely. "When I got there and saw it, I thought, well, there's a good chance you're not going home again. So I tried to put some distance between me and everyone I might not see again. Does that make sense?"

"Terrible, terrible sense."

"It's good to be home but hard to talk. I have to get used to not being alert all the time. You get hooked on that. I get startled easy. I haven't slept well. I get this feeling that snipers are lining up on me. I've got a temper now."

"I see it in your face."

"I didn't have it over there. I was too busy trying to not get killed."

"I think I understand. Are you are okay?"

He nodded.

"Pat, I'm glad you're going to help us rebuild this ranch. But I want you to know that if you walked out of here tomorrow to seek your fortune in a larger world, I would support you. And your father would get over it, sooner or later. You are young. Personally, I find your dream of guiding fishing excursions at sea to be, well . . . attainable and romantic."

"I wouldn't get shot at or have to kill anyone. But I think I need to be here now to help with the groves. I can get my old pizza gig and save the money."

She looked at him for a long beat. "If I had money I would help you with the boat."

"I have some money, Mom."

"It's humiliating, not being able to help your own children. None of the calamities that have fallen on your father hurt him as much as that."

19

"None of it's his fault."

"That's irrelevant to him. He's blamed himself for Ted since the day he was born."

"Ted's a grown man now."

"We train our men to accept responsibility for everything, don't we? Even things you can't control."

"I see some truth in that."

"Hold tight to your dreams."

Patrick poured a bourbon and took a flashlight and walked down the dirt road toward the outbuildings. The dogs trotted out ahead, noses down. The barnyard spread flat before him in damp moonlight and the sycamores towered into the sky. He saw the big barn and the metal storage buildings and the long bunkhouse. He walked past the barn and into the grove to see how close the flames had come. In the flashlight beam he saw that Ted's impressive brush-clearing had kept the fire from jumping from the grove to the buildings.

Ted had moved out to the bunkhouse when he was eighteen, having announced that it was time for him to be out on his own. Patrick had helped him. They'd taken apart and stored the old bunks, then filled up the big open room with things of interest to Ted – small animal cages, movies on tape and DVD and a big screen TV to watch them on, a computer and peripherals.

Now Ted sat at a wooden picnic table in the center of the large room, playing a computer fantasy game. Patrick approached and looked over Ted's shoulder at the monitor, where a massive upright humanoid with a bull's head and horns loped through pleasant woodlands eviscerating wild dogs. Ted paid his brother no attention. Patrick knew that Ted enjoyed being watched as he played, and that his brother's unacknowledgement was not rude but, oddly, somehow inclusive.

20

"Level eighty-one," Ted said after a while. His hands tapped the keyboard on his lap and the humanoid trotted and the wild dogs flew apart.

"What's the object of this game?"

"To create the best character you can. It's all about character."

"Why's he killing dogs?"

Ted turned. "Those are wolves, not dogs. Big difference. Dad seemed happier when you came back from your fire-damage tour. Bigger, somehow. Did you say you'd stay and help?"

"I did, yes."

Patrick watched his brother in profile, his hands brisk on the keyboard, the big taurine creature gliding through the countryside. After a while Patrick stood and went to the shelves of cages that lined two walls. This part of the bunkhouse was half-dark and most of the cage lights were off but he could see tarantulas stepping lightly and snakes both still and gliding, and the skinks and swifts peering out from cracks. Alligator lizards prowled. There were Pacific tree frogs and baby pond turtles no larger than golf balls. Patrick saw mantids and scorpions and black widows and pine sawyers. Ted only kept what was native and, as he said, "unlovable." The high handsome oak shelves were built years ago by his father, who had encouraged Ted's husbandry of creeping things – and oddly, Patrick had always thought – almost nothing else.

Ted talked without turning. "Pat, you did good for our country overseas, no matter what you think. And I want to do something, too."

"Like what?"

"I don't know yet. Something really big. And then, I think I'll leave. There's more to the world than Fallbrook. You should come with me. I'd like it if you came. Maybe if you

21

get that boat we can take it and just head out like for the territory."

"I think I'll be here a while. And you know what? The big thing you can do is help put this farm back together."

"Dad thinks I'm stupid."

"He gets his mind wrongly fixed at times."

"Just like I do."

"I already talked to him about this. It's up to us now, Ted. We've got to repair what we can repair, and when spring comes, hope enough trees make it. Otherwise we sell the whole place at a big loss and clear out."

Ted's creature hooked a wolf and threw it high and it hit the ground a broken, snarling thing. "Got him, Pat!" Ted swung around, his expression grave. "Dad really said that? He wants me to work?"

"He really said it."

"There's nothing in the world I'd rather do than help this family. *Nothing.* I'll give my notice to Friendly Village Taxi tomorrow after work. Cleo will have to understand. It may take her a day or two to find someone else, but I'm needed here. *Right* here *now.*"

"Yes. You are."

Ted smiled. "Tell me about the war."

"Later."

"I fully understand. You need to recover first."

Back in the house Patrick refilled his glass with ice and bourbon and lay in his old bed, the same one he'd slept in as a high schooler. As he waited for sleep to find him, the present stepped aside and his memory barreled in with an explosion of light, then Myers and Zane, and then a split second later the unforgettable sound of a bomb finding flesh. The roar startled him back to the now, where he smelled the smoke of many things native and distant that had burned. Much later, as sleep tiptoed toward him again, Patrick saw in his mind a white-with-black-trim Triton 240 LTS Pro Series fishing boat with the outboard four-stroke Mercury, twenty-five gallon bait well, plenty of deck storage, stainless steel hardware and grab rails, non-skid casting decks and gunwales. She was strong and capable. She streaked across the water with Patrick at the helm and she was his.

4

The next evening Patrick drove his pickup to City Hall for the council meeting. Not having driven in a year found him boldly speeding through Fallbrook's winding roads with the windows down and the cool evening air on his face. Snippets of joy.

Fallbrook city council met on the second Tuesday of every month and the meetings were covered by "Village View" reporter Iris Cash. One night not long before his deployment, Patrick had gone before the city council to ask for a setback variance for a new Norris Brothers grove fence, and he had discovered Iris. She had caught up with him after his presentation that night and asked odd questions about the variance, but had a spark of curiosity in her eyes. Six weeks later Patrick was gone, carrying his memory of that spark across the continents and into the hot desert of the war tucked away, a private jewel, something to have that was durable and good.

Tonight he wound through the crowded council chambers toward her, and caught her eye. She broke away from a small group. "Patrick Norris? It's so good to see you again! It's been a year."

"Thirteen months."

Iris was blue-eyed and curvy, with wavy blond hair. She wore a snug black T with the Statue of Liberty in red, white and blue sequins, jeans and black slip-on sneakers. Her expression was withholding. She held a small computer tablet in one hand. Her gaze roamed his own. "Are you back for good?"

"Yes. Done with all that."

"I thought a text or something might come my way."

"I just needed to get it done. I thought of you."

"Okay. You're looking well."

"So are you, Iris."

"I'm so sorry about the farm."

"We'll put it back together."

"You came back just in time for that."

Patrick nodded, picturing himself in the Domino's Pizza shirt, carrying a heat-insulated extra large to a Fallbrook front door. At least he wouldn't be sitting in an office. The tips weren't bad. It was the only job he'd ever had, other than being a high school student, a farm laborer and a killer with a choice of machine guns – M240 or SAW.

Neither spoke for a long beat. "Why did you come here tonight, Patrick? Another variance?"

"I came to see you. And what the town has been up to."

She gave him a look of assessment. "Stick around then! Fallbrook's been up to a lot. Call me at the paper sometime – there's a new coffee house we could try."

He sat near the back and on the right where he could see Iris in profile. The council chambers was a stately 20th century brick edifice with high coffered ceilings and an air of protestant thrift. The four councilpersons and mayor sat at a raised dais that curved along the far wall. They each had a slender microphone. The local cable outfit had a tripod and camera set up stage left, and an operator with a headset clamped on. The seal of the city – a robed woman with her back to the viewer, facing an avocado grove that stretched forever before them, the sun either rising or setting in the distance – hung on the wall behind the officials. Patrick estimated thirty rows of folding chairs, thirty across. He thought of how hard it was to find a place to sit at forward-operating-base Inkerman, which had three chairs, always taken, and rock-hard sandbags and Hesco blocks. He mostly ate standing up. As Mayor Anders called the meeting to order, the chairs were all but full and more citizens stood in the back and more outside the open doors, straining to see in over each other. Lew Boardman found a seat next to Patrick.

When the minutes were done the mayor opened with old business. A stocky man in his early-forties stepped to the podium. He wore a brown suit that looked too small, and a white button down shirt and a striped necktie. Patrick was surprised. He recognized the man as Cade Magnus, the middle son of one-time Fallbrook scourge Jed Magnus. The Magnus family had left town almost a decade ago – to the great relief of most of its citizens – but Patrick instantly recognized Cade's smug demeanor and haughty smile.

While the Magnus family lived in Fallbrook, Jed had published a racist newsletter and hosted a hate-filled radio show that had national followings. Young Cade, obviously enthralled by his charismatic father, was the heir apparent to the then White Crusade. Patrick remembered their car repair shop, Pride Auto Repair, where only American and German cars were worked on. Later a lawsuit had crippled the White Crusade but the Magnuses had stayed on in Fallbrook while father and son continued to publish racist literature and speak at Aryan, Klan and white separatist events across the country. Patrick had seen them many times over the years, walking around downtown as if they owned it, openly baiting people in their loud voices and braying laughter.

When Cade tapped the mic a low murmur came from the crowd then subsided.

Evelyn Anders looked down at him with some irritation. "Cade, I wish I could say it was good to see you again."

26

"Go right ahead."

"I heard you moved back here two weeks ago."

"I'll plead guilty to that."

"First you arrive, then we get the worst fire in our history."

"You're not implying I set the fire, are you?"

An uneasy murmur rippled through the room. Patrick heard a gaggle of laughter from up near the front where Cade had been sitting.

"So, you guys are the Rogue Wolves now, not the White Crusade?" asked the mayor.

"We can't use the words White Crusade or you'll take what little money you left us with."

"I'll take it?"

"Government will. Government is government – Public Enemy Number One." More laughter from his cadre.

"Cade, I read this Rogue Wolf proposal that you sent in last month, about the weapons ban protest. I see no merit in it at all, nor does this council. The city attorney says that legal carry of weapons would provoke violence and has no chance in the courts. We don't *want* people carrying guns around here. The City of Fallbrook is the avocado capital of the world, not the gun capital of the world. We will not sanction such a protest. We will not place this item on our agenda for public input."

"Yet the by-laws of this city allow me to address the council at this time."

"Don't trivialize our city, Mr. Magnus. Fallbrook has just suffered a major catastrophe."

"It was punishment from god for your ignorance."

"You have exactly two minutes."

"Thank you. Boys and girls, in these days of spiraling gun violence, such as in Columbine, Tucson, Aurora and Newtown, we believe more than ever that citizens must bear arms. The Supreme Court guarantees this as a Constitutional

27

right. It is not a privilege. An armed citizen is a protected citizen. A self-defense weapon locked in a safe at home is no protection against the rapist in a late-night parking lot. I would not be motherless now if Ellen Magnus had been allowed to defend herself in our family's place of business. But this is not about her or myself. So. Our society encourages a woman to defend herself against such an attack, yet leaves the crucial question of *weapon access* to the states and municipalities. Arizona an other states have the right idea – legal carry. California must follow suit. So, we call on the city leaders of Fallbrook to recognize November twenty-second of this year to be 'Self-Protection Day,' during which Fallbrook's good and law-abiding citizens over the age of twenty-one can legally carry, in public and on their persons, and loaded if they desire, the weapons of self-defense upon which this country was founded and built."

"Complete with the thirty-shot magazines?" asked Anders.

"Let's work out the specifics later."

"Did you choose the anniversary of President Kennedy's assassination on purpose?"

"Of course I did."

One of the city councilwomen moved to table the proposal for further study and it was seconded by the councilman sitting beside her. The council swiftly voted.

"Tabled it is, Mr. Magnus," said the Mayor Anders.

"You're just hiding your head in the sand."

"We appreciate your input. Welcome back to Fallbrook and behave yourself."

Anders whacked her gavel on the desktop and Norris heard the sharp ring of it over the jeers. Magnus remained at the podium and turned toward the audience, and Patrick had his first good look at the man in over a decade. He was handsome in a cunning way, his hair brown and full, his eyebrows disingenuously arched, eyes wide in feigned innocence. There was a trace of a smile on his lips. "You dumbass liberals with your cheap Third World labor don't know one thing about this country. Time to take it back, boys and girls."

Some people sitting with Magnus stood and clapped and hooted. Patrick saw a young pierced and tattooed skinhead couple. There was an older biker in chains and leathers with an obscure patch on the back of his vest. There were two fresh-faced man/boys wearing white shirts and black ties and they looked to Patrick like Mormons though this was doubtful. The man/boys couldn't be much more than teenagers. The big biker fell in behind Magnus as he left the podium and strode down the center aisle toward the exits. Magnus looked at Patrick on the way by and Patrick caught the gleam in his clear blue eyes – mischief or menace, hard to tell, he thought. "Welcome home, Patrick," Magnus said to him. "Thank you and well done."

"Go to hell," said Patrick.

When Magnus had passed by, Patrick saw Iris Cash looking at him from across the chambers. He waved at her awkwardly, as if trying to conceal his action from the hundreds present, many of whom were looking back in his direction at Magnus. After thirteen months of living in close quarters with men, it felt strange to Patrick to intend anything as private. Iris smiled. He smiled too and felt fortunate that he had carried her with him into the war and back, and that she apparently bore him no grudge for not calling. He had cast her as a weightless ideal rather than a flesh-and-blood human being, far easier to transport and protect, and he knew this was a selfish convenience even as he had done it. Now seeing her again she was exactly as he had pictured her: very real and beautiful.

Mayor Anders called the last old business on the calendar. A woman in the audience set up an easel on the dais, and set a foam-backed photograph on it. Even from far back Patrick saw that the image was a boy's smiling face, probably an enlargement of a school picture.

"That boy was killed on Mission Boulevard two weeks ago," said Lew Boardman. "Ten years old. It was late and dark and the car that hit him didn't stop. A late model white four-door is all the witness could say. It was weaving. The car threw him up and the windshield caught him again and he flew twenty feet. And the car kept on going."

A city safety engineer presented a PowerPoint proposal to construct two lighted crosswalks. On a city map he ran the pointer along Fallbrook's two busiest streets and stated that some stretches of them were hundreds of yards from the nearest traffic lights. He said that without stops or cross-walks, Fallbrook's pedestrians would continue to walk long distances, or take substantial risks to cross. He mentioned Clair Michaels, the elderly woman seriously injured by a car two years prior on Main. The safety engineer turned and looked at the photograph of the boy. The room quieted.

Patrick looked at the smiling boy in the picture, the gap where his front teeth would have soon been, the shirt collar buttoned all the way up. The safety engineer turned back to his mic and said the cost estimate was $84,000 per crosswalk, half paid by California DOT, another twenty-thousand for each coming from the county. The annual operating cost would be small because on-site solar panels would power the small lights embedded in the asphalt. Mayor Anders said such a project would leave a forty-four thousand dollar obligation to Fallbrook but the city had such money – barely – available from the general fund, earmarked for public health and safety. She looked at the councilpersons and noted that this sure seemed like a good use of that money. Public input?

A middle-aged woman was against this because the only thing any pedestrian needed to do was go to the nearest crosswalk – anyone could *say* they were too far apart. Did they need a crosswalk at every single corner?

A young man was in favor because he ran the streets of Fallbrook to stay in shape and the cars really were dangerous, especially at sunrise or sunset.

An older woman said that public safety was one of the sacred responsibilities of government, and if Fallbrook had the money and a boy had already died, then why *not?*

An older man said there were too many people in Fallbrook who didn't have cars – the illegals, mostly – so building crosswalks would encourage more illegal immigration.

An obese woman rose and said this was just another example of social engineering by democrats.

The young Magnus missionaries clapped and the man turned and glared at them.

From their seats in the audience, two girls stood and held up a banner attached to two broomsticks. The banner said "Who Killed George?" and Patrick heard a murmur of approval ripple through the room then a chorus of derisive grumbles and scattered boos.

"Friends of the dead boy," said Boardman. "From down in the barrio in the middle of town, where he lived."

A well-known art gallery owner spoke in favor of the lighted crosswalks: anything to increase foot traffic up and down Main is a good idea, she said. With a glance at the skinhead couple she added that even Tattoo You might benefit from easier customer access. The female called out something that Patrick couldn't catch.

The last person to weigh in said the whole boondoggle sounded like something the government would come up with, and he therefore stood opposed – it was expensive and unnecessary.

The councilpersons and mayor Anders gave their views and the motion was made, voted on and defeated – three against, two in favor. The girls with the George banner stood and raised it on their way from the room.

"Well," said Anders. "That's too bad. It really is. But, on to other things. Fallbrook, let's see how we can put you back together after this awful fire. We've lost three lives and three hundred homes and who knows how much livestock and farmland. We've got Fire Chief Bruck here to start things off . . ."

Patrick looked at Iris again, still tapping on the notebook balanced across her knees. Her fine fair curls caught the light. He had no idea so much was going on in little Fallbrook while he was out patrolling Sangin district. He settled further into the folding chair, positioning his shoulder blades to miss the uprights. He felt a small relaxation finally coming over him. It was more than jarring to jet from a violent, foreign world into a present that was also his past and possibly his future. He thought again about re-enlisting. Combat was better than a drug and he wanted more. In combat he had purpose. Everything was important and had to be done right. He knew that home was where he was *supposed* to want to be, but he felt no such purpose here. Everything seemed trivial.

He took a deep breath and looked up at the old stamped aluminum ceiling. Home is what we fought for, he thought. Whether it helped the people over there or not. Whether we were pawns in a game. Whether it will ever mean anything to me or not. I found my brothers. He saw the flash of light again. It was bright enough to obliterate the world during its sudden, brief life. Myers and Zane were not a part of it, this time. There was no sound either, as if his memory was being polite here in public. The ghosts in his heart rose suddenly, then settled. Patrick lowered his gaze to the tiled floor and closed his eyes and let the voices swim around him.

32

5

The next morning Ted steered his taxi up Reche Road, past the junior high school. Fire ash was still settling onto his car, but the morning was warm and pleasant. He had no fare. He thought again of Patrick coming down the escalator at Lindbergh Field two days ago. It was so obvious that the war had been hard on him. It bothered Ted that his brother had found no meaning in what he had done. That was the worst feeling in the world. To him, the young man he saw on that escalator riding out of the sun was a hero, pure and simple. And soon, thought Ted, he would be working alongside that hero, as a brother and a friend. To save the farm. He wondered how long that would last. He knew he'd miss this taxi but everyone needed to sacrifice. Cleo, who owned Friendly Village Taxi, had already said she'd give him weekends and some evenings, just to keep a little money coming in.

He pulled over and got the glass spray and paper towels from the trunk. As he labored away at the windshield he saw Mr. Hutchins far down the road, walking toward him. Ted finished the windows and circled back to pick him up. The old man swung open the front door and looked in. "Hello, Ted. Air still smells like hell out here, so thanks for stopping."

"Slow morning, Mr.Hutchins. Happy to."

Ted felt sorry because Hutchins was eighty-two years old and his wife was in a board-and-care downtown. Of course the Nanny State had taken away his driver's license, and his wife's facility was three miles from the Hutchins home. Which meant a six mile round-trip walk for Mr. Hutchins, half of it steeply uphill, through heat, cold and occasional rain. A man with bad feet understood the pain. Taxis were expensive and there were no busses. Hutchins was skinny as a minute and it riled Ted that government would do that to a man, and he considered himself patriotic in giving Hutchins a free ride now and then to see Alice.

Ted dropped him off at the board-and-care and Hutchins made a show of paying, but Ted put a hand on his arm and said no payment today.

"Sorry you lost your grove," said the old man. "Tell your mother and father to think about selling everything. Get a smaller place in a city, one that won't burn down. A place with a community pool. They can travel. Live off savings."

"They don't have any savings."

"Mine went somewhere, too."

He turned and waved as the automatic glass door slid open. Through the slats of a wooden fence Ted could see the patio area with its plastic chairs and tables, and the old people and their wispy white hair, their canes and wheelchairs and bottled oxygen. He watched for a while. It was nice to watch without being seen. That was part of the reason he liked driving the taxi, because he could watch life through glass, like on a TV or a monitor. On the wall of the building he saw still another offensive campaign poster for Evelyn Anders, which showed her face and proclaimed: "This Town is Your Town – Re-Elect Evelyn Anders for Mayor." She managed to look both professional and attractive, which Ted found underhanded.

Later he picked up Lucinda Smith at her condo on the golf course and took her downtown to Major Market. This was the fourth time she'd called Friendly Village Taxi in the last ten days. She was a pretty brunette, thirty-something, though

34

she hardly spoke to him. She never took her sunglasses off, never smiled or laughed. No ring on her finger. She was brief about her shopping today, as usual. In Ted's view she was either sullen or broken-hearted but he couldn't tell which. When she was done getting groceries he dropped her off at home and she gave him her usual two-dollar tip.

"Have a nice day," he said. Lucinda gave him a curt wave and headed up the stairs to her front door.

He looped around to Mission and drove back into town, the air still pale with ash. He drove past where the boy had been killed. The girls were there again with their banner raised, "Who Killed George?" Ted noted their cheerless expressions and wondered why the kid hadn't just gone to the nearest crosswalk.

Next he drove a squat dark pregnant girl from the Catholic Church to the Fallbrook Hospital. He tried to use his limited Spanish but got nowhere. She neglected to tip him. By the look of her she'd arrived in the U.S. just days ago, if not hours. She said nothing but she paid Ted in U.S. dollars, carefully counted, which he assumed were given to her by the same Nanny State that had taken away Mr. Hutchins's driver's license.

After that he took a family of four to the airport in Carlsbad and earned a ten dollar tip, though the round-trip took nearly an hour and a half out of his work day. Back in Fallbrook he got a fill-up and a wash at the GasPro station because nothing reflected more poorly on a driver than a dirty cab. He talked briefly with Ibrahim, the manager, who had escaped Saddam's police in Baghdad and fled to America. Ibrahim claimed to have been an oil engineer but the gas station job was as close to oil engineering as he could get for now. Ibrahim was a big man with quick eyes and he kept a Koran on the counter beneath the canned tobacco display.

Ted picked up his daily after-lunch fare, Mr. Rossie, a

cheerful older man claimed to be retired CIA. Rossie had had a stroke about a year ago, around the time Ted started driving, and he'd done physical therapy almost every day at 1:15 ever since. Rossie walked with a wide-stance quad-cane and offered a nod, smile and garbled words to almost everyone he met. Ted couldn't figure out how much of Mr. Rossie's mind was still good. But it was easy to figure the federal government pension and health insurance must be good indeed, because PT was one-hundred twenty-five an hour, which meant someone was coughing up $625 a week for the old spy's rehab. Ted thought about Mayor Anders and the cartoon he'd posted of her and suddenly more cartoon ideas came swarming into his mind. He laughed softly and vowed again, in honor of Patrick, not to draw another cartoon of the good mayor.

While Rossie was in therapy Ted got a sandwich from the market and drove out to the Air Park to watch the small planes take off and land. A beautiful yellow Piper Cub that often arrived this time on Wednesdays came tilting in like a bulletin from the past. He could hear the artillery thundering out on Pendleton, which he thought of as the sound of peace. He thought of Patrick and hoped he'd be okay. He ate in the car and listened to Cruzela Storm, the new hit singer. She had grown up in San Diego. She was unbelievably good, in his opinion, with beautiful melodies and mysterious lyrics and a voice the color of honey. Ted was prone to obsessing over small non-cuddly animals, certain people, music, books, TV, computers. He was about to start the CD again but remembered that he had to be waiting for Mr. Rossie at 2:15 for the ride home.

Later in the afternoon dispatch called Ted to say he had a fare waiting outside the smoke shop in Village Oaks. When he pulled up a big Mexican kid pushed through the door and came outside. Ted noted the pomade and the Killah wrap-arounds, the Raiders windbreaker, baggy black shorts, white knee-highs and Dickie work boots. Of course tatts everywhere. The boy threw open the back door and got in and Ted felt the car rock.

"Henry?" Ted asked. "Going to Ammunition Road?"

"That's what I told your boss."

"I'm making sure."

"Then make sure you take me to the liquor store first, the one by the Kyoto Restaurant."

"It's your time."

Ted hit the meter and watched the five-dollar pickup charge register. Henry – probably not even eighteen, Ted guessed – stared out the back window through his shades. Ted had seen him around, hanging out with the Fallbrook Kings, a street gang. The boy's name was actually Edgar, Ted was pretty sure. Edgar had a girlfriend who dressed provocatively and often clung to him in public. Hard to miss her, thought Ted. He wondered why Edgar used a fake name just to procure a taxi ride.

He parked in front of Lucky Liquor and the big boy-man got out. Ted watched him in the sideview. With both hands stuffed into the windbreaker pockets, Edgar looked around then warily walked into the store. He took a long time inside but Ted couldn't see him through the tobacco and beer ads on the windows.

And of course another Evelyn Anders campaign poster. There was also one for her opponent, Walt Rood. Rood had a warm smile. His campaign poster said: "Small Government That Works." He was an investor with a good reputation. Ted knew he was being endorsed by the Chamber of Commerce and that the "Village View" had called the race "a dead heat." Still it seemed that Anders' posters outnumbered Rood's three-to-one.

Finally Edgar came out and took a hit from a half pint of something in a dark flat bottle. The bottle glinted golden in the sunlight while he wadded and tossed the small brown bag into a trashcan by the door. Ted watched him slide the bottle back into his jacket pocket and stride heavily back to the cab. The kid climbed in and slammed the door. "Ammunition," he said again.

Ammunition Road was on the west side of town and ended at entrance to the Naval Weapons Station on Camp Pendleton. Ted drove along at the apartments where many of the Marines and their families lived. Not much to look at. The patios were littered with toys and barbecues and the drapes were almost always drawn. He could approximate the length of deployment by how neglected the yards and patios were. The military life was difficult, he knew. At eighteen, Ted had been embarrassed and angered at failing the physical for all branches of the armed services – his damned feet, of course.

"Pull into the lot and drive me down by the chain link fence," said Edgar. Ted pulled into the parking lot of the Parkside Apartments. It was full of the muscle cars that young men like, and plenty of little tiny economy cars too. Three Marines stood beside a late model Camaro with the hood propped open, looking down into the engine as if it was about to say something.

"This is the wrong place," said Edgar.

"Looks wrong."

"What's that mean? What do you mean by that?"

Ted's pulse rose and his breathing sped up. Anger. "This is mostly Marines, not Mexicans. We can drive around all you want, or you can just tell me where you really want to go." By now he'd guessed that Edgar had something specific to do. Something not altogether pleasant. Thus, using a false name to reserve a cab. And the stop for liquid courage. And the bogus run to Ammunition, clearly not his turf. And his nervous mood.

"Old Stage," said Edgar.

"That makes sense."

"'Cause that's where the Mexicans live? You're full of shit and I don't like you."

Ted felt his vision constricting – gun barrel vision, he called it. It always came with anger. Along with the fast pulse and the rapid breathing. And with anger his hearing became acute: now he could hear the crackling tin turn of the half-pint lid, then the gulp and swallow. "You can get out here if you want," Ted said. "But the ride is still nine dollars."

"You take me to Old Stage or you don't get paid."

"Do you have the money?"

"I don't have to show it."

"I don't have to take you to Old Stage, either."

In the rearview Ted saw him brandish a wad of bills. Ted drove Fallbrook Street to Old Stage and made the right. The little houses of the barrio slid past his windows, then the Mexican shopping center with the *mercado* and the *taqueira* and the *zapateria*. On the right was the American Legion Post 1924 where Ted assumed Patrick would soon be spending some time. Near the end of Old Stage, Edgar told him to make a left on Via Ventana, a small cul-de-sac rimmed by small stucco homes. There were cars parked along every inch of curb, and the driveways and garages were full of vehicles too, mostly older and American-made. Ted saw a nice lowered Impala painted candy-apple red. Four guys were in it, watching him.

"Stop here."

"Eleven dollars."

Ted turned to watch the big boy throw open the door and haul himself out. Then Edgar was at the window pointing a gun at Ted's face. "Turn it off and drop the keys on the ground."

39

Ted looked at the gun. His field-of-view had ratcheted down to almost nothing, but he saw in hyperfocus the black cave of the barrel, the age-worn bluing gone silver at the end of it like the muzzle of an old dog, and within the barrel the first spiral of rifling twisting back toward the hand that held the gun. Ted turned off the engine and dropped the keys to the sidewalk. They landed with a loud clank. He told himself to stay calm. "That's a big one."

"It's big enough to blow a hole in your head. Give me the bills from the box. No change. You got five seconds."

Ted opened the cashbox, which was just a small metal toolbox with the top shelf removed. Friendly Village Taxi had provided it to Ted but it didn't even lock. The change banged around loudly while Ted raked up the bills. He held them out and the boy snatched them away and stuffed them in his jacket.

"Gimme the tips too. From your pocket."

"But that's my money. I need it for the groves."

"Roll with it, fat boy."

Ted worked out his humble earnings and handed them over. His hand was shaking but still he thought: that's my forty-two bucks in there and I want them back. The red Impala started up and rolled slowly away from the curb. Ted aimed his gun barrel vision at the driver and committed the face to memory. "Those are the Fallbrook Kings," he said. "Is this some kind of initiation?"

"You're a genius, gordo."

Edgar stepped back and peeled a bill off the tip roll and dropped it on Ted's lap. He kicked the keys under the car then slid the gun back into his jacket and jogged off diagonally across one of the small lawns. He looked back then let himself through a chain-link gate that latched loudly. Through the mesh Ted saw the big drooping pepper tree in the back yard and the branches hanging low and the flicker of Edgar moving below them across the yard. A dog barked ferociously and Edgar cursed.

Ted heaved out and fished his keys from under the car. He ran as fast as he could across the yard but he was slow. Looking over the gate he saw that the yard was thick with foliage, and a brick wall ran along the back of it. He threw open the gate and ran for the wall and pulled himself up onto it and looked over. Something launched. He saw a hurtling cave of teeth and pink meat coming up at him, and he heard the loud snap of those teeth, then the pit bull fell away and gathered itself for another jump. Ted slid back down his side of the wall and heard the growls then the screech of tires from beyond the house.

He lumbered back across the yard, his feet already smarting from the exertion. He slowed and walked back to the car, trying to let his pulse slow down and his breathing relax and his vision return to normal. When he reached the open door of his taxi Ted took a deep breath, crossed his arms over his chest, tightly, closed his eyes and rotated his body counter-clockwise. He turned in circles as fast as he could. It was a tic from childhood. Pat said it was like he was unscrewing from the world, and Ted said he was trying to fly away. When he stopped turning and opened his eyes the world had changed not one bit that Ted could see.

He sat in his taxi and felt his mind starting to reassemble. At least I'm not shot, he thought. Not hurt. I only lost thirty-two dollars in tips and the charges for one day's work. Friendly Village Taxi is insured. Ted stared out at the fence. His vision relaxed, peripheries falling into place like a kaleidoscope shifting into a new pattern. He wondered: what's Edgar going to do when I see him around town again? In Fallbrook everybody sees everybody sooner or later. What am *I* going to do when I see him again?

Ted parked at the Fallbrook Sheriff Substation and waited

41

for his body and mind to mesh. He muttered the Lord's Prayer, which sometimes seemed to help. He made it half-way through. And by then some kind of timing belt seemed to have re-engaged inside him, and his inner engine started to run more smoothly. He could still smell his fear, ammoniac and bitter.

His feet throbbed as he crossed the parking lot. Twenty-six years, two surgeries and many expensive orthotics and Ted still couldn't walk faster than a chameleon without it hurting. Inside the Sheriff's department afternoon sunlight came through the blinds and hit the finished concrete floor, then laddered up the front desk and the flags of the United States of America and the great State of California. The black desk sergeant regarded him with frank suspicion. He had rousted Ted just a few weeks back for a failed brake light on his cab, then given him a nystagmus test in broad daylight, humiliating Ted in front of all of Fallbrook. My Government at work for me, he thought. He took a deep breath, nodded at the sergeant, then turned and walked back out.

6

Evelyn Anders sat in the back of the Fallbrook Fire Department sedan and looked out at Rice Canyon, where the devastating fire had started. The early October morning was warm and dry and the scorched earth wheezed smoke and ash. Rice Canyon was steep and rugged and serviced by only one paved road, which intersected Highway 76 six miles from the Fallbrook city limit.

She hadn't seen the canyon in two years, since she and her husband had gotten a sitter for the kids and come out here to hike and watch birds then gamble and spend the night at the Pala Indian Casino. Now she looked out at the utter destruction scrolling past the windows. She remembered Rice Canyon as a lovely, thickly wooded oakland, clotted with lemonadeberry and sage and ceonothus which, she knew, would all burn like matches in any drought month. And October was the absolute worst month of all. It looked like a hydrogen bomb had gone off.

Fallbrook Fire Chief William Bruck swung around in the front passenger seat and looked at her. "Evelyn, we've just learned something interesting that I'd like to share with you. Last week, an online English-language Al Qaeda magazine called for home-grown terrorists to start fires in the U.S. They published detailed directions on how to use simple timers and accelerants. The terrorist magazine is called 'Inspire.'"

"Good Lord. Why didn't you tell me earlier?"

"The DHS didn't tell me until about thirty minutes ago. They've sent an arson-terror specialist – Special Agent Max Knechtl. He told me that no one has claimed responsibility for this fire. But the good news is that NSA electronically monitors 'Inspire' readers here in the U.S. And they report to the DHS. So, if there's a connection . . ."

Evelyn wondered if NSA surveillence of e-magazine readers without a warrant was good news or not. But there were larger questions here, or at least more urgent ones.

"And the other good news," said Bruck, "Is that we've wrapped up the investigation and gotten everything into the lab."

"Well, Bill – *we've* wrapped it up," said Sheriff Stan Hazzard, who sat in back with Evelyn. The two men chuckled. The driver, a young buzz-cut fireman, glanced back at Evelyn in the rearview.

"What did you find out?" asked Evelyn.

"Oh, that's going to take some time," said Bruck. "We may have evidence of arson. But we've also got San Diego Gas & Electric power lines, apparently downed by the wind."

"How long until you know what caused the fire?" asked Evelyn.

"The lab is good," said Sheriff Hazzard. "A week at the most."

"But you can see right over there that the trees were higher than the lines," said Evelyn. "And we know they were swaying like crazy in the winds that night. It's the power company's responsibility to keep the trees away from their lines, right?"

"Exactly right," said Bruck. "Except Ashley found what may well be accelerant."

"Ashley?" asked the Mayor.

"Our arson dog," said Bruck. "We really can't discuss what she may or may not have found, Evelyn."

"Then, without *discussing* it, can you at least tell your

44

mayor what you found? We lost three lives here, Bill. And you're talking about Al Qaeda and home-grown terrorists."

He turned and gave her a granitic look. "The evidence of arson appears faint at best."

"Maybe that's good," she said. "A negligent accident is still better than a terrorist. It would be a silver lining for our little town to have the wind and SDG&E prove to be fault. They're insured for billions for this kind of thing."

"I know that."

She looked out at the broiled trees and earth and wondered who could start such a fire on purpose. The damage went on mile after mile. She knew that most wildfires were natural and they helped balance and restore the ecosystem over time – nature's form of self-government. She winced at her own thought. Since becoming mayor she'd felt that *she* was a governmental wildfire: cutting, cutting; trimming, trimming, no, no; I'm sorry we can't afford that, no! We can't even build a few lighted crosswalks to keep people from getting killed by cars, she thought. Mother nature and government can be cruel things. Who's to govern them?

Then the car came to a stop and she saw two uniformed deputies pulling away orange cones to let them pass onto a county fire road. They bumped along for maybe half a mile then parked. "We're pretty sure this is where it started," said Bruck. "You wanted to see it."

Evelyn got out followed the three men down into a shallow arroyo. The fireman/driver carried an extinguisher pack on his back and used a shovel as a walking stick. Evelyn's jeans were soon lashed with soot and her athletic shoes were blackened with ash. Single file they climbed a hillock. The fireman stopped and blasted a hot spot and Evelyn saw the ash and chemical dust rise and disperse. They stood on top of the rise and looked east.

"Some of the line went down right over there," said the fire

45

chief. "You can see the branch that came off that big oak and took down the line with it. You can see that the wind pushed the fire west – Santa Ana winds, strong offshore. Everything east, behind us, was spared because of that. The rest burned and burned. Drifted north as the winds weakened. Skilled arsonists wait for those conditions. Unfortunately."

Evelyn shot pictures. The digital SLX had been a Christmas gift from her husband, son and daughter and she thought of them every time she used it.

"We've got plenty of documentation, Evelyn," said Sheriff Hazzard. "Just let me know what you need."

Evelyn shot more pictures of the power lines tangled within the fallen branches. When she lowered the camera she caught the looks of annoyance passed between the fire chief and the sheriff. Let them be annoyed, she thought: this is evidence of SDG&E negligence and it's going to mean billions of dollars for Fallbrook and its citizens. Billions.

She skidded down the embankment to where a power pole stood. The downed line was nowhere in sight. She thought she saw a segment but it turned out to be a snake, caught above ground on the warm night and quick-roasted by the fire. "There's nothing worth seeing down there," the fire chief called out.

"Where's the power line that came down?"

"At the crime lab, Evelyn, where it belongs!"

She looked up from the snake to the blackened ridgeline and the muted sky and the vultures circling above with machined precision. Suddenly she was sickened by it all – by the stench and the ash and the death. The idea of terrorists doing this. Or any other sorry bastard. She angrily broke through a stand of scorched manzanita to find a private place, went to her knees in the ashes and threw up. Then again. She had to hold the camera to her chest so it wouldn't swing out on its strap and get puked on. A moment later, slack-faced and panting

46

softly, she stood and wiped her mouth with her hand then wiped that on her filthy jeans. She felt tears running down her face as she kicked some rubble over what she had ejected. She laughed at her simple human instinct – in spite of utter disaster – to not leave your messes for someone else to clean up. And when she looked down to check her work she saw the tangle of wires and fat D batteries and the old-fashioned wind-up travel alarm, all soot-blackened and weirdly fused to what looked like a small melted container. "Bill! Stan! I found something!"

After a quick shower and a change of clothes at home, Evelyn went back downtown to her office at City Hall. She could hardly focus on her duties after what she had found out in Rice Canyon. If that wretched ash-choked tangle of junk proved to be what Bruck and Stan said it almost certainly was, then three people had been murdered, Fallbrook was out billions of dollars, and a cold-blooded or even terrorist killer was lurking somewhere among them. Or, more than one? She Googled Al-Qaeda's "Inspire" magazine and found the most recent issue. Sure enough, the table of contents listed a piece calling for jihadi firebombing of forests in the United States. The article was dedicated to starting "huge forest fires in America with timed explosives and remote-controlled bombs." The magazine called for "Lone wolf attacks on American soil." Evelyn's heart jumped and fluttered. Wasn't Cade Magnus's group called the Lone Wolves? Or was it Rogue Wolves? Hell, she thought, in a weird way, what's the difference? Wasn't everybody a *something* these days? What reasonable person could be heard, with so many nutcase extremists of every ilk screaming and setting fires? Everywhere in the world! Even right here in Fallbrook! She wondered if this simple computer search would land her on some NSA watch list. She shivered.

47

She looked up to make sure her office door was propped open, very important, then started in answering the scores of phone calls and the hundreds of e-mails that awaited her. Talk talk talk. Tap tap tap. There were dozens more media requests for quotes and interviews – with Evelyn herself, not staff – they needed to put a face on disaster. She tried to accommodate them. Talk talk. Most of what awaited her was citizens complaints – citizens bereft with loss, citizens furious with the fire department, citizens wondering if the air and water were safe, citizens suspicious of fellow citizens. Tap tap. She answered each one as best she could before hurrying to the next: it was like juggling knives and bowling pins while balancing on a medicine ball. In Fallbrook, mayor was an elected, part-time position that paid two hundred and eighty dollars per month. Some weeks she spent three hours at city work, and some weeks twenty. Or thirty. The next few would be a test of her ability to govern *and* perform her full-time work as a "wealth manager."

She thought of her always-open office door as her way of healing the break in her heart caused by 9/11 and two bloody wars and the great recession and the mortgage meltdown and the real estate collapse and the bailouts of the big boys. These things had broken the hearts of her fellow citizens, too. God knew, they weren't shy about voicing it. But she was doing her part to fix what was broken: *she was leaving her door open*. The door to cooperation, the door to government *of, by and for the people*. Then why did she feel so helpless?

She looked up from the screen and saw Iris Cash and the two girls who had held up the "Who Killed George?" sign at the meeting the night before standing in her doorway. Behind them, tall and inelegant, looking as if she would rather be any other place on Earth than here, stood a young woman wearing only black, a thatch of copper hair jammed up into a black porkpie hat. "How can I help you?"

48

"I am McKenzie," said one of the girls. "And this is Dulce. We were George's friends. And this is Cruzela Storm. She has agreed to help us."

"And their idea is to do a concert and raise the forty-four thousand dollars for the crosswalks," Evelyn told her husband that evening as they checked the news on the kitchen TV and did the dinner prep.

"Cruzela Storm could sell out Warrior Stadium in a second flat," he said. Brian was a rocker by heart but an accountant by trade, and Evelyn's tireless partner in Anders Wealth Management. She knew that not every fifty-year old accountant would know of Cruzela Storm, but Brian would, certainly. He had a collection of guitars, mostly electric and vintage and valuable. He played them with voluble abandon through a large Marshall in their music room/den. And of course he had thousands of recordings and high-end audio gear to play them on. "Let me get that new one of hers."

Still an unrepentant CD listener, Brian came back a moment later with the jewel case and put the disc into the player. He turned off the TV and cranked the music to his usual level of too loud. Evelyn thought the opening guitar riff was dire and slightly head-banging, but when Cruzela Storm's voice kicked in it was low, pure and somehow honey-like. Evelyn looked at the picture on the CD cover: Cruzela Storm looked like Daryl Hannah in "Blade Runner," but with crazy copper hair instead of crazy white hair, all eyes and makeup. Nothing like she had looked in Evelyn's office.

"I like this bass line," said Brian.

"How much should tickets cost?" asked Evelyn. "If Cruzela Storm played at the stadium?"

"Her audience is older because she's relatively sophisticated – twenties and thirties, I'd say."

"Older? Twenties? God, what happened to us?"

"Hey hot stuff, I got ten years on you and I'm not complaining."

"That's sickening," said Ethan, heading for the fridge with half a smile. Ethan was thirteen, taller than his father and still growing, currently in size eleven shoes. He enjoyed castigating his parents but Evelyn rarely saw meanness in him.

"Get out of there," said Evelyn. "Dinner's in half an hour."

"Cruzela Storm is cool," said Ethan, tearing off a package of string cheese. "What does she look like in person?"

"She's tall and shy," said Evelyn. "She has beautiful pale skin. She's not exactly pretty. But she's . . . striking."

"I'd pay twenty to see her, but only for good seats." Ethan dropped the plastic sleeve into the wastebasket and walked out.

"Times two thousand at Warrior Stadium, if you put up chairs," said Evelyn. "That's forty grand right there. Then there's concessions, donations, raffles. Forty-four thousand? Easy. Lighted crosswalks – presto."

Evelyn drank some wine, thinking. She slid the sautéed pancetta, then the peas and olive oil, into the pan of bowtie noodles and started mixing. Cruzela Storm sang. "I think it's really more than cool of Cruzela Storm to help us build two new crosswalks," she said. "But why wasn't that little boy's life enough? Why did the people of his own town have to tell his family his life wasn't enough?"

"Because Fallbrook is full of racist pigs," said Gwen, following in her brother's footsteps to the refrigerator. She had her mother's thick dark hair, which she wore straight to her shoulders. "Cruzela Storm is half-Mexican, for your information. That's why she's going to sing. If George Hernandez had been white you wouldn't need Cruzela Storm. We'd have crosswalks leading *to* the crosswalks."

"I don't think that's true," said Evelyn.

Gwen dropped the string cheese wrapper into the trash

and bit the stick in half. "You can ask Cade Magnus if it's true, now that he's back in town."

"There are thirty thousand other people in this city besides Cade Magnus," said Brian.

"Yes. Half of them would agree with him, and the other half are afraid of him."

"That rings true in my heart, Gwen," said her mother. "And I'm ashamed of it. My own city council. And Magnus wasn't even there when we voted."

"Oh, he was there, Mom. Just invisible, like biological warfare. Like his dad."

"Aren't you a cheerful little girl?"

Ethan ambled back into the kitchen, tapping a pencil on his leg. "Cade Magnus just wants fame. It's the creepy losers he attracts that you have to watch out for. When's dinner?"

"I'd pay fifty dollars to see Cruzela Storm," said Gwen. "If I had fifty dollars."

"Tell you what," said her father. "If Cruzela Storm plays in Fallbrook, I'll buy us all good seats. Good singer, good songwriter, and a worthy cause."

Gwen glowered at her mother and walked out in her usual shoulders-forward, head-down kind of slouch. Ethan swiped an apple off the counter and followed her out.

"Can we leave our children with friends for a couple years and take a vacation?" Evelyn asked.

"Sure. Where do you want to go?"

"When I was in Rice Canyon today it made me think of Pala Casino. The hotel room, actually." She looked up at him with a small smile.

"With two child-free years we can do better than an Indian casino."

"Somewhere with room service and a good view of something."

Brian poured her a little more wine, then another full glass

51

for himself, and Evelyn saw the darkness cross his face. She had always loved his easy optimism but in the last couple of years she'd seen the growing frustration in him that he tried to tamp down with alcohol.

"Archie and Patrick Norris came by today for a big-picture look at where they stand," said Brian. "What a mess." He synopsized their plight. "And the Farm Credit Bank won't loan for replacement trees. So we sold off some of their retirement investments that had finally come back since the crash. That was a break-even. And some of the second-issue REITs we got them into – I had to dump them on the secondary market at a loss. That hurt. Evie? I'm getting really tired of watching our friends and clients take our advice then lose what they've worked for. The crash, the jobs, the drought, the freeze. Now the fire. It feels . . . endless."

"It's going to turn, honey," was the best she could come up with. She suddenly felt exhausted.

He drank. "But the good news is I paid our fed and state quarterlies today," he said.

"The ones due back in September?"

"Those very ones," he said softly. "We'll fall within the penalty grace period. Not worried."

"Did you have to raid the college account?"

Brian studiously did not look at her. "Yeah. And I sold three Gibsons and two Gretsches to replenish it. The Hummingbird. Ouch. But it's okay. How many guitars does one middle-aged bean counter really need?"

She came over and kissed his lips lightly and lay her head against his chest. "It's going to turn, baby. For all of us."

7

Patrick, Ted and Archie walked the reeking groves trying to guess which of the damaged trees might live and which would die. Archibald said that if there was a blessing in this fire it was the speed of it, leaving, possibly, a number of trees still alive. By spring they would see new growth on the survivors, few as they might be. Those without life by April they would cut off at the ground and Norris Brothers would try again to get a Farm Credit Bank to loan for replacement trees. Archie said if God smiled on them, which He rarely did anymore, half of the trees were still alive and would make it. A harvest from those trees was three years out now, but if spring showed at least half them alive, the bank would loan. The bank would *have* to loan on forty acres of good Haas avocados.

Patrick knew that if replacement trees were watered generously, and did not get *phytophthora* root rot, or stem canker or sunblotch disease, or fall prey to looper worms, amorbia larvae, thrips, mites or worms, they would produce fruit in three years. *Three years,* thought Patrick. And there had already been no pick earlier this year because of the March freeze. He thought of Pharaoh and wondered what his father had done to bring all of this down on them, knowing he had done nothing.

But in the meantime, there was plenty to do. First was to paint the southwest exposure of each tree with a fifty-fifty mix of white paint and water to prevent sunburn of the unprotected trunks and branches. This should be done quickly. Then they'd replace the damaged irrigation line, risers, sprinklers, valves and timers. When that was done the whole system would need to be flushed to keep the mains clean. After that they'd need to circle each tree with straw, out to fifteen feet per tree, to keep the fall rains from washing away the soil. All the while, Archie would continue to make the rounds to the other Farm Credit banks, begging them to do their jobs, as he put it.

The brothers started with the irrigation and Archie began the painting. Patrick worked with his shirt off and enjoyed the mild autumn sun on his back. He ducked under the seared branches and walked the grids looking for melted line and sprayers. Plastic was no match for a wildfire. He was soon as black as the trees, and the ash got through his bandana into his mouth and nose, and his safety goggles needed constant wiping. He saw that Ted was mostly black also, but he had some lightness in his step, in spite of his bad feet, and he was moving about with his shoulders back, attempting to hold his gut in.

Patrick's phone vibrated in his pant pocket and he was pleased to see platoon-mate John Bostik's name on the screen. "Boss."

"Hey Pat. What are you doing?"

"Labor."

"Everything burned up?"

"Pretty much. You?"

"Maria kicked me out so I got my own place in Oceanside. You should come over sometime. Party."

"That's too bad about the girl."

"It's cool. I just met her and I was driving her crazy. I can't sleep or concentrate. The littlest things freak me out. Fuckin' car backfired yesterday and I just about lost it. Everybody around me just pisses me off."

"Yeah, me too, the little things. I'm getting some sleep, a little. It's weird not being crowded in. Maybe you should see a doctor, get some pills."

"I already got more pills than I can take. Maybe we all could hook up after the Three/Five Memorial."

"We'll do that. I'll talk to Salimony and Messina. You hang in there, Boss."

Bostic had lugged and operated a heavy explosives detector known as a Minehound for thirteen straight months. He had often been silent, Patrick remembered – silent as he listened for the sound of metal registering through his headset. Bostic was the platoon's silent ears. Now Bostic was quiet again for a long moment. "I heard 'Paint it Black' in a bar and almost couldn't take it. That's how I feel. I hate this. I'd way rather be back in Sangin getting my ass shot at. At least I had something to do and training to do it. The only job I can here get is boxing groceries at the PX on base. And outside base, man, it's just children and grown-up children. America doesn't go to war, America goes to the mall. Everybody smiles and says thanks for what I did. They don't know shit about what I did and they don't want to know."

"That's a fact."

"Okay, Pat. Eat the apple; fuck the corps."

Patrick thought about Bostik as he and Ted took the truck down to the barn. They loaded up the valves, filters, water line, PVC cement, cutters, insulated wire, sprinkler heads, shovels and picks. With ten summers of such work behind him, Patrick could do this in his sleep. But Ted knew almost nothing about irrigation and he tried to do whatever Patrick did, then lost interest and turned over branches and rocks, looking for creatures he might move into the bunkhouse.

Back in the grove, the digging felt good to Patrick's

muscles and he was pleased by how many valves they had replaced by noon. It felt good to be necessary. "This isn't bad work," he said. "Nobody's shooting at us and nothing's going to explode. In Afghanistan you were either bored out of your mind or terrified. The thing I like about this work is it leaves my mind free wander."

"What was it like on your first patrol?"

"Just the usual."

"There wasn't much usual in what you were doing, Pat. You should at least tell me something about it, since I'm your brother."

Patrick dug in with his shovel. "When we first got there, the Taliban knew there had been a change of guard so they wanted to welcome us new guys. First full day at FOB Inkerman we were told to walk a hundred meters down road Six-One-One, then turn around and come back. Just our squad, twenty-one of us. One hundred damned meters. With that much gear, a hundred meters can smoke you unless you're used to it. We were supposed to get used to our stuff and the terrain. Six-One-One was narrow and rocky. Off to the east there was corn, high corn that time of year, all the way back to the Helmand River. Then hills. On our right, to the west, was all brown zone – flat desert and no cover. That hundred meters just about killed us. I carried a SAW machine gun, which weighs twenty-eight pounds. Plus ammo, grenades, water. When we started back we heard motorcycles out in the corn. That's a weird fucking sound – high corn with motorcycles revving inside it. We had ICOM radio intercepts and 'terps to tell us what the skinnies were saying to each other. They were setting up an ambush is what they were doing. But we made it back with no contact. We were disappointed."

"Disappointed you didn't get shot at?"

"Yep. We'd all gone there to fight."

"When *was* the first contact?"

56

"The next morning. It was a full-on op, with an early gear check and a map and orders to recon a village further up the Six-One-One. We were only five minutes out the back gate when we heard the motorcycles out in the corn again and the 'terps said it was Taliban again, a lot of them. They lit us up with machine guns, heavy fire, and we all hauled ass into the corn and dove in. Then everybody was firing blind and there was corn flying around but you could barely even see your own guys. Loud. It was amazing how we hardly ever *saw* the rag-heads. But we were happy to be shooting. So after a few minutes everybody's done and the air is full of dust and gunsmoke and everything goes real quiet. You could smell the shot-up corn. And goddamned Salimony screams out, *"America! Get some!"* We went another forty meters up the road and Messina saw a hajji in a man-dress digging in the rocks. Blew him onto his butt. It was our first kill."

"How many did you kill personally, Pat?"

"Eight for sure. Probably more like twenty, realistically. We could only do death confirmations maybe a quarter of the time because the contact was so heavy. They'd drag out their dead and we'd never know."

Patrick wiped the sweat and soot from his forehead then Ted did, too. "Wow, Pat. That must have been a rush. I wish I could do something like that."

Patrick looked out at the burned world that they were trying to repair, one sprinkler, one tree at a time. "Yeah, it's a rush."

Ted nodded and took up his shovel again. "I had a gun pointed in my face just two days ago. Right here in Fallbrook. I thought I might get shot for sure. I was driving my taxi and it was one of my fares. A young Mexican guy. He lured me to his 'hood on Ventana so his homies could watch him jack me. He took all the money I'd collected, and all my tips except for ten bucks. I was really scared but really mad, too. I could feel those two things fighting it out in me for what I should do. Scared and mad. I got short of breath and my vision shrunk down to like a tunnel like it always did, remember? I chased him but you know how slow I am. I went to the cops then turned around in the station and walked right back out. I'd seen the Mexican guy before around town, and I'm sure I'll see him again. His gun was old and the bluing was rubbed off the end of the barrel."

"How come you didn't say anything?"

"I just did, Pat."

"This happened the day after I got home?"

"Yeah, that day. I was thinking about you the whole time I was driving. And the next thing I know there's a gun in my face. I haven't told anybody but you."

"You didn't report it?"

"You know me and cops."

"What are you going to do, Ted?"

"I don't know what to do. I got robbed, so there's supposed to be justice. On the other hand, I didn't get shot and I'm only out some tip money. What do you think I should do?"

Patrick dug out a ruined valve as he thought. "Tough call. I'd go back to the cops. Report it. They'll question him. Maybe he's had other complaints."

"Then I go to court and a bunch of people stare at me? And the judge dismisses the case for lack of evidence? And don't forget, I'm the guy who got expelled for making fun of the mayor on the web, so they all would think I'm a whack-job."

"That wouldn't properly figure in, I don't think. But this wouldn't go to a trial. No witnesses except his buddies, and you know what they'll say. But you don't have to press charges to file a complaint, I don't think. You just have to let the law put this guy on notice."

"What if he robs me again?"

Patrick emptied a shovelful of good Fallbrook decomposed

58

granite around the valve. "Then that's a whole different story. If we're out and about and you see him, point him out."

"Sir, yes sir."

"Stop that, Ted."

"Okay. Should I get a gun?"

"No. Then things just escalate."

"Would you say that to anyone, or just to me?"

"To anyone. Speaking for myself, I can't tell you how good it was to check in my weapons in at the armory. I like being able to walk around without guns. It's a privilege."

They worked silently for a few minutes and Patrick wondered what would be right behavior for Ted, given the young Mexican man, the gun, the money, the fear and anger. He'd seen that anger spike. A gun for Ted didn't seem like the right thing. It struck Patrick that in many ways civilian life was more difficult than combat. In Fallbrook things were not clearly divided into us or them, friend or enemy, kill or be killed. In Sangin, the things he had done as a fighting man were simple and clear, bloody though they sometimes were. Here, things were complex.

They replaced the burned valve and walked to the truck for water. Patrick saw his father down in a swale two hundred meters away, painting a tree trunk with the sprayer. Something about it was amusing and sad at the same time: an aging man in a burnt grove, painting tree trunks white. White for Archie; black for Bostic. "Anyway," he said. "My mind wanders to Iris Cash a lot."

"She's very attractive," said Ted.

"Yeah. And she's a fighter. She thinks her stories are weapons. But for good, you know, to help people. She's trying get lighted crosswalks downtown, even though her own city council said no."

Ted glugged down some water and wiped his face with the back of his hand. "I heard about that. Evelyn Anders is behind it."

Patrick cut his brother a sharp look. "Don't."

"I won't. I'm not. I've got my orders." Ted nodded and pursed his lips but Patrick could tell that he wasn't going to be able to silence himself. "You know, Pat – Evelyn Anders is Mom's and Dad's financial advisor. Isn't it weird that with her, our parents have lost *so much money?*"

"Everybody has, Ted. It's a bad recession. Not everything is personal. Not everything is a conspiracy. Not everything can be blamed on a small-town mayor."

"Government *is* the problem, Pat. I'm sure of it."

"Work, Ted. Work."

At cocktails Patrick stood on the Norris patio and watched the sun setting over the distant hills. He was tired from the grove work but pleased with their progress. He thought about the fishing boat he'd seen for sale on the web last night. It was an older but very neat 17-foot Mako Pro Skiff, set up well for fly-casters, trailered and allegedly pampered. Thirteen grand.

Ted sat shoeless in a rocking chair, rubbing his foot through a blackened sock, a large tumbler of iced tea sweating on the deck beside him. He had brought a computer out to the porch to watch the San Diego news. "I've decided to drive the taxi on weekends and some evenings," he said. "It pays and I need the money."

Archie and Caroline both looked from the monitor to Ted, and the swinging love seat they shared swayed to a gradual stop. "If you have the energy for two jobs, like Pat does, then more power to you," said Archie. "I think all of you should know that I'll be talking to the farm bankers down in Escondido tomorrow. I'm hoping we can get a loan to order replacement trees."

"It's like a Government conspiracy to wreck our family," said Ted.

"In what way?" asked Archie. "I'm just talking to the bank, Ted."

"But it's funny how she bailed them out but not us."

"She?" asked Caroline.

"The Nanny State, Mom. Bailing out the banks."

"Look," said Archie. "I don't love the government either, son. But leave the whining back in the bunkhouse before work tomorrow. And wear some boots with better support."

"Do you still have the good orthotics?" asked Caroline.

"I'll find them. In the closet somewhere."

"I think this calls for a toast," said Caroline. They lifted their glasses and waited. "To the Norrises – back from one war and into another."

They clinked glasses and Patrick felt emotion in it, the simple act of touching. Then a TV story about the disastrous Fallbrook Fire came on the news and he saw Fire Chief Bruck and Sheriff Hazzard and Mayor Anders on the dais at city hall. The Fallbrook city seal was visible behind them. With the two men standing slab-faced on either side of her, Evelyn Anders announced that the fire was conclusively arson-caused and the current damages were three human lives and approximately two billion dollars in damaged property. She asked that anyone who had information leading to the arrest and conviction of the arsonist would get a reward of $50,000 from San Diego Gas & Electric.

"That's big government in bed with big business," said Ted. "Fifty thousand is nothing to them. She'll draw a fat pension and they'll raise the rates whenever they want. No wonder we the people can't win."

Patrick watched the next story, about an Al-Qaeda magazine calling for American jihadists to start forest fires in America in the summer and fall. Apparently, "detailed instructions" were published online. Patrick looked at the pictures of bearded, turbaned, smiling men who published

61

the magazine and they looked pretty much like the skinnies he'd spent thirteen months in Sangin trying to kill.

"You missed a couple," said Ted.

It was a relief to get away from all of them, to walk into the Domino's kitchen, get his blue-black-and-red work shirt on, pack the deliveries into soft-sided warmers and insulated pizza sleeves while he talked to Firooz. Firooz and his wife Simone were Iranian refugees who had come here decades ago, after the fall of the Shah. He had been a veterinarian and she a schoolteacher. They were humble people, willing to be of service, and now they owned the franchise. Firooz kept touching Patrick – on the arm, the shoulder, patting his hand. He and Simone helped Patrick carry out the warmers and set them securely in the cab of his truck. Patrick attached the Domino's sign to the roof of the polished black, Ford F-150 – used but low mileage, a graduation gift from his mother and father – then climbed in. He hit Mission and gunned it for Stage Coach. He'd never known, before deployment, what a pleasure it was to drive a good vehicle on wide safe streets, feel those V-8 horses stretching out, no IEDs to blow him to smithereens.

Three short hours later his work was done and Patrick sat outside in folding chairs with Firooz and Simone. The night air was damp, and in the down-spray of the parking lot lights Patrick could see mist and ash settling. They talked about town and business and the big election coming up and the several federal and state agents, not to mention local sheriff deputies, who had come around to talk with Firooz and his wife lately. Something about an online terrorist site they'd never heard of. Inspire.

"We can live through these suspicions," said Simone. "They are unfounded and ridiculous. And nothing, compared to what we have been through. This is our country."

8

Three days later, after ten hours of field labor, Patrick took the night off from delivery work. He showered and shaved and tried on clothes he'd left at home before deployment, which were too large for him after thirteen months of combat and meager rations. Zero hot meals a day. One cold shower a week. Some of his older high school clothes fit.

He met Iris Cash at Salerno's. The dining room and bar had few customers on this weeknight, even with several Fallbrook restaurants having recently folded. Iris took a barstool facing Patrick across a small round table. She launched straight into the arson evidence and the reward and who would do such a thing to this peaceful little town? Then she was off on Cruzela Storm and Georgie's brave friends and lighted crosswalks, and how she'd already gotten the school district to lock in a date for Warriors Stadium, and a pledge of deeply discounted food and drinks from Major Market; and she'd been promised page one, above-the-fold placement for an article and pictures in "The Village View" next Thursday, which would trigger the North County News and the San Diego Union-Tribune and the networks to follow and *kiss my exhaust!* Iris wore a frayed and faded denim jacket over a lacy blouse, and jeans tucked into boots. She had a quirky smile and smelled floral. Patrick earnestly faced this blizzard of words and expressions and sensations, easily the most pleasant minutes of his life for well over a year.

The waitress brought their drinks and Patrick told Iris about the irrigation and painting and how it took a long outdoor shower just to get the soot off him before showering inside. He tried to match her emotional energy but since coming home, he was having trouble staying interested in himself. It was hard to stay focused on things that couldn't kill you. Even when they were good things, and important. He found himself arranging the salt and pepper shakers and the bottle of hot sauce in the same relative positions as Myers and Zane and himself at 2200 hours on May 23 on the night patrol up to Outpost Three, wondering for the thousandth time, at least, how it was that Myers – touching down in Patrick's footprints while Patrick followed those of three other men ahead of him, and all of them behind Bostic with the Minehound and Zane with his splendid nose and instincts – had tripped the IED. How was that even possible? How had Zane failed to detect it? Bostic?

"So, are you going to stay in Fallbrook and work the ranch?" asked Iris.

"For now. I'm delivering pizza too."

This seemed not to faze Iris. "Do you like growing things?"

"Not really. I don't seem to have farming blood. I want to guide anglers on the bay. In a boat. But now, I'm trying to do what's right."

"I heard you lost almost all the trees."

"Just a few left for sure, out of eighty acres."

"You don't have to talk."

"I want to talk."

"If you say so."

Patrick returned from some far place. "Want to get a table and have dinner?"

"I'd like that. Can I ask you something?"

Patrick nodded and drank. He felt the strength of the liquor. After a year of almost no drinking, even a small amount hit him hard.

"Can you tell me three words that will help me understand you?"

Patrick thought for a moment. "I miss it."

Her expression went from concern to astonishment, which she quickly dropped. "That's . . . three words, alright. You *do* want to talk. Let's get that table. The *osso buco* here is terrific. Oh, can I just say one thing to you?"

"Please don't say thank you."

"Welcome home."

After dinner Patrick drove them out to Oceanside and they walked the pier to the end and watched the fishermen bring in mackerel and bonito from the floodlit sea. The landed fish spasmed wildly against their plastic buckets. Patrick nodded at some of the Marines in and out of uniform, and some of them acknowledged him. In town he took Iris to the Galleon, a bar popular with his fellow Pendleton Marines. They got two stools at the bar and Patrick bought a round for them and for the four Marines who were already there. The jukebox played a country song, then some metal, then "Satisfaction," the opening notes of which brought shouts of *I can't get no!* and raised glasses all up and down the bar. Patrick knocked back the bourbon and signaled for another round. Iris gamely drained her lemon drop, sat up straight and took a deep breath. "Don't let me get too stupid tonight. I have work in the morning."

"I've got your back."

She smiled at him and Patrick saw the doubt in it. The bourbons seemed strong to him. He ordered beer backs with the next round and Iris declined. The alcohol kicked in and Patrick felt calm and alert. He knew he was drinking for all the good things he missed, and he wondered what it said about him that what should have been the worst thirteen months of his life were in fact months of excitement,

65

purpose and selfless loyalty. Good things. Two rounds of drinks later the young Marine next to him asked where'd he'd been and Patrick told him Helmand, the 3/5 and the boy nodded respectfully. Patrick's 3rd Battalion, 5th Regiment had suffered more casualties than any Marine battalion in the war. They were known through history as the Dark Horse Battalion, and their motto was "Get Some."

"I wondered if that low fade made you a Dark Horse," said the young Marine.

"Yes," said Patrick, the low fade referring to his haircut – long for a Marine, and permitted only to grunts who had seen action. The low fade was not to be worn by new Marines, who were relegated to shaves or the traditional high-and-tight worn by most officers.

"You guys kicked serious ass," said the Marine. "Too bad we'll give it back to the terrorists and dope growers."

"It's their home," said Patrick. "And it's hell anyway. Let them have it."

"How many did you lose?"

"Twenty five very good men. Two hundred wounded."

"How many'd you kill?"

"Four hundred seventy confirmed but a lot more in reality."

Someone on the other side of Iris said something but Patrick couldn't make it out. Whoever said it, said it again. Patrick leaned forward and looked past Iris at the red-faced boy who was drinking Patrick's generosity. A high-and-tight cherry if Patrick had ever seen one. "I'd go and kill another four hundred if they'd let me," he said.

"You're a POG, so you don't have to worry."

"How do you know I'm a POG?"

"What's a POG?" Iris interjected.

"Personnel Other Than Grunt," said Patrick. "And I can tell by looking at you."

"I'm a Marine Air mechanic and proud of it. Jason Falk."

"Patrick Norris. You guys wouldn't land for our wounded in Sangin if there was fire, Jason. The Brits did it all the time, but not you."

"Watch your words. The pilots I know would fly down the barrel of a gun. All I said was I'd go over and – "

"Don't waste your time," said Patrick.

Jason considered this then chugged the last half of his beer. "Twenty-five is a lot of Americans."

"It's lot of Americans to waste."

"I don't agree it was a waste. Freedom is worth fighting for."

"But Afghanistan isn't worth dying for. That's what I'm trying to get through your thick fuckin' skull."

"E-Three Norris, there's a lady present," said Jason Falk. "That's in case you didn't notice. I told you once to watch your words. I'm Marine Air and I don't back down."

"Tell your pilots to grow some."

"What's wrong with you?"

"Boots like you," said Patrick.

"Time to clear out," said Iris.

Patrick turned to her and the blow landed blind. After that, pure reaction. As Jason chambered another punch Patrick crashed a fist hard into his face, then an even harder elbow. The sound whap-cracked through the music and Jason's face exploded with blood. Patrick heard Iris scream at him to stop but he hit Jason twice more on the way down and then he felt the weight of someone on top of him and he went to one knee and threw the first Marine over his shoulder. Then Iris was pulling him up and Patrick took her arm and guided her to the door but he hustled back and put the half-risen man back down with a short hook to his middle. Outside they ran down Sundowner to Pacific Coast Highway for the truck. The cuffs of Patrick's too-large pants flopped down past his ankles and almost tripped him. At the truck he opened the doors with the fob and they clambered up and in. Patrick made the u-turn too fast and the tires chirped and the headlights of a police cruiser parked across the street came on.

"Do not *consider* trying to outrace that cop," hissed Iris.

Patrick checked the rearview and saw he had about fifty yards head start, and the cruiser was coming fast, lights flashing and the siren loud. He looked at the Galleon and there was no one yet in pursuit. "I'm good. We're good. We're okay."

"Can you pass the test?"

"Pretty sure."

Patrick pulled into the Harbor House parking lot and the cop car whirled and screamed in behind him. He drove to the rear and parked. In the sideview he saw the cruiser flashing. He waited while the cop ran his plates and he hoped someone back home had paid up the registration in his absence. "Just be nice and be yourself," said Iris.

"Which one?"

Patrick watched the prowl car door open and a chunky uniform cop climb out. The cop had his hand on the handle of his sidearm in a casual way and in his other hand was a long flashlight. He stopped short of and slightly behind the driver's window and raised the beam of the flashlight into Patrick's face. Pat sat up with both hands on the wheel and looked straight ahead. His breathing was normal and his pulse felt right.

"What's the hurry?" said the cop.

"Just heading home."

"M'am. How are you tonight?"

Patrick saw her squint. "Just fine, officer. And you?"

"License and registration." Patrick dug out his wallet and handed over his military ID and driver's license. Iris had opened the glove box and Patrick leaned across and caught

68

her scent and the curve of her legs illuminated faintly by compartment light. He rummaged through the compartment and found the registration folder. "Step out."

Patrick opened the door and got out just as another police car pulled into the parking lot, lights flashing but silent. Then another. He looked across the tops of them toward the Galleon but still he saw no people or commotion there. The two new units penned him in. An officer from each car got out and stood between Patrick's truck and the first cruiser while the lead responder walked back for a warrants check. Patrick looked through the open window at Iris then leaned against his door and waited.

"Be cool," said Iris.

"How many cops does it take to arrest a jarhead?"

"I mean it, Patrick."

"They shouldn't leave those lights flashing."

"Did your dad ever tell you bedtime stories?"

"Mom did. Dad read me the Weekly Newsline of the California Avocado Commission."

The first cop came back and handed Patrick his documents. "Been drinking, Patrick?"

"I had two beers."

"Smells like more than that."

"Precisely two, sir."

"Are you returning or deploying?"

"Just home."

"I'm going to do a nystagmus test." The cop pulled a penlight stepped close to Patrick and played the beam back and forth, eye to eye. "Hmmm. Can you walk a straight line for me?" The cop stepped back ten paces. "Extend your arms and look up. Straight line now, walk directly to me."

Patrick heard muffled laughter from the other cops, who stood just beyond the lights and flashers of the first car. A group of people watched from the sidewalk. His plan was to focus on the north star but the marine layer offered him nothing but a pale fuzzy firmament. Marine layer, he thought: that's funny. He wished he could Marine lay Iris. He stared up into the fog as he walked but sensed he was just a little off course and when he lowered his gaze he saw that he was off almost thirty degrees. He stopped and sighed deeply and heard the truck door slam. Iris advanced through the flashing lights and the headlights with a hand out, proffering what looked to Patrick like a business card. "Officer, I'm Iris Cash with the Village View newspaper in Fallbrook? Can I talk to you for just about two seconds? Please?" Patrick saw the other officers converging in her direction and he felt his adrenalin spike and he was more than ready to fight again.

He heard the first cop say, "Yes, you may." The other officers moved closer to Patrick and he watched Iris and the cop talking but could not hear their words. They stood by his car just out of the flood of the headlights. The cop had that feet-spread, arms-across-the chest stance that looked non-negotiable. Patrick saw the red, white and blue bands of light flashing across their bodies. He looked toward the Galleon and he saw that the door was open now and there were men looking up and down the street. He tried to count how many drinks he'd had and could not. Iris came through the flashing lights, walking fast with her hand out, palm up. Patrick saw the men outside the Galleon looking his way. "Keys," she said. "Now."

Patrick held out the truck keys and saluted the officer, partially visible in the whirling colored lights.

9

Ted quit the grove work at noon and drove to Oceanside. He stepped inside Open Sights gun store and range, saw the glass counters along three of the walls, heard the muffled gunfire. The handguns were arrayed beneath the glass, all pointing in the same direction, like fish in a school. A tall man with a big head and a black suit came in. Ted thought he might have seen him around Fallbrook recently, then decided it was just his guilty conscience. Then he thought: what should I feel guilty about? The Second Amendment protects my right to keep and bear arms.

He looked through the safety window at the range shooters blasting away. There were several men, three women and two children who, it seemed to Ted, should be in school. He watched them through the imperfectly clear bullet-proof glass, their arms extended, all wearing goggles and bulbous headgear, guns jumping in their hands, shiny cases flying. He heard the pop-pop of smaller guns, then the booming thunderbolts of the magnums. Through all the soundproofing, he thought: what power. With the glass before him it was like watching on a monitor or TV or through the windshield of his taxi, thus hypnotic. He wanted to polish the safety glass so he could see better.

"May I help you?"

"I hope so. I was robbed at gunpoint three days ago. I'm looking for a gun."

"I'm sorry that happened. I hear stories like that a lot these days. I can help you be better prepared for that kind of situation."

"I'm Ted."

"Kerry."

Kerry was about Ted's age – assured, muscular and friendly – and Ted wished he was more like him. Kerry gave him general advice on a reliable, effective home-protection handguns and Ted liked the look of the Glocks. Kerry removed one of them, checked the chamber, popped out the magazine and set the gun on the counter. He told Ted that you could run it over with a truck, dip it in mud and hold it underwater, and a Glock would still fire every time. He praised the forty caliber as a versatile round, plenty of stopping power and it would carry fifteen cartridges in the magazine. He handed the gun to Ted. "It's like having your own fire squad," he said.

"I sure could have used it a couple days back."

"Tell me what happened."

Ted did, feeling his anger and fear again, and his embarrassment at having been lured into the ambush.

"That shouldn't happen in this country," said Kerry.

"I'd like it not to happen to me again."

"We teach weapons self-defense classes, right here."

"I'll take the gun."

"You do know if your decide to purchase, there's a ten-day wait while the state does a background check on you?"

"Right. So they can make sure I'm not a crazy."

"We offer a free test fire if you're serious about that sidearm. Have you fired a handgun before?"

"No."

"I think you'll like it."

Inside the range Ted watched Kerry fasten the Zombie Steve target to the motorized line and send it twenty feet out.

At the bench he watched Kerry ready the autoloader. The headsets were comfortable and made the gunshots around him sound distant but he could still feel the percussion in his body. Kerry stepped to the shooting stall with the gun, demonstrated the basic two-hand shooter's stance: feet shoulder-wide, weight slightly forward, right elbow locked, left not, grip firm but not tight. Squeeze, he said, don't pull. He fired one round. It took Ted a moment to find the hole, which was right through the middle of Zombie Steve's grimacing face. Ted smiled. Kerry set the gun on the shelf and Ted stepped forward and picked it up.

He listened to Kerry's instructions and squeezed off a round. He was surprised at the power, and at the immediacy of the recoil. A gun was a decisive thing, he realized – nothing hesitant or reversible about it. It impressed him that it could re-load itself so quickly, before the bullet got to the target, it seemed. Actually hitting the target was the hard part. Even at only twenty feet away, when he got the sights lined up, all it took was a split second to be aiming someplace else – the slightest breath or random thought and the gun barrel jumped far off course. So Ted held his breath but Kerry, speaking loudly through the gunfire and protective headgear, told him *don't do that*, just squeeze the trigger on the exhale and it's both eyes open, Ted, don't close that left eye of yours, you need them both to shoot well. Nine shots later Ted had hit Zombie Steve's body four times, and the white paper outside the body twice, and missed the target altogether with the other three. For a split second Zombie Steve became Evelyn Anders' campaign poster and this led to one of the body shots. Then Zombie Steve became Edgar and Ted hit the target again.

"Not bad for your first time," said Kerry. "That Model 22 in your hand is lightly used, so you'd save a good chunk of change."

Ted bought the gun and put the ammunition in his truck. He felt more capable now, and empowered by the idea that in ten days the Glock would be his.

A few minutes later he was back in Fallbrook, heading up Main toward home. The many poster faces of Evelyn Anders looked down on him with smug condescension. The face of Walt Rood struck him as caring and reasonable. He liked the slogan, "Small Government that Works."

Ted caught the red light at Alvarado and saw that Vince Ross Village Square on the corner was crowded. People were talking and drinking canned sodas and there was a long table with a red-white-and-blue tablecloth set out with what looked like brochures and DVDs. A banner facing the street proclaimed: *Carry Freedom!* He saw both men and women and there was something unusual about them. It finally dawned on Ted that they were all wearing holsters. No guns, just holsters. Some wore leg holsters like old West gunmen, others had detective-style shoulder rigs, some had holsters attached to their belts. Ted saw a man wearing shorts with a large holster strapped to his calf. Some even had empty rifle scabbards slung over their shoulders. They moved with an exaggerated ease, pretending too hard that they were not doing anything unusual. Ted wondered if nudists did that. He stared until the light changed, then rounded the corner, u-turned and parked on Alvarado.

Through the window glass he saw a man, head and shoulders above the crowd, apparently standing on one of the park benches. He wore twin leather six-gun holsters and bandoleers thrown over his shoulders. His arms were spread in oratory. Ted recognized him immediately as Cade Magnus. He hadn't seen him in ten years and he was heavier, but had the same stocky build and bushy brown hair. He remembered that Cade Magnus had eyes just like Cade's

74

father's – blue and clear. He had talked to them years ago, down at Pride Auto Repair, back when he was interested in the White Crusade. Now here was Cade, back in Fallbrook, a city that had rejoiced when he'd moved away.

Two Sheriff's cars pulled up and parked in the red along Vince Ross Square. Ted watched the four deputies get out, recognizing the black man as the one who had pulled him over for the brake light and given him the sobriety test in broad daylight, though his most recent drink had been half a year ago. One of the deputies was older, one was a stocky Latina and the other a young white man. They strolled casually toward the square. Magnus seemed to stop what he was saying then smiled and acknowledged them. Many of the bystanders turned as the deputies worked their way into the crowd.

Ted felt his indignation march in, and his vision beginning to constrict, and his heart rate climb. He trained his gun- barrel vision on the deputy who had written him the fix-it ticket – the black one, hiding behind the sunglasses. Anger overtook indignation. Ted felt that he had to do something. Should he go tell the deputies that this was a peaceful demonstration? Should he ask them why it takes four of them to raid Village Square when not one showed up when he was robbed at gunpoint two days ago? Should he tell Magnus he respected his right to stand up to the Government and exercise his Constitutional rights?

Ted got out of his truck and locked up and headed up the sidewalk toward the square. As he walked past, Cade glanced at him, as did two of the deputies and some of the crowd. Their eyes were hard on him and with every step Ted felt less protected – no layer of glass to shield him – and his anger and indignation fled. In their place he felt a constricting panic, almost like being lost. He thought of the box of .40 caliber shells in his truck. Was that a crime? Without breaking stride

75

he passed the square, turned the corner and kept going. When he felt safely past it all, he turned for a look behind him and saw a tall man in a black suit standing on the sidewalk, looking into the front window of the candy shop. From this distance, he looked like the man from Open Sights just an hour ago. Impossible, thought Ted.

His heart was racing by the time he got to Gulliver's Travels on Main. Mary Gulliver had no customers and she stood and smiled at Ted when he came through the door. Behind her was the wall of travel posters for exotic destinations. She specialized in cruises. To Ted, Mary was a beautiful woman, full-bodied, fragrant, always groomed to perfection. He had seen her around town for years but had talked to her for the first time only two weeks ago.

"Hello, Ted."

"Hi Mary. Busy? I just came to . . . say hello."

"Are you feeling alright?"

"Light-headed. I don't know why."

"Sit down, I'll get you some water."

He sat in front of her desk and looked up at a poster of Mykonos. He focused in on one small white building in the crowded cliff-top village. His carotid throbbed. She came back with a bottle and handed it to him, then sat down. "You might be feeling all that ash still in the air," she said.

"Probably."

"I'm so sorry to hear about the farm."

The water bottle was cold in his hands and his thoughts were swimming. He took a deep breath and let it out in a long fluttering exhale. "Mary, may I take you to dinner at the Cafe de Artistes tonight? The food is wonderful and they have very good wines. I'd like your company. I'll meet you there or pick you up, whatever's best for you. It's very French."

She smiled a troubled smile. "That is so sweet of you. But I'm not dating, Ted."

"Oh, I'm sorry – "

"Don't be, there's no – "

"You just never wear a ring and last week you mentioned going out with your sister. So I thought maybe you had some time on your hands."

"You are so sweet, Ted. That is so sweet."

"I'm really sorry." He stood.

"No, *I'm* really sorry . . . I just . . . well, Ted, I'm easily twice your age."

"I know. It was stupid. I'm stupid."

"I'm flattered."

Ted mustered a smile and saw the concern on her face. Her eyes were wet but nervous at the same time. "Maybe you can send me to Greece someday," he said.

"I'd love to."

"Do you like the Greek restaurant here in town?"

She was about to speak then stopped herself. The phone rang. "I should take this."

"Bye, Mary," said Ted with all the good cheer he could pretend. "I'll see you around."

"Stop by any time!"

He walked all the way down Main to the GasPro store, where he bought and drank a small, powerful energy drink. He talked briefly with the Iraqi-born manager, Ibrahim. Ibrahim was big and strong and usually good humored and helpful. But today he looked at Ted with a piercing suspicion. Ted felt as if Ibrahim knew everything about him: his anger and fear, his new gun, his overpowering urge to . . . *do something*. Ted dropped his change into a Muscular Dystrophy collection jar. Standing outside he leafed through a free pamphlet of cars for sale. Ibrahim looked at him through the window. Ted walked back toward his truck way down on Alvarado, keeping to the opposite side of the street from Gulliver's Travels, pausing at some windows to look in. He

77

saw himself and felt shame. His collapsed and graceless feet hurt again by then. When he passed Village Square there was no sign of Magnus or the protesters or the sheriffs.

Ted took a back way onto the Norris Brothers property. Bouncing along the dirt road he saw Patrick and his father two hillsides over, stooped to some task at ground level. He felt surprisingly secretive about having bought the gun and he certainly didn't want them to know about it, or see the ammunition. He swung over the rise and down into a swale and parked by the bunkhouse and barn.

Ted hustled the plastic bag into the barn and looked for a good hiding place. He thought of stashing it inside one of the bags of the pole-pickers, which were leaning against one wall. They wouldn't be used again for three years. Or, with the fire, he thought, maybe never used again period. He considered the fuel canisters and the many crates of fertilizers, soil amendments, vitamin additives and pesticides. There were also vehicles and heavy machinery – two tractors, a flat-bed Ford with fold-up sides for hay bales or crated fruit. Ted looked at the two dune buggies, the wood chippers, the Bobcat, and various tractor attachments – discs glinting faintly, a mower, a ripper, a front loader. Not here, he thought.

One shelf was taken up with his brother's fly-fishing gear. It was all covered by a blue tarp that was cinched down by its grommets but Ted knew exactly what was there: dozens of rods in their tubes and reels in their pouches and waders and boots and vests and so many fly boxes it seemed that every earthly insect and baitfish must be represented. Ted didn't feel right about stashing his ammo there.

The quad runners were parked in the back, along one wall. This section of wall was pegboard with moveable hooks for sundry items – extension cords, shop lamps, rolls of weed-whacker line, hats, mechanics overalls in several sizes. Ted thought for a moment then hung the bag of ammo eye-high, between the shop lamps and the weed string. Here, he decided, a white plastic bag could meant nothing.

10

Evelyn got to Anders Wealth Management early the next day and checked the S&P 500, up two points after yesterday's eight-point skid. The domestic tech sector was holding its own. The munis and state bonds looked good as bonds could look, given that soon-to-be bankrupt cities and states were, in her opinion, the dirtiest little secrets that financial professionals were trying to keep.

She saw that the foreign stock markets were all down except Brazil's. Almost all of Asia was a wreck, looking much like the U.S. markets had looked in '08. The roller-coaster lines of the Morningstar graphs taunted her from the screen, crazed and unpredictable. The Thomson-Reuters year-to-dates on three of her favorite large cap funds was depressing. Evelyn ate some of her low-fat scone and sipped a non-fat latte from Cafe Primo, knowing that those zigzagging fortunes on the graphs belonged to actual people, some of whom were trusting her to steer their ships between the clashing rocks of the Great Recession.

She checked mortgage interest rates and saw that they were still near all-time lows, though few of her clients could get these loans. What was left of the housing market was still constipated. The buyers – institutional investors and the lucky few individuals who had managed to dodge the Crash – were paying cash. It was bottom-feeding and there was nothing wrong with that, from an investor's point of view. But bottom-feeding was such a privileged and sorry substitute for the once-great, wealth-producing home industry that had vanished: the architects, builders, contractors, tradesmen, mortgage originators and lenders, appraisers, inspectors, realtors, and of course, the secretaries, office managers, clerical and support staff who kept all the wheels turning. Some were friends and acquaintances of Evelyn's and now they were gone from the business – their numbers no longer in service; their offices now for rent. She knew a full dozen Fallbrook real estate agents who'd folded over the last few years because homeowners couldn't afford to sell and buyers couldn't get credit to buy. And she knew there were more to come.

She drank down the latte and brought up the Norris Brothers file on one of her computers. She'd bumped into Caroline Norris just yesterday and had spent two whole hours very early this morning, unable to sleep, wondering how she could help. There had to be something more than selling off their real estate trusts at a loss on the secondary market, and cashing out Archie's and Caroline's retirement funds with taxes due and penalties for Caroline. Wasn't the whole idea of America geared to keeping this from happening? She just couldn't get Norris Brothers Growers out of her mind.

Then the whole thing with Ted. An unhealthy boy turned into an unbalanced young man, thought Evelyn. Somehow damaged. Evelyn wondered what she'd done to incur his disdain. When his behavior toward her became strange – say, five years ago – she'd sensed he had a crush on her. She'd tried to see it as flattering and harmless. Now, she was almost afraid of him, though this shamed her.

She'd been seeing him around Fallbrook since he was born and she was all of fourteen years old. Caroline used to push him around in a shaded blue stroller, shopping and meeting friends for lunch, and to events such as the Christmas Parade, the Independence Day fireworks show, the Classic Car Show. To Evelyn, Ted had looked like any baby – cute. And Caroline was striking. She was never casual but always well dressed and well groomed. Correct posture, expensive dresses that draped beautifully, tasteful jewelry. Even at twenty years old, she struck Evelyn as stately, more formal and cultured than most of the other Fallbrook women. Archie Norris was quite a bit older, and severe. He'd lost a young wife many years ago and was starting over. All of which made young Evelyn wonder if there was something wild in Caroline, something she needed to restrain. At age fifteen, Evelyn had begun to imitate Caroline's carriage and mannerisms, and to aspire to Caroline's presence and – someday, maybe – wardrobe.

Now, twenty-five years later, well-dressed Mayor Evelyn Anders picked at her scone and remembered that little Teddy was often sick, in and out of the hospital for tests. None had been conclusive, that she could recall. He limped.

Then he grew up, kind of. She felt bad for his aimlessness – still a live-at-home college student at age twenty-six – and for his faulty feet and pained locomotion. But the cartoon he'd drawn and posted online was mean and insulting and she would not dignify it or him by posting or returning his e-mails of apology. She wasn't happy that Cal State San Marcos had expelled him and she privately thought that the school had abridged Ted Norris's First Amendment right to freedom of speech. She had toyed with the idea of talking with the CSUSM Chancellor about having Ted re-instated but it seemed ill-advised, given his general state of weirdness. It was easy to imagine herself stepping into something she'd have trouble stepping back out of.

So. What could she do for the ailing Norris Brothers Growers? She reviewed Archie's and Caroline's investment portfolio. They had diversified, just as she had advised them. But the diversification had failed to fend off forty-percent losses in the Crash, which, added to drought, frost, fire and bad investments, were bringing the Norrises to their knees. She called up their history at AWM and confirmed that Archie and Caroline, as advised by her and Brian, were risk-tolerant investors in '08. Which of course had backfired magnificently.

She called her old friend Larry Williams over at the Fallbrook Farm Credit Bank and he told her that he couldn't lend to just anybody this soon after the fire. They'd all have to wait to see how bad the damage really is. Evelyn argued that Archie Norris wasn't just anybody, but one of the most respected growers in the whole industry. And that Archie would need to replace his ruined trees by late winter – whether it was ten or ten thousand of them – and the time to order them from the nursery is right now. Isn't that what the Farm Credit Bank was set up to do?

"Evelyn, can you imagine how many times I've had this conversation over the last four days? And with how many growers?"

"Well, I happen to know some of those same growers myself,
Larry, and your Farm Credit Bank is there with bells on for them."

"Each situation is different, Evelyn. I can't talk about specific clients. You know that."

"What I don't know is how to help Norris Brothers," she said.

"They should consider selling, and I hear there's an offer on the table – post fire – for a million three. Archie and Caroline play things close to the vest, but I'd have to guess that they could sell and live well. But I also know Archie, and my bet is he won't even listen to that offer."

"The ranch is what he *is*."

"Yes."

"What's it worth?"

"A four-bedroom built in the sixties on eighty acres of ag land zoned twenty-to-one? Barn and some outbuildings? Two million seven, tops. And don't forget there's going to be other groves and houses for sale after everything that's happened. So maybe two million five is closer. Yes."

"Hell, Larry. It appraised at five million dollars six years ago."

"So did Ryan Damon's spread out in Bonsall. He closed on it last week, two days before the fire broke out, for two point seven and it's no secret he was happy to get it."

"God."

"I wish I had His number for you."

Evelyn thanked him, rang off and brought up a summary of Norris accounts and holdings. She consulted the last few Fallbrook real estate MLS. She valued the ranch and house at $2.5 million, then added their three investment condos, which were worth a rough total of $650,000 in today's market. Then she added up in their modest retirement money and all investments with Anders Wealth Management. She included a hundred grand for holdings and investments that Archie and Caroline likely kept outside of AWM. The Norris gross worth was $3.3 million dollars.

However, Archie and Caroline were badly upside down in all three rental units, having paid dearly for them, just before the Crash. So even though the condos were bringing in modest rents, they were also unsellable at anything close to a break-even. The condos had been financed at a punishing 6.4% interest and no bank would refinance them with that kind of negative equity. Negative equity, thought Evelyn: what pathetic words. So, the Norrises had taken debt of $1.2 million dollars on three condos now worth $650,000, and secured the expensive sub prime loans, of course, with their home and business – Norris Brothers Growers.

Evelyn looked out her second-floor window and watched the Main Street traffic go by. It was rush-hour in Fallbrook now, which meant an orderly line of commuters headed out of town in each direction, and plenty of moms and dads, Brian among them, taking their children to school. Pendleton Marines and employees were stacked up westbound for the base. Main Street would be quiet again by nine o'clock. Back when she was girl there was maybe one-fifth of this traffic on Main at rush hour, which meant almost none. But she *liked* the way that her little town had grown to a whopping 30,000 citizens. In her opinion, it was every bit as good a place to live as it had ever been. A real Main Street kind of town. And she knew that without such growth she might not have been able to begin her professional career here. It was a vibrant little city and it had let her stay and become a part of it. She saw one of her campaign posters, wondered if she should have just skipped the picture and used text and colors instead. Not far away was a poster for Walt Rood and she had to admit he had an open and likeable face.

She turned back to her notepad and calculator, backing out the debt on the Norris's condos from the value of their home and property, projecting income tax on pension disbursements, coming up with an estimated net Norris worth of $1.3 million dollars. At sixty-six years of age, Archie was drawing social security, but not much. Caroline was only forty-six. They were both healthy so far as Evelyn knew. There were two universal variable life insurance policies in place but they had borrowed against them, gutting the cash-surrender values, and the death benefits were about to lapse.

If by "living well," Larry Williams had meant selling at market value, paying off their debts and buying a small home for $300,000 – and drawing down the remaining $1 million over, say, the next ten years of Archie's life, and the next twenty-five of Caroline's – then yes, they could do it. But if you figured inflation at even one percent a year, plus medical costs, and basic necessities, it was a pretty thin lifeline. A million dollars over twenty years was fifty grand a year. Out of that they'd have to pay taxes and utilities, supplemental health insurance, food, clothes and cars. They might want to go see their sons and grandkids. Maybe take a vacation. Fifty grand a year was not much money to do all of that, after a lifetime of work, she thought. Hard, hard work. Sell it all and live out your days, frugal and limited, looking over your shoulder? Things could be worse, and in fact they were worse for many. No wonder Caroline Norris had looked so intensely worried yesterday, Evelyn thought. No doubt she'd run these same figures herself since the fire. The latest purchase offer from the Newport Beach doctor really was low – ironically, bitterly low – $1,300,000. Just enough for the Norrises to pay their debts, walk away and begin their third act in life with pennies of the dollars they'd earned.

11

Patrick stood at attention and looked down at the sprawling tan hills of Camp Pendleton. The October day was warm and the Pacific was a silver prairie in the distance. Around him stood the surviving men of the 1st Marine Division 3rd Battalion, 5th Regiment. In the grandstands before them were their families and friends, and those of the twenty-five soldiers killed during the 3/5's most recent Afghanistan deployment. This "Dark Horse" battalion had taken the highest casualties of any Marine battalion in the war. Looking into the grandstand Patrick saw that many of the Gold Star family members – those who had lost sons – were quietly sobbing, dabbing their faces, trying to comfort each other. His parents and brother and Iris Cash sat near the front.

The battalion commander, a colonel, told them that these Marines had done what Marines always do. "They took the fight to the enemy. And they won." He spoke through a microphone and the hilltop breeze snatched his words from the speakers.

Patrick clearly remembered arriving in the Sangin district of Helmand Province. It looked like nothing he'd seen before, a strange combination of Arizona desert, Utah badlands and the moon. Distances were great and deceiving. The stars and planets were wrong. The creatures were a puzzling mix of the familiar and the exotic. The spiders were impossibly huge and the little saw-scaled vipers were mean and poisonous.

His unit was greeted by desert and the river and acres of corn that would become poppies later in the season. Sangin schools were closed by Taliban order, the marketplace was almost completely unused, and Taliban flags flew everywhere he looked. The villagers were furtive and distrustful, clearly afraid to signal anything like cooperation with the Americans or the Afghan National Army. The roads were already studded with hidden IEDs. Patrick and the Dark Horses arrived to mortar fire whistling down on them, a Taliban welcome. And snipers. The bullets made a snapping sound when they went by his head, and only later, he heard the distant report of the gun. Sometimes he saw smoke up in the rocks and sometimes shooters far, far away, unreal in shimmering heat. The whole place was crawling with the enemy – the Taliban, "hajjis," "skinnies," "rag heads," "woolies" – it didn't matter what you called them because all they wanted was for you to be dead. The next day Patrick's platoon got into a firefight not ten minutes into its first patrol.

The Colonel continued: "And nine months later, after hundreds of firefights, Sangin is secure. The schools are open. The Taliban has fled. The marketplace is busy. Your sons, and brothers, and husbands are heroes. You already know this, and now the world does, too."

Patrick looked at the men mostly standing to either side of him and he saw that all had solemn young faces, few of them over thirty years old. Many had been flown in from military hospitals around the country. Some had tears in their eyes and some were missing hands and fingers and feet. He saw amputees and double and triple amputees. There were wheelchairs and prosthetic limbs gleaming in the sunlight, and rebuilt faces and men with only one good eye and men with no good eye, and there were tears in eyes both good and bad, flesh and glass alike. Patrick saw brain-injured soldiers who could not easily process what they were doing here or fully control their bodies, and those so severely wounded they could no longer care for themselves.

Patrick also knew that many of the men sitting around him carried scars and damage that few could see, except maybe for the people who loved them most. They carried anger, distrust, boredom, frustration. They bore flashbacks and sleepless nights and fits of temper. They wondered why their countrymen knew so little about what they had done. They were embarrassed and angered by the sudden effusive thankfulness they received from strangers – the applause, the beers bought, the meals on the house – and the uneasy silence that always followed. They wondered why the civilians used their freedom to spend hours at malls or in front of televisions and monitors watching insipid entertainment and playing games. They wondered why there were no bond drives or food drives or rubber drives to aid the war effort, like in the past. They wondered why it was all up to them, why the war felt like some bizarre excursion that only they were asked to take. They worried about how they were going to handle growing families and mounting debt with soldiers' skills so often viewed as inappropriate for civilian work. They wondered how to make employers see that not every ex-soldier was a ticking bomb. They wanted something they could do and do well, something specific that had meaning. Most of them wanted, deep down in their burdened young hearts, Patrick knew, to go back and fight again, because war was by far the greatest excitement they had ever known and it was honest and selfless and brought meaning to some.

Patrick knew that there were other men here who, like him, had derived no meaning from the death and destruction. And he believed that this was a wound too – the shock of being hit by a truth that was difficult to speak and painful to hear – that these deaths and mutilations, these last full measures, had gained nothing. He remembered patrolling the enormous fields of opium poppies not to destroy them but to protect the crop and the farmers from the Taliban. And he remembered realizing, as the weeks wore on and they patrolled and fought and died for meager portions of ground, that after they went home the Taliban would come down from the mountains, and the poppies and the profits and Sangin would be theirs again and there would be no one strong and generous and brave enough to fight them off.

Then some of the returned soldiers came to the mic and spoke of their brothers-in-arms, and these tributes were tearful and filled with love and respect and gratitude.

"McClellan was a brother to me . . ."

"I think Corporal Lavinder was personally sent to me by God. He saved my life and because of that, his is gone . . ."

"Fenwick was one of those guys, he walked into a room and lit it up . . ."

"What hurts most is knowing that Randy isn't here . . ."

Patrick thought of Myers and Zane and the many others he had known who had died, and as the sunlight warmed his face he closed his eyes for just a moment and endured again the flash and the sound that strew Myers and Zane like rags to the steep rocky hillside. He let the sound ring in his ears until it quieted and he offered an open prayer to any God willing to hear it.

Then the families spoke. Wyatt Chukas, the brother of Pfc. Paul Chukas, brought Paul's bomb-sniffing Labrador to the podium with him. Buddy was yellow and small for a lab and he sat with calm alertness as the man spoke. Wyatt told of his brother being mortally wounded by a Taliban sniper, and how when he fell, Buddy ran to him and stood over him until help could arrive. The Marines had brought the dog back and delivered him to the Chukas family and Buddy had gravitated to Wyatt. Patrick wished he had Zane back here and thought, *you feel the tears piling up behind your sunglasses because Buddy was Zane, and Myers was Chukas and you were all in hell together but only Buddy and you are alive to remember it and who was it, exactly, got to make that fucking decision? You stand here now but you can't be blamed for living. You pray: don't blame me. Your throat aches and it feels like something inside is going to break loose but it doesn't. It hasn't yet. The breeze cools your face and your back aches from standing in one place for so long.*

Later Patrick excused himself from his family and Iris then drove Bostik, Salimony and Messina to a liquor store in Oceanside, where they stocked up. They doubled-back to the beach on base, which was open only to military and their guests. Today there were few people. Patrick used four-wheel and drove right down onto the sand. The waves were small and the surface of the water was burred by the breeze. They drank bourbon and tequila mixed with soft drinks and played two-on-two football and got soaked to their knees in the cold water. They dug into the sand around a concrete fire ring and slept.

By late afternoon the day was cool so they got to drinking again. They built a fire with the wood they'd bought and found some sticks to cook the hot dogs on. They talked about the war and the women they'd fucked since coming home but mostly the war. Patrick said nothing about Iris Cash because he hadn't even kissed her and he didn't like that word applied to her, even though he'd do that with Iris in a heartbeat. And he suspected that his friends were mostly just talk anyway.

"Well how about the hottie that was with your family back there, Pat?" asked Messina.

"She's just a friend."

This brought chortles and around went the bottle again, each man in turn upending it. "To friends, then," said Bostik. "To fuckin' Myers, man."

"And fuckin' Zane," said Salimony. He had a nervous leg that bounced whenever he sat and even now in the sand it twitched rhythmically. Salimony balanced the bourbon bottle on his knee and watched the liquid slosh. "I wish he could have made the party today. I loved that dog."

"I read this made-up fiction book once," said Patrick, "that said heaven is a big barn where you get to live forever with all your dogs and every woman you ever had."

"It'd just be one fucked-up brawl," said Bostik.

"Yeah," said Salimony. "Like when we grappled Sergeant Pendejo. And then, goddamn, two days later he's at the cooker yelling for us to come and get one of a burrito and the sniper hits him right between the eyes! I mean the spatula's still in his hands and his brains are actually on the wall! *On* it! Oh, man!"

"So here's a toast to Sergeant Pendejo," said Messina. "He was an asshole but he was our asshole."

"To our asshole!" they called out.

And so it went past dark and into the night until they saw headlights down by the waterline bouncing toward them. What with the wild up-and-down of the lights and the liquor swirling through him Patrick saw an entire enemy convoy but it turned out to be only two Jeeps. The Jeeps stopped and the headlights seared into them and four MPs got out and came to them. "Drunk Marines," said one of them.

"Says who?" demanded Bostik.

"You guys going to be cool? Because if not, we're getting out the batons right now."

"We're cool," said Patrick.

"Looking how fuckin' cool we are," said Messina.

"Alright. Get out your ID's, you drunk jarheads."

"Excuse me but we're United States Marines," said Bostik. "And we served in Helmand and we don't take one drop a shit from Boot POG rentacop cherries like you." Patrick watched him take a swig of the second bottle of tequila then hurl it at the lead MP.

The bottle missed badly but smashed the left headlight of the front Jeep. Patrick saw the glittering shower of glass and light, then the fight was on. He was drunk and stupid and slow against the sober MPs with their truncheons. The first time he went down he thought he'd just stay down, but he could hear Bostik moaning and Salimony cursing and a baton landing hard so he stood up and surged forth. Bostik was swinging into the blows and Salimony advancing on his attacker with a bottle he held by the neck, and Messina was besieged from two sides. Patrick whirled, realizing too late that the fourth MP could only be behind him.

He woke up on a concrete slab with a thin mattress on it and a scratchy olive green blanket bunched up under him. There was an unexplained and weird tightness to the back of his head. He sat up then eased himself back down, so great was his headache.

"You may as well stay up," said Bostik. "They're letting us out at o-six hundred."

Patrick looked at his watch but it was gone. "What is all this?"

"This is morning," said Salimony. "Before was beach. Drinking. Fight. Hospital. Brig. You got ten stitches in the back of your head. They're not going to charge us because they beat the shit out of us so bad."

"That seems fair," said Patrick. He sat back up and reached a hand toward the agony. He felt gauze and tape and shaven scalp. He heard a steel door open and shut then the sound of footsteps coming toward their tank.

12

With an iron headache and occasionally blurred vision, Patrick worked that full day on the groves. His father and brother offered him the easier tasks but Patrick worked even harder than usual. It was the Marine thing to do. He was black and dripping sweat after an hour and his scalp burned along the stitches. He guzzled water to help his brain fire right. The three men finished off the irrigation repair and half of the remaining trunk painting. But there was a heavy quiet between them as they rode back to the house in Archie's work truck, because Escondido Farm Credit Bank had refused to loan on the replacement trees.

Patrick skipped cocktails with his family, cleaned up and was waiting for Iris Cash in the Village View lobby at sunset. He walked her to his truck. Her face with the sunlight on it was lovely. His head ached all the way down to his toenails. He told Iris he dinged himself rough-housing with buddies the night before. "I apologize for ditching you yesterday."

"That memorial was one of the most emotional moments of my life," said Iris. "And you were the only person there I knew, and I've known you for less than a week. It was just really, really ... I'm not sure what it was, Patrick. I can't describe it. I'm writing a series about it for the paper. Trying to find words."

"I never expected anything like that. Even when I enlisted for infantry I never thought it would include such a thing. A ceremony for the mangled and dead and all their families."

Iris considered a long moment before speaking. "You must be terribly proud and terribly sad."

"Those words are good, Iris. And really, I'm sorry about leaving you there with my family and just running off."

"I've been reading about soldiers coming home."

"I'm a Marine, not a soldier."

"I didn't know there was a distinction. But I do know from my reading that after deployment, Marines really need their friends."

"I know I need to move on, get out of Afghanistan."

They came to the truck and Patrick held open the door for her. She put her soft fingers on his freshly shaven cheek and turned his head to one side for a better look at the wound. "Rough-housing with buddies? You've got *stitches*, Pat!"

"It was purely foolish."

He handed her up to the cab and watched her as she swung in. They set out for La Jolla. Patrick could smell Iris's scent and he felt like he was gliding down I-15 on it. Iris talked of the Marines of the 3/5 she'd seen at Pendleton, and how she'd like to talk to every one of them and put it all in a book. She said it would be fiction and Patrick wondered why you'd make things up about a war that was actual. You couldn't make it any truer than it was. Iris said she talked to some of the Gold Star families and absolutely refused to cry, even if they did, because she felt superfluous and trivial in their presence.

She told him the Village View was going to run her story on the discovery of the arson evidence front page, and Fallbrook Fire might even give them a photo of it to accompany the article. The point of the whole thing was to get people involved, maybe find a witness, or someone who had overheard someone saying suspicious things.

She said this DHS specialist, Knechtl, was a very intense man who wouldn't say much about his investigation. He wore

95

a dark suit and had a pale complexion and a big forehead and a small mustache. He looked more like an undertaker than a special agent of the DHS, in her opinion. Knechtl said that he'd questioned several persons of interest but he wouldn't say who, or where they lived, or if there were any leads. He addressed the whole Village View staff, then asked each of them to list three local people they thought might set a fire like this. He passed one sheet of blank white paper and one pencil to each person in the room, then asked them to meditate for one full minute before answering. About one minute into the silence Iris had peeked and caught Knechtl checking his wristwatch. She'd left her sheet blank, as had her editor, who was sitting on one side of her, and the art director, sitting on the other. She did note two people writing away, voluminously, it looked, arms around their papers for privacy.

Iris looked intently out the truck windows, often turning back to study something they'd just passed. She was alert and curious. Just a glimpse of her did something good to Patrick's heart. She talked about the latest developments in the Cruzela Storm benefit concert for the lighted Fallbrook crosswalks. She thought it was weird that some people were trying to make their town better while at least one other person was trying to burn it to the ground. Fire Chief Bruck had told her that no terrorist organization had stepped forward to claim responsibility for the Fallbrook fire. He doubted that Al Qaeda was behind it. He went on to say that eighty percent of arsonists lived within five miles of where they started their fires, which put this guy in Fallbrook, Bonsall, Rainbow or DeLuz.

"He said *guy*, because there are very few female arsonists," said Iris.

"You ladies have too much good sense to do that."

She looked at him dubiously. They made La Jolla in an

hour. Patrick looked up at the LDS temple aglow in the night, and the golden trumpeter fixed to the top of the east spire and he wondered if Mormons were anything like Presbyterians. They take care of their own, he thought. He followed his GPS toward the address, which turned out to be a mansion that stood in a neighborhood of mansions staggered high upslope above the city.

Patrick looked down at the ocean below and the lights of La Jolla flickering. He used the intercom and the gate slid open quietly. He came up the drive and spotted the Mako, trailered and displayed beautifully as a jewel in the driveway lights. He felt a quiver of excitement and he braked carefully and pulled up in front of the house. The front lawn was an emerald expanse and sprinklers hissed upon it. Patrick got out and smelled the ocean and thought it went well with the smell of Iris.

He walked slowly around the craft, port to starboard. It was a foam-construction skiff, seventeen feet long, with room for two clients and one captain. It was old but looked well cared-for. There were dents and scratches in the decks and gunwales but Patrick saw no patches or dark spots or other signs of waterlogged foam beneath. The cleats and latches looked new. The engine was a Mercury, to which Patrick was partial. Her CF tags were soon to expire but her name, *Fatta the Lan'*, was clear in black cursive and recently re-done. He felt dizzy with hope. He chanced a glance at Iris, who was looking at him.

A man came down the walk from the house. Patrick heard him before he saw him. He wore a white dress shirt tucked into dark slacks, suspenders and dress shoes, and he was not much older than Patrick, who half-expected the man's father to come out next. Instead, two small blond boys, dressed in matching red polo shirts, hustled through the door and came down the walk. The man introduced himself as Kevin

Pangborn and shook hands with Patrick and Iris. He had a small pot belly – not a couch-potato's pot belly, Patrick thought, but the pot belly of a well-off man, a man who ate well and played some sport – and his brown hair was short and brushed back. He wore gold cufflinks.

"Just back from overseas?" he asked.

"Ten days now."

"Thank you for keeping this country safe and free. I mean that from the bottom of my heart."

"You're welcome, sir." Patrick watched the boys watching him.

"You said you're going to guide fly-fishers in the bay?"

"That's right."

"Great."

"What do you do for a living?" asked Iris. "If you don't mind my asking."

"We raise capital and turn around ailing companies. I've done some fly-fishing. It's not easy. Maybe I can hire you to guide me."

"I'll need a boat first," said Patrick.

"No!" said one of the boys. "It's ours!"

Pangborn turned to face them and the boys looked down into *Fatta the Lan'*. "Well, Patrick, this Mako would be good for guiding fly fishers. Both casting decks are non-skid and that fore railing I had built will keep your clients from falling overboard. The Mercury's only got twenty hours on it. The beam is wide so it's a dry ride even when the chop is bad. The aerator for the bait tank is touchy. I've got the GPS and sonar inside the house, and they're part of the deal. I paid sixteen-two, have the receipts and service receipts."

"Why are you selling it?"

"I bought my dream boat, a Triton. And a slip down in San Diego. I don't need this one anymore."

The boys stood along the port side of the skiff, brushing

their hands along the railing and looking back and forth from their father to the skiff. "Why can't we keep her, Dad?" one of them said. He looked at Patrick sullenly.

"The boys love this thing," said Pangborn. An awkward silence followed. "Look, my listing price is thirteen grand but you seem like nice people, so I'll let her go for twelve-five. Trailer, electronics, cover, everything."

"No!" the boys hollered in unison. Pangborn pointed to the house and the boys marched up the walkway, muttering and clomping their athletic shoes loudly on the concrete. Patrick saw a tall blond woman gather them in and close the big wooden door.

Patrick thought of the fire, and his father turned down for Farm Credit loans, and the terrible financial shape the Norris family was in. How long would it take him to turn a profit on these eleven thousand dollars? In his mind he formed the sentence *I've changed my mind,* but when he spoke it came out differently. "I have eleven thousand."

"Ouch," said Pangborn.

"And another thousand in a month."

Pangborn rubbed his chin and studied Patrick. "You served our country."

Patrick said nothing.

"I'll take your eleven. That's more than good enough."

Patrick felt his spirits start to rise and he heard an old-fashioned dial tone come from Pangborn's direction. Pangborn pulled a phone from his pocket and checked the caller. "Patrick? Iris? I've got to take this. One of the elders. Give me five minutes, will you?"

Patrick backed the trailer and *Fatta the Lan'* into the Norris barn. In the sideview mirror he could see Iris standing by the door, framed in the barnyard lights. Her golden hair shone in the lights. Jack and Spike were on scene by now,

99

tails banging away, Spike sticking his nose up under Iris's sweater. She nudged him away with one knee and a smile. When the boat was in place Patrick cranked down the steel wheel and unhitched the trailer. Iris helped him muscle it over and down.

"Let me guess," she said. "Right now you want to tear into that engine and see how it looks."

He smiled and shrugged. "I could wait."

"I'll help. I'd rather do something than not."

"Take a walk with me, then. I'll show you what's left of the Norris Brothers groves. Just enough moonlight."

They walked the dirt road up the hillside to higher ground. In the moonlight the trees below stretched before them, thin and black. They stopped and Iris took his arm in both her hands. "That's a hard sight to see."

"We're hoping half of the burned ones live."

"Is that realistic?"

"The fire was really fast. That was the one good thing about it."

She leaned her head against him. "It baffles me that someone set it. What kind of person does that?"

"The Al Qaeda magazine had instructions for setting forest fires in this country."

"You'd think they'd take credit."

"Other than a terrorist, I don't know who would do it. A person who's really pissed off? Totally crazy?"

"They say angry, yes. And sexually underdeveloped."

"Hard to imagine how setting a fire solves that."

She nodded and Patrick felt the weight of her head against his shoulder. He freed his arm and put it around her and they stood for a long while, awkwardly, neither seeming willing to break off.

Later in silence he drove Iris to her car downtown. Someone hustled down the sidewalk in the dark, hunched in a loose white wrap that for a second could have been a tribal garment, and Patrick's heart jumped and his ears rang and his thoughts went AWOL, straight back to Sangin with Myers and Zane. He wished Iris would say something. Anything. Words in the air keep the devil gone. Sometimes. He stole a glance at her and caught her looking out the window, as usual, alert to who-knew-what? He was suddenly very aware of the space between them – he guessed it to be about twenty-two inches – and of the fine trembling in that air, which carried the weight of possibility in it, along with the chance, always present in his mind, that sudden violence would take it away.

13

In the purple dusk of the next evening, after ten hours of hard labor that displeased his father, Ted drove to Pride Auto Repair. Earlier that day in the grove Ted had been re-assigned to the tree-painting detail because Archie and Patrick could more quickly wire the new timers. Ted had gone to the barn to get a smaller, easier-to-carry sprayer, but not remembered to triple-rinse it before pouring in the paint and water. The triple-rinse was mandatory, Archie always said, because some of the sprayers had been used for a powerful weed killer just this spring. Even a trace of herbicide reside left in the sprayer could kill an avocado tree. Ted had then painted eighty trees when he suddenly realized he'd forgotten to triple-rinse the sprayer.

He ran and confessed the whole thing to his father. Ted could see the fury just behind the skin of his father's face, and he waited for Archie to explode. But he didn't. His father maintained patience. Archie put a hand on Ted's shoulder and looked straight into Ted's eyes and told him that all eighty of the newly painted trees were now much more likely to die. So, tomorrow's first task would be to pressure-strip *off* the paint. His father had told him to *get with the program, Ted. Please!*

Ted pulled into the parking lot. Pride Auto Repair was a big brick building, set well back from Oak Street. Parked near the front door Ted saw a familiar '57 Chevy Bel-Air, glistening white with aqua insets and abundant chrome. He remembered it as Cade's car from ten years ago. The shop had been boarded up for those years but now Ted saw that the plywood was gone from the window frames and the new glass was clean and clear.

He got out and walked toward the front door on aching feet. The old neon sign was up again too, he saw, depicting a blue Ford Model T doing a wheelie, red flames coming off the rear tires. The letters over the car were white and said simply, Pride. As a boy he'd always liked that sign. Now it was lit up in the near dark and Ted watched its colors play across the polished hood of the Bel-Air. The front door was wood and clear glass with blinds behind the glass. The blinds were rolled up. Ted looked through the glass and saw Cade Magnus looking back at him. Cade waved him in and Ted pushed through the door.

Magnus stood behind the old counter, which was strewn with a computer, printer and other peripherals, a new phone/fax, an answering machine, knotted cords and surge protectors. He wore a light blue short-sleeve shirt with "Cade" embroidered over one pocket, tucked into a pair of navy work pants. He was thick and muscular, as Ted remembered, and had the same smugly engaging smile. Through the windowed double doors behind Magnus, Ted saw the repair bay out back, the high ceilings and the parts racks and the big lifts resting at floor level. "Ted Norris," Cade said.

"Are you going to move back to Fallbrook?"

"I already have. I heard you lost your trees in the fire. Sorry. Those Lamb Haas avos you guys grew were the best I ever had."

"What about your father?"

"What about him? He's still up in Idaho. I got tired of it there. What about your father? Does he still believe you're mentally defective?"

Ted blushed. He'd confided certain things to Cade and Jed Magnus years ago, when he was fourteen and curious about the White Crusade, badly wanting to do something about the 9/11 attacks. He couldn't remember specifics but

103

apparently his relationship with his father had been a topic. "No, I wouldn't say that."

Magnus gave Ted a just-you-and-me smile. "Good for you, then."

"Do you have a family now?"

"An ex and two down in Oceanside, another ex and two more up in Coeur d'Alene. No more children for this white supremacist."

"I'm twenty-six."

"I saw your brother at City Hall Tuesday and he told me to go to hell."

"Pat's capable of that. He just came back from Afghanistan a few days ago. Third Battalion, Fifth Marines. The Dark Horses. *Get some*. He's got an edge."

"You were sixteen when I left. Pat was just, what . . ."

"Twelve. Why did you come back?"

Magnus gestured with open hands. "I'm a good mechanic. Got plenty of child support to pay. So I'm going to pick up where I left off. And this was the last place where I really enjoyed living."

"That's funny because most people here don't like you at all."

"They don't even like the *idea* of me. I've already pissed some of them off."

Ted looked around the big room. It had brick walls with framed posters of the Fallbrook Classic Car Show hung perfectly straight, the glass clean as the windshield of his taxi. The windows were the old-fashioned frosted mesh safety glass except for the front door glass, and the transom window over the door, through which Ted saw the neon Model T kicking up its red flames. He read edirP.

The pool table was there, just as he remembered it. He thought of seeing Jed and Cade playing one day when business was slow, and customers playing while they waited for their cars. The talk was all political. Ted remembered heated

104

words about the new pseudo-science behind global warming. He had always liked the sound of billiard balls hitting, so sharp and purposeful. Like the Glock. The cue rack, loaded with sticks, was bolted to the wall right where it had been. Ted saw the small blue squares of chalk in the bottom tray. Beside the rack stood the old jukebox, chrome with wood-look trim.

In the far corner of the room stood a pile of rubbish – flimsy metal shelving, defunct tube lights and fixtures, old electrical line, scraps of particle-board, a wooden desk with two broken legs, a rat's nest built of twigs and bits of paper and cloth. "Lots to do," said Ted.

"Check out the bay."

Magnus lifted the counter panel and Ted followed him through the open double doors. The repair area was large, with three lifts and plenty of shelves for parts and a big roll-up door in the rear. Ted remembered the new tires stacked halfway to the ceiling, scores of them. He smelled them now though this was impossible. The old-time vending machine was still there, whitened with dust. The couch sitting along one wall he also remembered, and the lamp next to it. One day when he was young – nine or ten, and riding his bike around town – Ted had seen, through the open roll-up door, Jed Magnus sitting on that sofa, reading. The lamp illuminated him in the darkened interior of the repair bay. Jed's wife, Ellen, sat close beside him, also reading. Jed's hand was on her knee. The Magnuses didn't look as bad as his parents – and almost everyone else in Fallbrook – said they were. Ellen was pretty. When Ted peddled his bike by, they had both looked up and nodded to him. The couch had been covered in red paisley upholstery then, and it still was today.

"I hear you drive a taxi. Bring your cab here for service so long as it isn't Jap or Korean."

"It's a Ford. I'm also helping Dad and Pat put the farm back together."

105

Magnus reached out to a wall panel and pressed a large black button. A motor groaned and one of the lifts rose on its great, grease-slicked piston. Ted looked at the steel stairs leading down into the workspace below, black with what looked like half a century of spilled engine oil and transmission fluid.

"I'm starting out on my own here, Ted. Then I'll hire as I grow. A shop takes at least two people, and someone on the books part-time. My father never liked car repair but I did. At least he took the time to teach me his trade. Your father shut you out, right? Bummer. But you know what I think? I think our fathers maybe aren't so different."

"What do you mean?"

"When I was a boy I could never really please mine. Then, when our civil trial got going up in Spokane, the prosecutors came up with a letter I'd written to a guy up there who had written me, and he wanted to join the White Crusade. I mentioned to him that a like-minded young man I knew was heading up his way and the next thing you know, that letter is the smoking gun that proves my father and I sent agents to Spokane to kill blacks. The letter didn't say anything about killing anybody. Dad didn't know anything about that letter until discovery. I'd pretty much forgotten it. It was written to an inconsequential man about another inconsequential man. I was trying to give some skinheads some positive motivation. You should have seen the look on my dad's face when they read that letter. He looked at me like I was the stupidest human to ever walk the earth, you know? Like it proved something he'd suspected all along. Like he'd finally had *enough*. He got over it. We got over it. But ever since then, when he looks at me I still see a little bit of that expression in him. So I know how you feel."

"I thought you two were tight."

"I'll tell you a secret, too. You know why I came back here, besides that I like Fallbrook and think it's a great place to live? I came back here to do something my father could never do.

106

Something bigger and more important than he ever dreamed of."

Ted felt a ripple of energy inside him, a little bump of adrenalin. "Like *what?*"

"I don't know yet. I'm working out some ideas."

"I know that feeling. It's my middle name."

Magnus hit the red button and the lift went down and clanked into place. "Well, don't be a stranger. Bring that taxi in any time after next Wednesday and I'll do you right. Tell your boss to bring in the other cars."

"There's two other cabs, and a black town car for people who don't want a taxi."

"Black, huh? Just kidding. Bring them all. I'll give you a fleet discount."

They walked back into the shop. Night had fallen and through the windows he saw the Model-T, still throwing red flames across the polished hood of the Chevy parked out front. Magnus took a flyer from the counter and handed it to Ted. It was a standard sized sheet of printer paper, white. The lettering was the Germanic Reich-style script favored by skinheads, death metal bands and motorcycle gangs.

TAKE BACK MAIN STREET!

November 22   Village Square   Fallbrook, CA

- – Speak Out for Legal Carry of Handguns!
- – Free Safety Inspections!
- – Wear Your Empty Holsters!
- – Exercise Your Rights!
- – Address by Cade Magnus!
- – Free Copies of Constitution!
- – Free Snacks/Punch/Gifts for Kids!
- – Drawing For 9mm Vintage Luger!
- – Browns, Blacks and Jews Stay Home
  or Better Yet GO Home!

"I got held up by a Mexican guy last week, driving my cab. He had a gun and he pointed it at my face. I believed he would use it. I could tell he thought I was a coward. He took most of my tips. At first I was scared, then later, I was mad at him. And at me."

Magnus put his hands on his hips and looked at Ted. "Get even."

"I went to the Sheriffs to report it but I couldn't stay. Cops creep me out. I've seen him around town, the gunman. He said his name was Henry but I think it's Edgar something."

"What kind of a small-town moron robs a cabbie where he lives? Maybe you should have filed a report."

"Probably too late now."

"Do you know him?"

"No. Just a high school kid, I think, maybe jumping in with the Fallbrook Kings. Some homies watched him rob me and they were smiling."

"Violent children, one and all. What's he look like?"

Ted described Edgar and his provocative girlfriend and the beat-up old Chevrolet Malibu he'd seen them in.

"It's okay you didn't tell the cops. You're almost always better off without them. Do you carry a gun in the cab now?"

"I pick up my new gun next week. It's a Glock."

"You've got a right to protect yourself. Even though spine-less liberals, from the president on down to our own mayor, will tell you different."

"Evelyn Anders is a curse on this town."

"I saw your cartoon of her. Someone sent it to the Rogue Wolf site. Great work, Ted."

The next words seemed to come out of Ted's mouth before he'd even thought them. "They expelled me from college for that drawing. I disagree with her politics, the way she throws public money around. Tax money. *My* money. She wants to control every thing I do. Actually, I like her face. She's pretty

108

in her own way. But I'm angry that privileged liberals like her have no idea what it's like to be me."

Cade gave Ted a long, serious look, leaned back against the counter and crossed his muscular arms. His eyes were the same blue Ted remembered from over a decade ago. "You know what happened to my mother here that night, don't you?"

"Everybody knows what."

"The government refused to let her carry a gun and she was murdered by a man she didn't even know."

"I get mine in a few days."

"Everything happens for a reason, Ted."

"I never believed that. I think things happen for no reason."

"Listen. Everything is connected but people don't always see the connections. Sometimes it's risky to let connections be known. Let me give this Edgar fellow some thought. And here, you give some of these to your friends, will you? Put some of them up around town, maybe when you're between customers. There's the website at the bottom. Don't stop drawing cartoons. Draw *more*. Post them, post them, post them. You're allowed to do that – the United States Constitution says so."

Ted took the flyers, nodding. "Anders has no right to take our guns."

Again Cade Magnus leveled his eyes on Ted and again Ted felt the boost of something optimistic inside him, something that could fuel action. "Ted, we call ourselves the Rogue Wolves now. Go to our website and see what my father has to say about our brave new, post nine-eleven, crash-and-recession- republic – run by a half-breed socialist who wasn't even born here. Our motto is Live Free, Fight Alone. We believe in the white race over every other. We are the opposite of Big Government. We do not ask you to vote for us, to pledge your allegiance or pay taxes to us. *Live free, fight alone,* Ted. That way they can't hurt us. Nobody connects with anybody else. No trail. They can't rob our bank accounts, or our imaginations, hearts or souls. Think about what you can do. What *only* you can do. And stop by, anytime. I'd like to see more of you."

When Ted was climbing into his truck in the Pride Auto Repair lot he saw a tall khaki-suited man standing across the street, seemingly intrigued by the front window display of the photography studio. Ted had sometimes stopped to admire the happy wedding pictures and wholesome family portraits and the flattering graduation pictures of high school students. The man certainly looked like the one in Open Sights and the one who was walking behind him after the Magnus rally the other day. Same big head. Ted wondered if his mind was playing tricks on him. Again.

He drove around the Carmella Street barrio looking for Edgar. He had the windows down and it was the first time since the fire that the air of Fallbrook smelled alive: trumpet vine and hillside sage, late-season roses. Young people cruised the fragrant evening, rolling along slowly in their cars, music throbbing. The youngsters walked or rode scooters or bikes. There was a big wheeled barbecue set up in a front yard, with a sign, and a husky man and a stout woman cooking and others waiting in line. Some of the girls and young women had Chihuahuas in their arms or on leashes and the dogs on leashes zigzagged the sidewalks, straining for freedom. Ted looked out at the small groups of people on the corners – all of them wanting to see and be seen. Cortez Market was bustling and the music blared from a small *disco* store with posters of musicians in the windows.

Ted put on a Cruzela Storm CD and turned the volume so Cruzela's voice would be part of the world but not dominate it. Her voice was low but smooth, but it could climb high and not lose its honey quality. Ted found it almost unbelievable that someone talented as Cruzela Storm would perform at Fallbrook High School. And just to build lighted crosswalks the city that didn't need. He'd still pay to see her. Although if arrogant Mayor Evelyn got up on her soapbox she'd probably ruin the whole show for him, and for everybody else.

Then there he was – Edgar – standing at the corner of Old Stage and Via Entrada, not two hundred feet from where he had robbed Ted. A streetlamp held him in a cone of light: shorts past his knees and a singlet and the killah shades even after dark. Ted felt his heart speed up and his hearing crank into overdrive. He turned off Cruzela and let the truck move at idle. Edgar's girlfriend was there, tight jeans and black boots, and they were arguing. Ted saw Edgar register his truck, then who was driving it. He braked and stopped at the corner where they stood. Before even thinking Ted raised his left hand, which was dangling out the window, and made a gun of it and pointed it at the big high school boy. Edgar tracked the motion from behind the dark lenses like a creature with compound eyes. "What do you want, man?"

Ted went brittle with anger. Or was it fear? Edgar's voice was loud and clear, and Ted was aware of the distant throb of the music and the sound of the truck engine and the sudden silence of the pedestrians at the intersection. When he finally heard it, his voice was high-pitched and wavering. "You owe me twenty-two dollars."

"I've never seen you. How can I owe you? Come on, Jessie, let's go."

"I want my money back," Ted said.

"Then get outta that car right now and try to take it."

"Oh, no. You might pull your gun again."

"I don't have a gun. He's trash-talking, Jessie. Let's go."

Edgar took her hand and turned away but she wrenched loose and stepped into the street and up to Ted's open

111

window. "Get fucked you fat shit." Edgar grabbed her wrist again and pulled her to the curb and up Via Entrada. Ted heard her laughter and her boot heels as they disappeared gradually into the darkness. *Get with the program. Get fucked. Get even.* He drove away with his heart beating hard and his ears ringing with defeat and rage. He would love to get even. Love to. And then some.

With everybody.

14

Evelyn Anders stood under a shade canopy at the Emergency Resource Center, waiting to tell her fellow citizens what the city could do for victims of the fire. It was a warm Saturday morning, eleven days since the blaze had been extinguished. The tables in front of her had stacks of informational pamphlets, anchored by rocks against the breeze. The Emergency Resource Center was set up in a church parking lot in the hills east of downtown. The centerpiece was a large gleaming trailer with the words "Certified Emergency Response Team – C.E.R.T." emblazoned across its flanks.

The mayor looked around at the olive drab National Guard trucks and uniformed guardsmen, the trailers and booths staffed by FEMA and various state and county agencies. There were sheriffs patrol cars, vans and SUVs, California Highway Patrol, police cars from outlying cities, and newspaper, TV and radio vehicles everywhere she looked. Iris Cash from the Village View waved at her then turned back to a fireman wearing a yellow helmet and a bulky fire-fighting suit. The cannons of Pendleton began booming in the west, a sound that made Evelyn cringe. They could go on for hours.

"Does anybody know who started the fire?" asked a tall boy whom Evelyn recognized as a classmate of her son.

"There has not been an arrest," said Evelyn.

"I don't understand why someone would do that."

"Here, watch this." She hit the play button on her laptop

and turned it to face the boy. She had made this video segment, "Arson," with the help of her son and daughter. They'd enlarged some of the photographs she'd taken out in Rice Canyon where the fire had been started, then used a Flip to shoot them. Also on the video were sketches she'd drawn of the weirdly fused triggering device and container for accelerant that she had found. The DA wouldn't release forensic photos to the public before trial, so Evelyn had drawn her own. Then they had recorded Iris Cash interviewing Fire Chief Bruck and two sheriff's detectives familiar with arsonist behavior. "Arsonists are often secretive, introverted individuals," one of the detectives explained. "They often derive feelings of power and superiority from the fire itself, as well as the human efforts to control the fire. Some arsonists join in to fight the fire as a way of enjoying their control. Some arsonists experience a sexual component when observing the fire."

"That's totally gross," said the boy. "It's murder if someone dies, right?"

"Some arsonists have been charged with homicide," said Evelyn. "And have done years in prison or in mental hospitals."

"Mental hospitals creep me out," said the boy, staring down at the monitor. Another boy, apparently a friend, came over and stood beside him. Evelyn watched the emotions play across their faces as they tried to understand the psychopathy of fire-setting. The first boy looked offended, the second amused. Onscreen the detective explained in a deadpan cop voice that mental illness and anti-social tendencies sometimes found expression in arson. "It's a crime of control and power," he said. "Most arsonists are repeat offenders. They begin with small fires and escalate. This Fallbrook fire is one of the largest arson fires in the history of California. It is likely that whoever set this fire has set others. The damage is

114

in the billions of dollars and three lives were lost. It is one of the most heinous crimes I've ever investigated. So please, if any of you saw *anything* suspicious at or around the time of the fire, please contact the San Diego Sheriff Department."

"How much is the reward up to?" asked the second boy.

"Ninety-eight thousand dollars," said Evelyn. "That jar there is for reward donations." She had spiked it with three fives earlier, and since then had collected a handful of change and two wadded-up one-dollar bills.

"I wish I had seen something," said the first. "That would have been cool. All I saw was smoke and Mom trying to catch the cat."

By noon there had been far fewer attendees than Evelyn had expected. She knew why, too – because the routed, exhausted, burned-out and grieving people of her city understood that, in practical terms, their government could do very little for anybody. The city could offer bottled water donated by Major Market. There were palettes of it stacked up beside her table, heavy 24-packs, all free. And the Red Cross had come through with bags of rice and beans, boxes of hot cocoa mix and marshmallows, though most if it was quickly claimed by people Evelyn knew to be the local poor, most of whom lived downtown, which was untouched by the fire. And that was about all the help the City of Fallbrook could give.

Evelyn left her table to check out the FEMA trailers, which were set up directly across from her position. She saw battle-ready ICE and DHS and Border Patrol agents and wondered how they fit into disaster relief. She approached and found the FEMA tables sagging under a bounty of puzzling dona-tions: box after box of ocean-scent deodorant bar soap, large bottles of cider vinegar, cheap socket-wrench sets, cotton balls, bagged garlic cloves, two-packs of aerosol air fresh-ener; bundles of week-old magazines, cartons of one-serving crouton pouches, and pile upon pile of new jeans all in one size – thirty-six inch waists, thirty inch inseams. Pawing through the jeans, looking for just one pair in a varying size, was like seeing into the mad mind of government itself, thought Evelyn. So much waste. So many good intentions. Who's governing *it?*

She went back to her table and straightened the stacks of pamphlets and sat. Her video detective droned on about arson. From this elevation she could see the blackened hills to the east and south, and the San Luis Rey River valley still mostly green and spared the burn, and a small housing tract, Meadows, to the north. Meadows was newer and hard-hit by the mortgage meltdown and real estate crash, and Evelyn knew two families who had lived in that tract and just recently sold short and left Fallbrook. The parents of one family were both in the mortgage business itself – loan originators. The other family's breadwinner was a project manager for a commercial builder, and was laid off with little chance of finding work in that moribund industry. *Adios.* Now the fire had raged through it and Meadows looked as if it had hosted a neighborhood war, some homes burned flat, some scorched but standing, maybe half of them left untouched. Even at this distance Evelyn could see a family picking through the rubble of one house, while across the street an older man stood and watched the sprinklers water his lawn.

"We're staying over at the Baptist Church for a few days," a bedraggled woman told her. She had two small children with her. She lifted a pamphlet and scanned it and set it back under the rock. "They've been good to us there. Hot meals and cots. It's chilly at night. We're not even Baptist but maybe we'll consider joining up."

"You're free to take all the water you can carry."

"We've got plenty of water, thank you. Did you see this?"

The woman handed her a flyer entitled TAKE BACK MAIN STREET!

"Cade Magnus," said Evelyn.

"I had no idea he was back."

"Where did you get this?"

"There was a stack of them at the Donut Bin this morning. And they're all over the telephone poles and bulletin boards in town."

Evelyn wondered why Cade Magnus would even want to come back to a town that disliked him. "It's like having a relapse of cancer. It was so nice just to be rid of his father and him."

"My husband has never met those people," said the woman. "But he wants to join the protest. He said Main Street needs taking back. Plus he has guns, so he'd fit in. He's a good man, don't get me wrong."

"The less he has to do with Cade Magnus the better. Oh, wait a minute – I'm the mayor and I can't oppose lawful assembly. I will not oppose lawful assembly, because that would mean Cade Magnus wins? Right? Just tell your husband to exercise caution. We don't *need* people carrying guns around Fallbrook."

"I agree."

"Thanks for coming by. I'm sorry there isn't more the city can do for you."

"Our house burnt to the ground and we're underinsured."

"Talk to FEMA. They're good at plugging those kind of financial holes."

"Already did. We're still a hundred grand short of a rebuild. Credit's completely shot. So, we can sell the lot or build something smaller. Real small, like a doghouse. You should have seen what a nice home we had. Not big, just . . . *home*. An actual white picket fence, roses, everything. I always loved that sentimental stuff. It stood for something."

"Good luck. I mean that."

"Too late, but thanks anyway."

117

Evelyn talked to several more people who were being sheltered in various churches, and in the synagogue. She asked lots of questions and concluded the worship centers were out-performing government relief agencies about ten-to-one. She decided to stop by the Presbyterian Church after this, the one that she attended on major Christian holidays, just to see if they needed her help. She vowed to go there more regularly, though she dearly loved sleeping in on Sunday mornings.

Special Agent Knechtl, pale-faced and wearing a gray suit, appeared at Evelyn's table. He was slender and tall, with a dome-like forehead, brief mustache and soulful, almost pitying eyes. He looked behind him then turned his attention back to her. "Mayor."

"So we meet again, agent Knechtl."

"It's *special* agent but you can call me Max."

"Okay."

"Tell me what you know about Theodore Norris."

"Almost nothing. I've known him since he was born but never well." Special Agent Max Knechtl inspired non-compliance in her. He looked embalmed but should she judge by looks? Maybe he had cancer. Maybe he was a great guy. She looked up at him, unable to fake a smile, and said nothing.

"Mayor, if you've known Theodore for twenty-six years you must have noticed more than that."

"More than what?"

"Than almost nothing." He waited, looking down on her with brooding concern. "I saw his cartoon on-line. It didn't amuse me. Has he ever threatened you?"

"No, of course not."

"Has he ever contacted you in any way?"

"I baby-sat him once and he sent me a thank-you card that he'd made."

"When was this?"

"Seventeen, eighteen years ago? I no longer have the card."

"He made it? What theme or motif did he use?"

"You're serious."

"Three innocent lives are serious to me."

"Exactly what department, or bureau or agency are you with again?"

"I'm a special agent of the Homeland Security Department, Homeland Security Investigations – formerly Immigration and Customs Enforcement, or ICE – which is part of the Joint Terrorism Task Force, or JTTF, Western Division, South Sector."

She was momentarily speechless, but slowly gathered her senses by an act of will. "Well . . . the card made for me by Ted Norris was a piece of red construction paper with a picture of a frog on it. I think it was a frog. He was nine years old or something."

"Why did you only baby-sit him once?"

"I mis-spoke. I meant to say, one time I baby-sat him and he sent me a thank-you card. Not that I babysat him only one time."

He nodded and turned around again to see if they were still alone. "Has he contacted you since the cartoon posting?"

"He apologized by e-mail but I chose not to respond."

"Did you know that Cade Magnus has moved back to town?"

"Of course. I'm the mayor."

"And you've known him for a long time also?"

"Yes. Maybe his whole life, too. We were in fourth and sixth grades together, right here in Fallbrook. It's a small town."

"Does Ted Norris seem like the kind of man who might enjoy the racist opinions of Cade Magnus and the Rogue Wolves?"

"I have no idea what Ted enjoys, except complaining that

the city spends too much public money on things he doesn't need. First it was the library. Now I'm sure it's the lighted crosswalks, or water and blankets for fire victims."

"Ted Norris spent some time at Pride Auto Repair two days ago."

"I think that's still legal."

Knechtl glanced behind him again. "Do you think it's interesting that in the last month, Ted Norris has publicly ridiculed you as mayor, Cade Magnus has moved back to Fallbrook, the worst arson fire in the history of North County has killed three, and these two fellows are assembling?"

"I doubt that either of them set the fire."

"Why? Someone did."

Evelyn felt affronted that this federal superman would accuse her citizens – though admittedly not her favorite citizens – of such a crime. But she also had the small wriggling thought that one of them could easily have done exactly that. "They just . . . didn't."

"Oh. Do you recognize these people? Press the arrow on the right."

He handed her a phone and Evelyn took off her sunglasses and looked at the screen. The first was a police mug shot of a thick-necked young man, freckle-faced and handsome in his own way. Next a mug of a slender dark-haired woman, kind of hard looking. Then a candid shot of another female, which, judging by the faint background, looked taken from far away.

"No. I don't know them. I've never seen them." She handed him the phone and put her sunglasses back on.

"Are you acquainted with Firooz and Simone Roshdieh?"

"They run the Domino's Pizza downtown."

"What about Ibrahim Sadal?"

"He manages the GasPro station. They're all legal middle-eastern immigrants, living here peacefully."

"Are you sure they're legal?"

"Well, no. I'll leave it to you to get to the bottom of it."

"Thank you." He held out a card.

"You gave me one of those days ago, at city hall."

He slipped the card between one of the rocks and a stack of flyers. "Call me if I can help."

"Help what?"

"Put this nice little town back together."

"Just catch the arsonist."

"Doubt not."

She tended the city booth until late afternoon, a long day indeed, her butt aching from the metal folding chair, her heart troubled. She was surprised that her colleagues in government had let her spend so many hours alone here, disappointed that Brian hadn't stayed around for long, and that neither Ethan nor Gwen had at least stopped by as she'd asked them to. Although she certainly understood that at age thirteen and eleven they had lives of their own. Selfish little lives, it often seemed.

She also didn't like that the DHS or HSI or former ICE or JTTF or whoever these people claimed to be, were all over Fallbrook, snooping rather than helping. Maybe it was just Tod Knechtl's non-radiant face and personality. Maybe she was just hungry. She walked over to the soup stand sponsored by Major Market. But the big kettles were empty, nothing but thin furrows of soup left drying on the bottoms where the ladles had last come through.

15

After church Sunday morning Patrick met up with Salimony and Messina in Oceanside. Bostik hadn't returned calls or messages and Salimony thought he might have just up and gone back to Crescent City. None of them had seen him since the beatdown on the Pendleton beach.

Bostik's new apartment was in a complex east of downtown, away from the Pacific. It was called the Timbers and Patrick noted the pine trees. The buildings were wood-sided and peak-roofed to suggest an alpine look, with the garages downstairs and the apartments above them. The wooden stairs were solid underfoot as he climbed. Patrick knocked on the door and they waited. He rang the bell but still no one answered and he heard nothing within.

He leaned against the railing as Salimony sprang down the stairs two at a time and Messina lit a smoke. Patrick could smell the pine trees that grew between the buildings. Bostik had grown up in a house near a pine forest and Patrick wondered if the Timbers reminded him of home. He thought of the Mako now trailered out in the barn, and felt the same giddy satisfaction he'd felt years ago when he saw the first bicycle that was his, brand new and black and gleaming, waiting for him under the Christmas tree. It was interesting to him that before he bought the Mako it was just a used boat of debatable value, but after he'd handed over the money and hitched the trailer to his truck, it became the most valuable inanimate thing in his life. His present and his future. And it added to Patrick's satisfaction that Iris had been there when he bought the boat, because she was his present and future too, in a way that felt real but almost too precious and fragile for him to look at straight on. She had been there. She had seen and approved. "I bought a boat," he said to Messina.

"Then let's go fishin'."

"You got it."

"We could have a perch fry."

"We can get yellowtail out there, even tuna when the water is right."

"I'll bet Boss went back to Crescent City."

Salimony came back with the manager, a husky ex-Marine who pounded on the door and got the same response that Patrick had gotten. He pounded again. "I don't know what to tell you. He paid his deposit and first month, and he didn't say anything about taking a trip. The policy here is, if the tenants want their mail collected or their patio plants watered, they have to let me know. Or set it up with a friend."

"Well, is his car here?" asked Salimony.

"The garage doors are remote and I don't keep spares," said the manager. "You can open it by hand, but if you damage it, you pay to replace it."

The four men went down the stairs and around to the garage entrance and Messina knelt and spread is fingers under the weatherproofing and lifted. The door rolled up noisily and Patrick first saw the upended patio chair, then the shoes and pants, then the limp white arms and bare torso and acutely angled head of E3 John Bostik, USMC, roped to a garage rafter. The smell was bad and his eyes were bloodshot protrusions in the purple swell of his face.

Patrick's mouth parted open as he looked at his friend but no words came. Then he was aware of setting the chair upright near Bostik and stepping onto it, his pocket knife out and open and in his hand. He heard himself order them to hold the body then he reached up and started sawing through the rope. He stood almost face-to-face with Bostik. The smell and the sight of him sickened Patrick. He heard himself speaking, words of comfort but no joy, a soft monotone, a caress. Then the knife hissed through and the rope jumped and Bostik glided down feet first, borne by friends. Patrick helped them settle Bostik to the oil-stained garage floor, then worked off his dog tags. Patrick found a roll of blue shop rags and broke off two and set them over Boss's face. Salimony went outside and puked in the bushes. Then the three of them sat down around Bostik, cross-legged, stunned and silent.

And you realize this is not what he had promised. This was not the mission he had accepted. He beat the Hajjis, beat the heat and the cold and the snakes and the odds, and he made it home. But the war came after him, across mountains, oceans and time. And it caught up. So he kicked the chair and finally got away. You know that a part of him will stay with you and a part of you will go with him. And this is what you all had promised, to be always faithful – Semper fi.

While Oceanside Police and Fire processed John Bostik, Patrick got the Bostik family number in Crescent City from 4-1-1 and made the call. He felt like he was in a nightmare but knew that it was real and he wouldn't have the blessing of waking up. He told Mrs. Bostik what had happened to John, and said he was very, very sorry but wanted her to hear it from somebody who knew and loved him. She was speechless. Mr. Bostik took the phone from her and Patrick explained again, then asked if they could stop by, very briefly, to pay their respects. Sixteen hours later the three men rolled into Crescent City in Patrick's truck. It was four in the morning and raining hard and luckily they'd brought jackets for the cold.

124

The Bostik home was off of Kings Valley Road, midway between town and Pelican Bay Prison. They found the driveway and parked away from the house. Patrick, who had driven the first five hours and the last five, spilled out of the truck and tried to shake the blood down into his legs then climbed back in. He lay his head against the rest but his stitches stung and he couldn't doze. He listened to the roar of the rain on the roof and looked through the fogging window at the darkness.

Sunrise came late over the redwoods and a small yellow house appeared. It was tucked back in the trees and smoke wobbled up from the chimney. In front of the house was a small square lawn with a concrete bird bath exactly in its center. It was raining lightly and the tops of the redwoods were intermittently lost in the shifting fog.

"Think they're awake yet?" asked Messina.

"It's almost eight hundred," said Salimony. "They have an afternoon flight out, right, Pat?"

Patrick nodded, this information given him by Jake Bostik yesterday evening when Patrick called to make sure they were still welcome to come by. He saw a light come on in the house.

Jake Bostik was tall and slender, a corrections officer at Pelican Bay. Janet Bostik was petite and pleasant-faced though here eyes were puffy and red. They were much younger than Patrick had pictured them. Mrs. Bostik put mugs beside the coffee maker and a stack of salad plates and two boxes of supermarket donuts on the kitchen counter. Jake set up TV trays in a living room with a picture window. While the coffee maker gurgled and wheezed Patrick listened to the rain tapping overhead and watched it spill over the gutters into a brick planter dense with ivy.

He heard shuffling and turned to see a boy come from

125

the hallway. His face was slack from sleep and his hair was peaked up on one side and down on the other and he looked very much like John Bostik. He was skinny and peach-fuzzed had a blanket over his shoulders. Patrick guessed sixteen. Without a word or a look the boy went into the kitchen.

"Nine-eleven was what got John going," said Jake. "He wanted to go fight. He was ten years old. I was thirty-one and I think *I'd* have enlisted if I wasn't married and a dad."

"Me too," said Salimony. "I really wanted to do something. I wrote Bush a letter saying I'd keep an eye out for terrorists at school. And I did. Never saw any."

"But later I had a bad feeling about the wars," said Jake. "It seemed right at first to go after bin Laden. Then Iraqi Freedom, the way they marketed it like a car or something . . . it seemed not necessary. Honey, we talked about this?"

She nodded and looked out the window. "And way back then, neither of us thought both those wars would still be going on by the time John could enlist, which he did, at seventeen. I was against it but there was no stopping him. Seventeen – that's a year older than Kirk is now. That's Kirk in the kitchen. I didn't think either war was worth John losing his life over. Or Kirk or any American boy. Not worth it. I'm just a non-political mom. That's what I thought about those wars. I still do."

Kirk came into the living room holding a cup of coffee in one hand and the blanket snug around his shoulders with the other.

"I'm still going to join up," said Kirk. "The second I'm seventeen."

"Why?" asked Salimony, one leg bouncing.

"Because this place is dark, cold, rainy, and gets tsunamis. I've had enough."

"I think that's a good reason to join," said Messina.

"Why don't you go to college?" asked Patrick.

126

"D's. I'll use the GI Bill when I'm out and know what I want to do."

Patrick wondered what John Bostik would be like if he'd gone to school rather than to war. Alive, for starters. Even young Kirk knew that a distant war had killed his brother, so what could Patrick say to dissuade him? Still he felt compelled to try. "There's only one reason to go to war, Kirk – to defend your country. Make sure you got a good war, one that does that."

"How will I know if it's good or not?"

Patrick had to think about that a moment. "I think the good wars come to you." The room went silent and Patrick felt six minds arching away in six different directions, like bright tendrils of one firework. "I'd like to say that the thing I loved most about John was his sense of humor. The first time we almost died together it was close. Real close. They caught us out in the open in the brown zone, not far from road six-six-one. Machine guns lit us up – must have been half a dozen of them dug in on a hillside. We hit the dirt and the bullets were thick and all we had for cover was this scrawny little fallen tree. And after about half a minute of this, Boss started laughing. Hard. And the bullets kept ripping past us and slapping into that tree and he said, 'I'm sorry Pat, but when I get this close to dying and I'm not dead, all I can do is laugh.' And I got what he meant and the bullets were still coming at us and I started laughing too and I couldn't stop. I just could not stop. Because it was absurd. Because we were supposed to be dead but we were flat behind a scrawny tree that was saving us. We finally returned fire. The air cover arrived and they laid down the rockets and killed every Talib on that hill. We lost two men in the ambush. Sisley and Ocampo. There were another maybe hundred times I should have died over there. At least. And every time death failed to get me, I laughed. John taught me to laugh right in its face."

127

Salimony told the family about John's easy kindness with village children, how he shared all the stuff in the care packages they sent, except for the peanut-butter filled pretzels, which he hogged for himself and his best friends only. Luckily, we all three qualified as best friends, said Salimony. Messina told them about the time their son ran to the side of a platoon mate, Salamanca, who'd set off an IED hidden in the rocks – got the tourniquet on him like right then – and saved his life *and* his foot. Patrick told them how he and John and would follow PFC Reichert out at night with SAW machine guns, to cover the crazy kid on his critter patrols. Reichert collected anything weird he could find, took pictures and made notes on them. He kept his treasures in jars and cans at the FOB – all sorts of lizards and snakes and bugs. He staged fights between the camel spiders, the Marines betting and cheering like it was UFC or something. "My brother, Ted, always had crawling things in cages when we were kids. Still does. So, when we covered Reichert on his night missions it was like we were covering Ted. And I thought it was an example of why we were in the war. How the war related to America and home."

Patrick saw that Kirk was listening to him. The boy had a pugnacious expression but he was alert. "Then are you saying it was a good war or it wasn't?"

"After going I know it wasn't good and it wasn't necessary. Before going I never thought about it. That's why I'm telling you to think about things first. It might give you an advantage. Maybe your brother sacrificed so you won't have to."

"I just flat-out disagree," said Salimony. "We kicked ass, made a difference and made our country safer. It's simple as that."

"I'm with him," said Messina.

Patrick shrugged. "Either way, John Bostik was a great guy and I'll remember him forever. I looked up to him."

"Amen," said Salimony and Janet Bostik in unison. Patrick handed Bostik's dog tags to his father.

They set out for home. Patrick steered his truck through the looming redwoods, which even near noon permitted little sunlight into the world. The rain had stopped and tufts of fog snagged in the tree tops. This place made Patrick feel sullen and nervy, and he saw why John and Kirk wanted out. At least in Afghanistan there was sun. He pictured Boss the last time he'd seen him, then quickly banished this horror.

Messina demanded they see Pelican Bay Prison because he'd heard about it in a movie. So Patrick found Lake Earl Drive and followed it out. "The prison's got a special cellblock, right in the middle," Messina said. "It drives you insane if they lock you in it too long. The cells are concrete cages with no windows." Patrick pulled onto the grounds which, upon first sight, looked tranquil and park-like. The parking lot was very large and only one-third full. Behind the electric fences stood the prison, which to Patrick looked efficient and not quite humane. "My old man took me to Joplin Prison when I was a kid," said Messina. "On account of I'd been doing some shoplifting. Just candy and football cards and stuff but he wanted me to see what was waiting for me. It pretty much worked. Except ever since I've been kind of fascinated by prisons. Well, that's good enough – I doubt they give tours."

They pulled out of the Pelican Bay parking lot in silence. Patrick followed the signs for the highway. Salimony got the sudden inspiration to visit Sgt. Pendejo's family too. He remembered that Pendejo had lived in Coalinga, where the big-ass earthquake happened a long time ago, and which was right on the way to home. "I mean, if we could tell Boss's family what a great guy he was, we could tell Pendejo's."

"But he wasn't a great guy," said Messina. "And his name wasn't even Pendejo."

"It wasn't?"

"No, pendejo means pubic hair in Spanish."

"I always wondered why his tag said something else."

"Pendejo was just a nickname, Salimony. You never knew that?"

"Pendejo's name was Alejandro Reyes," said Patrick.

"So it rhymed with pendejo," said Salimony.

"Kind of not very much," said Patrick. "He wasn't bad. I always thought, down under that guy who always did every damned thing he was told to do, was an okay human being. He wasn't mean enough to be a Marine. But he was terrific on that barbecue. He made the thing out of a fuel drum, remember?"

"He died making burritos for his men," said Salimony. "So let's go see his family and tell them he wasn't such a bad guy."

"Oh, they're going to love hearing he wasn't so bad," said Messina. "Sal? You really are full of shit. Maybe we could get some beers for the road."

"It's way past noon," said Salimony.

Heading south they played the radio and threw empties out the windows and stopped at rest areas. Patrick quit after two beers but the rest of the twelver was gone before Patterson. The two other Marines fell silent then asleep. After six hours on the road Patrick pulled off for Coalinga. The evening was warm in the central Valley and the land lay flat. He saw late-season cotton still in the fields but most of the soil was brown and groomed and ready to be planted. He saw the sign for the prison and the sign for the mental hospital then Messina's head pop up from the crew cab into the rearview. "How come they got so many criminals and crazies in this state?" he asked. "That's the third prison since Pelican Bay and I been asleep for three hours."

130

"Any of those cheese things left?" asked Patrick.

Messina held the bag upside down and nothing but orange dust came out. Next to Patrick, Salimony finally sat up, yawned loudly and burped. He took out his phone. A moment later he was leaving messages and talking to people, trying to track down the family of Alejandro Reyes.

Finally Salimony got Alejandro's mother, who gave him Alejandro's father, who gave him an address. Patrick drove to a convenience store and they bought a cold twelve-pack and three bags of expensive jerky and one artificial rose – pink, unrealistic, wrapped in a clear plastic cone and heavily scented.

The Reyes home was a travel trailer in a row of other trailers, all lined up for shade along a windbreak of drooping greasewood and oleander on the edge of a cotton field. Behind the windbreak was an irrigation canal. As he approached, Patrick saw that the trailers were old and faded, their shapes softened by weather and time. There were big air conditioners dripping water, some resting on wooden decks in front of the trailers, and some propped up on concrete blocks. Between the coaches, vehicles were nosed into the shade of the windbreak too, and they were older and dusty and some had folding sunscreens over the dashboards. He saw laundry drying on lines and children playing stickball and others sitting on upended wooden produce boxes in front of a TV that someone had set up under a portable shade screen. The sun hit the TV screen so brightly Patrick couldn't make out what they were watching. He saw a group of five or six young men, wiry in their singlets, heavily tattooed, drinking beer and eyeing him. "Pendejo wasn't exactly from Beverly Hills," said Salimony.

"This was your idea," said Messina.

"Who cares where he came from" asked Patrick. "The aqua colored trailer, right? Here it is, so let's do this thing."

131

They stood on the spacious deck and Patrick knocked on the door. He heard the roar of the big air conditioner sitting on bricks beside the aqua trailer. Overhead was a slatted roof intertwined with vines with fragrant white flowers. The deck had colorful pots of bougainvillea and geraniums and canna lilies. There were two barbecues and a fire pit made with the perforated canister of a clothes dryer.

A man pushed open the door and stood in the doorway. He was dark and slender, maybe fifty, Patrick guessed, with a weathered face and thick gray hair. He wore a white yoked cowboy-style shirt tucked into clean pressed jeans, and work boots.

"We served with Alejandro," said Patrick. "We just wanted to tell you he was a good man."

"I am Raydel, his father. It's too small in here. Wait, please." Raydel pulled the door shut and a few minutes later he came outside followed by a thin dark woman. She had black hair and wore a light blue dress and she smiled without looking at the young men. She carried two white resin chairs from inside and Raydel set out three more from the stack on the deck. He introduced his wife as Theresa. She went back into the trailer and returned with a framed portrait of Sgt. Reyes in his dress blues. She set it on the railing of the deck, facing them. The ghosts stirred in Patrick's heart. Pendejo looked proud and happy. He was not a hard man.

They sat in the shade and Salimony gave everyone a beer, and the rose to Alejandro's mother, and he opened the jerky and passed the bag. "He hated the rations," said Salimony. "Alejandro got those packages from you, with the spices and dried chilies and those weird pickled carrots you Mexicans eat. And he'd mix it with field rations and come up with real food. He was the best cooker in the whole battalion. I think you should know that he was doing something he liked when he died. He was cooking for us jarheads. Standing right out there by a barbecue he'd made all by himself. He was brave."

Salimony's leg bounced and he drained his beer and crumpled it and got out another.

"He was honored at the Three/Five memorial at Pendleton," said Patrick. "Two of his best friends spoke about him. I didn't see you there."

Raydel nodded and sipped his beer. "We decided not to go," he said. "It is a very long way."

"It's only about six hours from here," said Messina.

Raydel looked at him and Theresa stared down at the deck. Then she looked at Patrick and he saw she was fighting something back. "We have no papers. When we go somewhere there is the chance we will be stopped and deported. The Marine Base would be very dangerous. Here, people know us and we are safe. So we don't go away from here."

"Half the laborers in Fallbrook are illegal," said Patrick. "It's a tough way to live."

Alejandro's father set his can on the deck and crossed his hands on his lap. He had the relaxed, conservative posture of a man who had worked his life outside. "Alejandro was born in Tijuana. We brought him here when he was one years old. I always have work because I know farming and I work very hard. But he did not want this. He wanted something better. He join the Marines because he wanna become a citizen here."

"He wasn't even an American citizen?" asked Salimony.

Raydel and Theresa both shook their heads. "We have three more children," she said. "And they were born here so they can always stay. But Alejandro, he live under the same fear we have. He wanna be a cook."

"They should make him a citizen even though he's dead," said Salimony. He upended his can and drank the last drop.

"I wondered about such a thing," said Raydel. "But I don't want to cause attention. My other son, he's gonna join too

133

when he's old enough. He don't like to work but he wants to fight."

"Well," said Salimony. "Alejandro is a citizen of my country no matter what nobody says. He made me some kind of soup when I got sick over there. God knows where he found anything good to put in it. A whole pot of it, enough for me and ten other guys. I didn't get why Alejandro wouldn't stand up for himself. He was older and us young guys kinda pushed him around. Four of five of us jumped him one day, roughed him up good. It's for fun, but he acted like he wasn't there. Now I get it – he was afraid if he fought back they'd find out and toss him out of the country when he came home."

"There is a program for soldiers who come home to be citizens more quickly," said Theresa. "That was his plan. Then to open a restaurant."

Raydel had the same thousand-yard stare that Bostik seemed to have so often. Patrick looked at the picture of Alejandro then stared down into the opening of his beer can and tried to banish the image of pink brains on a tan wall behind a barbecue. He was thankful that Alejandro's dad didn't have to see that. The ghosts in his heart swirled up suddenly, agitated and wanting out.

16

The morning was the coolest of the month and Ted felt winter in his feet. His task was to strip off the herbicide-tainted paint he'd put on some eighty tree trunks. Archie patiently demonstrated how to use the pressure sprayer, cautioning Ted that a direct ninety-degree blade of compressed water would cut into the tree surely as an axe. Archie fired away at an angle, "lifting" off the possibly poisoned paint that Ted had applied. "If the bark starts coming up, your angle's wrong."

"I got it, Dad."

"I'd like to get a full day of work out of you."

"Moving the compressor will be pretty hard on my feet."

"You think the compressor is heavy, Pat and I will be lugging bales and putting down straw."

"The compressor is heavy, too."

Ted grunted and as he pulled the heavy wheeled contraption tree-to-tree over the leafy, ash-frosted earth. He got the thing going but the pressure seemed insufficient so he put on a different nozzle. And sure enough, once he got the hang of it the paint came right off. He was surprised how thick it was and found it hard to believe he'd failed to triple-rinse the spray canister. He had no knack for practical physical things. Ted put in his ear buds and cranked up Cruzela Storm. A voice like new motor oil, he thought, clean and smooth and durable, and a similar color, too. Her main theme was: keep going in adversity, keep your cool and your faith. Her sub-theme was: people will try to take what's yours, so learn to stand up for yourself.

He moved beneath the spindly naked canopies. Lifting off the dried paint took longer than spraying it on in the first place, but Ted worked diligently. He stopped now and then to lift rocks to see what creatures were living underneath. He caught one big tarantula, one small scorpion and an alligator lizard, and put them into separate cottage-cheese containers with air holes punched in their lids. He had always loved unlovable things. They were humble and expected nothing, though some of them packed secret stings and poisons. He set the containers in the shade of the truck and got right back to work.

Later, close to lunchtime, through the music streaming into him, Ted suddenly and clearly heard the sharp report of his father's voice. He lifted off one bud. *"GoddamnsonofaBITCH!"*

Ted dropped the nozzle, yanked off the earbuds and pawed open the low-hanging branches in the direction of the yelling. Through his sweat-and-soot smudged goggles he could see Archie far downhill of him, and Patrick a hundred yards to the east. His father stood looking at Ted with both arms out, palms raised in an unmistakable question: *what in the hell is this?* Ted burst through the black limbs and hustled down the slope, sidling down the steep granite escarpments, his feet swaddled in pain but soon he was standing before his father, panting. He stripped off the goggles to see what Archie was holding in his outstretched hand. It was one of the thick slabs of dried paint that Ted had lifted from the tree.

"Paint, Dad!"

"This isn't paint, Ted. It's bark! Formerly living bark! You've killed thirty trees today, son. *Congratulations.*"

Ted took the white fragment and turned it over. The inside was colored a very pale green that suggested life. The whole thing was no thicker than half an inch. He held it up closer to make sure it wasn't just paint. But he could see that it was not.

Patrick arrived and took the bark from Ted and saw the problem. "Took off a bit much here, brother."

"I thought it was paint, Pat. I swear."

"Christallmighty Ted!

"Screaming doesn't help," said Patrick.

"Nothing helps."

"Then stop being an asshole," said Patrick.

Archie glared at his sons, Patrick and Ted in turn.

"I didn't mean it to happen, Dad," said Ted. "It was an accident."

"You're both worthless." Archie snatched the painted bark from Patrick and backhanded it against Ted's ample belly, off which it bounced. Then Archie shook his head and turned and headed muttering toward the trucks.

Ted closed his eyes and clutched his arms tight to his chest and began turning counterclockwise.

Patrick grabbed him by the shoulders and slowed him and held him in place. "Goddamnit, Ted – that won't do you any good. You can't just go away."

Ted closed his eyes tight and waited for lift-off.

Ted switched jobs with Patrick and worked furiously through lunch, breaking apart the heavy bales and spreading the straw under the trees with a pitchfork. Occasionally he stopped to watch Patrick removing the paint from the tree trunks, and from this distance Ted couldn't see what his brother was doing differently than he had. It looked as if Patrick had switched nozzles, and that was about all. But the real difference, thought Ted – is Pat won't create a disaster. Pat will do it perfectly. Ted snapped through another nylon tie with the heavy cutters, threw the pieces into the back of the pickup, then rammed the pitchfork into the bale, broke off a load and heaved it under a tree.

It was easy to think of a bale as someone who wished him harm, like one of the rapacious takers in the Cruzela Storm songs cranking in his ears, like Edgar or his foul-mouthed girlfriend or Evelyn Anders or his father. It felt good to impale them over the next hours, spreading them evenly around the trees that he had tried so hard to save and only managed to put at even greater peril. It was good to focus anger on a person, to have a face to use for a target. And thanks to me, he thought, when the rain comes, this soil and these trees will be protected by this straw. Just as when the fire had come, the Norris residence had survived because he'd trimmed back the trees and bushes around the house and outbuildings. And what exactly had Dad said about that? Not one word, Ted thought. Only his mother had had the good manners to thank him for what he'd done. And Pat. Patrick had said something right off about him doing a good job. Or had he?

Near sundown Ted carried the pitchfork back to the truck. He checked the creatures in their containers and set them up front. His phone rang. He checked the caller, took a deep breath and spoke in a low voice. "'Lo, Cade."

He ditched family cocktails, showered and shaved and drove to Pride Auto Repair. There were three cars in the lot, Cade's white-and-aqua Bel-Air, a Dodge Magnum and a red Dodge pickup truck, late fifties, beautifully restored. Ted heard music inside, hard and reckless. He stood under the neon Model T sign and looked through the open front door. The overhead lights were strong and lit the room like a stage. Cade was in there, shooting pool with a man while two women sat on stools and watched. Cade wore a holster low on his leg like a gunfighter and a six-gun glinted in the leather. The women wore halter tops and small skirts and their pale legs shined in the overhead light. They held bottles of beer. The man playing pool with Cade was young, all muscles and freckles. He wore a black leather vest over his naked torso, and a black cowboy hat, and a large handgun on his belt, holstered high and back, like a detective. They all looked at him standing at the open door. Cade smiled. "What do you want, Ted, an engraved invitation?"

Ted stepped in. Cade bent to the table, formed his bridge and sunk the seven ball with a clack so sharp it pierced the music. The strong man ignored him but one of the women, the brunette, smiled and held up her beer. "Want one?"

"Sure."

"The fridge is in the back, cold ones up front."

"Can I get one for you?"

"Bring it on, big guy."

"Anyone else?"

No one answered so Ted got two cold ones. He pressed them to the opener on the wall while he looked around the repair bay. There were two cars up on the lifts and two more waiting, hoods up. Back in the lobby he gave the woman the beer and pulled up a bar stool a respectful distance from her. The muscular man eyed him then looked back to the table. Cade leaned against the wall by the cue rack, twisting a cube of chalk onto his stick. The jukebox played hard fast music from a band that Ted wasn't familiar with, something about brass knuckles, red blood and a flag that still waves. He leaned over for a look at the selection and saw that the old retro jukebox was in fact a newer one, outfitted to play CDs.

"I'm Joan and that's Amber and Trevor," said the brunette. She had a compact face and a pleasant smile and she was older than he had thought at first. "Friends of Cade's from Idaho. Spirit Lake."

"Are there really spirits in it?"

"Indian ghosts is the legend. It's beautiful there. Cold in

winter. We came to talk Cade into moving back but we're already in love with this place and we only been here two days. This is like America used to be."

"Before government took over."

"Absolutely. Are you a friend of Cade's?"

"I've known him my whole life, pretty much, so, yeah."

"Then you know all about what happened here."

"Yep, right out back. Mrs. Magnus was locking up and he surprised her."

"Yes, and she wasn't armed to defend herself."

Ted nodded and saw the glance between Amber and Cade. Amber slid off her stool, shut and locked the front door and made sure the blinds were closed. Joan set her beer on the counter and dug into her purse and produced an empty .45 caliber cartridge casing and a small glass vial. Looking intent, she unscrewed the vial and tapped some shiny white powder into the shell and sniffed it up her nose. She shuddered and grinned at Ted and loaded one for him. Ted peered down into the casing. There wasn't much white stuff down there. "Crank?"

"Best there is. Cooked not all that far from here. Smooth and silky and it'll keep you talkin' into next week. Just kidding. There's hardly any crash."

"Really," said Ted. He wanted to sound knowledgeable though he'd never tried methamphetamine for fear he might like it too much. He saw Cade and Black Hat watching him. Joan smiled crookedly. He brought the shell to his nose and sniffed it up. There was an explosive burn that made his eyes water, then nothing.

"It'll take a few seconds," said Joan. She took the casing and put the works back into her bag. Ted watched her, listening to the billiard balls knocking around the table and trying to hear the muttered comments of Cade and Trevor. The singer on the CD screamed on about *cleaning up America and taking out the trash!* Suddenly Ted's heart had shifted into a higher gear and he felt a great torque unleashed inside him, like horses coming down the stretch – power, and clarity and confidence.

"Woah," he whispered.

"Woah is right," said Joan. She had straight shiny hair held back with a barrette, and a cute nose and pretty hands. "You'd think the Magnus family would have gotten a little help after the mother was raped and murdered by a psychopathic killer," she said, turning to Ted. "A *black* psychopathic killer. Instead, the monster got a fancy state hospital room and the Magnuses got bankrupted by the courts. Thank you, government. The liberal press didn't cover that angle, though. Hardly a word of sympathy for the family because they believe in their own white race, right? Then later in court they made it sound like Jed Magnus was sending killers around the world to kill black men. Bankrupted him. Absurd."

"Joan?" said Cade, settling in for his next shot. "Shut the fuck up, will you? That's old news."

"Which relates directly to our own present times," said Joan.

"Be a dumb shit," said Cade. "You have the right."

"I was eleven when she was murdered," said Ted. He really wanted to talk. *Had* to talk. The crank brought out old feelings. Suddenly it was like he was here, fifteen years ago, age eleven. The crank seemed to bore out his brain, clean away the clutter and increase the capacity of it. "I rode my bike down here from home the next day and the whole place was still behind crime-scene tape. The deputies were there to keep people from coming in, so I sat in the shade across the street and watched all the people wanting to see where the murder happened. People driving and walking, and tons of kids on bikes and scooters, like me. And news crews, dozens of them. And by the time – "

141

"I was eighteen, living in Spirit Lake," said Joan. "Everybody knew about it because Jed's newsletter was popular. When Jed moved the family there later, we were honored to have them. There was a nice welcome party, home-cooked potluck and a bluegrass band. People showed up, like they're supposed to. The whole town. Half of them were retired cops from ugly cities. Like my dad. So don't you diss me, Cade Magnus."

On top of the crank, the beer hit Ted surprisingly hard, not having drunk alcohol for nearly six months. He hopped off the stool and got another bottle and strode back. He felt seven feet tall, sleek and extremely intelligent. No foot pain at all. Cade banked in the eight-ball, set his cue on the table and raised a fist. "Ted, you're up. Ladies, doubles?"

The women came off their stools and headed for the cue rack. Trevor set his black leather cowboy hat on the counter, crown down, and wiped his forehead with the back of one big freckled hand. His hair was red and cut close. His handshake was powerful and Ted watched Trevor's tan eyes roam his face. His voice was soft. "I heard you had some trouble with a local gangster of the Mexican variety."

"He robbed me at gunpoint."

"You should take him to the next level, Ted – white man style. I can help. Do you know where to find him?"

"He hangs out on Carmella Street. Or along Old Stage, behind the MacDonald's. I've seen him there."

"Not good enough. Can you get his home address?"

"Easy."

"Give me your cell phone." Trevor took Ted's phone and started pushing buttons. "Here is Joan's number. When you get it, give her the wetback's address. Not his name, just his address. I've never heard of you and never seen you."

"I get it."

"You and me will fix it so he doesn't want to bother you again."

142

"Yes."

"Mostly you are going to fix it. I won't fight your fights for you."

Ted was amazed that the white powder would bring him so much power, then more, and more, and more. It was like being plugged into a wall socket for an endless charge. "I don't want you to fight my fights."

"Tell me about the mayor."

"I hate her politics. And maybe her, too."

"Your cartoon was cool."

"Thanks, man."

"Maybe you should take *her* to the next level."

"What does that mean?"

"Whatever you need it to mean. This band is Hate Matrix. They might give you some ideas."

"Well, I've thought about certain things I could do."

"Thought is for the weak – *act*. Make a list of people who need to be dealt with. Hold onto your anger. It's the only thing that'll get you through."

Ted felt the power prowling around in him like a tiger looking for a way out. Wasn't that tiger his life, his passion to do a big and meaningful thing? He was the tiger and the tiger could do the big thing. He smiled.

"As of right now none of this ever happened."

"I appreciate it."

"I don't know what the fuck you mean. I'm a Rogue Wolf, Ted. I live free and hunt alone. You should too."

Ted teamed up with Joan. She won the lag and broke and took solids. While she played Ted couldn't help but notice the beauty of her, the harmonious proportions, the fair skin and the light sheen of perspiration on her neck. She had Pegasus tattooed on her shoulder. He had another beer, and then another. Amber was lovely too, curvier than Joan, with wispy blond curls and a dazzling smile. The women raised their cues and beer bottles and bumped hips each time they passed by each other, and Ted was certain that their laughter was getting him higher than the crank and beer were. He concentrated as hard as he could on the shot-making, and the drugs gave him plenty of confidence and even some steadiness. Between shots he sat on a stool with a half smile and the cue propped up beside him, watching the women and letting their sweet scents drift over him, occasionally looking at Cade and Trevor. He liked these people. Sound judgments on society but no judgments of him. Like-minded individuals but not in lockstep with anything or anyone. Strong but fair. *Rogue Wolves*, he thought. *Live free and hunt alone.*

Buoyed by camaraderie, meth and beer, Ted drove west out Mission Road. Near the San Luis Rey River he pulled into Riverview Stables parking lot got out. He went to the railing and looked down into the arena and saw that he was in luck. His heart did a little giddy up. Dora was there! Two months ago he had given her a ride into town after her car had run out of gas near here. And of course a ride back to her car after she'd bought a fuel can that he filled for her. Since then, once a week, Ted had come out to watch her teach the night students under the lights. He could tell she liked him. And he liked watching Dora's mastery over the huge, unpredictable animals.

Now he saw a big chestnut mare ridden by a girl, cantering around Dora. He heard the hollow clop clop of hooves and the music of Dora's voice floating up toward him. The air was sweet from the river and the moon was a sliver caught in the sycamore branches. He padded softly down to the grandstand and sat in the front row and watched.

Dora was a pretty red-haired woman in her late twenties. Tonight she was wearing jeans and paddock boots and a red cowl-necked sweater. Her hair shined in the arena lights. Ted smiled with pride. As he watched the horse and rider circle her, Ted thought of the first and only time he'd gotten on a horse. Why it had reared up, nobody could say. But the gelding's neck had broken his nose and he had landed hard on his back, his breath knocked out of him. When he came to his senses he was looking up at his mother. He could hear his father cursing and the departing thump of his boots and the more distant thud of hooves. Now he pictured his mother's face, her beautiful face, the furrow of her brow and the throb of the vein in her forehead, and beyond her the blue sky and white clouds. The horse was named Feather and it was the last horse he'd ever touched.

The lesson ended with a quick hand of applause from Dora. Ted watched the girl lead her horse toward the boarding stalls. Her parents were waiting for her on the other side of the arena and the dad put his arms over his daughter's shoulders and they all walked slowly past the dressage arena. Dora glanced at her watch as she came from the lighted arena toward him. With a giddy tickle in his heart Ted waited until she was close, then jumped from the darkened grandstand, stumbling slightly. "Hi, Dora!"

He heard the intake of her breath. She stopped abruptly and it took her a moment to identify him. "Ted? *Ted?* Don't be jumping out at me like that!"

"I'm sorry."

"Yes, so what are you doing?"

"Watching, Dora. That's all. I came to see you."

"You scared the hell out of me."

"I'm so sorry, I thought you would see me, even though the light's not good."

"Yeah, okay, well I didn't see you. My heart's still pounding. Jeez . . ."

Now Ted felt a twinge of fear too, a little tremble in his gut and a flutter in his heart, as if someone had just jumped out

145

of the darkness at *him*. "You're right, Dora. I should never have done that. I'm really sorry. Can I walk you to your car?"

She looked at him but in the half-light Ted couldn't read the expression on her face. "I guess," she said.

He fell in beside her and she moved over and they headed for the parking lot. Ted looked up at the clubhouse and restaurant on the hill that overlooked the property. Through the windows he saw a few diners, candles on the tabletops, a waitress delivering something. He shifted his glance down to Dora to see her jaw set tight and her lips firm and her brow bent into a frown. "Dora, can I buy you a drink or dinner? I really didn't mean to scare you."

"I've eaten, Ted. No thanks."

"Glass of wine? Decaf?"

"No and no. I think you've had enough to drink, too."

"Maybe a little too much. Good lesson tonight?"

She didn't answer. Ted listened to the crunch of their feet on the decomposed granite walkway. He looked down at her petite, lace-up boots, then at his own special-order, extra-extra wide walking shoes which, even fitted with unbelievably expensive orthotics, let his collapsed feet slosh and yaw with every step.

"I asked you not to come here again, Ted. What part of that was I not clear about?"

Ted still felt her fear and now he was feeling her anger too. He didn't know why other people's emotions got into him so quickly and strongly but they always had. They could drown out his own. "I just came by to say I won't be coming by anymore."

"That's lame, Ted."

"I know. I'm starting to get mad at me too."

"I'll call the sheriffs. You know that, right?"

"Please don't."

"This is the last time you come here, then. The next time

I'm pulling out my cell phone and calling them on the spot. Do you understand that?"

"Yes, M'am. Yes, Dora, I do." Do I ever, he thought. He needed to calm her. He cupped her upper arm very softly. "The moon is nice tonight, isn't it?"

She tried to pull away but Ted's grip automatically closed. A reaction. His hands were very strong and always had been. She yelped and wrenched her arm free and he heard the clink of keys. She whirled. He'd never seen her angry and the anger spoiled her face and he felt responsible. "Ted, you're a nice guy, and I thank you again for giving me that ride weeks ago. But it doesn't entitle you to follow me around the rest of my life, touching me. We've been through all this. You scare me. You're drunk. You're *weird*."

They came to the car that ran out of gas, an old Jaguar Vanden Plas into which Dora quickly disappeared. The door locks clunked and the engine started and Dora backed up fast, gravel blasting up against the chassis. In seconds she was far down the road, making a left onto Mission and punching it hard up the hill.

17

The next day Patrick spent ten hours pitching straw and four hours delivering pizza. Driving home from the pizza place someone slammed a car door. Patrick cranked the wheel sharply right, jumped a curb and slammed on the brakes, the grill of his truck stopping inches from the Gulliver's Travels shop-front window. He was breathing heavily, sweating hard. Myers and Zane were up the sidewalk under the theater marquee, looking at him. How the fuck did they get to Fallbrook? They merged with shocked pedestrians, whose drop-jawed stares brought Patrick back. It was terrifying to lose control of his mind and memories and even body. He unlocked his hands from wheel, repositioned them, and backed onto the street, thanking God he hadn't hit anyone.

By the time he began pulling apart the Mercury outboard it was ten at night. The light in the barn was good and Patrick was pleased to find the motor in decent condition. The artillery on Pendleton commenced and Patrick flinched and went to one knee. Steady, he thought. Steady. The ghosts in his heart roiled and wavered and he was back in Sangin – Myers and Zane lying shredded against the rocks, Pendejo's brains on the wall, Sheffield's boots lying yards from the rest of him – all knots in the outstretched line of his memory from Sangin to Fallbrook, from Fallbrook to Sangin. He hauled that line back, across continents and oceans and time, hand-over-hand, dropping the slack into the larger hold of his waking mind. When he was done he closed the lid. His breath was short and his body washed in sweat. He took a deep breath and felt the flutter of his heart.

He cleaned the points and injectors and hooked up the new battery. The carburetor needed cleaning so he disassembled it at one of the workbenches and let the parts soak in solvent. He ate another piece of the pizza that Firooz and Simone had pressed upon him, as they did after every one of Patrick's shifts. The smell of the solvent reminded him of cleaning the SAW and the 240 and his mind went AWOL again and he couldn't pull it back this time.

By the third day in theater you get your preview vision. Which is when you see something happen that really didn't happen, and then it does happen, exactly how you saw it. So you're seeing an event ahead of time. The problem is sometimes you're think you're having a preview vision and you're not. So that turns every single thing that you imagine into something real, and if your imagination is filled with death and mutilation and agony, which in combat it will be, then you see ugliness and mayhem everywhere you look. So these things become your starting lineup you can't make substitutions. On patrol you see Sheffield trip an IED about fifty feet in front of you. And when you open your eyes Sheffield is still walking and there was no explosion. And then five seconds later an IED goes off and Sheffield crumples over smoking and screaming. Lots of us grunts had those preview visions. Our theory was that you're aware of more than you think you are, so things register on your senses without you knowing. I don't know how I could have seen that IED, though. It was buried in the rocks and rocks were everywhere you looked. The skinnies made the IEDs out of wood and plastic so our mine detectors couldn't pick them up, and they covered them with their own shit so if they didn't kill you whatever was left of you got infected. Preview visions were common for machine gunners like me, because we usually patrolled to the rear, to put down the fire when the contact came. Later on the tour I saw Lavinder shot by a sniper and I hit the ground. Bostik was behind me and next I know he's looking down at me laughing his ass off. There was no shot and Lavinder was fine. Thirty seconds later Lavinder gets shot dead by a sniper up in the rocks just about exactly how I saw it happen. We put some heavy fifty on the rocks and for once the air strike came fast. When the Blackhawks cleared out we climbed up there and went rock-to-rock killing Talibs whether they needed it or not. I felt like taking scalps but didn't. I put fire into a corpse just because. You just get pissed and lose it sometimes. Later I felt shame. Lavinder was one of those guys you hated to lose because he was happy so much. A happy guy was hard to find. It could be contagious but annoying too. Once I asked Lavinder why he was always happy and he said it was because he knew he was going to die over there. And once he'd accepted that fact, the pressure was gone and every minute he wasn't dead yet was another minute to be happy.

Patrick swirled the coffee cans of solvent to get the carburetor parts clean and ate another piece of pizza. He heard a truck park outside and thought: where's my weapon? A moment later Archie was standing in the doorway with a bottle of bourbon in one hand and two glasses in the other. The dogs barged past him, all tongues and tails. "Mind if the asshole comes in?"

"Not one bit."

Archie nodded and walked in. He was a purposeful man, always on task, but tonight he seemed uncertain. "Ted gone to bed?"

"Think so. We tired him out the last couple of days."

"Just as well. I wanted to talk to you first. Splash?" At the workbench he poured two bourbons neat. Patrick came over and took a glass and they leaned against the bench facing the Mako. The dogs patrolled the barn, sniffing things. "That's a nice craft, Pat. Eleven grand. Well done. How's the engine?"

"Low hours and clean."

"Don't overload the oil mix on those two-strokes."

"Never. I learned that from my old man. What's up?"

"I feel rather shitty about what happened out in the grove yesterday. I'm going to try to apologize. I think you understand my anger, but how could Ted? Sometimes I'm not even sure I do. When I saw those big chunks of tree bark all over the ground . . ."

"He's always had a blind spot in his common sense."

His father nodded and sipped the bourbon. "That's a good way to put it. You know, right from the get-go Ted wasn't fortunate."

"The seizures and fever."

"Your mother and I thought we might lose him." Archie looked at Patrick then back at the boat. "I had very high hopes for him. I wanted him to not just survive, but to flourish and fly someday. I wanted to make it happen. I saw in Ted a chance to be a hero."

"A hero to your own son?"

Archie was staring at the boat but Patrick could tell he wasn't seeing it. Over the years Patrick had noticed the thousand yard stare in his father and but only since the war did he recognize it for what it was. He'd seen it on Bostik and Salimony and Messina, on every man he'd known in the 3/5. It was a strange thing: distant and focused, aware and oblivious, outer and inner, present and absent.

"Did I ever tell you about meeting your mother?"

"Sure, Dad. It was in a restaurant and love at first sight."

Archie gathered his attention on Patrick and smiled. "Well, that was the party line. There was a bit more going on. Some of which may be pertinent. May I speak frankly?"

"You should."

"It wasn't a restaurant. It was a biker bar in Oceanside. Kind of a dump. I'd gone there with a buddy. I was forty years old, ten years widowed. The farm was making me some good money. I had plenty of energy and girlfriends. I was steering solo and happy with that. I'd loved my first wife perfectly, I thought. Or as close to perfect as I could manage. She died young. Cancer, as you know. And because our love was young, she was ideal. Even in death and after, she remained ideal. So who could compete with that memory? Well, when Caroline walked into the biker bar she was beautiful, troubled, drunk and about half my age. But she had indefinable *thing* that was absolutely unmistakable in spite of the ideal love I'd once had. My heart registered it immediately. My first wife welcomed her. I felt things I hadn't felt in years. Helpless, for one. I berated myself for foolishness but it did no good. Does it ever? Caroline's boyfriend was with her, a biker, a big guy who seemed to think he was in charge. When she took off her sunglasses I saw the smudges of bruises near her eyes. I'll confess to being unimpressed by the boyfriend and saying so. The short version is we took it outside and I gave him a terrible whipping. Caroline called two days later with a story to tell. We made a date for the telling. Among others things it involved mental and physical cruelty, and pronounced recreational drug abuse." Archie drank and looked at his son. "But she was something, Patrick. Sobered up, she had the looks and brains and appetites I'd intuited. Her heart was good and hungry. What a match for mine. And she was about to have something I had resigned myself to not having. She delivered him into the world approximately seven months later."

"Ted."

"None other."

"I suspected."

"As did many others. We were married before she showed. We delighted in our wicked little mystery. No confessions but nothing hidden, either. No explanations, nothing revealed, then the arrival of our little Ted. I pledged to save him from his own . . . unfortunate nativity. Ted's father was a charming, brutal pig. Like Caroline's father, he humiliated and hurt her. Her father was from money and of money. Layers of privilege and recklessness. Staggering unaccountability. The biker was intended as an antidote. Imagine. But you can't satisfy swine of either type because they only want more. It takes a lot to fill a tiny heart. So she broke, Pat – right here in the house, right in front of my eyes. She broke, utterly and completely. And then she started over. Began to make herself again. To make herself *herself* for the first time. The baby was my project, my contribution to turning Caroline's life around. It was my job to make that baby right. She chose me to accompany her on that journey. I have been honored. She's become the strongest person I've ever known. She still frightens me in every good way and I would still lay down my life for hers in an instant."

Patrick felt history falling into place behind him, followed by a strange liberating pleasure, like looking down from a cliff but feeling fully capable of flight. "Not sure what to say, Dad."

"The upshot is I couldn't do anything for Ted. His seizures or fevers, or his feet or his odd inabilities. And over the years I went from hope to forbearance to disappointment to annoyance to resentment to hostility. The headshrinkers assigned him different mental maladies, some of which seemed accurate. Others not. No consensus. Your mother has always worried that he'd do something bad to himself or someone else. There's an anger in him he rarely lets show. I don't think he's a bad person. I don't think he's severely retarded. I did love him and I will learn to love him again. And I've punished him enough for disappointing me. I know that, and I intend to stop."

Patrick let all this rattle around his brain. He took another slug of the bourbon and felt the good warm passage of it. "You've never told Ted?"

"He asked me when he was eleven years old, if I was his father. Once. I lied once and that was that."

"You should tell him the truth. And forgive him for disappointing you."

"I will. I hope he can forgive me for being such a pure and unalloyed sonofabitch for so many years."

Patrick nodded and Archie poured more bourbon into their glasses and they touched them. "He's got a good heart," said Patrick.

Archie nodded and stared out past the things around him. He knew what his father was going to say before Archie said it – like he'd seen what would happen to Sheffield and Lavinder. "I hope I don't have to sell all this," said Archie. "Your mother and I would walk away with almost nothing. Nothing for us and nothing for our sons. Sixty years of Norris blood, sweat and tears come to *nada*."

"We're doing what we can. It's up to the rain and the trees now."

"Farm credit bank in El Centro turned me down today. We've got enough money in savings to pay the bills for four months. That'll take us through February. No more. If we get a good survival rate, the earliest we could start selling would be two whole years from then, but we would be able to borrow against the surviving trees. Even the Farm Credit banks can't say no to living avocados. We'll see signs of life by February, on any trees with life left in them, and we'll know where we stand in the eyes of God. If His curse continues and all the trees are dead, your mother and I will sell off our modest investments with Anders Wealth to buy replacement trees. That would make real a forty-percent loss in the current market. Or, of course, we just sell the whole damned place and walk away."

"I didn't know it was this bad."

Archie sipped. "Time is running out. This makes me

154

fearful and angry. So I take it out on the people I love. I've never felt this way before, Pat. Never this low for this long. I never thought that I would prove to be a miserable failure, and turn into a furious little man. I detest my reflection in the mirror. I despise my God. I often have dreams now where Caroline has simply vanished."

"What's it take to stay afloat for a month, Dad?"

"Six grand or so for the basics."

Patrick looked at his skiff and saw almost two months of living expenses for his family. He figured his pickup truck was worth maybe seven, given the low mileage. Another month plus change. So he could contribute three months. And what, ride his bike to Domino's and deliver pizzas on it? Although, he thought, there was the old red Honda 90 over in the corner, a beloved Norris family relic. Not much more than a scooter, but it was street legal and he could rebuild the engine in a few hours, rig some sort of pizza rack to the back. He wondered how Iris would like being a passenger on it. "I'll sell the boat and kick in eleven grand. That would give you two more months."

"I note you don't say, give *us* two more months."

"I don't want to farm, Dad. I never did and never will."

The silence was abrupt and dense. "No. Then don't sell your dream to float the dreams of your mother and father. That would be ass-backwards."

"I'll do it if it makes a difference."

"I pray every night it won't be necessary. To a god that I . . ." Archie refilled Patrick's glass then carried his own and the bottle to the big open door of the barn. "I see light in the bunkhouse. Maybe I'll have my talk with Ted. I'm on a roll tonight, aren't I?"

"We're fishing Glorietta Bay tomorrow. You'll have to do without us for a day."

"That's a good thing."

Patrick fished out the carburetor parts and let them dry on the bench. He poured the solvent into a bucket so labeled, snapped the lid and set it back with those for motor oil, two-stroke oil, gasoline and diesel. He hoisted himself up on the bench and sat for a while, drinking the liquor and pondering things. He wondered how Myers, following so meticulously in his own footprints that night on patrol, May 23, 2200 hours, had tripped the IED but he, Patrick, did not? Then again the flash and for the thousandth time Patrick saw Myers come apart in all directions and Zane flayed in the light. He hoisted the memories into the hatch in his brain and tried again to close the lid forever.

After getting the carburetor back in place and their fishing gear together, Patrick stood at the workbench with a pencil in hand and his new pad of graph paper. His Business Plan, lacking college finesse, was a series of short sentences pertaining to how he'd like his guiding career to evolve. He read through some of them: *By age thirty you will have three boats, and by forty, four, and by fifty, five boats and that will be enough ... remember as a guide you must be optimistic but predatory and never lose track of your purpose, which is to make sure your clients have a good time on the water ... be generous with casting tips and instruction but don't micro-manage ... remember that the fishing can be good even when the catching is bad ... invest 30% of your profit to build your business, and save 30% for when you can't work ...*

This all seemed well and good but Patrick was too tired to add anything now, so he took two blankets from one of the rough-hewn storage cabinets built fifty years ago by his grandfather, folded one lengthwise twice and laid it on the deck of the skiff. He turned off most of the barn lights but left the door open, then set a wide sheet of plywood from the low point of the boat to the floor. He climbed in and laid down and covered himself with the second blanket. The dogs came up the ramp and curled up beside him for short while, then clambered back down the plywood and trotted off. He thought of Zane and how he had loved him purely, how the war had demanded that pure love, then refused to let him take that love home. Another good reason to hate the war. And he thought again of Myers and Pendejo and Sheffield and the others, how his heart was heavier for Zane than for any of them. This was one of his several shames, and one for which he judged himself harshly. He heard the coo of a pigeon high in the beams, a flutter of wings then nothing.

18

At sunrise Glorietta Bay was a silver mirror and *Fatta the Lan'* glided confidently upon it. Patrick swung into the bay and looked out to the Coronado Bridge arching from mainland to peninsula, the night lights still on, traffic steady. The eastern sky was indigo over orange. He gunned the Mercury, felt the propeller bite and the bow lift.

Ted stood on the fore deck, legs braced on the railings, a six-weight fly rod at the ready. "This thing rides sweet!" he called back to his brother.

"We'll see how it does offshore!"

"Are we going outside the harbor?"

"After we fish the bay. You're good with that?"

Ted turned his big body and looked back at Patrick. "Guess I better get my sea feet."

"We'll take it easy."

Frowning, Ted turned and squared himself against the railing. Patrick brought the boat west and anchored almost under the bridge. He logged his coordinates on the GPU then into a small notebook he planned to keep in a plastic bag near the radio. It felt good to be inventing a future. Cars thrummed high overhead.

Ted cast out a perch fly and Patrick watched the sinking line slide deeper and deeper out of sight near one of the bridge caissons. Sea bass were ambushers and tended to cruise structure so the caissons were a good bet. There were halibut, perch, corvina, mackerel, barracuda, occasional bonefish and sharks, and the lesser skates, rays, dog fish, lizard fish. The bigger game fish were mostly offshore and not commercially accessible in Patrick's 17-foot skiff. His business plan called for a new boat, double the size and range of this one, by his twenty-seventh birthday, five years from now. He planned to keep the Mako so that a partner, or even an employee of his, could continue with the bay clientele. The offshore sharks, dorado and tuna promised tougher fishing and bigger money, but the client base was smaller. The bay was where he'd find clients, run up some numbers, build a base and a reputation.

"I just got bumped," said Ted.

"Bring him back."

Ted stripped in his fly, paused, then stripped in again and the line tightened straight. *Oh yeah … come to Theodore!*

Ted set the hook then let the fish take line. Down in the blue Patrick watched the animal flash and be gone. *"Trophy, Pat?"*

"Monstrous. A website fish!"

"Yeah, BABY!" Ted looked over at Patrick, his face merry. The tip of his uplifted rod dipped with the strength of the little fish. He was up on the balls of his substandard feet, back straight, his left arm tucked formally behind him, his right arm raised like a conductor. Patrick smiled at the simple pleasure a fish can bring. Gift from a hidden world, he thought. A fish on the line keeps the demons gone, and that's what he would offer his clients. It was a mystery to him why all people did not fish.

Ted let the bass take the line for a sound, then brought him up in long firm strips. Patrick looked down at the animal still trying to break free, gills pumping, its freedom cut down to inches. Ted lifted the fish out and swung it into him, gently catching its lower jaw between his big forefinger and thumb.

159

He set his rod against the railing and held the fish up to the new sunlight and removed the perch fly with a pair of hemostats. He turned to Patrick with a conspiratorial wink then lifted the fish to his lips and kissed it. He kneeled and set it back into the water. Patrick watched it hover for a second, there then not.

"Tastes kind of fishy, Pat."

"What if we catch fifty?"

"Remember that lizardfish that got me?"

"I thought you'd learn after that."

"You going to fish or what?"

"Immediately and right now."

"Pat, when I'm out here with you I'm as good as I get. Maybe that sounds dumb."

"Good is good, brother."

"Out here nothing gets into me but the good stuff."

"Don't start all that."

"Out here the bad things never even start, is what I'm saying."

Ted turned and leaned into the rail and Patrick took his five-weight from the rod holder. He pried off his sneakers and stepped aft, flicked out his fly and patiently stripped line onto the deck while he watched Ted cast. For all of his big brother's bulk and general gracelessness he had a nice delivery, side-armed and languorous, with hard stops on both the back cast and the fore. Patrick thought of last night's revelations from Archie, and of Ted's biker father, and as Patrick watched, the damaged beginnings of his brother made Patrick love him in a new and different way.

As the sun rose they caught and released bass near the bridge, and later perch near Marina Park and bonito off Shelter Island. Patrick used the electric trolling motor for stealth. He caught a legal halibut and let it go with a glancing thought about tonight's dinner. Ted tied on a steel leader and landed a nice barracuda, cavalierly kissing its dangerous snout while Patrick watched, vowing to disallow such foolishness on his guided trips. That shouldn't be hard.

Ted carefully unhooked the fish and dropped it back into the bay. "I've kissed women more dangerous than that!"

Patrick wondered. Not far from the Nimitz Marine Facility they each caught bonefish that sizzled off like rockets and made long runs. Bones were picky eaters, but fast, durable and experts at throwing a hook. They were shaped like projectiles and had goofy faces and were probably the most coveted game fish in the bay. Patrick knew a good percentage of his clients would want to target them, though their numbers were small. He felt the strength and wild purpose of the fish as his line hissed through the flat water, opening a wake and throwing a plume of mist into the air. Pound and a quarter, he guessed: a nice one. He stood rocking gently with *Fatta the Lan'* and felt the joy of fishing, which for him had always been the bringing in of a wondrous thing from an alien place. He'd been trying to explain his love for fishing in more detail for most of his life but had failed, even to himself. As he knelt and set the bonefish free Patrick heard the sea lions croaking in their pens over at the training center where the Navy taught marine mammals to detect mines and enemy swimmers. He wondered if the mammals were drafted or if they volunteered. The ghosts inside him stirred and he pushed them back into their places. Be gone, not now. Ted seemed to sense a struggle going. He turned around and looked at Patrick with concern, then grinned and shrugged, as if asking Patrick to throw off his problems and get with the day. Patrick saw something in him that Archie had probably never owned and that Caroline had long ago imprisoned. Crazy joy? Abandon?

Outside the harbor the Pacific was gray and heavy with chop. The wind came from the west, cool and weighty. *Fatta the*

161

Lan' hit the open water and recoiled like a puppy sensing danger. The swells moved her easily, her weight vanished and at speed she was skittish. Ted sat on the bench facing aft, hunkered in his windbreaker as the boat dipped and rose and the cold spray lashed his back. "I hate it out here in little boats like this," he said.

Patrick cut their speed which did little to improve things. It was a long charge north along Fort Rosecrans and Patrick knew the Navy could run him out at will but they usually didn't. He steered toward the rocky cliffs of Fort Rosecrans National Cemetery and by the time he dropped anchor fifty yards offshore Ted was up with his rod, bracing himself on the railing as best he could while *Fatta the Lan'* climbed and fell in the swell. Ted swayed, dropped to one knee to hold the rail, then heaved himself up again and turned to Patrick. "If I fall over and drown, tell Mom I loved her and tell Dad I'm sorry. I'm not sure what for but I sure am sorry! Naw, second thought, tell him life is hard so tough shit, old man."

"If you fall over, just swim! Shore's a hundred and fifty feet that-a-way."

"Anything can happen at sea."

"If you're dead set on drowning then, do I get all your critters and the computer?"

"Yeah! And tell Dora at the stables I didn't mean to scare her. And tell mayor Anders I hope she loses the election and never builds those lighted crosswalks we don't need!"

"Catch a damned fish, Ted."

Ted turned and raised his rod and false cast to build line-speed in the wind. He was rocking mightily but still managed to keep plenty of line in the air. Patrick heard him bellowing: "Fish can tell when you don't have the mojo, Pat! Even from a hundred feet away. It's something to do with the way your personal vibrations travel down the line and affect the fly. Which is directly related to the way ideas get into my

162

brain. But I'm not sure how they're related. Geronimo!" Ted double-hauled briskly and let the line go and Patrick watched the loop unfurl and eighty feet of line and leader turn over to place the fly above the rocks.

Patrick cast too, the wind carrying his fly toward shore. He let the weighted fly and fly-line sink as he rocked with the boat. Ted had a harder time balancing in the slightly raised bow. He took a knee to ride out a strong swell. Patrick felt the hump of water moving under him, and he saw it lift the bow as it rolled toward shore, where a long moment later it surged onto the rocks and exploded.

When the boat had settled enough, Ted stood up and leaned into the railing, slipped, and fell overboard. Patrick heard his quick yelp and the snap of his rod against the boat and the splash of him hitting the ocean. Ted reached his free hand over the gunwale but the next swell pried him loose and carried him toward the rocks. Patrick pushed his rod into the holder and got the gaff and scrambled fore. Ted was side-stroking toward *Fatta the Lan'* with the broken rod and reel still in one hand but the swells pushed against him. He was already half sunk in his heavy clothes and coat. Patrick leaned far out with the handle-end but Ted was out of reach. *"It's cold in here, Pat!"* Patrick stashed the gaff and got the rope from the bow compartment and hurled it to his brother. It slapped over him and the next swell lifted, then dropped the boat into a watery bowl. The same swell lifted Ted and carried him fast toward the rocks. He was riding lower in the water now and breathing fast. He found the rope with his free hand and tried to haul himself forward but the rope was long. *"Drop the rod, Ted! Drop it and use both hands!"*

But Ted held fast to the rod, grabbing short lengths of rope with his left hand while the surge moved him faster out. Patrick swayed greatly on the casting deck, stripping rope with both hands. A swell dropped him so steeply that his feet left the deck and for a moment he was mid-air, then the deck jumped up under him and he crashed to his knees, jaws crunching, but still hauling. When the rope was tight he stood again and put his back into the tug of war. The swells pushed Ted toward the rocks, then Patrick pulled him closer. Ted still held the rod butt and reel. After a long minute Patrick had him halfway back. Then the fly-line flew off the stump of the broken rod, and the reel screamed. *"I'm hooked up, Pat! I'm hooked up!"*

"Hang on! I've got you! I've got you!"

Patrick felt the swells lose some of their power as he pulled Ted into deeper water. Then Ted dropped the rope and tightened up the drag on the reel to better fight the fish. Patrick yelled to pick up the damn rope. Ted began to sink and a strong swell dragged him back toward the rocks until he took up the rope again. He was gasping deep and fast while Patrick pulled mightily, sweat pouring off his nose. A long minute later Ted was close to *Fatta the Lan'*, holding out the rod to his brother. Patrick took it and felt the heavy pull of the faraway fish. "Jeez, Ted, nice fish."

"I told you. I'm thinking snapper. Rocks. Deep."

"Me, too. Can you hold on? I'm going to back us out of here so we can get you aboard without the surge."

"Amen, Pat!"

"Feels like ten pounds of fish down there."

"Oh, at least."

"Hang on, I'm going to weigh anchor and get us out of here."

"I hope it's a snapper! Mom's favorite."

"Just hold on, Ted."

"Dad shouldn't of yelled at me for taking the bark off the trees. That was a mistake anybody could make."

"It's over."

"It's never over! I scared a woman out by the stables a

164

couple a nights ago. Dora. I like her a lot. I feel everything she feels, like a connection. I didn't mean to scare her."

"Pay attention, Ted. Don't lose the fish!"

Patrick reversed them further offshore, steering with his hips, one hand on the rope and the other on the rod. The fish had taken half of the backing but it was losing strength. When he felt less turbulence he raised one foot and put the motor in neutral. He drew Ted close and cut the engine and pulled his brother around to the stern where the gunwales were lowest. Ted was able to get both hands up onto the boat railings but he was too tired and too heavy to hoist himself up and over.

Patrick let go the rope and pulled on Ted's jacket and felt his brother's legs pumping and his feet flailing against the hull. Ted panted with this exertion and Patrick put his shoulder down and latched his free arm around Ted's big neck and pulled. He felt Ted's heavy exhales on his skin and he crouched for lifting power. There was a moment he thought he might go over, rather than Ted come in, but then Patrick felt his brother's legs stop moving and a sudden lightness to him. Patrick pulled with all his strength and Ted came up. Patrick slipped and hit his butt hard as Ted surged in and flattened him. They screamed and fought for breath and laughed, Patrick with the broken butt of the rod still up and the line tight to the fish, Ted crushing the breath out of him. Patrick was weak with suffocation and laughter by the time they got unraveled.

It took Ted another twenty minutes to get the fish in, a bruising red snapper from the rocky depths, twelve and a half pounds according to the Boga grip that Patrick deployed from his tackle box. Patrick took a dozen pictures of Ted and the fish. Both men were still breathing hard when Patrick pushed the camera back into his shirt pocket and buttoned it.

"We gotta take this home for dinner," said Ted.

"I'd say so."

"You'll make a good guide, Pat. Maybe I could be your first mate."

Patrick muscled the spent fish into the cooler in the hold and closed the lid. He had put in a block of ice just in case. Patrick loved being prepared for things, as he was in Sangin, twenty-four hours a day, even on the burn-shitter, even in his sleep. "I'd like that."

"You don't need a mate on this little boat, though."

"I'll have bigger ones someday."

"I'd probably screw up."

"No, you wouldn't, brother. Look at that fish."

"Okay, Pat – you and me on a boat, fishing and making money and having fun. Now I got something to look forward to. I'm cold."

"Get that jacket and shirt off."

Patrick worked off his jacket and handed it to Ted then started up the Mercury. "Hold on, big brother."

The sun hung orange in the west as they rode back to the ramp. Ted sat on the aft bench and every time Patrick looked back he was shivering in the too small jacket but still chattering away. Patrick was used to him not speaking for days or weeks, then unleashing a river of words and now the river came.

"But you know, Pat, there's this other woman who's a mystery and I really like her, too. Lucinda. She called Friendly Village Taxi like over two weeks ago and I got her. And she's called other times – either Tuesdays and Thursdays. We've gone to the market, the pharmacy, the dry cleaner, Joe's Hardware and either Las Brisas or Rosa's for take-out. She doesn't hardly talk. Doesn't take her sunglasses off, so maybe she's hiding something. I think she's troubled. I can almost feel it but I'm not sure what it is. She lives in a condo and with flowers on the balcony. She's very pretty and healthy

166

looking but really unhappy. She has great sadness. I can feel it, but it's more than that. I'm driving tomorrow just in case she calls. I can't take much more of Dad. And I know he can't take much more of me. I wonder if Mom will do that snapper Veracruzano style."

19

Under a gray-bellied sky Evelyn Anders began her walk from the Post Office on Mission Road toward the largest shopping center in Fallbrook. She took long strides and counted each one. It was six on a Tuesday evening and the traffic was steady and swift. She paused to look at the burn marks left by the flares that had marked the place where George Herrera was killed three weeks ago now – right there in the first southbound lane – carbon-gray flowers scorched into the asphalt. She thought she saw a bloodstain, too. Was that even possible? Oil, she thought, surely. Or transmission fluid.

It was downhill in this direction and ahead she saw the proud retailers of the republic: the KFC bucket in the sky, Albertson's and Blockbuster and Baskin-Robbins, Verizon and AT&T, Taco Bell and Carl's Jr. and Payless shoes. And so on. She was long resigned to franchise America here in Fallbrook, and often patronized some of these places just like everyone else. But her heart stayed in the older part of town, back on Main with history and art galleries and public sculpture and most things mom and pop, such as Anders Wealth Management. And I'm the mom, she thought: class of '85 to Mom in the blink of an eye.

After step one-hundred fifty five she stopped and looked back. She was about halfway to the shopping center, and sure enough, not twenty feet from where George had been killed, waited a young woman with a stroller and two very young children, ready to cross. Another mom, thought Evelyn. The woman was already off the curb and onto the asphalt of Mission Road, waiting to run for the relative safety of the median strip. Her hair lifted each time a car sped by.

Evelyn watched her take two little hands in one of her own, grab the stroller handle mid-way and push off. The hole in the northbound traffic looked good. The woman locked her stroller arm and bent her back and dug in with her legs. The children hustled along tethered and unafraid. The woman's face was steadfast at the approaching cars and her hair stood out behind her. The stroller bounced along and Evelyn pictured a tire coming off but before it could happen the woman was standing in the safe zone, cars roaring by on either side. The problem with this median Evelyn knew, was that it was also a turn lane, so you never knew when a harried driver might swing in. Harried drivers were looking for cars in front of them, not people. Evelyn saw that a lighted cross-walk right *there*, activated only when someone needed to use it, could save a life.

She continued downhill to the next safe place to cross, which was the traffic signal way down at Ammunition. She had no idea how far it was between crosswalks until walking the distance herself. Looking back toward the Post Office where she'd started – what? – a half a mile?

She waited out the light then crossed. She dashed across the wide entrance/exit of the Happy Jug Liquor Store – WE SELL LIVE BAIT! – then started up the sidewalk for the climb back up Mission. All of this to get to the trailer park where George had lived, and to where he was returning, in the dark, on the night he died.

Evelyn waved to Iris Cash, waiting at the entrance to the Meadowlark trailer park as planned. With her were George Herrera's two young friends, McKenzie and Dulce, who had contacted Cruzela Storm about a show to benefit

169

the crosswalks. Evelyn shook their small hands, then Iris introduced her to photographer Natalie Llanes, who had a nice Canon DSLR slung around her neck. Iris and Natalie positioned the girls for a photograph with the battered Meadowlark sign in the background. Evelyn stood back and watched the two girls smile momentarily, then catch themselves.

Looking past them Evelyn realized she'd never set foot in Meadowlark, though she'd driven by it thousands of times, as had anybody who lived in Fallbrook for long. It was right in the center of town but because it sat in the low creek bed, Meadowlark was easy to miss if you were in a car. She looked at the closely spaced trailers, many colorfully painted, some stout and some slouching. Eucalyptus and palms grew high amid them, and the trailer awnings hung heavy with mandevilla and nightshade and jasmine. Satellite dishes stood on nearly every roof, sometimes two or three of them, old models big as flying saucers and newer ones small and sleek.

Iris waved Evelyn over to pose with McKenzie and Dulce under the Meadowlark sign. Natalie wanted the pretty evening sky as a backdrop. The girls had obviously dressed for this and Evelyn sensed their nervousness. McKenzie wore a dress and Dulce a hint of rouge. Their black hair shone even on the gray day. They were twelve. Natalie the photographer chattered away with them in Spanish.

Evelyn brushed a fallen flower petal from the hair on McKenzie's shoulder. "I spent some extra time on myself too, girls. A good Village View photo one week from the election can't hurt."

"You'll win," said McKenzie.

"Absolutely," said Dulce.

Evelyn wondered about that, given the wildfire that had occurred on her watch, the arsonist lurking unchecked, her defeat on the crosswalk issue, and the rife public anger at government incumbents in general. Next week's Cruzela Storm fundraiser could be a factor with the undecided. She wondered if she needed to nail up another fifty "This Town Is Your Town – Re-elect Evelyn Anders For Mayor" signs before election day. Her opponent, Walt Rood, with his pleasant face and "Small Government That Works" posters, seemed to be watching her from everywhere she looked. Natalie fired away.

"Can we shoot a few in front of one of your houses?" asked Iris.

Evelyn saw the girls glance at each other but neither spoke for a moment. Dulce looked down at the patch of brown grass under the Meadowlark sign and McKenzie looked back at the trailers as if she'd heard someone call to her. "They're trailers," she said.

"Trailers are homes, too," said Iris.

The girls looked at each other again and Dulce shrugged. "Okay."

Evelyn followed them in. The road had been paved years back but had crumbled away to half-paved. She wondered why the city hadn't maintained it – privately owned, probably. The creek ran through in a trough of cattails and she could smell the dank wet smell of it. She heard Mexican music and television voices and smelled food cooking. A boy sped by on a bike and rattled off something in Spanish to the girls. Evelyn was surprised how subterranean and out-of-sight she felt down here. Just a few yards away, but high above, SUVs and luxury sedans and snappy hybrids sped up and down Mission, the drivers – if they were anything like her – largely unaware of the hidden world below.

"It's called the cans," said McKenzie. "Because of all the metal and aluminum. *Las latas*. As in, *vivo en las latas* – I live in the cans."

171

"That's funny but not funny," said Evelyn.

The girls self-consciously glanced at each other again then continued walking past trailers of many colors – lime green, tangerine, yellow and pink. They were crowded tight but most had tiny gardens out front or decks. Many of the decks had sides and roofs made of trellis, shot through with vines. Evelyn could smell the blossoms, faintly, mixed in with the aroma of the fast food places above them on Mission. Most of the decks had patio chairs or old couches and lavish potted plants and flowers. McKenzie stopped in front of a slouching sky-blue coach with a rainbow and puffy white clouds painted on it. "George's house."

Evelyn heard thumping sounds inside and a moment later three children spilled from the blue trailer to the deck. She guessed the oldest, a boy, at about McKenzie's and Dulce's age, and the two girls were younger than George had been. They smiled when they saw Iris, who climbed the wooden stairs yapping and herding them into place, then stepped back out of range. Natalie aimed her camera up at them. The boy stood straight, chest out and chin up, giving McKenzie then Dulce his hard look.

"Felix is the boss until his parents get home from work," said McKenzie. "He makes his sisters do their homework and keeps them from fighting over the TV."

Iris turned. "Come on up here, Evelyn. We need all of the crosswalk crew."

After the photo shoot Evelyn said goodbye to the girls and declined a ride to her car from Iris and Natalie. Instead she walked alone through *Las Latas*, filling her eyes with this secret barrio she'd hardly even noticed before today. A gaggle of children ran among the trailers, yelling and laughing while grown-up voices chased through the windows after them. She heard a TV in English and another in Spanish. She followed the road around to where the creek widened into a pool under a bridge, the water shiny and smooth. There was a rough-hewn bench and table on the bank, wrappers and cans and plastic bottles collecting at the downstream outlet. The couple sitting close on the bench looked back at her, the boy large with pomaded hair and the pretty girl wearing a hot little outfit. They had take-out bags and looked happy. She gave a sorry-to-bother-you wave and they turned back to the water. Around the next bend in the threadbare road she saw a woman standing on her front patio between two large picnic tables stacked with laundry, folded and labeled and ready for pick-up. A washer and a dryer labored outside the trailer. Evelyn smelled the laundry breath of the dryer and the scent of KFC wafting in from above, where the power lines sagged heavily and the violet bracts of a bougainvillea overgrowing an old satellite dish reached skyward, vibrant with color, hungry for the fading sunlight.

She walked back up Mission toward her car. The climb was steep, even in mild weather and casual shoes. She stopped across from where George had been hit near the post office, which is where she'd parked her car. Then Evelyn got a sudden idea, and stepped off the curb.

It was nearly seven and almost dark now and to her left headlights charged uphill toward her while on her right brake lights snaked downhill in the far lanes. The median lay between. Waiting for an opening, she glanced down at the trees and rooftops of *Las Latas*. At forty-six, Evelyn was near-sighted but hadn't seen a doctor because most of her work was up close, and because she could practically drive the streets of Fallbrook in her sleep. When they left town at night, Brian did the driving. So as she looked into the oncoming traffic she saw headlights and cars and the spaces between them, but to judge their speed and threat level was difficult. Cars were just way faster when you weren't in one.

She thought of her old tennis injury, the torn ACL in her knee, and how an ill-timed twist could put her on the ground with a bullet of pain.

She chose her moment and took her first step. She planned to take the near lane when the last car in a knot of five or six was safely past. When it whizzed by she accelerated into the lane, accelerated *somewhat,* she found, suddenly worried about her knee. She was almost to the next lane when a pickup truck burned rubber from one of the many driveways that lined the other side of Mission, turning left against the traffic. The truck jumped and the tires screamed as it peeled across lanes for the median to which Evelyn had committed herself. The speed of the truck seemed to nullify her own; she was in less than slow-motion now, even though she had run cross-country at Fallbrook High School just a few short years ago. No, she realized, a few long years ago – long, *long, LONG years ago!* She calculated that the truck would kill her in the median in mere seconds unless she stopped right here and let it go by first, which would also mean certain death by another vehicle. She saw the onrushing constellation of headlights coming up Mission toward her and she knew those drivers were looking into headlights coming at *them,* and a pedestrian was practically invisible until too late. She lifted her knees and lengthened her stride, cutting across lane two at a perilous angle, trying to cut behind the truck.

Suddenly the world synchronized: the pickup truck blew into the median right front of her, the driver's eyes wide with surprise; the closest of the uphill cars swerved into the next lane to miss her; tires squealed and horns blasted and somehow that car skidded, screeching sideways across the far lane and the narrow shoulder, jumped the curb and come to a stop blocking the sidewalk.

Evelyn, aware of all this and of nothing else, stood panting in the median. The pickup truck stopped not twenty feet

174

from her and the emergency flashers went on and the door flew open. Down from the cab came a stocky blond woman in jeans and a plaid flannel shirt. She crunched across the median dirt and gravel and took Evelyn by the arm. "Are you okay?"

"Half-way there!" She sounded daft even to herself.

"I couldn't see you. I'm so sorry. Let's get you outta here."

"Ready when you are." Evelyn watched the downhill cars slow for the flashing truck lights. Two of the drivers stopped and Evelyn, released by the woman, crossed the lanes and stepped onto the sidewalk. She turned to see the southbound drivers allow the woman in the pickup truck back into lanes, and the flashers go off and the truck pull away.

Still trembling she called Brian from her car in the Post Office parking lot. He heard her fear immediately. She explained what happened in a detached voice, her adrenalin-moderated panic only now free to bust loose. Brian was the calmest and most capable man she knew, her rock and anchor. Evelyn felt as if she hadn't seen him in weeks, maybe years. Had she? Really *seen*? He said he would be there in two minutes to bring her home.

"No," she said. "The Econo."

"The Econo?"

"Please."

"The kids are done eating and homework is light. Give me ten."

"I'll get number twelve."

She was waiting for him at the door of room twelve of the Fallbrook Econo-Suites when Brian knocked. Her heart thumped crazily and her nerves buzzed. He came in, set a bottle of wine on the table and Evelyn attacked.

20

Iris Cash lived in a freshly painted green bungalow with white columns, a spacious front porch and late-season flowers still nodding in the planters. A pumpkin carved with a toothy grimace stood on the railing, candlelight steady within. Patrick parked in the steep short driveway and set the brake and looked at the house. It was up on Skyline in an older part of Fallbrook and when Patrick got out of his truck he could see the rooftops of downtown and the cars on Main, headlights on in the near darkness. He went around and got the bouquet off the passenger seat.

She met him at the door wearing a forthright smile and a snug yellow dress. Her hair was up. She made a fuss over the flowers, which were sunflowers, protea and purple stattice. Once inside Patrick liked the burnished walnut floor, the stout beams and wrought iron brackets above, the framed paintings and photographs, the built-in bookcase.

"Mom said I'm supposed to put those in a vase for you," he said.

"Right this way."

"Great house."

"I grew up on a farm so I like the old things."

"You're the farmer's daughter."

"Except I don't like farming and don't want any part of that life."

"I feel the same way, except I do have a part of it."

176

"You have a disaster to deal with. That's a little different."

In the kitchen she handed him a heavy cut-glass vase and Patrick filled it half with water. She handed him a pair of curve-bladed pruners and Patrick looked at them and figured he was supposed to trim the flower stalks. Advanced manners were something he hadn't learned, having gone from high school straight into the Marines then to Afghanistan. He'd graduated from a laptop to a machine gun in a matter of months. So he'd also missed a lot of everyday things, like how to balance a checkbook or make something to eat other than a sandwich. Or how to pick out cool clothes or order a decent haircut. Or how to talk to a pretty woman without your blood pressure spiking. "Maybe just like an inch or so?"

"Perfect. I see you got your head fixed. The stitches, I mean."

"Good as new, Iris."

She showed him the house, though he got just a peek of her bedroom. The house reminded him of an old TV show or maybe a magazine feature on the homes of yesterday. There was no stainless steel and few hard edges. Lots of fabric and curves. He liked the aerial photograph of the Cash family farm that hung in the dining room. Also in the dining room stood a majestic china cabinet, lit from within. Through the windows Patrick saw plates and bowls of all sizes, flower vases, platters and mugs. "Great-grandma's," said Iris. "Hand-made. Mom let me have it early." Iris's place reminded him of the Norris home, although some of Iris's artwork was modern and baffling. He wondered what Iris would make of the big portrait of his grandfather and great uncle glaring down from above the mantle. He pictured her standing in that room in the yellow dress she now wore, and in his imagination she drew the light from the windows and the room was dim – she alone was specific and clear.

They walked into the backyard. Small copper lamps threw

light in neat low circles. Patrick saw a brick patio with a picnic table and benches beneath an arbor that was owned by a fat grape vine twinkling with lights. Downhill was a small lawn with a good-sized magnolia tree in the middle and more lights dangling in the low branches. The fence was overgrown with bougainvillea. Patrick looked at all this, surprised to be interested in it. The ordinary really could be awesome. The picnic table was set with a fancy cloth, utensils, two bottles of wine and four glasses. "Do you like red wine or white, Pat?"

"Yes, I do."

"But which more?"

"Oh, both about the same."

She smiled and handed him a corkscrew. "Then maybe you could open that white and we'll have a glass before dinner."

"No screw top? Just kidding." Although he wasn't. Opening wine bottles was another skill that, as an eighteen-year old on his way to becoming a platoon machine-gunner, Patrick had not learned. He found the foil cutter and folded it out and got the heavy metal wrapper off. The opener was pretty much self-evident. The pop of the cork surprised him and he felt a quick bolt of adrenalin shoot through him. "Look, I didn't dive for cover!"

She looked at him uncertainly.

"Just kidding," he said. "Again."

He poured two glasses, slopping some on the nice table-cloth and trying to mop it with his finger. Iris lit candles and turned on music that played through a pair of tiny speakers. They sat side-by-side at the picnic table, looking out over the rolling hills of Camp Pendleton. It stretched all the way to the beach, which he pictured, wincing as he remembered the brawl with the MPs. He could feel the now smaller bandage up there, obnoxious on his skin. He banished the incident from his mind and concentrated on what was before him: the U.S. Naval Weapons Station, the railroad tracks stitching to the coast, the broad black sky above. He could feel Sangin reaching back for him through Pendleton, where it had all started – enlistment, training, deployment. From here Pendleton looked peaceful and sparse, a face put on for civilians, not at all like the war machine it was.

"We're not in Kenton, Ohio, anymore," said Iris. She told him a few things about her childhood and she used good words, which made it easy for Patrick to see: the endless corn fields with the farmhouses built up close to the straight flat roads; the barns and outbuildings further back; the streams wandering by, sheltered by green thickets of poison ivy and sumac, copperheads, water snakes and turtles. She told him that summers got so hot the asphalt edges of the roads would bubble and melt and stick to your shoes. She had a big black horse named Elmer and he was gentle as could be. And after he died she got a yellow mare named Calliope. There in Ohio, said Iris, it was all about the Browns, the Reds and the Indians, and of course the Buckeyes. If she never saw Kenton again it would be too soon.

"Except to see family," she said. "It's funny, though – I have good memories of a place I never want to go back to. Mom and Dad, they were married to the corn crop, but they sure got us kids around after harvest. We went to D.C, and New York, Boston, Chicago, all through the south, to St. Louis and Denver. Then later to L.A. and San Diego. Patrick, I took one look down at San Diego when our plane was landing and I knew I was going to move close to there. I was twelve. Here's another funny thing. Years later, when I came out here just after college, I drove around the whole county for two weeks, looking for just the right place to find a rental and a job. And of all the extra cool places in San Diego County, I picked Fallbrook, which is the most like Kenton. Oh yeah, I'm a brave one. Not exactly Magellan!"

"It all comes down to what home means," said Patrick,

startled by his lameness. He now felt required to say half-way intelligent things. "I mean, you know it when you see it, like you did. But I never had that. I never went to a place and knew it had to be mine. I got to see places too – mostly in the west. I liked it all. My favorite city was Missoula, no ocean but tons of rivers. My main thing was the fish. Besides the Pacific and any river that has fish in it, my favorite place was the Grand Canyon. And my favorite place in the Grand Canyon was halfway down it, where I could see up to the top and down to the bottom in one look. But I never thought of moving there."

"They say it's harder to stay than to go. I'm glad you stayed. I'm staying too. I've got a trip to Kenton planned soon, and I *already* can't wait to get back."

She took his hand and Patrick felt an strange rush go through him. Not the terrible bone-freezing excitement of combat, but something warm and unrelated to self-preservation or death. It made him uneasy. He fished his phone from his pocket and showed her the pictures of the carburetor from *Fatta the Lan'*, before he'd refurbished it, broken it down in the bucket of solvent, then reassembled and put it back in place in the Mercury.

"Nice," she said.

"And check these." Next he showed her the fishing pictures of Ted and Glorietta Bay and the swells and the big snapper that had just about done them in. He wasn't surprised how many fish pictures there were. "Sorry. I always take too many of the fish."

"You're proud."

"That thing weighed twelve and a half pounds."

"Was it good?"

"Oh, man, it was illegal good."

He put the camera back and she took his hand again and again he felt that wholesale foreign rush go through him.

Cruzela Storm sang a love song. When it was over Iris went to the kitchen and returned with a heavy red French oven. Patrick stood and when she leaned to set it on the table her honey hair fell forward and Patrick couldn't take his eyes off the play of the candlelight on her extended arms, the bend of her body in the yellow dress. She wore padded mitts. She set the lid upside down on the table and steam roiled up from the pot. Iris stripped off the mitts, glancing at him. "Caught you looking."

"I can't not."

She smiled and brushed her hair off her face. "Please kiss me."

Patrick wasted no time on this direct order. It was a young couple's kiss, awkward then strong then hungry. Patrick felt weirdly, blessedly anchored. Time passed. Without breaking the kiss he blindly tapped his fingers around the tabletop for a mitt and found one. He set the lid back on the pot with a sharp clank. "It'll keep," he said.

"I won't." She led him inside and across the hardwood floor and down the small hallway to her room. There it was dark except for a small lamp by the bed, and the room smelled clean and there was a window with nothing but hills and sky beyond it.

"I'm not super good at this yet," he said.

"No worries. I've done it a millions times." They were both grinning when she turned off the lamp. "Now I'm the one just kidding."

They undressed each other cautiously. Patrick released the backside bra hook with minor struggle. Her whispers were warm in his ear and he got meanings but not words. He whispered back calmly, crazily ready, biting his tongue for painful distraction. Her bed was a foreign country, its surfaces and smells clearly no part of Patrick. The new nation welcomed him. Invasion. Surrender. Occupation. Oh, Iris. Nothing like

181

this, ever. Window in wall, sky in window, stars in sky. Again and again then sunrise.

She handed him a cup of coffee. "Never been this wrecked for work before," she said, kissing him lightly on the lips. Sway of Iris, scent and dream-blur, out the door.

21

At ten o'clock that Thursday morning Cleo from Friendly Village Taxi called Ted to say that their semi-regular fare, Lucinda Smith, would be ready for a ten-thirty pickup. Ms. Smith had asked for "the big guy" if he was available. The image of Lucinda's pretty, dour, sunglassed face came into focus in Ted's mind's eye like a close-up in a movie.

"I am available!"

He gunned the taxi. In the rearview he Mr. Hutchins' hoary old head rock against the backseat. With only minutes to spare, he sped Mr. Hutchins to the board-and-care downtown to visit his wife, refused the man's money, then sped over to CVS for breath mints. On impulse he picked up a TV/DVD combination from a display by the checkout line, with a sweet 13-inch screen and a remote – $99! Lucinda would love it.

Ten minutes later Ted pulled into a guest parking space across from her building and shut off the engine. Her condo was on a golf course outside of town. Beyond the condo he could see the course and one of the greens and a man striding toward a ball with a club in both hands. It was a warm day and there were wispy cirrus clouds high in the blue.

A moment later Lucinda stood amid the potted plants and flowers on her front porch, fiddling with her keys. The sunlight bounced off her shiny black hair. Down the steps she slowly came, sunglasses on, purse slung over a shoulder, reusable shopping bags wadded in one hand, her usual joylessness apparently in place. She wore jeans and a loose black T and flat black Chinese slippers. She climbed in and shut the door.

"Village Market, then Rosa's."

"You got it. I'm truly honored you asked for me."

Ted backed into the quiet street. In the rearview he saw her looking at him – at the back of his head, anyway – through her blackout glasses. "I wish they hadn't told you that."

"Oh?"

"I asked for you because you hardly talk."

"I'll hardly talk all you want. Don't worry. I'm just happy to have the work is all I meant."

"If you say so."

Ted put on his own sunglasses. He drove three wordless miles to Major Market and let her out at the entrance. "I'll pick you up here." She shut the car door and walked away. She moved like someone wishing not to be seen. She was inside, pulling a cart from the line when the automatic doors slid shut. What was devouring her? He felt it strongly but couldn't identify it. It was something powerful, too, it felt like she'd left some of it right here in the cab. Anger? Fear? He wondered often if people sensed the same thing in himself. He parked in the shade where he could see her come from the store, resting his arm on the TV/DVD player box on the seat beside him.

She came out with a bag in each hand. Ted pulled up and stopped curbside, offering to handle the bags for her but she swung them into the backseat ahead of her and closed her own door. He pulled out of the lot and got onto Mission, headed for Rosa's Mexican restaurant.

"Keep going," she said.

"What about Rosa's?"

"Drive past the air park and the tennis club and turn at the high school."

184

"Where are we going?"

"You weren't going to talk."

"But I need to have a destination."

"Rosa's."

"We already drove past Rosa's."

"Please just drive."

Ted followed Mission out of town, past the Econo Suites and the deli and the nature preserve at Los Jilgueros. "A jilguero is a goldfinch. Oops." She was looking at the back of his head again.

"I was rude. You can talk if you have to."

"What's bothering you?"

She sighed and went quiet again. Ted thought he'd lost her. Why couldn't he just keep quiet? Because the same forces that made him want to *do something* also made him want to *say something*, he thought. He turned on Stage Coach and drove by the high school and Duke Snider Field and Warriors Stadium. He came to the stretch of Stage Coach that the locals called "Holy Hill," where many of the churches stood. The Baptist was Ted's favorite because of the weekly aphorisms on its marquee. This week's was a good one: "Where Will You Be Seated For Eternity? Smoking Or Non-Smoking?" Ted imagined sinners writhing in flames. "I'll probably end up in smoking," he said.

"See you there."

"Look at the hills out there. Black from the fire. Somebody set it."

"That would be heavy burden."

"To set a fire?"

"I would think."

Ted looked south to where the ruined foothills stood against the pale blue sky. The Fallbrook air looked clear and clean but the burnt smell still hovered. "Are you new here?"

"No."

185

"Do you have a job?"

"Please. Please don't."

There was so much Ted wanted to ask but he didn't want to scare her off. He followed Fallbrook street into town and picked up Mission again at the Post Office and headed down the hill to Rosa's. "Go around one more time," she said. "The same way you just did."

"I have to charge you. No, never mind. I won't."

She ignored him. In the rearview he watched her pull a cell phone from her purse and dial from contacts. She ordered a number ten and a Fanta. Ted heard Lucinda putting her phone back into her bag and when he looked up at the mirror she had taken off her sunglasses. She was looking down, and from the small motion of her shoulders Ted could tell she was doing something with her hands. He heard the hiss of aerosol spray. Her shiny dark hair hid her face. A moment later she lifted her head and looked in the mirror at him. Her eyes were brown, beautiful and charged with grief. "Life is like a day," she said. "It has light and dark. You can re-arrange them for a while but the portions never change." She slid the clean sunglasses back on.

"No, they don't. That's why you need a place to go where the dark can't get you. For me it's on a boat with my brother. His name is Pat and he's a war hero. I may be working with him someday."

"You understand, then. Where the dark can't get you. I like that. I changed my mind. Go to Las Brisas."

He made the loop again in silence and parked at Las Brisas taqueira. Ted watched the shoppers come and go from the little grocery with the soccer posters in the windows and the chilies hanging on the eaves. Lucinda came out a few minutes later with a white plastic bag. A few minutes later, parked behind the narrow garage below her condo, Ted lifted the TV/DVD player in one big hand and – with no privacy partitions in the taxis of the Friendly Village – reached back and set it down on the seat beside her groceries and lunch.

"This is for you."

"I – "

"It was on sale at CVS and it looks like fair quality, for the price."

"Look . . . Ted . . ."

Ted felt the thrill of his name spoken in Lucinda's voice, coming from Lucinda's mouth, carried by Lucinda's breath. "Remote and everything, you even get batteries."

"I can't take it. Give it to someone who can really use it. I can't. Thank you, but I can't."

Ted felt like he had been dumped into deep water with an engine block chained to his ankles. "Maybe you could just put it somewhere out of the way for now, then give it to someone later. Christmas is coming up. I can put it in your garage here – "

"No. Do not."

"Okay, Lucinda. Not a problem, Lucinda."

She got out and slammed the door and climbed the stairs two at a time, bags in hand.

"Lucinda?"

"*What?*"

"You forgot to pay me."

She looked down on him from the patio and he saw her shoulders sag and heard her sigh. Her bags clunked to the deck. She unslung her purse and came back down the stairs.

Ted finished off his shift at five o'clock, drove his truck to Open Sights in Oceanside and picked up his new Glock. Kerry sold him a clip-on holster, cleaning kit, a locking transport box and a padded cloth pistol bag. The range was busy and the sharp reports of the guns came muffled but forcefully through the walls and safety glass. He thought of Lucinda coming down her stairs. She had asked for him.

"We've got some terrific classes coming up next month," said Kerry. "Self-defense, safety, all the laws you need to know. Plenty of those to learn and more on the way."

Before leaving the store Ted made sure the gun was empty then locked it in the hard case. He locked all of his purchases in the toolbox bolted to the bed of his truck. Driving back toward Fallbrook he felt different. He felt calm, capable and equal. He felt that he had a powerful secret. He felt that he could protect himself and his family and Lucinda against criminals and government. He thought how different it would have been – the day that Edgar held him up and took his money – if only the Glock had been there with him.

She had asked for him.

22

He stopped and bought a twelve-pack of budget beer and drove to Pride Auto Repair. Cade's Bel-Air and Trevor's Magnum were there, along with a gleaming red-on-black Harley-Davidson he recognized. It was dark enough by now for the neon sign to show up beautifully, the blue Model T throwing out red flames. Standing between his truck and the building, keeping a weather eye for cruising cops – especially the one who had given him the nystagmus test in broad daylight after he'd been six months sober – Ted holstered the unloaded gun and clipped the rig to his belt. His XXL aloha shirttail – hula girls in grass skirts playing ukuleles – covered the gun nicely.

Inside there was no one at the front desk but behind it, through the open double-doors to the repair bay, Cade Magnus fiddled with the engine of a van and Trevor rolled a new tire toward a white pickup truck. A biker couple Ted had met – Screw Loose and Psycha – sat on the old paisley sofa with their legs splayed and beers resting on their thighs, watching the men work. Ted walked into the bay and opened one of the refrigerators, set the twelve-pack inside then broke one off for himself. He lifted a white resin chair off the stack and set it down by the sofa. Cade and Trevor were watching. Ted lifted his shirttail. Cade nodded and Trevor gave Ted one thumb up.

"New iron?" asked Screw Loose. He was a short and

stocky, with long orange hair and a short orange beard. Ted had noticed that, contrary to most bikers, Screw's leather was always clean and his gear always shiny, right down to the buttons on his vest.

"What's it look like to you?"

"Don't shoot yourself in the foot."

"I could shoot you."

"Funny," said Psycha. She was thin, with lank brown hair parted down the middle and a face brined by wind and sun.

"True, too," said Ted, enjoying the familiar tightening of breath and vision that presaged anger.

"What's got into you, Ted?" asked Screw.

"It's the gun," said Psycha "He's got stones now. He's not the shuffling moron he was yesterday and the day before."

Screw Loose laughed loudly. Ted shook his head and cracked his beer. The beauty of having power was you didn't have to use it. You could just glide. Cade cursed at the Chrysler engine and Trevor started bolting on a new tire with the half-inch impact gun. Ted considered the paisley couch and again remembered seeing Jed Magnus's sitting on it, reading, with one hand on Mrs. Magnus's knee. Through the raised back door he saw the street where he'd sat on his bike all those years ago, looking in.

Cade and Trevor finished up the work and everyone filed past the refrigerator for beers, then went into the lobby. Joan and Amber showed up a few minutes later in tight jeans and snug tops and heady perfumes. They brought a friend named Icey who was slight and fair-skinned and had tattoos running up the backs of both legs – serpentine plaits like an old-fashioned silk stocking – disappearing under her shorts. Her hair was a bleached buzz cut and her face was studded and serious. The three women sauntered in and headed straight for beers, then the pool cues. Joan slung her purse onto the counter and dug in for some you-know-what. Trevor put on some hate rock, a new band called By the Neck Until Dead. To Ted they sounded even worse than Hate Matrix, although the lyrics were rousing.

Ted whiffed a .45 casing of powerful methamphetamine and chugged a beer. As the crank blistered his brain Ted danced awkwardly in place and clapped his hands to the music. *I can do anything!* He and Icey, the tattooed woman, won their game against Cade and Joan, though Ted wondered if Cade threw the game by missing an easy put-away of the eight ball.

When Ted knocked it in Cade nodded approvingly and said something to Trevor, who checked his watch. The music was too loud for Ted to hear what was said but everyone else seemed to understand. The women gathered their purses and jackets and headed out to the parking lot. Cade and Screw Loose followed and a moment later Ted heard the Bel-Air and the Harley roar to life. The headlight beams cut across the Pride Auto windows and the car and motorcycle rumbled away leaving Ted and Trevor in the wake of noise.

"Where'd everybody go?" asked Ted.

"It's time to go see your friend."

A visceral, muscle-rippling thrill shot through Ted, almost as strong as another whiff of crank. "The next level? Yeah, let's do it."

"Come here."

Ted followed Trevor back into the repair bay. In one corner, leaning upright near the old-fashioned soft-drink machine, were a half-dozen baseball bats. Ted saw that some had been cut short. Trevor lifted one of these and gave it a discerning half-swing, more of a chop, then handed it to Ted. "Use this aluminum one."

"What if he has his gun?"

"I've got it all figured."

191

"I have the Glock just in case."

"You won't need it."

"But just in case."

Back in the lobby Trevor closed the front-door blinds then the men stepped into the evening. Trevor locked up. Ted drove his truck down Old Stage. It was just after seven, and the street was quiet tonight. He swung into the shopping center and parked by Robertito's Tacos where Trevor told him to. He cut the engine and looked out at the busy taco shop. "Have you had their burrito fries?" Ted asked. "They're so big I can't even finish one."

"I eat healthy, not Mexican."

"You got all those muscles to take care of."

Trevor looked at his watch again. "Edgar comes here most week nights, about right now, according to a friend of a friend of his slut girlfriend, Jessica. He gets food for himself and her. She lives in that trailer slum in the middle of town and they eat at a picnic bench by the creek. They eat, then breed in his car, then Edgar drives home."

"They're gonna recognize me" said Ted.

"That's the whole point. You're you and you're white and brown doesn't mess with white. That's your gospel. You're going to beat this truth into his ignorant head."

"You're not going to be with me?"

"I can't fight your battles for you. This greaser stuck you up at gunpoint, friend. Don't forget it."

"This was going to be you and me."

"This was never going to be you and me. Don't worry."

"I want a mask. Like in the movies."

"Then next time get yourself a mask, Ted! Do we have to feed and clothe you, change your diapers? Are you a Rogue Wolf or a baby? This is a simple thing we're trying to accomplish here. Are you going fail us?"

"I'm not going to fail."

"Good, Ted. Because Edgar just pulled up. That's his old Malibu. Here, take this – then switch seats with me."

Trevor lifted a snort of crystal to Ted's nose but didn't take one himself. The top of Ted's skull lifted off cartoon-style then slammed down and Ted pictured brain-dust puffing out his ears. He came around the truck and Trevor slid over to drive. Trevor leaned across and put a small baggie in the glove box and told Ted not to forget it was there. Trevor steered them through the parking lot to Mission and drove the short half-mile to the Meadowlark trailer park. Ted's mind was racing toward doubt all of a sudden, so he touched the Glock at his hip and looked at the baseball bat leaning against the seat, and, in the company of a friend, felt a rip-tide of confidence.

"Okay, Ted. Let's do this."

They pulled into the trailer park. Ted hadn't been in Meadowlark since he was a boy on a bike. He remembered the many colors of trailers and the butterflies that were drawn to the lantana that grew down by the creek, and the purple spikes of pride of Madeira limned by sunlight. There were plenty of tree frogs back then too. He knew his mind was wandering off again, deliberately trying to avoid duty. He took a deep breath and felt the oxygen and the chemicals speeding through his blood. It was like having God loose inside. Trevor guided the truck down the narrow, barely paved road. Ted looked at the big funnels of the trumpet vines blossoms dangling over a yellow trailer. Up ahead he saw the pool and a bench.

"Get your hood up, Ted. That'll keep them from recognizing you until it's too late. Go sit on the bench like you're just enjoying the night. Keep the bat out of sight under the table."

"What if he has the gun?"

"Bash him as soon as he gets close enough, man. Do I have to explain every damned thing to you?"

193

Ted lifted the hood over his head. He slid from the truck and carried the bat with the cut-off end cupped in one hand and the handle tucked up along his arm. He sat on the far end of the bench where he could keep at eye on the pool and on the road down which Edgar and Jessica would come. The bat lay across his lap, hidden by the table top.

It was dark here, away from the lights of Mission Road. He looked back to his pickup truck, parked inconspicuously along a chain link fence between a battered old station wagon and a neat subcompact. Through the windshield Trevor's face was a smudge in the dark. The traffic up on Mission hissed along and Ted smelled KFC and a hint of nightshade. His heart throbbed fast and hard but the deeper he breathed the faster it went. He stood, looked around, sat back down, watched the flicker of moonlight on the pool.

Then he heard footsteps and voices coming down the road in the darkness. Turning slightly he saw Edgar and Jessica. Edgar wore pale pants and something black on top. The girl wore dark clothing that wasn't yet visible in the darkness. When they came closer Ted saw that they each carried a plastic bag and that Edgar had already noticed him. Ted tried to ignore the wild rush of blood so loudly coursing in his ears. Their voices came through the night. He turned his face toward the water.

"*Who's that?*"

"*Victor?*"

"*Victor's in Elsinore tonight. Mike? Is that you, Esse?*"

"It's me, Edgar," said Ted, his back still to them.

"Mike? What are you doing here, man?"

"You bring me burrito fries?"

Ted heard Edgar's plastic bag hit the far end of the table top. "You shouldn't have taken my money," he said, turning.

"What? Taxi guy?"

Ted rose and swung the bat and the cut-off barrel whipped

194

through the air. Edgar caught it inches from his face and held on. Ted wrenched hard but couldn't break it loose. Edgar grunted, his face just inches from Ted's, and Ted used all his strength but their wills were locked and their weights and strengths were equal. Jessica screamed and crashed into him and punched him hard in the ribs. Ted felt his strength surge and he slowly muscled Edgar away from the bench and toward the water. Jessica hit him again and it hurt but neither man let go the bat.

Suddenly the world was two bright eye-rattling beams of light and Trevor advancing through them. Ted heard Jessica gasp and yelp and a moment later something heavy landed in the water. Then Edgar suddenly stiffened and let go of the bat. Ted fell away and Trevor took his place, pounding Edgar with short, practiced blows. Edgar dropped to his knees, then to his hands, too, head snapping and blood flying in answer to Trevor's kicks. Jessica splashed noisily toward shore. Ted righted himself and tried to draw his gun but he couldn't find the holster snap. Then Trevor was shoving him toward the idling truck. Ted stopped and closed his eyes and crossed his arms over his chest and tried to unscrew from the world but Trevor slapped him sharply across the face and pushed him. Ted clambered up then Trevor came around and in, his leather gloves smeared with blood, yanking the truck into a tight u-turn. As the headlights raked them, Ted saw Jessica dripping over Edgar, who was still on his hands and knees, shaking his big head like a man in disbelief.

"I had no idea you were that fucking slow," said Trevor. "Did you panic?"

"He was faster than me."

"Shit, Ted. You had a *club!*"

They were down Fallbrook Street almost to Main when Ted felt the hot sharp pain in his side. He braced his feet on the floor and pushed himself back and lifted the hoodie

195

and T-shirt. On his lower ribs were two swollen bumps about the size of cherry tomatoes, each with a neat slice in the top. Blood trickled steadily from both.

"Woah, Trevor. She stabbed me."

"I saw the knife. The hospital's close, Ted. You'll be okay."

Trevor swung onto Main and made the right at Alvarado. He gunned the truck up the hospital entrance and pulled alongside emergency. "You're on your own," said Trevor. "No use dragging me into it. Whatever you say, *don't* tell them you were at Pride tonight. I'll leave this truck in the Wells Fargo lot, keys on the left rear tire. Think of your wolf pack, not of yourself. Gun and holster off, Ted. I'll lock them in the toolbox behind us."

The knife wounds burned hotter and Ted felt bad in his heart, too. "Okay. I'll go alone."

23

At four that morning Patrick wheeled Ted from the emergency room to his truck. Fallbrook slept in dark and fog. Patrick could smell the ocean and the burned land around them and the combination was rare and jarring.

"It hurts when the chair hits the sidewalk cracks," said Ted.

"We'll be home soon."

"I don't want to go home."

Ted's wounds had been treated and he'd made his statement to the Sheriffs. His luck had been good: no veins or arteries cut; no organ or GI damage, although the knife had come close to doing both; nothing broken off inside; the antibiotics would help him fight off infection and he was given pills for pain. No strenuous physical activity for a week.

Ted told the deputies that he had parked at the bank last evening to go to the Irish pub across the street – all set for the roast beef on rye – when two young gangster-types had jumped him and he'd fought them off. One of them pulled a switchblade and poked him twice and they'd taken cash from his wallet and left it on the ground. He'd walked up the hill to the hospital himself. No, he did not know them. But he could certainly identify them. He seemed disinterested and he rarely looked at the deputies. Patrick listened to him doubtfully but said nothing.

He helped his brother up into the front seat. Ted grunted

dreamily. Pat rolled the wheelchair back to the lobby and climbed into the truck a moment later.

"Can we go fishing, Pat?"

"No."

"Can we just drive out and look at the ocean? I'm hungry, too."

"Let's eat in Oceanside then we can go down to the water if you want."

They ate at a 24-hour place on Coast Highway then walked, slowly, to a bluff overlooking the beach and pier. They sat on a cold concrete bench. The waves slapped the shore below, hidden in a gauze of fog as the sun rose behind them imperceptibly. Ted asked for a war story and Patrick told him about patrolling at night, racing against sunrise, single-column and single-file, with the point man working a Minehound and the number two man backing him up because the sweeper couldn't quickly return fire. And about how when they took contact everyone froze right in place, single file, lined up like ducks but not wanting to step off the path and get blown up. Which is what the skinnies wanted, because single-file Marines made easy targets. And he told Ted about the various IEDs the Talibs made – the pressure plates, the crush boxes, the saw blade IEDs. Ted listened without interruption but telling these things was a burden to Patrick and his heart was far from in it. He'd rather forget than provide entertainment.

"What the fuck really happened last night, Ted?"

"It was just like I said."

"Two guys with a knife outside a bank with security cameras all over? At dinner time? With the restaurants open? Two blocks from the Sheriff station?"

"Yup."

"Bullshit, brother." Patrick had taken a toothpick from the counter of the cafe. He picked at something then let the pick dangle from his lips. Ted had taken one, too, and Patrick saw him do likewise.

"I want to confess," said Ted.

Patrick just shook his head.

"I've been hanging around with Cade Magnus and those people at Pride Auto Repair. I'm a Rogue Wolf, pretty sure."

"Why? Why do that, Ted?"

"We believe the same things."

"Christ."

"Christ was white, according to the Wolves. And to history. None of this olive-skinned stuff you hear."

"Did the Wolves put you up to something last night?"

"Oh, no, Pat. This confession isn't about last night."

"You're a terrible liar, Ted." Patrick glanced at his brother, then looked out to the Pacific coalescing in the early light.

"It doesn't take much to fool most people," said Ted. Patrick studied his brother in profile. "Pat, that guy who robbed a few days ago that I told you about? I took him to the next level."

"What does *that* mean?"

"It's a technical Rogue Wolf term. It means I beat up Edgar. But Jessica stabbed me. So I threw her in the pond."

Patrick leaned forward, elbows on knees, and looked down at the damp, gum-stained concrete. He knew how his father must feel. "Was Cade with you?"

"I told you he didn't have anything to do with it."

"But he was there, wasn't he?"

"I swear on our parents' grave. No. But Trevor was."

"Trevor?"

"One of Cade's Rogue Wolves."

"You beat up the robber? Or Trevor did? Your knuckles aren't even skinned."

Ted sighed and put his hands into his hoodie pockets without looking at them. "I used gloves. Maybe you could

199

just say something like, good job. Or, way to go, Ted. There are more heroes in this world than just you."

"I not a hero and I don't want to be."

"It's how you were born, Pat. Me, I have to work harder."

"So he robbed you with a gun. Now you say you've beaten him up and thrown his girl into a pond. Are you satisfied? Does this make it even now?"

"Yeah. I really got him good."

"So you're done. You're not going to do this again."

"Oh, absolutely not. We're even-Steven. I just remembered when I was in fourth grade and I got in a fight with Ronnie Stevens and we became friends later."

"Is that what you want to happen?"

"This went a little too far for that."

Patrick could see the whitewater below, washing ghost-like up the beach. The caissons of the pier were individuated, and lights came on in the restaurant far down at the end. A surfer stood knee-deep with his board under his arm, as if he'd been trapped there all night awaiting release by sunlight, then fell forward on his board into the water. Two more paddled out through the shorebreak. "I don't want you down at Pride Auto Repair anymore, Ted. Do you understand?"

"Naturally."

"I'm ordering you away from there."

"Okay. I'll stay away."

"You have to control yourself, Ted. If you won't control yourself, who will?"

"Not government, that's for sure."

"Who's talking about *government?*"

Ted shook his head back and forth quickly, then rolled the hood over his head and snugged it tight. "They get in! They get in!"

"What are you talking about – your ideas again?"

"Yes! I got this new idea in the hospital a few hours ago

– how if you make yourself believe a lie to make the world look the way you want it to look, you've started to go insane. And after you believe that first lie every other lie gets easier. And in you go, deeper and deeper. My first lie was that I would become a meaningful man. That I had something that was all mine and really important I was meant to do. That *thing* I was telling you about on the way home from the airport. I was eleven when I had the meaningful man lie. Can I make another confession? You think I won't control myself. But sometimes I get really, really angry. You don't know how angry. I want to do terrible things. And I see how they can be done. Exactly how. And usually I talk myself out of them. Usually. I'm afraid someday I'm not going to be able to. And then I'll mix up my anger with the really important thing I was meant to do. And then, wow, what a random mess that's gonna to be."

Ted unzipped his sweatshirt and touched the wounds beneath the clean olive T-shirt his brother had brought him. "Three/Five. Dark Horses. Get Some. I got some, Pat."

"I don't know what I'm going to do with you. You fuck up everything, Ted."

"That's Dad's line."

"I didn't mean everything. Not everything. Just some things. I wish there was a way for you to not try so hard."

"You mean give up?"

"Not give up, but . . . hell . . . I wish there was a way for you to just put one foot in front of the other and get the mission done. And quit worrying about every damned froggy thing that comes into your head. And just *be* in the world without having to change it. Man, just be here and let other people's problems be other people's problems. Not yours."

"That makes really good sense. I'm going to try it, Pat. You know, in a way, I've been trying to do it almost my whole life! When I turn fast counterclockwise? With my arms crossed and my eyes shut? Really fast? Like you said, it's unscrewing from the world."

Patrick felt exasperation and nothing more. This was what he hated most about civilian life – the incredible slowness; the numbing discussions; the goop-thick assumptions that there was plenty of time for all things to be considered, no matter how idiotic and useless and destructive they might be; the truly awful belief that everyone had a right to express themselves any time they felt like it, to unscrew themselves from the world if they wanted to. In civilian life, how long did you have to wait for a thing or a moment to truly matter? In Sangin the way you tied your boots could decide whether you lived or died. And those around you. That's why you electrical-taped yourself and your gear before patrol, slapping the tape on every surface that could reflect light back to the enemy, everything that could make a sound and give you away. Then you jumped up and down and listened for a rattle, and Myers would watch and listen for even so much as a twinkle or a rattle. It had to be perfect. It mattered. In Sangin, if you simply forgot the extra tourniquet, someone could die. In Sangin if you let even a small patch on your goggles get sanded so dull you failed to see the Talib sniper in the rocks far away, someone could die. If you walked imperfectly and knocked a rock down a slope, someone could die. It all mattered. And that, the *mattering*, was the greatest pleasure there was. Not the adrenalin-rush of combat, or the mind-blowing alertness it took to survive it. But the knowledge that *everything was important and you had to do everything right. You had to be perfect for yourself and the men around you. Because you knew they made themselves perfect for you. It was pure dedication and pure belonging, to be ready, and to risk your life to save another.* Your greatest humility was your greatest pride. Nothing else came close. Combat was life at its most meaningful and everything else was an approximation.

"You're thinking about the war, aren't you, Pat? How in the war the enemy was the wooly-heads, but back here at home the enemy is me."

"Enough horseshit, Ted. Let's go home. We've got ten more hay bales to pick up and a whole lot of pole-pickers to oil and sharpen."

"You think we're ever really going to need them again? Those pole pickers for avocados?"

"What I think doesn't matter. I'm just going to be ready if some of the burnt trees live. Or if Dad can get a Farm Bank loan and there's any planter stock left on the market. And if the rain comes."

"I don't think Dad believes any of it is going to happen. He's already given up. He's just going through the motions because it's all he knows how to do. It makes him mad. And he enjoys being mad."

"That's his kind of faith, Ted."

"I brought a bat to take Edgar to the next level but I never landed a blow. We both got a hold of it and tried to get it away from the other. We were up close and our eyes were about level and it was me against him. We're big guys. And when I called on all my strength it came to me, and I was able to move him back. Then Jessica stabbed me and Trevor butted in. But I had that guy. I had the whole thing going my way."

"It's the last time you see those people. The last time you go to Pride."

"That's exactly what I was going to say. That's right, Pat. The last."

Patrick and Ted sharpened picker blades until eight a.m., then Patrick sent his brother downtown to get the hay bales. He told Ted the feed-and-tack store men would load them in. After Ted's truck vanished around the bend Patrick waited a few minutes then drove to Pride Auto Repair.

203

He'd been here as a boy with his dad, though not often, because his parents didn't care for Jed Magnus's race hate. He wondered how long it had been. Twelve, fifteen years? Outside it looked the same, with the racy neon Model T sign up again, and the windows cleaned. Inside was also like he remembered it, except for seeming smaller, with same high ceilings and brick walls and the pool table, jukebox, counter and stools. The counter was the same scarred oak, and the framed Vintage Car Show posters looked just like the ones from his boyhood, only with more recent dates. The lobby had been made to look old when he was a boy and it looked even older now. But now the man behind the counter was Cade and not father.

"Patrick Norris! Good morning."

Patrick walked to the counter and Cade offered his hand. Patrick took it, yanked hard, grabbed Magnus by the collar with his other hand and pulled him face-first onto the countertop. He put his back and legs into it, dragging the man the length of the counter before launching him to the floor. Magnus crashed hard in a storm of pens and flyers and business cards, complimentary calendars, candy. "Leave my brother alone. Don't look at him or talk to him again. Ever."

A muscular young man came from the repair bay through the double-doors, holding a red shop rag in one hand. He stopped and the rag dropped to the floor. Magnus was already up in a shooter's stance, a handgun leveled at Patrick's chest. "I could shoot you right now, Patrick, and be within my rights. You've assaulted me on my property without reason. I've got a witness."

"You won't shoot me. And you won't call the sheriffs. I'll tell them about Trevor's adventure last night with Ted. I take it you're Trevor."

The big man looked at his boss, who lowered his gun then and put it behind his back from where it had come.

He brushed off the front of his blue work shirt, making sure the 'Cade' patch was clean. "You're an asshole, Norris. You come into my place of business on a nice Friday morning. You break my pen jar and mess up my 'Take Back Main Street' display. You dump my customer-appreciation candy on the floor. And it wasn't cheap drug store stuff – it's real avocado fudge made here in Fallbrook. You throw me around and accuse my employee of who knows what. All because of your dumbass brother? Let me tell you something – we can hardly keep him out of here. He just slinks back again and again like a whipped dog. So, if you don't like the company he keeps, take it up with him. But I own this place. When I'm in it, I look at who I want to look at, and I talk to who I want to talk to. My country has a Constitution that protects people like me from people like you. It protects your brother too. So get lost, jarhead, or I *will* blow a hole in you. You want a war to fight, fight it against America's enemies. Until then, you're just a trespasser."

"Rogue Wolves."

"That's right."

"The skinnies weigh half of what you do but they're twice as heavy." Patrick looked at each man in turn and walked back out.

24

Patrick and his father and mother walked the realtor through the family home. The revised offer had come one day after the fire. It was afternoon and the light came through the windows in pleasant autumn angles and Patrick tried to see the place with fresh eyes. The realtor's name was Scott Dormand and he had worked with Archie and Caroline for twenty-plus years. He had a sad face and depleted hair, dyed blond and combed over. Patrick could tell that Dormand was concerned with an as-is sale, noting the wear on the hardwood floors, the unpopularity of wallpaper below the chair rails, the unusual "sea foam" color of the tile in the master bath.

"The sonofabitch doctor can do what he wants with it," said Archie.

"Very true," said Dormand. "Very true."

"We won't take a million three for something worth three million."

"I know you won't, Arch. I just wanted to see it again before we make the counter. There's a lot here to love – the location is magnificent, the home has terrific bones, the kitchen has been remodeled and the plumbing and electric are sound. You've got double-pane windows, and the gorgeous old fireplace. On the other hand, we don't want to scare them off."

"By asking them to pay what it's worth?" asked Caroline.

"Before the fire, his offer of two-million was low, according to the comps. Asking three million, you were high. But I presented his new offer of one million three to you because that's my job. And, well, the buyer looks at the ranch and sees the same house he made an offer on before the fire. But he also sees eighty burnt acres of avos that may not come back. He wants those trees. He wants to be a grower."

"Goddamned Newport Beach doctor wants to be a grower," said Archie. "Just tell him full asking price – three million, even – take it or leave it."

"I'll tell them exactly what you and Caroline want me to tell them. But three million is pretty high, Archie. Prohibitively."

"Honey?" asked Archie.

Patrick heard his mother sigh. She was wearing her usual white blouse, a pink kerchief around her neck, pressed jeans and black boots. Her makeup and lipstick were minimal and tastefully deployed. "I'm with you, Arch. Three million."

"Patrick?" asked Archie. "What do you think?"

"I don't think you want to sell it."

"Not for a penny less than three, I don't."

"Then hold out, Dad."

In the silence Dormand cleared his throat. "I really have to doubt that anyone will pay it, in this economy, after this fire. Just so you understand, Archie."

"I'm not as stupid as I look."

"Hope the trees live and the rain comes," said Patrick.

Archie looked at him in assessment. "And if they don't and it doesn't, I'll have to sell it all to salvage three worthless condominiums. A fire sale, literally. God knows what kind of lowball offer *that* might be. Tell the old sawbones we're firm at three, Scott."

"Will do."

"Would you like to walk the groves, see the trees?"

"There's no real need for that, Archie."

Patrick and his parents walked the scorched western boundary of Norris Brothers Growers anyway. In this second full year of drought now cursed by wildfire, the dust and ash rose with their footsteps and hovered in the parched air. Even the weeds and wild grasses that crept to life each year with the first drops of rain were long missing from the untrammeled center of the dirt road, and from the shaded, life-friendly soil beneath the avocado trees, even from where the irrigation valves leaked their tiny surpluses into the ground. The earth beneath Patrick's feet looked like something he'd shovel from a fireplace – dead powder without promise. He thought of the infernal dust of Sangin and the spiders big as his face.

They stopped on the high ground and looked down on the eighty acres. Far below, the San Luis Rey River serpentined toward the Pacific in its path of green. From here Patrick could see the barn and the bunkhouse and some of the outbuildings. Ted's truck was parked in front of the bunkhouse.

"What's wrong with your brother?" asked Archie. "How can he spend all day inside like that?"

"Some kind of side ache," said Patrick. "I'll let him tell you."

"He eats a lot of take-out," said Caroline.

Archie shook his head. "Well, I'm sorry his stomach is upset, but the Farm Credit Bank in San Diego passed on us, Pat. They were our last real hope for a loan. The Norris family is now officially unleashed and on its own."

"I'll work extra hard tonight," said Patrick, checking his watch. "Fridays are big money."

"What a joy to be unleashed," said Caroline, draping her arms over their shoulders. "Woof."

Patrick was right about the big money. He found himself racing between pickup and delivery then back again for more. How fast he could do the job seemed important. A Sheriff's Deputy pulled him over on Alvarado for doing sixty in a forty-five. They talked about the wildfire then Afghanistan, where the deputy had a cousin who was deployed. His cousin knew the Marine who was murdered last week by one of the Afghan army soldiers he commanded on patrol. Slow down, he told Patrick, handing back his driver's license – woolies aren't worth dying for and neither is pizza.

But it was hard to hold down his speed. Firooz and Simone had three vehicles going, and every time Patrick came through the Dominos door they were making and baking pizzas as fast as they could, ordering each other around in Farsi, trying to keep up with the phone and internet orders in English. On his next run he swerved to miss a Chihuahua darting across Main with its leash still attached, then pulled over and ran down the witless dog, which bit him before he could hand it over to its owner.

He came home at nine o'clock, counted his tips and slipped the bills into an envelope he kept under his mattress. Seventy-eight dollars and change. Not bad.

He showered and walked down to see Ted. The night was close and smelled of soot and an owl huffed through the darkness above the barn. Patrick knocked on the bunkhouse door and stepped in, the dogs wedging past him. Ted sat at his computer table, as usual, playing one of his games. He said he was feeling okay – the pain pills worked like magic and he'd just made it to the next level of the game. Patrick crossed the big rustic room and set a hand on Ted's shoulder, looking down at the monitor, where the running bull-headed figure tossed wolves into a starlit sky. Patrick saw that Ted had hung several Evelyn Anders campaign posters on the bunkhouse walls: "This Town Is Your Town." A tall stack of "Village View" newspapers sat on the computer table and Patrick noted the front-page picture of Evelyn Anders and George's two young friends. Article by Iris Cash. Ted looked up at him, smiling.

209

"Why all the pictures of someone you don't like?" asked Patrick.

"Reminders that I need to do something big and meaningful."

"Collecting pictures of Evelyn Anders is big and meaningful?"

"Come on, Pat," Ted said meekly.

"Why do you dislike her so much?"

"Well." Ted went back to the game for a long moment, guiding his character through the ruins of what looked like a medieval castle. "Evelyn babysat me once. I remember it. Very clearly. You might, too. She kept coming to the bathroom door to ask me if I was alright. She really cared. I was in the bathtub just taking my time, washing everything extra good. You were watching TV in the den. The next day I made her a thank-you card with a frog on it. I mean I cut out a picture of a frog and glued it on, not a real frog. I don't remember her ever sending me anything back. Like a card or something. Nothing. Nothing. I asked Mom if Evelyn could baby-sit me from then on but Mom wanted Agatha, the old one. Ick. She smelled like lilac and she wore orthopedic support stockings to hold in her varicose veins. Always asking if she could make me something to eat but her just being there totally like took away my appetite."

Patrick wasn't sure what to say to all of this. "You're not drawing more cartoons of the mayor, are you?"

"I promised you I wouldn't."

"Leave her be, Ted."

"Yes, sir."

"I talked to Cade and Trevor. You're not welcome at Pride Auto Repair anymore."

"Not welcome? Or banned by you?"

"You're better than the Rogue Wolves any day, Ted. You don't need them."

"They're not the Dark Horses."

"They're angry children."

"Maybe that's why I like them."

Patrick went to the door. "Are you playing straight with me, Ted? No cartoons of the mayor? No more hanging out with those people?"

Ted looked at him, the monitor light playing off his face. "You have my word, Pat. So . . . can I ask you a question?" Patrick waited. "What do you think I would have to do to make Dad respect me?"

Patrick thought a moment. "He respects hard work."

"There isn't anything I can do. Nothing I'm good at. I mean, besides driving the taxi."

"He's got more in his heart for you than he can let on. It's the Norris way of being a man."

"He makes me feel bad."

"You shouldn't. You're a good man. You just haven't found out what you want to do yet."

"Naw," said Ted, turning back to the screen. "I'm not good. But thanks. Thanks for saying so."

Patrick set his hand on his brother's shoulder again and watched him play another minute of his video game. He looked over at the cages and saw minor movements inside them. When he glanced at Ted's face he saw how far away he was, how lost in a one-dimensional world that didn't exist, with beings that had no equivalents on this planet.

"You can leave the dogs with me," said Ted.

Out in the barn Patrick turned on the lights and sat a while with *Fatta the Lan'*, noting her fine overall shape and condition. Her gunwales were smooth to the touch. He wiped down the engine housing and waxed it, then took a light rubbing compound to the hardware and railing. The aft drain was developing a stain so he used rubbing compound to that also, and it came right up. With a file he ground a small ding out of the prop of the electric motor, running his finger over it to make sure it was smooth. It was nothing that would have effected her performance but a blemish nonetheless.

Later he poured a tall bourbon and got the blankets from the workbench and made up his bed in the boat. The night was cooling so he got a sleeping bag too. In the dark he lay face-up on the deck, safely enclosed by the curving sides of the craft, listening to the crickets and the muted hoot of an owl somewhere out in the trees.

25

Saturday night Iris threw a dinner party for two of her girl-friends and Patrick, Salimony and Messina. Arriving before the other guests, Patrick saw the spit-shine that Iris had put on her bungalow. There were fresh cut flowers and music from the stereo in the living room, and many candles. The candles were electric and for amusement Iris kept dimming them and turning them on and off with the remotes. She wore a periwinkle blue dress and flat sandals with rhinestones on them. She was happy and nervous. She was leaving early the next day for her yearly fall trip back to Kenton to see family and friends and Patrick saw how important to her this party was.

"I'll help out all I can," he said. "I brought wine and beer. The guys are easy."

"I hope it's all okay. I made enchiladas and salad and dessert. If you can just talk to everybody and maybe change up the music, that would be great. Oh, and make margaritas out back. Do they smoke?"

"They do whatever you order them to. They're Marines."

"They'll love Nat and Mary Ann."

Iris smiled quickly and dimmed the candles. "I'm going to miss you, Pat."

"It'll be good seeing your family."

"I'm really looking forward to later tonight." Patrick blushed.

213

Her friends arrived together, bearing more wine, flowers and food. Patrick helped them unload and shook their offered hands. Natalie was a tall Latina, Mary Ann petite and blond. They worked with Iris at the Village View – Natalie as a photographer and Mary Ann in display advertising. Natalie was pretty and full-bodied, and her jeans and blouse made no apologies for this. Mary Ann wore a red cowgirl shirt and a denim skirt, and one side of her hair was held back with a comb while the other fell free to her shoulder. Patrick watched the three friends converge mid-kitchen to view, touch and converse with one another in the way that women do. They forgot he was there or acted like he wasn't but either way, he enjoyed being there.

Salimony and Messina came together too, close-shaven, scrubbed clean and bearing twelve-packs of premium beer. Salimony was tall, and though bone-thin in Sangin, had filled out some. His trousers and shirt looked new. Messina was a short knot of muscles, proud in a tight black T-shirt and Harley boots. Patrick introduced them to Natalie and Mary Ann, and short Messina kissed the back of tall Natalie's hand, which made all three women laugh, which made Messina blush and smile and punch Salimony in the gut but not hard.

In the back yard they drank and ate guacamole made from Fallbrook avocados. Patrick noted the small labels identifying the fruit as that of *Manos del Sol*, or, "Hands of the Sun," which happened to be Lew Boardman's ranch, which bordered the Norris Brother's groves on one side. Patrick wondered again why Boardman had stayed lucky through drought, frost and fire, while the Norris Brothers had suffered mightily. In Sangin he'd decided that God was Luck and this seemed as good an explanation as any. Iris had a light hand with the spices and the guacamole was excellent. Patrick made margaritas and manned the music. He followed the recipe on the mix bottle and tried to play upbeat songs. Iris had strung small twinkling lights in the big magnolia tree. The evening sky was a gray blanket drawn down over the orange ball of sun. Salimony and Messina moved one of the picnic benches end-to-end with the other and the six of them sat across to watch the sunset. Photographer Natalie fixed her camera to a tripod and set the timer and got a shot of all of them lined up with the last of the sun on their faces. The men stole glances at each other because this time of the evening was special at FOB Inkerman, just before patrol. They'd smoke and crack dark jokes and say awful things about each others' mothers and sisters and girlfriends. But never about the wives, never the wives because they all knew the high odds of their marriages being destroyed by the war, the high odds of their wives no longer being able to live with them after deployment, the reasonable odds that, even as they smoked and joked and waited to go kill or be killed, their wives back home were being talked up by a man, some guy with hair and kind eyes and a few bucks in the bank. So you only joked about that at your own peril. Then, as soon as the light was gone they'd set out, the enemy less able to shoot them. And they fell into that jagged mix of hypervigilance and grinding patience that it took to be up all night, moving quietly along the ratlines, looking for the best cover in which to hide and fire, knowing they had to get the job done and get back before the sun rose again or the Talibs would cut you to ribbons from the rocky hillsides before you could make Inkerman.

"How about a toast to the United States Marine Corps?" asked Iris.

"How about to the three prettiest girls in California?" asked Salimony. He smiled broadly and his nervous leg bounced up and down like it wanted attention.

They raised their wide sloshing margarita glasses to the sunset and drank and Patrick heard the French door to the house open behind them and a woman's laughter.

He was surprised to see the two men stepping out to

the patio. They were Marines he knew from Pendleton. Not Dark Horses. A woman walked along between them, arm-in-arm with each. Patrick looked to Iris, who was more than surprised. She rose as if to confront them but Messina jumped up and said he'd invited them – sorry he forgot to say something but these are great men with nothing to do tonight! Patrick saw Iris try to hide the disappointment. The men and woman ambled across the yard toward them and Patrick noted that they were drunk. Messina introduced them as Grier and Marcos and told Patrick to whip them up some drinks. "And who the heck are you?" Messina asked the woman.

"I'm the stripper!"

Christ, thought Patrick. Iris looked at him very doubtfully.

"Not really." She giggled. "Just Mindy."

Iris's table only sat six so Patrick brought in chairs and the crashers got corners and plates on their laps. Everyone drank at speed except for Natalie, who was sober three years. Messina watched her intently. Patrick kept an eye on the interlopers and kept getting up to fetch and pour more wine. He'd learned to twist the bottle at the end of the pour to keep it from dripping. He felt grown up. The table talk was spirited and from the bleachers the three crashers offered a chorus of drunken but good-natured commentary. When Grier leaned back he nudged the framed aerial photograph of the Cash family farm with the back of his head and it fell off the wall but he hung it back up, undamaged, with exaggerated care. In the kitchen Patrick helped Iris get the trays ready. *That dumbbell Messina,* she whispered. *How could he do this?*

"I'll get rid of them if you want."

"We can't be rude, Pat."

"Yes, we can. This is your dinner, Iris."

"Then I'm sure not going to let them ruin it."

216

"I have bad feelings about this."

"I won't cave in to negative thinking."

Patrick ignored his anger. Back in the dining room he poured the red wine and Marcos held out his empty margarita glass and offered a glassy grin. Patrick didn't serve him. Finally seated, Iris asked Mary Ann if she'd like to say a prayer and everyone around the table joined hands. It was brief and heartfelt. In the silence after "amen" Grier burped and Mindy shushed him.

"You three," said Patrick. "If you can't behave yourselves, you'll have to leave."

"Says Colonel Patrick Norris of the 3/5!" said Grier. He was a big man, heavier and older than Patrick.

"We're not so bad are we?" asked Marcos.

"Patrick is right," said Mindy. "So we're going to behave starting right now."

"Man," said Salimony. "These enchiladas are good."

They passed the dishes and the food dwindled quickly. Messina handed a bottle of white wine back to Mindy and she poured some into her margarita, her little finger raised preciously, then set the bottle on the floor, empty.

"Mind if I turn up the music?" asked Grier.

"No, thank you," said Iris. "I'd like to hear the conversation."

"In that case I'll tell you what I did today," said Messina. "I worked my butt off training my replacements. See, I'm twenty-six years old next month and the Corps doesn't need me anymore. Not when they got eighteen-year old cherries to do what I did. They don't want third-tour men. We're washed up and too expensive and even the brass thinks were too crazy to fight anymore. Plus, it's all winding down."

"Maybe it's time you left the Corps anyway," said Natalie.

"I don't *want* to leave the Corps," said Messina. "All's I'm good at is fighting. I can't exactly get a job as sniper, can I?"

"In the French Foreign Legion you can," said Salimony.

217

"Ain't fighting for no Frenchmen," said Messina. "So, Natalie – pretty genius Natalie. Did I embarrass you when I kissed your hand upon our recent introduction?"

"I've never had a man do that."

"Oh boy," said Messina. "I could say something on that subject, but I won't. Anyway, you're the most beautiful woman I've ever seen."

"Why thank you!"

"I just want to be on the record."

There was scattered laughter to this, but underneath it the silence was uneasy. At one quiet moment Patrick was aware of several glasses being lifted at once. He went into the living room and forwarded the music player to a peppier song. When he sat down he saw that Iris had gathered herself – shoulders in, forearms on the table, hands steadying the base of her wine glass. Her smile was fraudulent.

The men talked who was short and who might re-up. Patrick and Grier were already out of the Corps for good. Grier had a part-time job as a night watchman at Qualcomm headquarters, said he mostly read between rounds, boring as hell but perfect after Helmand. He offered flamboyant descriptions of combat violence for which he kept apologizing to the women, and Patrick quickly deduced that Grier was just a Bagram jarhead stationed north of Kabul in the biggest American base in-country. Which, in spite of his gory posturing, made Grier just a Fobbit – a Forward Operating Base Marine – who'd never seen combat, fired a gun and probably never been outside the wire. Patrick had learned that the more emotional the detailed the description of combat action, the greater the chance it was mostly, if not totally, second-hand. He stared off through the living room and the French doors to the night.

The women listened and asked questions. Salimony told a carefully edited story of the Labrador, Zane, saving a

218

life. Patrick talked about crazy Reichart collecting gigantic spiders in empty ammo boxes, naming them and trying to feed them MRE leftovers. To Patrick this didn't seem like terrific table talk but Iris and her friends were plainly interested in their lives in Sangin. They started out curious about everyday things: was it hard to live on one hot meal a day and one shower a week? With all those spiders around, how did you sleep? What was worse, the heat or the cold? Then their questions got harder and came faster: Was it hard knowing that the Taliban would murder and maim villagers they suspected of collusion? Was it true that Afghani women could be stoned to death for conversing with anyone in the Coalition military? Why all the amputations? Was it strange to protect fields of poppies instead of destroying them, as the military had done in the past? What could be done about the "insiders?" Was trust even possible anymore?

"If you chicks are so interested, why didn't you sign up and go?" asked Grier.

"Natalie and I talked about covering the war for the Village View," said Iris. "But they had no budget for it."

"You'd need a whole budget just for your hair and makeup," said Marcos. "You didn't really want to go. You wanted to stay here and decorate your little play house."

"You don't know one thing about what she wanted," said Patrick.

"You only think you do."

"I saw some of the press corps babes," said Messina. "There was some stone-ass hotties. I saw one do fifty-one pushups."

"Any more tequila out there?" asked Mindy. She lurched up and knocked over the empty wine bottle beside her chair. It rolled and echoed brightly, dribbling the last of the wine, but she was oblivious to it and walked in short, weaving steps

219

toward the patio. She wore high wedge heels and it looked as if she might tip over.

Grier rose to pick up the bottle but hit the Cash farm photograph with his head again, and again it slid down the wall and hit the floor. "You ought hang this thing higher, Iris."

"There's one above it and I like it there," she said sharply.

Grier tried to hang the photo but he missed the hook and it hit the floor for the third time in half an hour, and the frame broke into two L-shaped pieces. He picked them up and sat back down and held them back to together. "I can glue it."

Mindy wobbled back in from the patio with the tequila bottle in her hand. "Do you ever think that we were all put here to learn certain lessons?"

"Sure," said Marcos. "The lesson a Marine learns in California is he isn't going to get a date with any of the really hot babes. They're already hooked up with lawyers, actors and tech nerds. All the jarheads get are leftover idiots like you."

"Fuck you," said Mindy.

"But that's not true," said Salimony. "Just having dinner at this table is a good thing for us. Look around you, Marcos. You should be thankful to be alive and not blown to smithereens."

"Marcos is right," said Grier. "Bitches like these aren't going to roll out the welcome mat for me. Patrick, I think you must have drugged Iris here. At the very least."

Patrick stood. "Time for you Marines to hit the road."

Grier stood too. "Sir, yes sir, General Pat."

Marcos said: "You don't get it, do you? After tonight, you guys won't see any of these high-end cunts again."

Messina threw back his chair, wheeled and hit Marcos in the nose with a terrific cracking sound. Iris screamed: *"STOP!"* Marcos charged through the blow, stomped on Messina's foot, then raked his fingers across Messina's eyes. Patrick and Grier met each other half way around the table and locked up. Grier, heavier, bulled Patrick back into the China cabinet, which shattered as if hit by a grenade. Patrick felt the frame collapse under his weight, the shards of glass spraying against his neck and rattling down, heard the woeful explosions of plates and bowls on the hardwood floor. He gave in to his anger. He flew into Grier's slower, drunker body, throwing kicks and punches that landed and landed again. Blood flew. Salimony and Messina pummeled Marcos into the living room, knocking an heirloom mirror to the floor with an explosion of glass. Iris and Mary Ann fell on top of Mindy, who screamed nonsense and flailed away with a table knife in one hand and a napkin in the other. Grier swiped the blood from his face and smiled, then shot in low to grapple Patrick, but Patrick caught him with a knee square to the forehead and elbow-piled him to the floor. Grier dropped to his hands and knees on a bed of broken glass. Patrick lifted one of the heavy oak chairs and crushed the man flat with it. Then he registered motion on his left: Natalie snapping action shots.

Oh Jesus, he thought.

Iris and Mary Ann had Mindy pinned to the floor and she was sobbing. Patrick ran into the living room. The TV had fallen from its stand and burst. Glass vases and cut flowers littered the floor and several of Iris's new electric candles bravely continued to beam in the wet debris. Salimony and Messina had Marcos backed into a bookcase, blows and books and photographs and knickknacks all raining down on him. Patrick shouldered in, kicked Marcos squarely in the groin and showered him with his fists and elbows. When Marcos fell the three men dragged him, groaning, outside to the porch, then down the steps and dropped him into the planter. Iris and her two friends lugged unstruggling Mindy down the porch steps, her wedge shoes clunking down each craftsman plank, then launched her onto the grass. *"Get out*

221

of here and don't ever come back!" Iris screamed. Her face was a grimace and her fury sent a sobering jolt through Patrick. What should he have done? *"And you bastards get out of here too and don't you ever come back. And you, Patrick, Patrick Norris? You NEVER come back here again or I'll call the cops and file charges. I swear to God I will!"*

Patrick watched Natalie and Mary Ann squeeze through the front door and into the house. Iris gave him one last furious look before she slammed the door and drove the deadbolt home.

Grier had pulled Marcos to his feet and they staggered toward a white Camaro parked at the curb.

"Sorry, Pat," said Salimony. His new shirt was torn and splattered with blood.

"Yeah, Pat, sorry," said Messina, with bloodshot eyes and a jaggedly split lip. "We gotta help fix it. We gotta."

"You heard her," said Patrick. "Get the hell out of here. Go."

Patrick waited until the Camaro and Messina's Mustang had both disappeared down the hill. He listened for sirens and was surprised to hear only silence. Neighbors left, right and across the street stood on their lit porches and neat lawns, looking at him, their voices riding softly on the damp night air.

He strode back onto the porch and knocked on Iris's front door, then knocked again, harder. Natalie called through the wood. *"You better go, Pat. You better go like now."*

26

Evelyn looked up from her desk at Anders Wealth Management to find Ted Norris standing in the doorway of her office. She flinched. The morning light coming through her windows illuminated him. "Ted?"

"Yes?"

"Are you okay?

"I'm good as new."

"Can I help you?"

"I want to get a few things off my chest."

"I'll let Brian know you're here."

"But I don't want to talk to Brian."

"You're not here looking for trouble, are you?"

"No. Not in any way."

Brian appeared in the middle distance behind Ted, glancing up from his tablet. He gave Ted an interrogatory stare. Ted sensed him without turning. "Don't worry, Mr. Anders. I come in peace."

"I'm sorry for what happened," said Brian. "I saw it on the Village View website."

"I lost eighty dollars but saved my life by fighting hand-to-hand."

"The Sheriffs are going to step up the downtown patrol," said Brian. "Not everyone can do what you did."

"I'm not a hero and I don't want to be." Ted folded his hands together at his waist. He was wearing another baggy

Hawaiian shirt and loose jeans and his huge therapeutic shoes. The shirt hung oddly distended on his right side.

"Come in and take a seat then," said Evelyn. "I have an appointment in half an hour."

Ted stepped in and put a hand on the doorknob.

"Leave it open."

"I was going to."

Brian circled his index finger around his ear then made the 'call me' sign with his free hand and walked toward his office. A spark of fear flickered inside her and she wished that Brian had done something more. But what? Call security? The landlord had terminated the service months ago, and the tenants couldn't afford security on their own. She'd put "Patrolled By Fallbrook Security" stickers on the windows and a larger sign by the mailboxes in the ground-floor entry, but any bad guy with half a brain would figure them for what they were – bogus.

Ted sat heavily in one of the chairs in front of her desk. "I'm not drawing any more cartoons of you."

"Thank you, Ted. Good decision."

"Patrick ordered me not to."

"Then I thank both of you."

Ted adjusted himself on the chair, as if something was physically bothering him. "I disagree with almost everything you've done as my mayor."

Evelyn felt instantly crushed, but the feeling disappeared quickly. Four years in elected office had made her skin much thicker. Still, there was pain in disagreement: democracy hurt. "I'm sorry to hear that. But I was elected for what I believe. And I'm expected to act on those beliefs, for the good of Fallbrook."

"I'll probably have to vote for Walt Rood."

"That's your right."

"I like your campaign posters. Your picture is nice."

224

"You should vote your . . . I'd like to have your heart, Ted."

"Have my heart? You really would?"

"I meant your vote. I was going to say, you should vote your heart – but then I tried to say something else and it came out mixed up."

"I do that all the time. The big important words in your thoughts, they come out, but some of the other ones don't. So what you say isn't complete. It isn't what you tried to say."

Evelyn smiled. Ted really did have a good heart in there. "No, things come out wrong all the time. I'd still love your vote, though."

Ted looked at her with an unreadable expression. He half-stood, reached under his shirt. Before Evelyn fully registered what he was doing, Ted drew a plastic sandwich box and held it up toward her. "I brought this for you," he said. Something thick and slow moved inside the opaque container. "It's a tarantula."

"Oh! Well, I'm really not a big tarantula fan, Ted. Incredible as that may seem."

"This one is a female. The males are skinny and die. These females are plump and live a long, long time. She eats crickets you can buy at the pet store."

"I'm . . . can you keep it for me? Or can I let it go in the nature preserve or somewhere?"

"Let her go?"

"Just asking."

Ted reached out and set the container on Evelyn's desk. She watched the thing feeling its away around. "When I was young I fell in love with you," he said.

Evelyn felt her face change color but she wasn't sure *what* color – discomfort pink or creeped-out white? "Oh?"

"When you babysat me. And after."

"I remember that. And I remember the card you made me."

"I wanted something back from you but instead I got nothing."

"The card had a frog on it."

"It was a Pacific tree frog. They're all over Fallbrook but they only come out when it rains."

"I hear them in the creek by my house. Is there something specific you came here to talk about?"

"The concert by Cruzela Storm. I want you to cancel it."

"That's a terrible thing to say, Ted."

"It's my honest opinion and I vote. You are not my mother or my nanny."

"The concert is to help pay for two lighted crosswalks, Ted. George Herrera lost his life right there on Mission for no reason. No reason at all! You should be asking to help, not to hinder."

"To help you?"

"Help Fallbrook."

"Are the lighted crosswalks big and meaningful?"

"Yes. They're big and meaningful and *affordable*. If we have the concert, that is."

Ted looked around as if considering. "I'd like to join your re-election staff."

"But Ted, you and I disagree on almost every issue. Besides, the campaign work is mostly done. It's just a matter of taking down the posters after the vote."

"Then I would like to show Cruzela Storm around Fallbrook after the show. A tour of our city, in my taxi. For free."

Evelyn's scalp cooled and tightened. "That's sweet of you. But she'll have lots of security."

"They can come, too. My cab has room for four adult passengers. So – me, you, Cruzela and two security guards. It's clean and comfortable."

"She's a very private and in-demand person, Ted."

226

"Will you at least ask her?"

"No. I won't."

"You are everything I don't like about government and women," said Ted. "All you say is no, no, no and no. You should be ashamed of yourself."

"Sometimes I am ashamed, when I can't do enough. I'm trying here, Ted, with the crosswalks I'm *trying* to say yes to something good." Evelyn's phone chimed and she listened and rang off. "My nine o'clocks just got here." She looked past Ted's shoulder at Brian, standing out in the hallway, phone in hand. She could hear footsteps coming up the old wooden stairs, their echoes climbing the stairwell and spilling into the lobby. God bless the LaPointes!

"I also don't like that you've lost all Mom and Dad's money," said Ted. "They're losing everything, because of you."

Evelyn stood. "I have not lost all their money. And I won't discuss anything more with you."

"No, you won't. Because you're government and a woman, and a thief and a liar."

"Leave now."

Ted grabbed the tarantula off the desk and looked at Evelyn as he worked the sandwich box back into the waistband of his pants. "I'll do something big and important. I don't need you."

227

27

Ted clomped down the stairs, through the lobby and onto Main Street. His stab wounds hurt. His vision had constricted and he was short of breath. When he got to his truck, the dome-headed man he'd seen lurking around Fallbrook was sitting on a sidewalk bench in the late morning shadow of the buildings. As before, he wore a suit, this time olive. His complexion was pale and he had open, expressive eyes and a small neat mustache. He held up a badge holder then slipped it back into his jacket pocket. "Hello, Ted. I'm Homeland Security Department, Homeland Security Investigations Special Agent Max Knechtl."

Ted stopped and looked down the long rifled tunnel at the end of which sat the agent. He didn't think Anders would get him that riled up. My government, he thought, working for me. Now more of it. "I'm Theodore Archibald Norris. Citizen."

"What's that under your shirt?"

"A tarantula for the mayor. She didn't like it."

"That's an unusual gift."

"You must be the arson expert. Your boss was on the news but they didn't show you."

"Yes, I am that expert."

"I didn't set the fire."

"Sit down and talk to me. Take a load off those feet and those stitches in your side."

Ted reached under his shirt. Knechtl's hand was already on a gun holstered within his suit coat, and his expression had gone blank. Utterly. His face was nothing but two eyes with sunlight coming into them. Ted could see dark blued steel twinkling behind the olive lapel. "The tarantula," said Ted, slowing extending the sandwich box for Knechtl to see. "She's a female."

"Nice one. I'm relieved. Sit, Ted." Knechtl smiled but left his hand inside his coat for a moment. Then he crossed his hands over his knees but he still had the empty look on his face. Ted took the opposite side of the bench and set the sandwich box next to him. "Tell me about the fire."

"I just told you I didn't set it."

"I know *you* didn't set it. But someone did. And I think you're a smart man. You know every inch of this little town and the people in it. You know its streets. I see from your political cartooning that you're a student of current affairs and a man of clear and strong beliefs. Talk to me about this town and the man who set this fire, Ted. Educate me."

A Sheriff's patrol car went by, driven by the black deputy who'd given him the nystagmus test for all of Fallbrook to see. The deputy nodded behind his sunglasses and Ted nodded back, then noted that Knechtl nodded back also. Ted felt suffocated by government: the mayor – formerly his own babysitter with whom he had once been in serious love – spinning financial webs upstairs in her lair; domed Knechtl ambushing him on Main Street; and of course the cursed black sheriff's deputy on scene, on scene, *always* on scene like a character in a repeating dream. Ted yearned to be in his cab, for motion and protection, to be watching the world through heavy glass. "I was driving the taxi when the fire broke out. You can check my Friendly Village Taxi time card."

"Oh, I've done that. And your call-in log, too. You had five fares that morning."

229

"I was too busy that day to set a fire."

"If you say so." Ted's vision began to reassemble and he took a deep breath. It was beginning to seem possible that Knechtl was not here to arrest him for anything. Across the street, Mary Gulliver stood outside Gulliver's Travels, sipping a mug of something, getting some of the morning sunshine on her pretty face. Yes, she was twice his age but who cared? "Oh, there's Mary," said Knechtl. "I've talked to her about you. And I've talked to Dora Newell and Evelyn Anders and Lucinda Smith about you, too."

Ted felt as if he was naked now, sitting on a bench on Main Street, with everybody able to see his naked, pale, flabby body, his shy little penis, and his open, unprotected soul. God he could use some protective glass. He reached into his pocket for his sunglasses but had left them somewhere. "I hope they said good things, agent Knechtl."

"It's *special* agent. How do you like the Glock?"

"It's legal. It's for self-defense. I was robbed at gunpoint not long ago."

"And at knifepoint just two nights ago."

"I passed the background check for the gun. I've never been convicted of a crime. I had a high D average at college until they kicked me out."

Knechtl took a cell phone off his belt, checked something, put it back. "You had a C-plus going in the media and politics class."

"I loved that class."

"And I saw that almost every book you checked out of the library was about current events, recent trends, our nation."

"I read books because I don't trust the media. There's always more than they're telling us. The truth is always on the back page but TVs don't have pages. I don't like you knowing what books I check out and what my grades are. It doesn't seem American."

Knechtl nodded and uncrossed his legs. He picked up the plastic box and tilted it up and down. "I can assure you it is. You're defensive, Ted. Is there a reason?"

"Because I'm innocent."

"Of what?"

"Everything."

"Then why be defensive?"

"I don't like being followed by you. You're a pit bull of the nanny state. It doesn't matter how nice a guy you are, Max. I didn't do anything wrong. Nothing. Except, well, a few days ago I painted some of the burned trees without triple-washing the sprayer. Then I stripped off the bark when I was trying to get the poison paint off. Killed about thirty trees in less than a day. Talk about making your dad mad."

Knechtl set the container back on the bench. "Why did you go to the 'Inspire' magazine website?"

Ted was suddenly amazed that the DHS could have found out about that digital visit. But just as quickly he realized that he'd read somewhere, or maybe heard on TV, that *every single email, cell call and website visit in America is recorded.* "I researched 'Inspire' because it was on the news. I'd never heard of it. I wanted to see if it really was trying to get people to set wildfires in the United States." He looked across Main Street to the pedestrians walking by and he could feel Knechtl staring at him.

"Did you read the instructions on how make a fire-bomb with a timer?"

"I'm not interested in things like that."

"But you saw them, the instructions?"

"Because they were part of the site."

"The timer on the Fallbrook device was similar to the one described in 'Inspire.'"

"But I went on the 'Inspire' website after the fire, not before." Ted turned and faced Knechtl, saw the strange

231

neutrality on his face, like when the special agent had put his hand on his firearm.

"I'm not accusing you, Ted."

"Sounds like you are."

"I'm trying to let you help me. Domestic terrorism is our number-one threat. Tell me about Ibrahim Sadal down at the GasPro Station."

"Ibrahim? I don't know him."

"You've spoken to him many times, Ted. And yes, he's spoken to me about you."

"He's a good gas station manager. He always fixes the carwash when it breaks, and the window-washing water is always clean and he never runs out of paper towels. He's always a few pennies a gallon higher than the Arco across the street, but I think his station is better."

"He came to this country from a violent Muslim nation. His family has ties to militant mullahs."

"I thought Saddam killed them all."

"Maybe we should have let him."

Ted picked up the sandwich box and lifted off the plastic lid and gently spilled the big spider onto his lap. She methodically started creeping up his aloha shirt.

"Aren't they poisonous?" asked Knechtl.

"Mildly. Their fangs are big but they're not interested in biting people. They just want to be left alone. If I grabbed her now, she'd bite me. Or if I badgered her into it. Just like if you badger people too much, they'll bite you, too."

"Have you and Ibrahim Sadal talked politics?"

"Why would we do that?"

"Has he made anti-American remarks?"

"Not that I ever heard."

"What's your gut tell you? We know for a fact he's a practicing Muslim. He keeps the Koran behind the counter at the station. I've seen him reading it when business is slow. Would Ibrahim set that fire?"

Ted gingerly scooped the tarantula off his shoulder. He opened his hands and let her walk from palm to palm, over and over again, while he thought. Her feet felt dainty but purposeful on his skin. He liked the way her first and third legs on one side rose in unison with the second and fourth of the other. Like she was compensating for sore feet. He set her on his lap again.

"Tell me about Cade Magnus, Ted. Do you find it interesting that the fire broke out exactly seven days after he moved back here to Fallbrook?"

"Not really. I don't think he set it."

"Why not?"

"He isn't sneaky."

"Interesting observation. Have you talked to Cade about the fire?"

The tarantula had summited Ted's shoulder again, and again he lifted her off. "No."

Knechtl steadied Ted's arm for a better view of the tarantula. His grip was surprisingly strong. "Is she warm or cool?"

"Slightly warm. Sun."

"What are those two little things sticking up under the rump?"

"Those are spinnerets, Max. They dispense silk."

"Do tarantulas spin webs?"

"No way. They line their tunnels with silk. Then they decorate the tunnels with whatever they find. I found a tiny plastic soldier in a tunnel once. A prone rifleman."

"What do you talk about at Pride Auto Repair when you shoot pool with Cade and Trevor and the women?"

"Why don't you just hide a bug in the place?"

"Expensive and time-consuming. I don't think Cade Magnus set the fire either. But I do like to keep tuned to what

233

he's up to. I'd appreciate you passing along anything that strikes you as unusual. Domestic terrorists are our number one threat."

"You said that twice."

"It can't be said too many times."

Once again the spider had climbed Ted's shoulder. She now seemed to be considering a climb up his neck, her two foremost legs raised as if to take the first steps. Ted angled his head and looked down and saw the eight stacked eyes looking up at him. "Are you good enough with that gun to shoot a tarantula off my shoulder?"

"Piece of cake. Nice talking. I'll be in touch." Knechtl headed down the sidewalk.

Ted slid his hand under the spider and tilted her back into the box. "I'd never let him do that."

He stood at the Pride Auto Repair counter and watched Cade barge through the windowed double doors. Cade flung open the counter walk-through and pulled Ted outside by one of his ears. Ted yelped and tried to duck away but was forced to stoop and crab along to the front door or have his ear torn off, and to keep the spider from getting slammed around. Once they were outside Cade let go of his ear and pushed Ted to the ground. "Don't come back here until you can account for yourself."

"What did I do?"

"I don't want your brother here. I don't want the DHS or FBI here. I don't want *you* here. You're not worth it."

"Account how, Cade?"

Cade looked like he was about to say something, then he slammed the door. Ted looked up at the neon sign of the blue Model T doing the wheelie, throwing the red flames. The sign was turned off but the sunlight played through the tubes and brought the colors to life. Ted gathered himself and stood. His knife wounds throbbed and he wondered if they were leaking. He checked the spider in the box and she looked hunched and afraid. He set the box on the seat of his truck and put a ball cap over it to give her some shade and peace. Standing by the open truck door he lifted his shirt and saw the pink discharge soaking through the dressings.

He drove out to Lucinda's condo on the golf course and parked well away from her unit but with a good view of it. He looked at the security screen door and the curtained windows, and he wondered where her potted plants and flowers had gone. He could feel her consuming pain from here, he thought, and he wondered again what was gnawing away at Lucinda's soul.

After an uneventful half hour he drove out to the stables on east Mission in hope of spotting Dora. He cruised through the parking lot, looking down on the riding arenas and he saw equestrians and their mounts but Dora was not among them. He went back downtown and walked past Gulliver's Travels and waved at Mary at her desk but didn't stop. He ate lunch at the Irish pub and overtipped the friendly waitress. He got his hair trimmed at California Cuts and overtipped the stylist, too. At the salon desk he saw Cruzela Storm concert tickets on sale. He read the flyer and pursed his lips: Fallbrook clearly didn't need lighted crosswalks, but Cruzela Storm made crazy good music. The tickets were modestly priced at $30. He felt his brain battling his heart and his heart won out. He bought two. He drove out to Bonsall and saw a movie about a super-hero who gets the girl, then drove back to Fallbrook to hit the GasPro for a fill up and a wash.

It was nearly five now, and the traffic was heavy leaving Pendleton and Mission was buzzing with cars. He pulled into the gas station and saw Ibrahim Sadal out re-stocking the paper towels in one of the service islands. Ibrahim was a big man and he did his work quickly and efficiently, and he had to, what with half a dozen cars taking on fuel and customers heading inside to pay and buy snacks and drinks and smokes. Evelyn's rejection had made Ted angry. Knechtl's interrogation had left him dazed. Cade's dismissal had re-ignited his anger but now all he felt was betrayed. By everyone. His feet hurt.

He pulled up to pump two, got out and waved. Ibrahim recognized him and waved too, then hustled back into the mini-mart. Ted got the gas going and leaned against his truck. The line at the car wash was three cars now, which was quite a wait. He saw Ibrahim run from the store into the supply room of the car wash, come out with a new window washer, charge over and hand it to the man at pump seven. Then he sprinted back inside the mini-mart. The door to the supply room had banged when Ibrahim shut it but now Ted watched it slowly swing open. He saw a pail on wheels and a jumbo flat of paper towels and a bucket of what looked like new window washers. Someone could walk right off with those, he thought. When the nozzle clanked off Ted slapped it back in place and collected his receipt for the wash.

28

Monday morning Patrick stood on the front porch of Iris's wounded bungalow. She was one day gone but he knocked anyway. She had not returned his calls. But he had seen where she hid her extra house key and now he guiltily fished it from under a flower pot and let himself in. He closed the door behind him feeling like a stalker.

Inside, the casualties were worse than he'd thought, though he wasn't surprised that five jarheads and four women could cause this much destruction in a few short minutes. The dining room was the worst, especially the once-beautiful China cabinet that now stood upright again, but with its glass gone and shelves dashed loose and the frame badly cracked. Its shattered treasures had been swept into a hillock in the middle of the gouged and lacerated hardwood floor. The women, with gallows humor, had set a decorative stainless steel crucifix atop the mound. The dining room walls were scraped and dinged. The dining room chair Patrick had used on Grier lay on its side, two back rails broken clean in half.

He heard the tapping on the front door. When he opened it Salimony and Messina and another man trailed in with the stealthy lightness of men on patrol. They followed him into the dining room. Salimony looked at Patrick solemnly, then touched the pile of ceramic and crystal shards with the toe of his running shoe. "Wow."

Messina, stitches above his eye and mouth, stared

swollen-lipped at the aerial photograph of Iris's family's farm, which looked as if it had come through a bombing, the glass radiating fissures from a ragged central hole, the photo torn, the frame propped against the wall.

"Can you fix the cabinet?" asked Patrick.

Pfc. Albert Taibo, an alleged master woodworker from Los Mochis, Mexico, and medic to Patrick's 3/5 platoon, touched the splintered frame of the cabinet with his fingertip. He walked around the cabinet, twice. Albert was a stocky blue-eyed blond who looked more Irish than Mexican. "How long would I have?" he asked.

"Five days," said Patrick. "It all has to be done before she gets back on Saturday. Everything."

"Whew," said Taibo. "She'll be able to tell the cabinet's been worked on."

"How will it look?"

"It will look good. But Patrick, this is going to cost some money. Just the materials will run you a grand. If I charged my usual that would be another thousand but I'll do it for free."

"In five days."

"That's only if I can get the bird's eye maple and good oak. Which means I should get to the builders' supply like, right now."

"You need to fix the floor too," said Patrick. "All these scrapes and cuts. It has to look like it did before. And also that chair I broke on Grier's head."

"You gotta hire floor and furniture guys to do that, Pat. I can't work that fast. And, sorry, but I'll need the materials money up front. I've got almost nothing."

Patrick pulled the wad of tip money from his pocket and handed it to Taibo. "That's five hundred fifty-four bucks. Buy what you need to get started. I'll have the rest by the end of the day."

238

"Gonna rob a bank?" asked Messina. He took out his wallet and gave Taibo a twenty.

"Maybe just sell his truck," said Salimony, handing Patrick all twelve dollars from his wallet.

Patrick got the Fallbrook phone book from the kitchen counter and took it outside. The back yard looked idyllic compared to inside, nothing smashed or broken, the picnic benches still arranged for the six-across sunset photo taken by Natalie. In his memory Patrick returned to that wonderful sun-lit moment just a few hours ago, and to Iris, and his heart sank with the weight of what he'd done. The sunlight was far different, now the sky had a flinty look to it, the kind of distant icy whiteness that his father had told him meant a storm.

He called the glass store and the art framers and the flooring people and painters, and set up times for them to come out, promising cash for priority scheduling. He called and got a price on a comparable big-screen TV at a big box store in Oceanside: another $589 plus $179 for the DVD player. Back inside he wrote down a list of broken things, guessing that some would be pricey to replace and some impossible. Next he called Kevin Pangborn down in La Jolla and explained his situation.

At noon he was traveling south on Interstate 15, bound for La Jolla, with *Fatta the Lan'* trailered securely behind his truck. He looked back at her in the rearview. The way she bounced along jauntily, as if she were heading out to the water, made him angry at himself. How did he get so fucking dumb? Then he was just sad.

The matching Pangborn boys clambered screaming over the boat while the father, young and pot-bellied, strolled around her twice, looking for damage. "I can't go the full eleven. I can only give you five."

Patrick's heart fell down and out of him and landed half

239

a mile away in the cold Pacific. "Five thousand dollars? You made me a fair deal at eleven. Now I'm offering the same fair deal back to you."

"But I can't take her."

"Why can't you take her?"

"It would be against my principles as a man, and my training in finance. I no longer want the boat. But I'll give you five thousand dollars for it."

"I need the eleven thousand, right now."

"I understand that."

Patrick weighed the satisfaction of kicking Pangborn's flabby ass against his own responsibility to Iris. At the moment, the asskicking was winning out. Pangborn gave him an uneasy look. The boys tried to push one another off the captain's chair and claim ownership of the wheel. Pangborn snapped at them and they stopped fighting and focused their sullen stares on Patrick. "I expect you to pay what I paid you for the same boat."

"What lesson are my boys going learn from that?"

"How to do the right thing."

"They'll see me as weak."

"Get back Fatta the Lan', Dad!"

"Yeah, Dad . . . we want our boat!"

Patrick turned his back on the boys and the craft and looked down on the pink mansions and the heaving Pacific. He tried to think of anything but his anger. He thought of Iris far away. He thought of Zane panting in the shade of the Hesco blocks, eagerly awaiting his next patrol. He saw that the La Jolla sky was an unusual gray down low, graduating higher up to storm-white. Good distractions all, but he still thought the only answer here was to beat Pangborn.

"I have to be frugal and firm," said Pangborn. "In the church I'm known for my generosity."

"I need the money for something very important."

240

"I'm sure you do. Okay. Six thousand. Best and final."

"You're a hypocrite and a coward, Mr. Pangborn."

The boys looked at their father. "I'll go write the check. My bank is down there in town."

Patrick got back to Iris's house that afternoon with a new flat screen and DVR and all the right cables; dishes and place settings for ten that looked somewhat like the broken ones; good quality wine glasses, tumblers and margarita glasses; three crystal vases that, based on the shards Patrick showed to a suspicious clerk, resembled the causalities; two table-cloths not unlike the one drenched by wine and tequila. He had also bought things that were not replacements but he thought Iris might like: a costly hallway runner; a stone vase made in Italy; an electric massage pad with "shiatsu" rollers. Thirty-three hundred and change, gone just like that.

While Salimony and Messina brought the boxes in and started setting up the TV and DVR, Patrick paid the painter half of his twelve-hundred dollars up front. Work would start tomorrow. Patrick also paid the glass-and-mirror man two hundred against his estimate of four hundred to replace the mirror glass and repair the frame – work to be completed no later than Thursday. The flooring guy called to say he couldn't get there today as promised but would be there first thing Tuesday.

Out on Industrial Way he arranged with a furniture maker to repair the oak chair for an estimated two hundred dollars, work guaranteed by Friday. On Main, the art framer said he could build a new frame for the aerial farm photo – two hundred fifty dollars was a cash-only price – but the picture itself was beyond his skills to repair. He suggested a print-maker in town who might be able to do something with it.

The printmaker had a gallery that sold original California watercolors and poster-like copies of them. The walls were hung with them and good light streamed through the windows and seemed to project the paintings onto the white walls. Patrick's eyes wandered to the paintings as the young man examined the farm photo. He told Patrick he could glue the clean cuts from the back but the punctures had destroyed some paper, and this would require small patches and hand-painting. The repaired photograph would still be bent and the reconstruction work would be visible, but he could make a computer-generated *giclee* that would be nearly perfect. He would personally see to the color corrections. Patrick could have the repaired original and the swanky new copy of it all ready by the end of the workday tomorrow. Patrick gave him one-hundred fifty dollars, half of the job. "Is that one for sale?"

"The horses? That's 'Free Spirits' by Millard Sheets. Steals your eye, doesn't it? It's a lithograph, which makes it afford-able and collectible at the same time. Signed and numbered by the artist."

"How much?"

"It's eight hundred dollars." Patrick attempted an unim-pressed nod. "We can change the frame if you'd like – there's no charge for that."

Patrick walked over for a closer look. There were two horses, one light and one dark, both graceful and spirited. They were running or playing. There was power in them, and a spark of the wild. The animals were engaged with each other and paid not Patrick nor anyone else one bit of atten-tion. They were not meant to be perfectly realistic, which took some getting used to. But the horses said something to him – the dark and the light. He wondered if this was an artist's trick. They reminded him of some of the other works of art in Iris's home. But did he truly like the horses or mainly think Iris would like them? Well, mainly he wanted Iris to like them. Was this a bad thing?

"Just back from overseas?"

242

"Afghanistan."

"We have a military discount of twenty percent. So it would be six hundred and forty dollars. And I'll pay your tax."

"Thank you. I'll take it."

"If you don't like it after a few weeks, bring it back and I'll refund your money."

"She'll like it."

"A gift?" The young man shook his head and smiled slightly. "She'll *love* it."

It was almost dark by the time Patrick and his two friends got the electronics working, the wall dents patched and the debris taken to the dump. Taibo had set up his table saw and sanders in the garage and some of the newly cut shelves and splines were already stained and drying. Patrick smelled the varnish and thought they just might pull this off.

He marched into Domino's Pizza just in time for his six o'clock shift. He wolfed a small pizza while attaching the Domino's light to the top of his truck, then donned the blue-red-and black uniform shirt.

"You look tired," said Simone. She handed him a large can of iced-tea from the cooler. "We have three deliveries ready to go when you are."

By nine he was back at Iris's with two large left-over pizzas and twenty-one skinny Monday dollars in tips. Salimony was asleep on the living room floor, the still-bagged Sunday paper for a pillow. Messina was almost done putting away the new dishes and cookware. Taibo still labored in the garage, the cabinet frame glued, doweled, clamped and drying. *Banda* played softly from his boom box.

Patrick was back before sunrise to move furniture out of the way for the flooring specialists. No sooner was this finished than the man called to say he wouldn't be able to get to Patrick's floor until mid next week.

"It has to be done before Saturday."

"Not by me it doesn't. Get someone else," he said, and hung up. Patrick left messages at three other places but two hours later not one had called back.

When Salimony and Messina showed up Patrick drove fast to Joe's Hardware, where he chose the most expensive wood finish in stock, a rich dark color like Iris's, marked "Walnut." He bought liquid stripper, a heavy belt sander and five grades of paper, wire brushes, big sponges, paint trays, brushes, paint thinner and a jumbo package of red shop rags. Another two-hundred and sixty bucks flew from his pocket, leaving less than eight hundred dollars from *Fatta the 'Lan.*

By eight-fifteen he was sanding off the old finish in the living room, hoping to finish by the time the painting crew got done with the dining room. The painting boss morosely examined the drywall patches and added another hundred to the job to finish them off professionally, unless Patrick preferred for them to show. Taibo's table saw screamed from the garage. Salimony and Messina attacked the living room floor with coarse sandpaper. Patrick leaned into the hot screaming belt sander, still believing they could pull this off. They were United States Marines.

By Thursday the walls and foot rails had been painted, the chair had been returned, the mirror rebuilt, the China cabinet was ready for its glass, the aerial Cash farm *giclee* was hanging in its new frame, and "Free Spirits" had a place in the newly beautified dining room. The kitchen cabinets brimmed with new dishes, glasses and goblets. The Italian vase looked good in the living room.

But the refinished hardwood floors were not right. The three men stood in the foyer studying the still-tacky floor. Very clear in Patrick's memory was the burnished warmth that had once come from the wood – like it had candles

244

underneath. But now the wood was brown and flat and invariable. "Looks like we drowned it in cheap paint," said Patrick.

Messina looked down on it, nodding. "Or in shit."

"And look where it meets the hallway," said Salimony. "You can really see the difference."

"Maybe it will look better when it dries," said Patrick.

"Yeah, like dry shit," said Messina.

Taibo came to the French doors of the patio, open for ventilation, and looked in. "You need to match the old finish, you idiots," he called across to them. "The old finish had more red in it. So Patrick, go back to Joe's and buy red mahogany stain, and cherry wood stain too. And get more of the walnut, and ten gallons of stripper and some more trays. I'll help you get the color right."

"That sucks," said Messina. "Just these two rooms took two whole days."

Patrick looked at his watch. "She said she's getting in at seventeen hundred Saturday."

"Back when she was still talking to you," said Messina.

Patrick gave him a hard look. "We've got twenty-four hours to get this off, mix up the right color, and slap it on."

"She won't ever say another word to you if we don't get these floors right again," said Messina. "And that Natalie, isn't she sweet as a honey sandwich? She probably won't say another word to me, neither. So, let's get some, Dark Horses."

Twenty-three hours later, at five o'clock Friday, the four Marines stood in the foyer watching the wood dry. They were half-stoned from breathing fumes close-up for an entire day. Their backs and knees were sore and their hands were stained and scalded by the finish that found its way into the rubber gloves. But Patrick could see the old warmth back in the wood. It was radiant.

245

They sat exhausted and tipsy in the back yard, drinking tequila and beer left over from the party and eating Jack in the Box food that Patrick had fetched. The sky to the north was the brittle white of a storm foretold, but the sunset was a red-and-orange wonder far out beyond Pendleton. They lined up at the wall to watch. "Sangin's sunsets were just as good but here we won't get killed," said Patrick.

"Not by woolies, anyway," said Messina, lighting another cigarette.

"I saw Pendleton for the first time when I was eighteen years old," said Salimony. "It was exactly eight years since I wrote President Bush that letter after nine-eleven. Right to the day – September twelfth. And when I first saw Pendleton, after growing up in Indiana, I thought: hot damn, I want to stay in California and live here when I get out. And now that's what I'm doing. So this is my dream come true. According to this new study California is the most poorly managed and fucked-up state in the whole union. But it seems fine to me. Just look at it."

"You been sniffing too many fumes, Sal," said Messina.

"They don't effect my dream." He passed the big bottle to Taibo, who drank and passed it to Patrick.

"When I drink," said Patrick, "I think of Sangin. And when I think of Sangin I think of you guys, and Boss and Zane and Myers. I think of Zane more than I should. I've got two cool dogs at home but I don't love them the same way as I loved Zane. Once in a while I feel bad for loving a dog more than I loved most of the men. But it never was about love, not even crawling out through fire to tourniquet Prebble's leg. I didn't feel any love for Prebbs about that, but I did it."

"You did a damned good job of it, too," said former medic Taibo. "It saved Prebble's life. Love is what you do, not how you feel about what you do. And you wouldn't have run through fire to save the dog."

246

After a long moment during which the sunset lost small gradients of light, Patrick said: "Before your time, Albert, before our first medic Adams went down, we were on a patrol and Zane dropped to the ground fifty meters from us. I could see he was onto something. Somebody whispered, oh, the heat's got him. But I knew from the way he was looking at this twisted-up little tree that he was on a bomb. And he wouldn't come off it. Crittendon couldn't yell after him and call every skinny from miles around right to us. Then a sniper opened up. At Zane, not us. To this day I don't understand why he did that, shoot at the dog, apart from pure meanness. So Crittendon yelled his head off trying to get Zane up but it did no good. The sniper kept missing – probably some village kid making extra money. Like having a paper route. We put the fifty all over him and I went and got Zane myself. God knows how many IEDs I walked over but the fifty kept the sniper down. I got to Zane and picked him up and carried him back. And I stayed away from that tree. When the Apaches came and sent the sniper to paradise, our bomb guys followed my footsteps back to the tree, and what did they find but a goddamned saw-blade IED dug in underneath it. So, actually, yeah, I *did* save the dog."

"So you were like a dog medic," said Salimony. "There ain't nothing wrong with saving a dog."

Patrick took another swig of the golden liquid. "If I could name one thing that the war stole from me that I miss most, it would be loving my own dogs."

"Maybe you'll learn how again," said Salimony. "So, here's to Zane and Myers and Pendejo and Adams and all the others who left it out there. Man or dog." They touched their beer bottles and watched the rump of the sun settle behind the hills.

Patrick and Messina looked in on the newly finished living room floor, found it acceptable, bumped fists. To keep from walking on it they went around the house to the front door. They came in and followed the hallway down, and in the closet of the spare bedroom found blankets and two rolled-up sleeping bags.

They drank and talked late and lay face up to see the stars through the patio lattice. Every word went back to Sangin, and every space between the words. Twice they traipsed around to the garage and turned on the lights to see the Iris Cash's heirloom China cabinet, made newly resplendent by Taibo. Each time, Patrick circled it again and again, hawkishly looking for the tells of rebuilding but he could see none.

Later back on the patio they drank and talked more. "This would be heaven for me, to live in this house in this place," said Salimony. His restless leg bounced up and down beneath his blanket. "I don't mean with Iris, Pat, don't think that. I'm not saying with *her*. I'm just saying this is where I'd like to start over."

"Patrick's saying with *her*, don't worry about that," said Messina. "And I get Natalie, so cross her off your list too, Sal."

"She's twice as tall as you," said Salimony.

"You wanna fucking fight?"

"No. I'm in a good mood."

"If Iris ever talks to me again it's thanks to you guys," said Patrick.

"But we're the ones who broke her place all up in the first place," said Salimony.

Patrick thought about that for a long moment. "Naw. It was those dumbass jarheads from Pendleton." They laughed. "Men? I love you all but we gotta get past this shit. Past Sangin. Past all of it. Into the future."

"I'm going to end up some place just like this."

"I'm going to end up some place like Natalie."

"I'm getting a job with county paramedics," said Taibo. "Soon as I get my certs."

248

"How many blown up men you treat in Sangin?" asked Patrick. "Dodging IEDs and getting shot at?"

"Can't even count."

"And that isn't good enough for the county?"

"Nope."

It was cold for them on the concrete in their clothes and blankets and lightweight sleeping bags, but not as cold as Sangin, not even close. Patrick dreamed of a gleaming white ocean liner leaving the dock, honking and steaming like in the movies, with Iris and Ted and everyone in his platoon, living and dead, waving goodbye to him. So he just climbed into *Fatta the Lan'* and keyed the engine alive to catch up with them but real life barged into his dream and reminded him that the boat was no longer his. *Fatta the Lan'* vanished and Patrick tread the cold water and the ocean liner kept on going.

He woke with first light, stood and kicked Salimony awake. Minutes later he and his friends were standing side-by-side, looking through the open French doors and into Iris's living room. Patrick reached in and hit the lights. Even in the man-made incandescence, Iris's hardwood floors were magnificent. Patrick let his gaze wander the rich planks, saw the warm illumination that came from within. He laughed quietly: mission accomplished. Salimony, Messina and Taibo laughed too.

Later in stocking feet they re-installed the China cabinet in the dining room. To Patrick's eye it looked perfect. Brushing a fingertip over the bird's eye maple and nodding, even Taibo seemed to approve his own work. They picked up after themselves then shuffled – shoes and plastic trash bags in hand – across the dining room to the living room to the foyer and out.

249

29

By late morning Patrick and the rest of the Norris clan were in the grove filling sandbags. The special NOAA forecast was calling for a two-part storm – a large Alaskan front heading down from the northwest, aimed to collide with an unusually strong late-season hurricane coming up from Baja. The meeting point looked to be offshore San Diego. Too early to tell, said the TV forecasters, but it could be substantial. They promised to track this thing by the hour.

Patrick was always amused how San Diego citizens treated rain as an insult, while the farmers treated it as a birthright. But the forecasts aside, Archie had had a dream two nights ago about a deluge hitting his groves and sweeping them all the way down the San Luis Rey River valley to the sea. Thus, preventive sand-bagging and lots of it.

The morning was damp and the reeking ash and earth clotted their boots and weighed them down. Patrick labored and brooded about Iris and what he had done and failed to do. He willed his phone to ring but it did not. The dogs dug up a gopher hole, dirt and ash and straw flying between their back legs, faces caked with dirt.

"Sorry," said Ted, dropping his shovel into the bed of his truck. "I can't work anymore. The stabs."

"I told you to have them checked again," said his father.

"Hurts."

"Of course it does, son. You don't have to be out here right now."

"Rest the wounds, Ted," said Caroline. "Maybe you'll feel better tomorrow."

"Yeah, almost for sure, Mom. I'm sorry I can't do more work." Ted slowly rounded his truck and climbed in. He looked forlorn. Patrick watched the truck roll over the rise and disappear.

Caroline came over for more sandbags. "I've been worried about him," she said.

"Let's stand by him," said Patrick.

"We always have," said Archie.

"He needs us," said Caroline.

By afternoon they had begun building sandbag walls along the contours of the slopes. Next they would fortify the downhill roadsides, and finally, build up both sides of the gorge that drained the groves when enough rain fell. It was backbreaking work, worse than stacking the Hesco blocks for security at Inkerman. The blocks over which the sniper still hit Pendejo, Patrick thought. He saw that it would take at least two more days to pile the sandbags high enough to do real good.

He had trouble paying full attention. He figured Iris was getting into San Diego just about now. He tried to put himself in her shoes and guess how she'd feel when she walked into her house. Dazzled by the improvement, or even more pissed off at what he'd done?

He looked up to see Lew Boardman on a distant hill, watching them. Boardman held his palms up and out, wondering what all their labor could be about. Patrick slung the bags with a vengeance. The hardest part was dropping forty pound bags accurately enough to not have to stoop and wrestle them around by hand. His father was strong and apparently tireless and strong in his faith that this

251

much-needed rain would come. Archie kept looking skeptically north and south, as if to daring it not to.

Hours later darkness closed in. On the drive home Patrick looked out at the dark skeletons of the trees but in his mind's eye he pictured Iris stepping into her refurbished home, her face in a wondrous smile that told him everything he needed to know. The image was very much like the memory of her face that he'd carried overseas, but now it was more detailed and more real, and far more valuable. But, what if she didn't like what she found at home? What if she had been traumatized by his violence? What if she'd experienced violence before, making his unforgettable and unforgivable? Certainly she had been humiliated in front of her friends. What if she was ashamed of him and of her own misjudgment of him? What if she just disliked the floor? Or "Free Spirits?" What if Taibo's China cabinet wasn't masterful in her eyes at all? And the *giclee* of the Kenton farm? Why should she treasure something that had come out of a copier? How could she possibly be drawn to an electric shiatsu massage pad? Why did he feel like a fool?

Patrick set out for the bunkhouse with the dogs panting alongside him. Ted was at his usual place in the big darkened space, at the picnic table, face thrust into the computer monitor. He didn't turn when Patrick came in but he dropped on hand to Jack's thick Labrador head when the dog came up.
"You okay, Ted?"

Ted finally swiveled around and looked at Patrick. "My feet are killing me, and so are my back, my hands and my knife holes. I checked them today and they weren't leaking. But they're still swelled up."

"Well, you tried to help. You showed good courage and conviction, Ted."

"You sound like Dad now except that you might mean it. He doesn't ever mean it."

252

"I meant what I said."

Yellow Spike, heavier and a bully, barreled in between Jack and Ted, trying to hog the affection. Ted pet each dog's head. Patrick went to the terrariums and watched the critters watch him. He remembered when they were boys how flustered Ted would get when some of his animals got away. It seemed to happen a lot, mostly to the snakes and scorpions. Only later did Caroline confess to carrying the cages outside when the boys were at school, and releasing the animals that scared her, shooing them into the groves with a broom. Ted had thrown a memorable tantrum at that. Now a small frog eyed Patrick then sprung to the opposite glass wall and stuck perfectly, still eyeing him.

"Have you been back to Pride Auto Repair?"

"No, sir, Pat. I told you I wouldn't."

"Have you posted any more online cartoons or insults to Evelyn Anders?"

"No! But I actually apologized to her a couple of days ago. Face to face."

"Oh, no, Ted."

"No worries. It went really good. We're good. Everything's good. Except . . . I need to ask you a question."

Patrick saw the dark hard cast of Ted's face, a haunted look that had visited him, off and on, ever since Patrick could remember.

Ted climbed off the bench and stood. Patrick came over and saw the game now paused on the monitor – a first-person shooter in what looked like Afghanistan. The shooter brandished an M-240, as had Patrick in real life. "Uh, Pat, I saw you drive off with *Fatta the Lan'*. Now you're back and she's still gone. What happened to her? Did you take her out without me?"

"I sold her to pay off some debts."

"*Sold her? Debts?*"

"Just stupid stuff I did."

"But you don't do stupid things."

"I manage my share."

Ted looked at his brother. *"Fatta the Lan'?* We were going to sail out for the territory. We were going to fish and make money and get big tips from the clients. And go drinking back on the waterfront. And eat too. Then work our way down to Mexico where the water's always warm and there's lots of fish, and the women are friendly and beautiful. And then back up the California coast until it got too cold. *Remember?"*

Patrick considered his brother's troubled face brushed by the monitor lights. Tears welled in Ted's eyes but didn't spill over. "I'll get another boat, Ted. I've still got five hundred bucks left."

"But, Pat . . . what's five hundred going to get us?"

"I'll need to make more. We'll get something decent. And I still have to take the captain's test and log more hours, and do the CPR course and fill out all the state forms and get the insurance. There's tons of paperwork. And a website. It's all time-consuming. And expensive, if you're a little guy."

Ted shrugged and looked back at the game for a moment. "Alright. I can do something important without you, Pat. You're not my keeper. Mostly I just feel bad for you losing your boat."

"I'm going to get another boat, Ted. We'll fish. You can help me guide now and then."

"Not every time though, because sometimes you'll have three anglers and the boat'll be too full. Right?"

"That's right."

"I'll be a part-time first mate."

"Yes, you will."

Ted sighed and paused the game. "Okay. That's something to look forward to. Now, I'm going to go soak my feet in the bathtub. Those sandbags are the heaviest things on Earth.

254

Maybe that's because they're filled with earth. I'll get over you selling the boat, Pat."

Patrick was early for his Domino's shift but the evening was already busy. He helped Firooz and Simone answer the phone and take internet orders and make pizza. Patrick checked his phone again – no call or text – and again felt the tug of his heart.

"Did you hear?" Simone asked. Patrick looked up from the bag of frozen Buffalo wings he was pouring onto the baking tray. "Police arrested the manager of the GasPro for setting the fire. I saw the arrest. I was getting gas and suddenly they were bringing him out of the store. He had his uniform on and he was handcuffed."

"The Iranian?" said Patrick, thinking: the skinny? He'd seen the man at the GasPro station since before he'd enlisted. It seemed like every time Patrick filled up, the big man was working. He was a big solid guy who looked you in the eye.

"There were six men. I notice things when I'm afraid. These men wore armor and helmets. They carried machine guns. Their clothing had the big letters – DHS, HSI, DEA, ATF and FBI. They brought him from the store and put him in a white van. So, when I came back here I turned on TV and listened to the radio and got on the Internet. There was nothing. Like it didn't happen. Just like in Iran. I called the Fallbrook sheriffs but they would not say anything about an arrest. Then, one hour ago, the radio said that the arsonist had been arrested. Ibrahim, the gas station manager – they say he set the fire. Look!"

Channel 10 came on and there he was, Ibrahim Sadal, looking wild-eyed and angry. Next came video of Sadal's arrest, courtesy of the Department of Justice. Six heavily armed federal agents swiftly moved him out of the mini-mart and into the van. He looked down to avoid the camera.

"From Baghdad," said Firooz. "He was an oil engineer under Saddam then he escaped to America. This is what he claimed. It is a terrible thing that he set the fire."

"But what if he did not?" asked Simone.

"Then this thing is terrible, too," said Firooz.

"In Iran I saw arrests like this," said Simone. "And I never saw the arrested person again. And there was never an explanation or news of it. Only rumors."

"Only rumors." Firooz nodded.

Patrick carried the two four-packs of pizzas to his truck and set the red insulated packs on the passenger seat. Firooz followed with two more and a rectangular carrier for side orders. Simone lugged the soft-sided cooler of drinks. She set them in the truck and slammed the door and Patrick flinched but he saw they did not notice. He attached the Domino's sign and hopped in.

His tips on ninety-six dollars' worth of food amounted to eight dollars and change. After the last delivery he argued with himself out loud, while unerringly tracing his path back downtown and straight for Iris's street. When he was close he pulled over and removed the Domino's sign from the roof of his truck. He drove past and saw lights on inside. The garage door was closed. Down the street he u-turned and drove by again, then gunned his truck back to work. In the Domino's parking lot he finally caved in and called her but she didn't pick up. He left a brief message: welcome home, hope it went well, I missed you, you don't have to keep any of that stuff if you don't want. He punched off and headed back into the pizza place with Taibo's words ringing in his mind: love is what you do.

30

Ted drove the taxi to Open Sights on his lunch hour Tuesday and shot up fifty rounds of forty-caliber wadcutters. Kerry was patient and encouraging even though Ted was erratic. He had trouble shooting with both eyes open, which Kerry told him was the foundation of sound marksmanship. Ted continued to yank rather than squeeze.

Blasting away from twenty feet at a zombie Bin-Laden target, Ted felt strong emotions, and they changed almost as quickly as he pulled the trigger – exuberance, anger, satisfaction, shame – in no logical order. A lot of the anger was at Patrick for selling *Fatta the Lan'* without telling him. It seemed like a sneaky thing to do. What was he going to do with the money, buy Iris Cash an engagement ring? If he added Patrick's betrayal to those of Evelyn and Cade, and what did he have left? He wished he'd brought an Evelyn Anders re-election poster to use as a target. Wouldn't *that* bring all those government police, deputies, agents, special agents, marshals, jailers and torturers running! Kerry ordered him not to quick-draw with a loaded gun unless he wanted a big hole in his foot.

"They're pretty big targets," said Ted, looking down at them and wiping the sweat from his brow.

Driving home, gun and leftover ammo locked in the taxi trunk, Ted had a sudden premonition that another terrible thing was about to happen to him. But two minutes later,

Cleo called from Fallbrook to say that his regular fare, Lucinda Smith, needed to be picked up at home in half an hour. She had asked for him *again!*

Ted swung into the Rite Aid and bought their least expensive bottle of men's aftershave and breath mints. Outside he touched just a dab of the weirdly blue-green liquid to his Adam's apple before locking the cologne in the trunk beside the Glock. Crunching the breath mint, he studied himself closely in the rearview then drove east on Highway Seventy-Six for Fallbrook.

Lucinda came down stairs with her usual reusable grocery bag and air of gloom. She was wearing nicer clothes than she had worn before, and fashionable boots. She had a small embroidered Chinese satchel over one shoulder. He thought she looked lovely. She told him Major Market and Rosa's restaurant after that. The fare clock registered one point six miles before Ted could no longer be quiet. "And how are you today?"

"Good. What's that smell?"

"Probably ash from the fire. Are you going to the Cruzela Storm concert on Sunday?"

"No. It smells like someone shaved in here."

"That's better than ashes, isn't it? I have two tickets to Cruzela. The show is to raise money for the lighted crosswalks Fallbrook doesn't need. Would you like to go with me? I'll pick you up, do all the driving."

There was another long silence. "How do you know we don't need them?"

"Just by using my own two eyes."

Another long moment passed and in the rearview Ted saw her looking out the side window. She wore her sunglasses as always. He had never seen her eyes except that one time when she cleaned her glasses in the back of his cab. "No. I can't go to the show. But thank you."

"Why not?"

"I'm busy."

"I thought you'd say no. Though I'd really like to know what you're so busy doing, that you can't see Cruzela Storm. She's good. Do you have a job? Wait, that's none of my business so I'm not going to ask. I take that back. I unsay it. I'll be quiet now. I promise. It isn't that hard if I concentrate. Like driving a car. More or less. Well, to be honest, it is hard, Lucinda. Do you ever think other people might have problems too?"

"I don't have the capacity to care about them. And I hate that in me. I wasn't always this way."

He dropped her off in front of the market and watched her walk in, then parked in the shade and turned on the news. The San Diego PBS station had a story about the arrest of Ibrahim Sadal in Fallbrook. Federal charges were being readied. According to Department of Homeland Security Investigations Special Agent Max Knechtl, they had recovered from Sadal's place of employment a timer, batteries and accelerant "similar" to those recovered from the flashpoint of Fallbrook's devastating Rice Canyon Fire. Also found were print copies of an Islamic jihadist publication called "Inspire," two of which contained explicit instructions for building firebombs and urged "native jihadists" to deploy them in hot, dry, windy weather. Knechtl said that Sadal had been granted political asylum fifteen years ago, after fleeing Saddam Hussein's regime, and there were obvious concerns that he might be part of a larger sleeper cell operating in the U.S. Ted thought of Sadal working away at the gas station, right in front of everybody, for years. It made him even angrier to realize that the government could make Ted take a nystagmus test in broad daylight in front of his friends and neighbors, and let the local gangsters jack him, but couldn't secure the borders.

Lucinda came out with her bag lightly laden. She climbed

259

into the back seat and Ted shut the door. This door-opening was a new courtesy she was allowing him. At Rosa's she came out with two plastic bags, and again Ted got the door for her.

"Would you drive me around the town again like you did before? Along holy hill with all the churches?"

"I'll drive you anywhere you want."

Ted swung onto Main then Mission and looped around past Los Jilgueros nature preserve, turned left at Fallbrook High School and followed Stagecoach. On holy hill he noted the new Baptist Church aphorism: "Trespassers Will Be Baptized" and found it amusing. He wondered why Lucinda Smith always wanted to take the long away around.

"Let's go back and eat these lunches at Jilgueros," she said. *"Really?"*

"I like the native plants. Please turn around before I change my mind."

The nature preserve sat between downtown and the high school. There were trails and two big ponds and all of it was planted to California natives. They parked in the lot and walked in past enormous sycamores and stout oaks. Rounding a curve the trees gave way to more open land – grasses and white sage and big stands matilija poppies. Ted watched two red-shouldered hawks wheel and cry above them. From behind him a hummingbird shot over his shoulder so close that for a second it sounded like a car going past his ear. Then the sound drifted off. Ted lifted some promising fallen bark to see what was under them and uncovered a large potato bug. "They can give you a painful nip."

"It looks shiny and waxed, like a car."

"When you lift things to find creatures, you have to put the things back the same but different. So you don't squash what's under them."

"I had two blue parakeets. A group of parakeets is called a chatter."

"Bats don't make good pets."

"They're noisy creatures. There's a bench on that hilltop. Let's eat there."

"The bats are generally quiet and mostly eat bugs."

"I miss them, the parakeets."

They climbed the hillock and sat. The day was muggy and warm, strange for October, and he felt the drop in pressure that presaged a storm. The latest from the weather people had rain beginning Sunday, and possibly lasting five straight days. Ted had heard one San Diego TV weather caster call it Stormageddon and another Stormocalypse. The low pressure made it feel as if his body cells were less tightly held together. Like his brain had more freedom, not that this was necessarily good.

"Stormageddonocalypse-oramathon is on the way," said Ted.

"So they say."

They sat at opposite ends of the same bench, facing town. Ted could see part of Main, Evelyn Anders' office building, the spire of the little church up on Fig and the American flag over the post office. Lucinda had a light, almost inviting scent that ran contrary to her general joylessness. Ted let the warm breeze bring it to him. He hadn't spoken in a few minutes and he wondered if silence was all they could agree on. Silence as communication. That lasted exactly thirty seconds – Ted timed it on his watch – then he suddenly felt like sniffing a big load of pure crank and talking to Lucinda for a week straight. Play some music loud enough to melt his face, and dance to it. Maybe take a deserving person to the next level. Then he could sleep for another week straight. Sleep a lifetime. Instead Ted went to work on the taco. He poured a little green sauce on it.

"I liked what you said last time about finding a place to get away from the darkness," she said. Ted nodded. "I think I know where to find that place."

261

"Where?"

"Not far from here. I think I'll be going there for a while."

"A quest like?"

"Not exactly, no."

"Exactly what then?"

"It will be clear soon enough."

Ted felt her heaviness, her great private freight, trying to take her down. Lucinda was not usual. Mary at Gulliver's Travel was lonely, and horse-lover Dora Newell was scatter-brained, but Lucinda Smith was sad. *Sad.* He half expected to see a dark aura surrounding her but when he glanced at her there was none. "Are you involved in drugs, Lucinda?"

"God, no. But I do like my wine. Used to, anyway."

"You have a bad secret," he said. "That you've never told anyone. And you are thinking of killing yourself."

"I've thought about it a lot."

"Oh, don't do that, Lucinda. That would be a shame."

"No. Just yesterday I decided not to. No." She dropped her fork and napkin into her foam box and snapped the top shut. "I want to thank you for reaching out to me."

"I never touched you!"

"It's a way of saying you – "

"I really want to, though."

"That's out of line, Ted."

"I was afraid so."

"But I still want to thank you for being kind to me. It's meant something to me these last few weeks. My family isn't close and they don't live around here. I haven't made friends here yet. So, just to have this guy not talking too much and being courteous to me and even buying me a TV I don't need, well, it meant something. So thanks, Ted. For everything."

"You mean I get to see you again?"

"No. Not like this."

"I don't get women."

262

"Someday one will get you."

"You get me."

"Yeah. I kind of do."

Ted heaved closer and set a hand over hers. It was a small-boned, chilly hand. He leaned in close. She turned to look at him and all he saw was her sunglasses. He slid them off and set them on the table. Her eyes were brown and bloodshot and he saw the darkness around them. They were beautiful. When he touched his lips to hers they were firm and dry. He smelled her scent and the aftershave and Rosa's green sauce.

"No, Ted."

"Yes?"

"Absolutely no."

"Okay." He pulled back and she slid her sunglasses back on.

"Let's do this thing," she said.

"What thing?"

"Drop me off at the Fallbrook Sheriff Station."

"Why?"

"I'll explain on the way."

"It was a beautiful September day. The skies were clear and it was hot but not too hot. You could feel the fall coming on. The children were back in school and I always like seeing the kids out and about, walking and riding their bikes to school. I like their energy and chaos. I always wanted to have children but it didn't work out. My husband turned out to be a cheater. Divorce. I'm only thirty-five years old so there's plenty of time for it to happen, biologically."

Ted could hear the gravity stealing into her voice.

"I wait tables at the Pala Mesa Resort, where my condo is. I can walk to work and back. It's mostly nights. That day I got up early, even though I'd worked late the night before. I did my workout then drove downtown for a few things. Came back and worked the lunch shift for another waitress who wanted off. It was busy. I got home about three, took a quick nap, then showered and dressed up nicely and had a glass of wine. It was a Paso Robles blend and I really liked it. I felt good about working late the night before, and I'd made solid money at lunch and I had the night off. So I decided to treat myself to dinner downtown. I like Salerno's. I sat at the bar. I don't like sitting alone at restaurant tables, especially here in Fallbrook where it's all married people and families. You know what I'm saying . . ."

Her voice had cracked. Ted looked into the rearview and saw Lucinda wipe her nose with a tissue. He wondered why talking about working and eating dinner had made her so sad. She continued, low and throaty and somehow dazed.

"I had calamari and a couple glasses of their Chianti classico to start. Then a Caesar and the linguini and one more glass of the wine, then that killer roasted chicken in garlic and lemon. I should explain that I have a fast metabolism and I work out a lot, and waiting tables is physical, too. So I *love* to eat and I eat a *ton* and never gain weight. I demolished the chicken and two more glasses of wine then the tiramisu with a very nice cognac. I talked to an airline pilot and his girlfriend. I felt good and sociable and not a bit sleepy. It was about eight. So I swung over to Murphy's for an after dinner drink, nothing fancy, just a glass or two of good California zin. Had a cup of coffee, too, to keep me sharp. Listened to the band. Then I left and drove up Mission toward the post office to make the right on Fallbrook Street. The radio was on and the windows were down and I was having one of those wonderful, out-of-nowhere moments when you're just plain, *happy*. You know? Happy. I was simply happy. And I hit a kid running across the middle of Mission."

"And you'd had two bottles of wine and a cognac."

In the mirror she nodded, clenched the tissue in her

264

fist, and her fist to her mouth while the tears ran down her knuckles. "I know. I *know!* I'd never had that much before. Ever. Or since."

"So you're going to surrender."

"Yes. I am."

"They'll put you in a cage."

"It's the least I can do. George Herrera. George Herrera. George. My car's locked in the garage, dented, and his blood on it. I mean, I wiped it off, but . . ."

"It's hard to see at night. The headlights coming at you. And glaring in your rearview. And all the cars going fast."

She nodded but said nothing.

"I'm sorry," Ted said.

"Not as sorry as George or his family. Or me."

"But letting the government put you in a cage won't help them any."

"It might help my soul. A little."

Ted drove past the substation on Alvarado.

"You passed it," she said.

"I think you should you reconsider."

"I've been considering very hard for three weeks, Ted."

"Everyone has the right to keep and bear secrets."

"None of us has a right to a secret like mine. You will not convince me I'm wrong. Turn around or let me out."

Ted pulled over and into the shade of a magnolia tree. "I have secrets I've never told."

"Then I pity you. Maybe you should come with me. I didn't mean that."

"Some of them aren't so good."

"Any worse than mine?"

"It depends how you count."

"That makes no sense."

"Lucinda, I think we're all better off with you not in a cage."

265

"How on Earth could you believe such a thing?"

They sat for a while in silence. Ted looked at her again and wished there was something he could do. "What about the parakeets?"

"I gave them and the plants away last week. Rent is paid, notice is given, condo is clean. The things in this bag are for you and fare cash is on the seat." She got out and slammed the door and headed back toward the cop house.

He watched her go and wished there was something he could do. He reached back and swept up the shopping bag up with one finger and swung it onto his lap. Inside he found a pack of two extra large orthotic foot pads, and a small toy boat for children ages 4-7. Apparently she had noticed that his feet hurt. So that meant she was at least partially able to get outside herself and see other people's problems. He remembered telling her that he got away from the darkness on his brother's boat. Was the plastic boat an insult or a joke? Was she saying he was child-like?

31

Ted dropped off the car at Friendly Village Taxi, then drove home to the bunkhouse. He lay on his bed and looked at the ceiling and tried to ignore the urges, both benevolent and malicious and all things in between, boiling around upstairs. Dismissed by Evelyn, his formerly beloved. Harassed by Knechtl. Rejected by Cade. Demoted by Patrick. Jilted by Lucinda in favor of a cage. He got up and found the stash that Trevor had given him, and he crushed the rock, loaded the pipe and fired it.

Lung-swell, ear roar, lift of skull. Eee-hawww. He put Cruzela on the player and did an in-place dance. Then he stopped and crossed his arms over his chest and closed his eyes and rotated counterclockwise faster and faster, unscrewing from this shackling world and shooting toward a higher, better one, a human bullet.

Suddenly a great idea came to him. It came as so many others had come, barreling right into his brain from who knew where. He sat down at the picnic bench and created a new document on the computer and wrote a letter to Lucinda. He talked about his strong emotions for her and how sorry he was for what she had done and that she'd have to go to prison, probably for a long time. He said he couldn't imagine anything more horrible than that, having to live in such close proximity to people you don't know or like. He also confessed to sins of his own, things he'd never been caught at, things he'd never, ever told anyone before. He printed and signed it and put it in a letter envelope and wrote "Lucinda Smith" on it, "C/O", but he wasn't sure which jail or prison to send it to so left off the address and slipped it under his mattress. His body was buzzing in an unusual way, something to do with writing something honest to a woman he loved.

Then another great idea came to him. He went to the computer and did a San Diego escorts search. He'd done this before but never with a sense of purpose. Never like now.

Amazing.

Her name was Jasmine, though Ted suspected this was just her stage name. She met him in the Primo Cafe that evening and Ted accompanied her back outside where she counted the money and make a quick call to her boss. She was tall and green-eyed and had silky straight blond hair to her shoulders, with bangs. She had a good tan and her knit dress was not short but snug and almost the same color as her skin. Into the fabric small coffee-colored beads were woven, which made it look like she was wearing nothing *but* beads. She had a loosely woven shawl over her shoulders, and carried a small beaded purse. She had beautiful arms. Her necklace and earrings were freshwater pearls. Ted did not gape.

She turned away from him to make the call. Ted studied her partially revealed back, athletic-looking, lightly brushed by tiny jewels of perspiration, or perhaps a body spray. He disbelieved his good fortune. Earlier on the phone with Edie of Edie's Escorts, Ted had been flustered and unwilling to specify his choice of race, body type, age or "look," but Edie said she had a very special escort that Ted would certainly appreciate. And here she was. He was wearing his suit, a navy wool summer-weight fabric of average quality, a white shirt and clip-on tie. Of course his orthotic dress shoes.

Edie had told him the charge was $175 per hour with a two

hour minimum, plus an "expected" 20% tip and a $75 travel charge to North County. She told Ted that Jasmine was used to being treated and tipped very well. Also, said Edie, Jasmine was a companion, *not* a prostitute. Should Ted mention prostitution or sex for money during this phone call Edie would hang up and his calls would not be returned. Was Ted with any law enforcement agency? Had he ever been? Had he ever been convicted of a felony? Edie took Ted's credit card number against any problem with the cash. If Ted wanted more than two hours of Jasmine's company, then the rate was $150 per hour. If he wanted anything particular during their time together, he should take it up with her.

They walked up Main, her hand lightly on Ted's arm. The daylight was fading and Ted felt the warm density of the hurricane far to the south. They passed the Irish pub and the Anders Wealth Management building and a women's boutique.

"I've never been to Fallbrook," she said.

"I was born five hundred yards from this exact spot."

"Should I have dressed more conservatively?"

"No. This is a liberal town, for being so conservative."

"I was a Navy brat. I've lived all over the world."

"Then you'll like the restaurant I've chosen. It's called the Cafe de Artistes because it's French. It's the most important restaurant in Fallbrook. If you go there you're somebody."

"How wonderful. What do you do for a living, Ted?"

He looked at her, then away, distantly. "I'm just back from Afghanistan."

"Navy?"

"Dark Horse Battalion. Fifth Marines out of Pendleton."

"You'd get along with my dad, for sure."

"I bet I would."

"I never did. But that doesn't mean you and I won't."

They strolled down Main to Alvarado, rounded the corner

and came to the entrance of the cafe. Ted held open the door. He had reserved a mid-room table and as the hostess led them to it, he noted that every single person on the dining room looked at Jasmine, and then at him. He saw familiar faces. Fire Chief William Bruck had a four-top. Mary Gulliver and her sister were there. He ignored them. When they were seated Ted stole a look at Jasmine over the top of the wine menu. His heart was beating strong but the first shadows of doubt were falling on his mind. He excused himself and went into the men's room, had a blast in the stall, straightened his clip-on in the mirror and headed back into the restaurant.

The owner came over and welcomed them. He wore jeans and an open-necked sport shirt and a smile that looked genuine. He had no trouble looking at Jasmine which was okay with Ted. Ted asked Jasmine what type of wine she liked, and ordered one of the good bottles of Bordeaux. He was now up to $495, not counting his tip for Jasmine, dinner, dessert, after-dinner drinks, coffee and tip for the waitress. And probably more wine. Only an hour and forty minutes left on his clock! But no regrets. When the wine came he drank the first glass quickly, and it went so well with the nerve-jangling meth that he drank another, then they ordered.

It was easy for Ted to picture himself in early 20th century Paris, with the big colorful oil paintings on the walls and the curvy wood furniture and the cabaret piano music playing through the PA. The walls were boldly painted and each table had cut flowers and a candle. When the wine had been poured they touched glasses and Ted looked into Jasmine's beautiful green eyes in which the candle flame flickered.

Then, in a low and gentle voice, he was able to open about his time in Sangin with the Dark Horses of the 3/5. He admitted his tour was the defining event in his life. He described combat as occasional heart-stopping seconds of terror separated by eternities of boredom. Highest causalities of any Marine unit in the war, he said. Longest war in U.S. history. He spoke of seeing friends die, and taking enemy lives. He talked of loyalty to the unit, the sacredness of the mission, the way he felt not just significant but indispensable for the first time in his life. And of his dog, Rossie, who saved him from death not once but twice, and who had finally perished in a blast that also took Pfc. Hutchins with it. He told Jasmine about a village boy named Hamid who was brave enough to help them, and the asylum in the U.S. that the Marine Command was able to arrange for him and his family. He told her about red and pink poppies dancing on the breeze and about spiders the size of those salad plates. He tried to describe the jagged, orange-drenched beauty of Sangin at sunset, the heat, and the odd arrangement of stars that looked close enough to pinch between his thumb and finger. Then he was silent for a long moment, again watching the candlelight play off Jasmine's eyes.

"I can't say any of it right," he said. "I don't have the words."

She smiled and tapped his hand. "Excuse me. I've got to take this call but I want to hear more."

Ted pulled out her chair and Jasmine strode across the dining room with a phone to her ear. Smiling, he turned to Mary Gulliver, who quickly looked away. Ted saw the cafe owner watching him from across the room, a look of disbelief on his face. I know what you're thinking, thought Ted – I'm thinking the same thing! He sat and finished his glass of wine and ordered another bottle.

A few minutes later Ted was pushing in Jasmine's chair when Evelyn and Brian Anders came into the dining room behind the hostess. With them was the Dean of Admissions at the college that had expelled him for his Internet cartoon of the mayor, and the dean's companion, a large sturdy man with a shaven head and a goatee. Ted nodded curtly to the

271

mayor, then focused all of his attention on Jasmine. She studied his face and glanced at the new arrivals. "Friends?" she asked.

"I haven't seen them since the war."

"Maybe we can say hello to them when they're settled."

"Maybe. Please tell me about yourself."

She'd grown up on Navy installations – Norfolk, Pearl Harbor, Qatar, Saudi Arabia, Coronado, Pensacola. Her father was a colonel and her mother a homemaker. Two brothers. When it came time for college she came back to San Diego, her favorite of the cities she'd live in. She was dead tired of moving every few years. She did two years at UCSD, a business major, but she quickly tired of "retarded college boys and being poor," so she got a full-time waitress job at an expensive La Jolla restaurant. She said the money was good but the work was "mind-numbing," so she took a job selling BMWs at a dealership but that didn't work out because of the sales manager. "Jeez," she said. "Married guys." Then a stint dealing blackjack on a cruise ship, where she'd met Edie. They kept in touch and a few months later Jasmine signed on as an escort. She expressed herself with a combination of toughness and femininity that he admired. "I like the escort work okay," she said. "I really do like meeting new people and helping them feel comfortable in social situations. I'm a good dancer and I speak French and Spanish. But the money is in the, ah . . . other stuff, if you know what I mean."

"I understand. This has been a magical night for me. We're down to our last hour and twenty minutes."

"I'm up for more if you are."

Dinner passed dreamlike and euphoric – Jasmine in candlelight, the gay paintings hovering around them, the murmur of conversation and the upbeat music. To Ted, the room tilted slowly and corrected gently, like an ocean liner, and he gave over to the sea of sensation. They talked about

272

childhood. He was surprised to find the second bottle gone and ordered another.

Ted sensed motion and a change in light behind him and when he looked up Brian Anders was at their table. "Hello, Ted. How do you do, miss – "

"Jasmine," she said.

"Right. Ted, I just want you to know that if you ever post another sick cartoon of my wife, or come into our place of business with a poisonous spider hidden in your pants, I will personally kick you up one side of Main and down the other. In broad daylight, for all to see." Suddenly, Shaven Head was there, too, hulking, his hand on Brian's arm. Brian yanked it free. "Go sell hate somewhere else, Norris. We don't need it here."

"Come on, Brian."

"Do you understand, Ted?"

Ted could see the anger in his eyes and the severe clench of his jaw. "I understand that you're trying to wreck my dinner."

Shaven Head took one of Brian's arms again and Evelyn arrived and grabbed the other. Ted had never seen her this flushed and beautiful and in control. "Come on, honey."

"Let go of me," he hissed, with a hostile wrench of his arm.

"Brian!" called out the owner, waving his hands like a fight ref. Ted saw that the other diners were watching them and the servers had frozen mid-action to see what would happen next. Mary Gulliver looked pale. Fire Chief Bruck brusquely pushed in next to Brian. "Enough."

"Brian, damnit, come with me," said Evelyn.

"Damn *him,* not me."

"Brian, come on," said Bruck. "Nothing you say is going to change this guy."

"Whack job," Brian spit out at Ted. "Why don't you get out of here and take the whore with you?"

Ted tried to stand but Bruck held him down. He wanted to

273

speak but his thoughts were a knot. His breath was short and he looked up at all of them through the familiar rifled tunnel. What he felt most was shock at his own stupidity: he'd left the Glock in the truck. He looked at Jasmine, who had a fierce expression on her lovely face, still sitting there at the table across from him, but now a thousand miles away. She had not abandoned him. He was aware of Brian taking Evelyn by an arm and turning away, knocking into the owner. The servers resumed motion and heads turned away.

"Okay, people," the owner said, steadying himself. "We're all grown-ups, last I checked. Let's enjoy our dinners now."

"We should get dessert somewhere else," Ted managed.

"I'm ready when you are."

He waved the waitress over.

Ted used the bathroom again and they walked out onto Alvarado in the dark. He felt the Glock calling to him from his truck, just a few blocks away. He looked at Jasmine and weighed her company against the lure of the gun. She took his arm and they walked up Alvarado in the balmy darkness. The stores were closed but the streetlamps cast their steady light. She had the shawl over her shoulders. "I'm sorry for what happened," she said.

"I am, too. And I apologize. I thought my town would have better manners."

"People can be like that. Like new schools when you move when you're a kid. Pow. They want a piece of you before they even know who you are."

"What happened is, Jasmine, they mixed me up with my brother. We're twins. He's the one who put political cartoons of the mayor on line. He's the one who scares people with critters sometimes. So I just bear it, for him. For Patrick."

She looked at him. "I can feel your arm shaking."

"I was ready to fight."

274

"I'm so glad you didn't."

"It infuriated me what he said about you."

"You want to know something? I've heard worse. Lots."

Ted nodded. "We only got ten minutes."

"I can't go over on the time, Ted. Edie will fire me."

"How much for another hour?"

"One-fifty. If you want something special, then there's different rates for different things."

"I want you to meet a friend of mine."

She looked at him with frank suspicion. "A three-way?"

"No. No. Just a friend."

Ted pulled the wad from his pocket. He saved most of his work money because living at home was free. Regardless, he'd taken out a thousand cash from the bank earlier in the day and had already paid $750 for company, wine and dinner. He would owe Jasmine a tip of at least twenty percent of her combined time, according to Edie. Ted had never been good at math, and the wine and methamphetamine were not helping him think any straighter.

"Um, I paid for two hours at one-seventy five, and I want to get one more at one-hundred fifty. What's twenty percent of all that?"

"One hundred."

"Jasmine, you sure put a dent in a thousand dollar bill!" He handed her the whole roll of $250, which left him with the $15 that had been in his wallet before the bank run. She flipped through the bills, nodding, then slid them into her clutch. "Come on. I hope he's still at the shop. It's right around the block."

"Better be a short block, Ted. These shoes aren't rated for actual walking."

Ted could see the red-white-and-blue neon sign flashing down Oak Street. Cade's Bel Air, sleek and gleaming, stood near the entrance of Pride Auto Repair. He took her hand

and hurried her across the parking lot. At the front door window he cupped his hands and looked in. Through the open double-doors of the repair bay saw Cade sitting alone on the old paisley sofa, reading from a tablet of some kind open on his lap, the lamp casting a cone of light down onto him. Ted remembered Jed and Ellen Magnus. The front door was unlocked and he held it open for Jasmine to enter.

"Cade? Ted here! I'd like you to meet someone."

There was a short silence. Then, "Alright, Ted. Be right there."

Cade came through the double doors. "Hello," he said. But his tired-looking eyes went to Jasmine and stayed there. "I'm Cade."

"Jasmine."

"Jasmine's my companion tonight."

"You're a lucky man," said Cade.

Ted looked at her proudly, saw her smile at Cade in a way that said she'd heard that line several hundred thousand times. "We just had a real good dinner at the Cafe de Artistes. Except Mayor Anders was there and she mistook me for Patrick again. Made another one of her scenes." Ted winked at Cade.

"Again."

"You'd think after twenty-six years in this town they could tell us apart."

"You would. Jasmine, can I get you something to drink?"

"Just some water would be nice."

Cade went back into the bay. Ted told Jasmine that this place had been here since he was a boy, but he didn't say anything about what had happened to Cade Magnus's mother. "Cade's dad is Jed Magnus. Jed is very well known in political and racial circles. He's a patriot-philosopher. He moved away ten years ago and now Cade's back to continue his work."

276

Cade returned with a bottled water and two beers. He set them on the counter and motioned for his guests to sit. Ted pulled out a stool for Jasmine and she settled in gracefully. Cade stayed on the other side of the counter, leaning back against the wall, a Fallbrook Classic Car Show poster from 1985 on one side of him and the 1986 poster on the other. They talked about the arrest of Ibrahim Sadal and the evidence found at the gas station where he worked. Ted said he felt relieved. Jasmine had seen the TV news report that showed the suspect being hustled from the mini-mart to the plain white van. What spooky looking guy. She said terrorists should be shot. After a fair trial, of course. Cade smiled and raised his beer to her and Ted joined in.

Cade said it was no surprise they caught the rag-head, what with all the law enforcement descending on Fallbrook after the fire. What a bunch they were, Cade and Ted agreed. Ted told Jasmine of the very weird Department of Homeland Security Special Agent Max Knechtl, who thought he could wear suits in Fallbrook and not be noticed. Cade had been questioned by two DHS-HSI special agents, Chennoweth and Landsea, who allowed that Knechtl was "different." Cade had also been visited by an FBI duo out of San Diego, but they'd seemed more interested in Jed Magnus than in the Fallbrook Fire. Cade's friend Trevor had been detained and interviewed by FBI National Security Branch Counterterrorism Division CTD special agents out of San Francisco. Trevor said that these hard-working agents had discovered Las Brisas taqueira and were usually crammed into a booth there every time he went in, hiding behind their sunglasses, raiding the salsa bar over and over. Jasmine laughed and asked them how they remembered the initials for all of the departments and agencies and bureaus. Cade said all she really needed to know was that DHS was all the people who couldn't get jobs at the post office.

277

For Ted, the time shot past like a bullet train. It was like getting glimpses of himself and Jasmine and Cade through the windows. Just a smear, a streak. Jasmine excused herself for "the sandbox" and Ted told her it was through the double doors and back on the left. As she walked away the men watched her glistening body and the lazy sway of her knit dress, and heard the clop of her heels on the polished concrete floor.

"Patrick as your crazy twin brother? Now that's genuinely funny."

"I had to say something."

"What the hell are you doing here, Ted?"

"I want to be friends again. With you and Trevor and everyone. I want to be a Rogue Wolf. I want another chance."

"But all you bring us is suspicious feds and your pissed-off ex-Marine brother. You flub up an easy thing with the Mexican, get yourself stabbed instead. What do you want from me?"

"Just a chance to prove I'm good enough."

"Prove away, then, Ted. Please. Surprise me. Impress me."

"How?"

Cade sighed and looked at him, eyebrows raised as if in exasperation. He drank some of his beer, then crossed his arms and fixed Ted with his blue eyes. "How about something with the mayor at the concert? She's giving one of her little speeches before the show, the paper said."

"I'm ready for anything after what she did tonight. What did you have in mind?"

"That's what I want *you* to do, Ted! Figure out something on your own. Show me the distance you're willing to go. Until you can do that you'll continue to be a nobody. But, if you want to impress me, really write your name big on the wall of history – how about you taking Mayor Anders to the next level when she's making her speech?"

278

"I thought of doing that. I swear I did. Before you even said it. I dreamed it once too. I was able to do it."

"I'm talking way next level. Think the representative in Tucson. I know you have the tools. But do you have the balls? The concert is Friday, three nights from now. Three nights to think hard about it, Ted. About who you are and who you want to become."

Ted said nothing. He'd certainly imagined such a thing. Ever since trying to apologize to Mayor Anders in her office, and being rejected and dismissed by her, the idea had been inside him, looping endlessly along like a bass line, just barely audible. Then tonight, after being assaulted by her husband, the sound came stronger and more clearly. "Tucson. I can do that."

Cade looked toward the sound of Jasmine's heels coming toward them across the high bay concrete. "Which service?"

"Edie's in San Diego."

"Sweet. Maybe I underestimated you, Ted."

"Everyone does."

32

Patrick got to Warriors Stadium early Friday evening to help Iris with the concert. He had not seen her since the dinner party and they had talked just once on the phone in the last six days. She had sounded calm but distant. Kenton was Kenton. Best friend Carrie was getting married. Family was good, friends fine. So far as the Cruzela Storm show on Friday went, she could use some help and get him seat. But nothing about herself or what had happened. Was she furious? How furious? Or, by some miracle, was she pleased by his work? She gave no hint nor clue. Patrick wanted to do as he was trained – to take the fight to the enemy – but how exactly do you do that with a woman you're in love with?

None of his old clothes fit because he'd lost so much weight in Sangin, so on Thursday his mother had taken him shopping in Escondido. Away from home and alone with him, Caroline was light and forthcoming and she bought a new scarf and took Patrick to lunch in the swanky cafe at Nordstrom. She said she enjoyed shopping much more than filling sand bags, but not to tell Archie. Patrick noted that she drew looks from men of different ages and she seemed both aware and impervious.

As they roamed the crowded mall she took his arm and told him a story about herself at eighteen, one week out of high school, the same week that Patrick had joined up. "My father was vicious when he was drinking, which was always.

He disliked women. They were sexual things or nothing at all. He treated my mother like a child, and in some ways she was. Their fights were violent. My older brothers were his life and future, and I understood this, on paper anyway. I was invisible. In a way it was a relief. But I tried extra hard to please him. I was class valedictorian. I played varsity volleyball. I learned Spanish and French and I learned to dance and sing and ride a horse. I tried to be beautiful. I kept my, um . . . honor. The Sunday after graduation he took me to brunch. Santa Monica, upscale place. He told me he was proud to have done his part with me. He said I wouldn't amount to much but if I could marry right I'd be okay. And if I married right a portion of his fortune would follow me. He leaned in close and whispered something in my ear."

Caroline leaned over and whispered in Patrick's ear: "He said, *'Caroline, remember, there's a hot little fuckdoll in every profitable marriage. Practice up and learn how. If you don't believe me ask your mother'*. Well, Pat, he and mom had given me a new red BMW convertible for my Stanford career up north. Two hours later, and with my best worldly possessions, I was speeding due south from LA to San Diego, which I knew to be party central. I said nothing. His comment at lunch wasn't the only reason I left. The least of them by some measures. Just the last straw. Well, once in San Diego I searched hard, and it only took me a few days to find the worst boyfriend any virgin valedictorian could wish for. Just like Dad, but meaner! Not only alcohol, but drugs too. A little physical, that boy. Let's just say I happily morphed into my opposite and within a year I was a very serious wreck. But I was putting the screws to Daddy alright! I'm not sure what would have happened if I hadn't stumbled into a biker bar in Oceanside one day and been spotted by your father. I truly don't. My blessing and my miracle, staggeringly undeserved. And that, Patrick, is how you got your mom. That is why I'm so careful in what I do. Why I control everything, from the way I knot my scarf to what I read to how I hold the book. What I say and how I say it. From the way I set a water glass in the sink to the way I rinse it. It's not composure or serenity, certainly not vanity. No. Control is my vaccine against becoming that way again, the way I was before Archie. Which I know I am . . . prone to."

Patrick was speechless past the shoe store, the cell phone kiosk, the luggage store and the food court. He felt like hiding behind a Hesco block and smoking cigarettes.

"Did I embarrass you, Pat?"

"No. Some. I've never seen you blush, Mom."

"I don't exactly tell *that* story every day."

"Um, did your dad know you did all that?"

"I tortured him with it."

"That's a story, Mom."

"I'm glad Archie opened it up with you. Regarding Ted. I love you, Patrick. And I hope you love me. That was the whole point."

At a young-persons store with suggestive posters and throbbing music she bought Patrick a new outfit that was expensive but looked cool, he thought. He showed his ID and handed the clerk the money himself in order to get the ten percent military discount. The new sport coat fit well and the shirt was cotton but smooth as silk. Hundred and fifty-dollar jeans!

"If you don't melt Iris's little wooden heart in *that* outfit, you're going to have to find greener pastures, Pat."

"We're just friends, Mom."

"Ho, ho. Don't tell *her* that."

Later at the mall hair salon – Messina had told him not to go to barber shops unless he wanted to look like an ex-jarhead forever – Patrick was pleased to find that his hair had grown just long enough to be styled. And to mostly cover the patch where his stitches had been after the beach brawl with the MPs. He looked at himself in the salon mirror as the stylist made tiny snips, itemizing his recent bad behaviors. He wondered if the world might be better off with him back on patrol where he knew what he was doing. A structured setting. It sounded good in many ways.

Now he walked across the parking lot toward the stadium entrance, saw the little band of protesters near the gate with their signs: WALK THE WALKS WE HAVE! NO GIFTS FOR ILLEGALS! SUPPORT POLICE – NOT JAYWALKERS! There were some ELECT WALT ROOD signs, too, though Patrick didn't see the candidate. The people and their energy unnerved him and he was tempted to turn around and go home or to a quiet bar. He wondered if the loud concert music would set him off. He thought how Ted always said that things just got into him against his own will, and now Patrick saw how that might happen. Things are big, he thought. They have power. You can't turn everything off. The guns of Pendleton started pounding away to the west, and Patrick flinched but steeled himself and his control held.

He went around to a side entrance and squeezed through the loosely chained gate, then ambled onto the Warriors Stadium turf that he'd last played on just four years ago. Wide-receiver, decent hands. The turf was the same vivid green and the yard lines straight and white. He stopped midfield near the fifty and remembered catching a pass right here in the homecoming game, to no avail in their narrow loss. He looked at the scoreboard with the Warrior in the head-dress, and the snack bar and press box painted barn red with white trim. He'd always liked the bright stadium lights. It was easy to wander back into that past. It seemed so small now, but safe and pleasant, like a small nest he'd jumped from. Could it be only four years? But down by the goal line everything was different – he saw the elaborate scaffolding and stage, and the big amplifiers, the drums and congas, the keyboards and the colorful guitars in their stands, all twinkling in the stage lights.

He found Iris talking with a group of volunteers setting up VIP chairs near the stage. She had on a blue silk blazer over a navy blouse, and jeans and knee-high boots, and the sight of her made his heart ache and his mind wobble. He stood there in his new clothes, feet together and back straight, waiting. The evening was cool and breezy and the sky was a heavy, fretful gray. Finally she turned. She studied him, curiously, as if she'd never seen him before, or perhaps had known him once and forgotten almost everything about him. A strange look. He felt skinned. She approached and Patrick smiled but inwardly he wasn't sure whether to meet the threat, hold his ground or retreat. Please nothing bad. He'd never been this unsure of what to do, not even in the chaos of combat. She came up close and he saw the emotion in her eyes but couldn't identify it. Just could not. "We can help set up these chairs," she said.

"I'm sorry."

"Me, too. We can talk later. I love the horses. Let's get this done."

Patrick worked with the energy of the hopeful. Natalie and Mary Ann joined them but neither of them offered him more than a wave. Natalie took pictures of Iris and Mary Ann working, for the Village View. It was dark by the time they finished. A few minutes later the crowd was filing in. Iris gave him his ticket and pointed out their seats, a third of the way back and in the middle. She excused herself to follow Natalie toward Cruzela Storm's trailer for a brief interview and photo shoot. Evelyn Anders fell in behind them. Iris turned and looked at Patrick, and again her expression was inscrutable to him – his twenty-two years of worldly experience no

284

match, he sensed, for millennia of female evolution resulting in Iris Cash. He waved, lamely.

Evelyn followed Iris and Natalie, squeezing past two body-guards and into Cruzela's Storm's trailer. It was roomy. Cruzela sat on a loveseat with an acoustic guitar propped on the cushion beside her. In her daring stage clothes Cruzela no longer looked awkward and uncomfortable, but strong-limbed, sexual and dangerous. She made Evelyn feel neither young nor particularly attractive anymore, but these were not bad feelings. It was good to see a woman who was all of that and more. Cruzela's hair was a shiny copper mane, her face heavily made up, her lips black. She rose and shook their hands formally, half a head taller than tall Natalie. "Help yourself to the food and drink."

Evelyn backed away and stood near the food, unsure of whether to offer herself a seat in the presence of a star. Iris sat down across from Cruzela and started in with her questions. Natalie started shooting. One of the bodyguards, well muscled and his black hair in a ponytail, carried a chair over to Evelyn with one hand, and it seemed to weigh no more to him than a glass of wine. Boy, could she use one of those. She disliked public speaking but half an hour from now she'd be up there in front of two thousand plus people, trying to thank them for something they just wanted to get on with. They sure weren't here to listen to *her*.

"Glass of wine?" asked the bodyguard.

"Oh, please, yes."

"You look like a red wine woman."

"You've read my mind twice in ten seconds."

She pulled her tablet from her purse and brought up her speech notes. She read through them, half-tuned to the interview, half-aware of the flashes of Natalie's camera. "*When I heard about Georgie Herrera half my heart broke and the other half just got pissed off,*" said Cruzela. Evelyn heard the crowd

285

outside burst into applause but had no idea why. She couldn't believe there were protesters out there. Now, she told herself, when you get up there, just let them know the basics, then get off stage. The basics were: welcome, sold out, will raise over fifty grand, which will pay for Fallbrook's share of lighted crosswalks *and then some*. Also, remember to thank bigger sponsors: Village View News, Major Market, Pro-Tire, Martial Arts Concepts, Rotary, American Legion Post 365, Democratic Club, Soroptimists, Kiwanis, Fallbrook Wood Carvers, Gem and Mineral Society, AAUW, the synagogue, the many churches and the many charitable groups. She knew that the people she didn't thank by name tonight would complain to her, but that public service, now, wasn't it?

She took a drink of the wine and listened to Cruzela talking about growing up in Barrio Logan. She watched Natalie shooting her pictures, trying to be unintrusive. She studied Cruzela Storm and wondered what it would be like to have a talent. As she spoke to Iris, Cruzela's emotions seemed to crash right through the heavy makeup and onto her face. She doesn't have only talent, but heart, too, thought Evelyn. For a moment she felt good, knowing that she had helped her people help themselves, and that everyone had come together here to do a good thing that needed doing. Well done, Mayor Anders, she thought, and drank a toast to herself and thought a brief prayer for Georgie.

By the time she climbed the backstage stairs and began her journey toward the ferocious lights before her, Evelyn's stomach was in knots and her legs had gone heavy and cold.

"They're gonna love you, Mayor!" Cruzela called from behind her.

She had no idea of what walking into a stadium of applause would be like. She'd never bothered to imagine it. But it hit her with the force of a blow and she stopped for one moment before continuing. By the time she reached her mark her

286

citizens were clapping and yelling her name and some stood, then more rose, until all were on their feet. Their voices hit her as one voice, and their clapping as a two thousand votes of confidence. Maybe all that approval would last until the election! She waved her tablet at them with one hand, and brought the mic to her mouth with the other.

Fans had left their seats and clustered up close to the stage right below her, mostly young girls with bouquets for Cruzela, but there were some boys and adults, too, and the sheriff deputies on either side of them watched, unconcerned.

"God bless you Fallbrook!" she called out and the volume rose as if someone had turned a knob. "I'm your biggest fan!"

Smiling and still waving her tablet, Evelyn opened her mouth to speak again. At the same moment she recognized Ted Norris, wrapped in a heavy winter coat, working his way toward her.

Ted plodded through the rowdy crowd. Evelyn Anders stood up there in the lights with the gleaming musical instruments, her tablet held high. Her ten-thousand commandments, he thought: what I shalt and shalt not do. She wore a black dress and a short white jacket. She recognized him, and he heard the falter of her voice as she began her speech. She cleared her throat and started again. He'd smoked the last of his crystal in the parking lot, drank half the pint of bourbon and slid the flat dark bottle into a coat pocket. The stadium and stage lights sent bright fissures across his mind's eye, like lightning crackling down on a city. My world, he thought: my moment.

He glanced at the deputies standing with their backs to the stage, surveilling the crowd. He noted that they were very young and unarmed – not deputies at all, in fact – but so-called Explorers, earning their credits for academy. The Glock waited beneath his shirt and coat, firm against his belly.

He turned and looked at his brother and Iris, seated maybe a third of the way back. Even with the mayor up there chirping away, they were talking intently. Patrick had an earnest, optimistic posture. Even from this distance Iris looked stern. And they seemed separate from what was going on around them, like they were the only two people at the show, thought Ted, or on the whole planet.

Evelyn blathered: *"Georgie ... tragedy ... lighted crosswalks ...fifty-thousand dollars ..."*

He shuffled around a group of teenaged girls, their scents finding him. He stopped just short of another gaggle of girls. They looked at him with an incomprehension he understood their incomprehension because to him they seemed like penguins or aliens. The stage was ten feet away, and maybe waist-high. Evelyn reigned above them all, bathed in light. *" ... and Joe's Hardware, and all of the churches and Beth Israel have been so generous, also ..."* Surrounded by the giddy children, Ted ran his hand up under his coat and shirttail to the handle of the Glock – so solid, so unchanging, so *there*. Evelyn yapped on. She was beautiful. He remembered her voice on the other side of the bathroom door the night she'd babysat him, *just making sure you're okay in there, Teddy,* and it was the same voice he heard now. Now, seventeen years later, that same woman looked down on him, trying to hide her fear. What a gift that fear was now. *"Fallbrook, you've done a wonderful thing ... give yourselves a round of applause before Cruzela comes on ..."* Evelyn loomed there, searching his face with a frozen smile. He looked up the long rifled tunnel of his vision at her, drawing breath deeply, trying to get enough in so he could exhale slowly, like Kerry had told him.

He tightened his grip on the gun. It was warm and heavy and encouraging. The time was now. The crowd burst into applause for itself, and in the roar he commanded his hand to withdraw the weapon and shoot Evelyn Anders. This is for all of you, he thought: for you who hated and betrayed me. His command was clear and his heart was undivided. But the gun

288

did not move. He commanded again. Nothing. He squeezed the grip tighter, finger outside the trigger guard as he'd been taught. Evelyn lowered the mic and tablet and bowed. As she leaned over she held the mic to her chest but the beginnings of her breasts were still visible, like in the cartoon he'd drawn of her. When she straightened she was looking right at him. He summoned all his will and courage. *Her. Now.* She turned and strode away and the crowd began chanting for Cruzela.

Ted watched her go. Her white coat was a good target, clean and bright in the lights. With every step she took, a voice inside said: *You are nothing.* He took his hand off the gun and jammed his fist into his coat pocket. As the applause and chanting grew louder he felt smaller. And smaller. He listened to the sound of the world.

You are nothing.

You are nothing.

Invisible now, he turned and patiently worked his way through the cheering crowd. He took slow steps so as not to look in a hurry, though it was evident that not one soul in this stadium was aware of him. Well, his brother, maybe. Maybe. Even the cops and explorers barely looked at him as he walked down the wide aisle along the stands, toward the bathrooms and the exit. When he got to his truck in the parking lot he closed his eyes and crossed his hands over his chest and tried to unscrew himself from it all. Of course it didn't work. But he understood that he could use some friends right now, friends like the Rogue Wolves, and maybe a cold beer and a little jolt of crystal and a game of pool. They'd have him back, wouldn't they? At least for a while? At least so he could explain what he'd . . . not done?

You are nothing.

The neon red, white and blue of the Pride Auto Repair sign glowed clearly in the Fallbrook night. Cade's Bel-Air was

289

parked in its usual place along with a light blue Volkswagen Beetle convertible that Ted didn't recognize. He parked and went to the front door. The blinds were drawn and it was locked but music pulsed. Loud. Through a thin slice of space between the blinds and the window he looked in. Cade, shirtless, his back gleaming with sweat and his pants around his ankles, plunged into the backside a woman wearing only high heels, her arms braced on the pool table, hair swaying. Cade pulled her hair like a rein and her face came around. Jasmine.

Ted covered his head with his elbows and bashed through the front door in an explosion of shards and slats and pull chords. Jasmine was already scrambling away as he found his balance on the slippery glass and pulled the Glock. Cade reached down for the pistol holstered on his belt but his belt was down at the floor and Ted shot him twice in his naked ribs, and when Cade spun away screaming Ted shot him twice more in the back. Cade's gun spun loose as he crashed facedown on the pool table, blood lurching and arms spread and his anguished screams cutting through the music. Ted shot again but missed and the green felt jerked. He wasn't seeing right and his ears were roaring. What had just happened? He didn't know how he'd gotten here, or why he'd come. Instinctively, he strode after the woman, into the repair bay and it was only half-light in the big room but he tracked her by her sobbing and the sound of her heels retreating from him on the concrete floor.

"Don't, Ted. Don't, please don't."

"I can barely hear you."

"Let me get around you to the door, Ted. Remember me? I'm Jasmine."

"I don't remember you."

"Please don't kill me."

"You should go." He felt the gun, suddenly heavy in his hand, and looked down at it.

"Can I get by you?"

"Go."

Her pale naked body shook by. He stood for a moment looking at the paisley couch and the reading lamp. They meant something to him, something from his past, but what? When he got back to the lobby the woman had already thrown open the ruined door and ran out. He could see her unlocking the Volkswagen, shaking her head and talking to herself, naked and clutching a handful of clothes to her chest, eyes wide and her face slack-jawed with terror. The wounded man had slid off the table and was now on the floor, curled in on himself, breathing fast. It looked like enough blood for two men, or three.

Ted turned off the music and sat down on one of the bar stools. He set the gun on the counter and put his hands over his ears and watched the man on the floor. A moment later headlights came down Oak Street and raked across the still-open door with the broken glass around the edges like shark teeth and its blinds snapped and dangling and the pull strings swaying in the warm breeze.

When the man came through the door everything came back to Ted. A flash. An avalanche. Everything. "Oh, hi, Pat. I messed up pretty bad this time."

Patrick stepped into Pride Auto. He registered Cade in the lake of blood, Ted and the gun on the counter next to him, the heavy smells of blood and gunpowder and solvent. "I saw a car leaving."

"Jasmine, the escort. I let her go."

Patrick called nine-one-one. While he spoke to the dispatcher he studied Ted, who slumped at the bar like a common drunk, dreamy and deranged. Patrick knelt over Cade Magnus and he saw the look of death in his eyes – a gaze locked open on the faraway. "You've got help coming,

291

Cade. If you can hang in there they can help you. Hang in there. Can you do that?" Cade coughed a mouthful of blood across the floor and whispered, "Christ . . ."

"I got mad when I saw him with Jasmine," said Ted. "Doing that stuff to her. I thought you were my friend, Cade. I introduced you to her, you sonofabitch."

Patrick put a hand on Magnus's shoulder, felt the tremble. Taibo would have slammed a vial of morphine into him, eased his way onward. But there was nothing he could tourniquet or do with wounds like this. "If you can hang on just five minutes, Cade." Magnus said nothing. "What happened at the concert, Ted? What were you doing up close to the stage like that?"

"I was going to shoot the mayor but I couldn't. My hand just wouldn't move."

"Where'd you get the gun?"

"Open Sights. Marked down. Shooting Evelyn was going to be my big important thing but it didn't work out." Patrick watched Ted pick up the gun and heave off the stool and come over. "I liked Jasmine."

Patrick stood. "What are you going to do now?"

"I know what my big important thing really is. Not Evelyn at all. Now I get it. It started a couple of days ago with this woman I know. She told me you have to tell the truth about what you've done. Even if it's bad. And she didn't just tell me that, she *did* it. She told the police what she'd done."

"Well, isn't that great?" said Patrick. Cade Magnus sighed once and shivered hugely and his throat rattled and caught. Patrick knelt and touched his bare bloody shoulder again and felt the buzz of life stop. "Look, Ted. What you did." A shadow moved over Patrick. He turned his head to see Ted leaning down. Patrick stood and tried to swipe the gun from his brother's hand but Ted was quick. He backpedaled and braced against the bar for balance, weapon still in hand.

"That isn't all I did." Patrick heard sirens and he saw his brother glance in their direction. "Ibrahim Sadal didn't set the fire. I did. Later I put an accelerant and timer and the Al Qaeda magazines in the supply closet at the gas station. Then I called Knechtl from a pay phone. I wanted to see it all burn, Pat. I needed to. I did my research and waited for the right weather. I wanted to burn this city down. And the houses in the city and the people in the houses. Mayor Anders' house for sure. And every avocado tree we owned. Most of all I wanted to burn Dad to ashes and watch the wind blow him away one puff at a time every day for the rest of my life. And every time a puff of him went up I would know. I couldn't ever do much right, Pat. I tried. So I just went with wrong. Big wrong. Important wrong. Of course I messed it up. I was worried about Mom and the dogs and my creatures so I cut back the bushes around the house and barn. My fire never made it downtown. I don't know why. I set plenty of others. This was best by far. It's all written down in a letter under my mattress. Everything. The letter is to Lucinda Smith but you can read it before you send it to her."

The sirens wailed, closer. Patrick tried to make all of this useful, get it into workable condition, but could not. "Three people died in your fire."

"Four now total."

"God damn you, Ted."

"I love you Pat. You're what I wanted to be."

"Damn you again, then."

"I felt damned my whole life. But now my big important thing is half accomplished. I'm almost done. I'll be remembered for it. And it will make the world better. Sound good?"

"Okay, Ted. You make the world better now."

"Do you know what I'm saying?"

Patrick studied his brother's face for the clues he had missed. Missed for a lifetime. Again and again and again.

Even now he didn't see them. But he thought he understood what Ted meant about making the world better. "You have to mean it."

"Oh, I mean it. But I want it to come from you. Here." Ted held out the gun unsteadily. Patrick heard the sirens bearing down, out on Main Street now.

"I won't do it, Ted."

"I can't do it alone."

"It has to be from you."

"But is it right?"

"It's right, Ted. It will matter."

"Really? It's right?"

"I think it is."

"You and me, then? Pat?"

The sirens screamed and the cars barreled down Oak Street, their flashing lights cutting through the open door.

Patrick grabbed Ted's wavering gun hand. He pressed his finger alongside his brother's, through the trigger guard. The barrel of the weapon dug into Ted's heart. For a moment they looked into each others' eyes and Patrick saw the damage and confusion in someone whom life had mostly cursed. He knew there was some goodness among the darker things. He wrapped his free hand around Ted's head and clutched him close. "I love you." For a moment they were one, cheek to cheek, heart to heart and hand to hand. Together they pulled. The explosion cracked through the lobby and out the open door into Fallbrook.

33

The storm lumbered in from the southwest early Monday morning, heavy with blessing and menace. At sunrise the sky was black over the Norris Brothers groves and the wind blew warm and strong. Patrick and his parents stood on the front porch in rain gear, the steam from their coffee cups rising, the dogs alert beside them. Patrick noted the porch thermometer at 72 degrees and the barometer was the lowest he'd ever seen it.

He glanced at his mother and father, then up at the infinite black clouds, which covered every inch of sky in every direction, as far as Patrick could see. A vast numbness had descended on Patrick and he couldn't free his mind from what had happened. He felt stuck and weighted and sinking, a brute mammal caught in tar. He was exhausted by deputies, reporters, sympathizers and mostly, by grief itself. He had lied to them all, even to his mother and father and Iris, about his part in his Ted's death. Or, rather, he had failed to report the full truth.

"I'll die before I let this storm take the last of what I have," said Archie. "Pat, do you think we should stage from the Big Gorge or the upper roads?"

"It's up to you."

"I'm asking your advice."

"The high ground, then. Is the tractor ready?"

"Gassed and ready in the shed below the gorge."

"Let's hope it doesn't come to that," said Patrick. He knew that his father's vow was not made lightly. The Norris Brothers Growers had lost a man, Frank Webster, in the winter of 1957. A saturated west-facing hillside had broken away and buried him and his tractor under ten feet of mud. The spot was marked by a concrete cross, now fully exposed and blackened by fire. The tragedy was recalled only occasionally and briefly, as if there was shame on the family for letting it happen, Patrick had always thought – something in which they were complicit and maybe an accessory. Like Ted.

"And we ought to lock the dogs in the barn," said Patrick. "They can't help and they might get hurt."

"I'll get them food and water," said Caroline.

The wind lifted ash and straw from the grove and the air around them grew dark with soot. It looked like dustbowl windstorm coming. From the kitchen Caroline brought steel containers of coffee and a big cooler filled with food and drinks. Down at the barn they loaded shovels, a hundred empty sandbags, scores of four-foot lengths of reinforcement bar, and three sledge hammers into Archie's truck. They jailed the dogs, who howled in frustration as Patrick climbed back into his truck.

He took the lead, the defroster on and coffee jostling over his fingers. The Norris groves were nearly all slopes, some gentle and others steep. He climbed the narrow road in long switchbacks, Ted hugely present in the seat next to him. Ted's voice and some of the words from his letter to Lucinda Smith coursed through Patrick's brain: *I am attracted to you like my dogs are attracted to birds, because of nature . . . now that I know your secret you make sense to me . . . too bad it had to happen to you . . . I never felt like I was part of my own family, but they mostly tried to make me feel like I was, except maybe Dad . . . it wasn't the first fire either, I set others but none of them did what this one did . . . I didn't have any talent for fires . . . I want to*

*be famous for a few hours so I'm going to confess like you did
... don't want Ibrahim to sit in prison either ... He never did
nothing to me ... I'll make sure Patrick sees this letter and he will
make everything right as he always does ...*

As he always does. They parked the trucks side-by-side on
the high peak near the center of the property. As boys, Ted and
Patrick had nicknamed this hillock "Everest," and climbed it
using unnecessary ropes. They'd planted an American flag
here. Now the eighty Norris acres flowed down from them
in blackened corrugations spiked with scorched trees, their
branches bare and sharp. When Patrick looked to the south
he could see Lew Boardman's adjacent acres, green and
verdant and untouched.

He idly wondered if God had saved the Norris home.
Wasn't that God-like? Roughly a year ago Patrick had
wondered something similar, on his seventh patrol in Sangin,
when Dahl had brushed up against an IED and been blown
so high into a tree it took them a while to spot his body.
Yet Sloan, Fortner and Graff, all right there with him, were
spared. Hand of God at the expense of Dahl? Things like
that happened again and again, and Patrick came to believe
that God decided everything by deciding nothing, that the
specifics of your life and death on Earth were no reflection
of you or God at all. You could call God Luck, and though
it might a good approximation it didn't explain much. The
most important truth he'd learned was the simplest too and
it applied anywhere you went – get through the fucking day
alive.

The rain started, blown one direction then another by the
strong tropical wind. Patrick trotted to his father's truck and
squeezed in beside his mother. Archie cracked the windows
and turned off the engine and set the wipers low. They
refilled their cups and listened to the rap of the rain on the
roof and the hiss of the wind in the leafless trees. The rain

had already turned the ground to gray-black slush, and the smell was strong.

They watched and waited a long while and the rain came faster. Beyond the bare and bloody facts they hadn't talked about what had happened. Words were feeble. Patrick still smelled the blood on himself and it seemed to come from inside. But now silence was intolerable, made somehow obsolete by the coming storm. Patrick was about to speak but his father spoke first.

"I feel that he is here with us."

"He was in my truck on the way here," said Patrick.

"I keep waiting to wake up," said Caroline. "And none of it is going to be true."

"It's the worst truth I've known, Caroline. To date."

"And we'll all be . . . like before. Right?" She wiped under each eye with a different fingertip. She sat bolt upright as always, shoulders back and chin up. "There was so much pain I didn't see."

"Me neither, Mom. And we were close."

"None of us saw," said Archie.

Caroline stared. "I still don't know how I raised a boy tormented enough to destroy so much of the world around him. Then himself. There's blood on my hands."

"There most definitely is not," said Archie.

"I didn't see, but *I knew*," she said. "They gathered up some moms on TV after one of the school massacres. From across the country. They all had boys who were wrong, they said. They were afraid their whole lives. Really afraid that their sons would hurt themselves, or worse. They watched them and loved them and helped them. Talked to doctors, some-times cops even. The boys didn't commit crimes or serious violence, that they ever knew of. The boys just kept plodding along, barely keeping in their lanes. And the mothers kept waiting for that terrible thing to happen, for their sons to make hell on earth for innocents. And that show hit me like an atom bomb because those moms were me."

"You did everything on Earth for him," said Archie. "I won't let you take blame."

"Five dead by his hand," she said.

The rain drummed on the truck roof. "When I was a boy I thought my father was the meanest man in the world," said Archie. "I promised if I was ever a father I wouldn't withhold the things he withheld from me. I did just that to Ted. I tried not to but I did. I became . . . what I set out not to become. Love is not enough. You have to use it correctly."

Patrick set a hand on his mother's knee. The wind gathered speed and the rain came harder. Blood on hands, he thought. He always knew Ted was different. Always knew Ted had that anger, a secret streak of crazy in him. But what should he have done differently? Or his mother or father? What?

Where was your preview vision for Ted? Like your preview vision of what was going to happen to Sheffield and Lavinder? How come you couldn't do that for your own brother?

Blood on all of us, thought Patrick, from Sangin to Fallbrook, and from Fallbrook to . . .

"None of us lit that fire or shot that man," he said. "Or killed Ted." With this partial truth Patrick privately and forever renounced the whole truth, in strange honor of his brother, for the sake of his family and himself. It would be his secret forever, his portion of the burden Ted had left behind.

"No, we didn't," said Archie. "It just feels that way."

"Can I just miss him for awhile?" From the corner of his eye Patrick could see her snugging the black silk scarf she wore around her neck, fussing with the knot, flaring the ends, then wiping her eyes again.

Patrick and his father switched seats and Patrick guided the truck into the mounting wind and rain. Patrick figured if the

299

forecast of four inches was correct, and it fell over twelve hours, they'd be okay. But with more, or a faster rate, they might have to reconfigure the sandbag walls to guide the runoff. And they might have to fill more bags, an onerous task when sand was mud. In a full deluge, the upper roads would wash out and Big Gorge could overrun or collapse, taking the mid and lower roads with it. At that point only the tractor stood a chance. Worst case was an earth slide, which would destroy everything in its path. But slides were rare on the Norris ranch, the last one bringing Frank Webster's death, well over half a century ago. In that case even the tractor became an enemy.

Patrick stayed in first gear, looked out at the slanting rain and the black sky. Up high the clouds roiled and rose, like waves peaking, ready to crash down. He thought of Iris. He touched the cell phone in his pocket to make sure it was there. Pictured her face. Remembered her words just before he had left her to follow Ted from the concert. *I can love you, Pat. But I don't know if I can survive you.*

Now he thought of Iris bursting into Pride Auto Repair and, against odds, prevailing. She was clear-headed and rational. The deputies asked her to stay outside but Iris politely refused and brandished her press credential. Over the next hour she not only got the story, and cell-phone photos, for the Village View, but managed to comfort him. Patrick, as a possible suspect, was ordered to sit on an old paisley sofa back in the repair bay and so he sat, dazed, trying to keep the blood-drenched details of his story straight for both Iris and the cops, trying not to hear the final report of Ted's gun thundering over and over. Even through all that, he had registered Iris's clarity of mission, the way she was able to accomplish it even with a choked voice and a makeup-streaked face. She'd shuttled back and forth between him and the crime scene proper, part friend and part reporter. Grief-numbed as he

300

was, Patrick was aware that the sum of his love for her was being added to.

The rain roared against the metal roof. Patrick imagined the tropical and Alaskan fronts colliding as on the weather maps. Maybe right here in front of us, he thought. "This is going to be a whopper," he said.

"The road's already boiling," said Archie. "I hope it holds."

"Where's the thunder?" asked Caroline. "I love thunder. Ted loved thunder too. We tape recorded it once when he was four so we could hear it whenever we wanted. He'd play it when he . . . went potty."

The truck slid on the steep higher roads but Patrick countered with the four-wheel drive. They crept along, gear low and wipers high, watching the water cut runnels in the roads and splash up against the sandbag walls. Patrick noted that the walls now looked about half enough high. Radio reception was poor but the L.A. news said two inches of rain had already fallen there, with another two-to-four inches expected before noon. There were reports of wind damage in Antelope Valley. Orange County was getting blasted too, power out in parts of Huntington Beach and Fountain Valley. San Diego public radio reported widespread destruction in Tijuana, San Ysidro and National City, and an inch-and-a-half of rain downtown with more to come. Fashion and Mission Valleys were already flooded and closed, and a downed tree up on Banker's Hill had landed on a car and killed a man. NOAA radio estimated winds at 90 mph at the storm's center, and upgraded it from tropical storm to hurricane Harley. Her center was now just off Todos Santos, a brief thirty miles from the border and winds were expected to increase closer to landfall.

Patrick goosed the truck around a snug downhill turn. The wall of sandbags in front of them broke away and a stream

301

of black, ash-stained rain flooded through the break. He slid the truck to a stop on level ground and set the brake and they piled out and wrestled the bags back into place. The bags seemed twice as heavy to Patrick and even with the heavy leather gloves they were hard to hold. When the wall was up they used the sledge hammers to drive in the rebar.

Patrick grunted as the rain found its way past his slicker and onto him. Their hammers clinked sharply on the steel and with every blow Patrick imagined he was demolishing Ted's long history of bad fortune, which had started his own body in his own crib. What kind of a beginning was that? Maybe life wasn't random at all, as he'd decided in the Sangin Valley, but something ordered and invariable, like a book that you have no say in the writing of and can't revise. So that what happened inside Pride Auto Repair on Friday night was a closing chapter, long fixed and waiting to be read. Same with Boss and Myers and Zane, Dahl and Pendejo and Prebble and Adams and Sheffield and . . . well, it added up to a lot of books. But was this notion of a book of life any better than the idea of one big game of chance? And if so, how?

Suddenly the storm shifted gears and became a faster and less resistible thing. Even on high the windshield wipers were insufficient and Patrick had to lean close to the glass for brief snapshots of the way forward. Another sandbag wall had collapsed above them and he caught a snippet of the waterfall cascading proudly down. The runoff was clearer now that the rain had washed the trees and earth of ash. The truck slipped and slid down the road toward the Big Gorge.

Patrick rounded a curve and drove into the face of the storm. The wind tried to pry the vehicle from the ground and for a moment the truck shivered as if it might lift off and take flight. "I always wanted to see Munchkinland," said Caroline. Tree branches whirled through the air and whapped against

302

the sheet metal. Patrick saw a section of the bunkhouse roof rotating corner-to-corner through the sky. "Goddamn you!" cried Archie, looking up through the windshield. "This is how you answer me? This? Go straight to the hell you made!"

By noon the sandbag walls were collapsing everywhere they looked. They couldn't replace them fast enough to matter. They ran out of empty bags and rebar stakes anyway. The wind had backed off but the sky was even blacker and the rain seemed more solid than liquid, not drops but sheets of water stacked back-to-back as far as Patrick could see. Everywhere he looked the water rushed across the ground and it was not clear anymore but brown with precious soil. Patrick saw this and his spirit sank even deeper: Norris Brothers Growers washing away to the sea.

They huddled in the truck with the heater going on full and ate the sandwiches and drank the coffee that Caroline had made. Their heat condensed on the windows and the world outside was a dark roar. It seemed impossible to Patrick but the rain ratcheted up another notch. Archie started laughing – an accusatory, lowdown laugh that had more defiance than joy in it. Patrick understood this sound and felt what his father felt and he laughed too. Then Caroline started up.

They stood on the road where it passed over a large galvanized culvert that marked the narrows of Big Gorge. From here Patrick looked uphill to see the runoff overflowing the sandbags, rushing down into the gorge, roaring through the culvert below. Sandbags broke away and fell into the dark current and vanished. An uprooted avocado tree tumbled over the falls and the water swept it across the gorge, pinning it against the culvert. "It's twelve feet in diameter," yelled Archie, though Patrick could hardly hear him.

"About two feet to go!" called Patrick. He knew that if the

303

torrent overflowed culvert and the road they now stood on, it would take the road with it.

"If the water gets one foot from the top, you two get out of here," said Archie. "Promise me. One foot!"

"I'm prepared to die with a shovel in my hand," said Caroline, her shovel held fast between her legs as she re-arranged her drenched hair.

"Get me to the tractor!"

The tires spun and the truck slid on the downhill slope but Patrick kept the truck on the road. He glanced up to see a raven pinwheeling across the sky before them, bouncing wing-to-wing as if on something solid. They passed another section of the bunkhouse roof lying in the grove nearby, the metal sheared violently away from its beam, some of the rivets still in place. "That bunkhouse was eighty years old," said Archie. "I shall not be defeated. I utterly shall not."

"God bless you, Archie," said Caroline.

"I defy Him to bless me. Caroline? I love you very much. You too, son."

Patrick slid to a stop. Archie pressed through the door and staggered into the wind. The tractor shed had been blown away leaving nothing but a concrete pad and two six-by-six uprights. But the Ford was there, staunch in the rain, the blue paint faded and touched by rust, the oldest non-human employee of Norris Brothers Growers. Through the slashing downpour Archie climbed on and started it up. Diesel smoke billowed black at first and struggled up through the solid downfall. Patrick worked his phone from his pocket and sent a text to Iris: *Bad storm we fight I love you.* He dropped the phone into the center console, glanced at his mother and aimed the truck back up the hill.

Back at the culvert they bent to their shovels but the earth was so drenched they could capture little more than slurry to fortify the upslope bank. It was like using teaspoons of sand

304

to hold back an ocean. Patrick saw that the water had risen since they'd dropped off Archie at the tractor. He stopped shoveling long enough to look at his watch: 2:44 p.m. Almost eight straight hours of rain, he thought, and what – six, eight inches? Did it matter? He squinted up into the silver darts hurtling down from a black infinity.

"Another six inches and we'll be swimming," said Caroline. She stopped working and handed Patrick her shovel and gloves. Standing straight, shoulders back and head erect as always, she pulled back the hood of her poncho and straightened her bandana, which was soaking wet like the rest of her. Her fingers patiently loosened and re-tied the knot, then fashionably slid the whole thing over to one side. Her hair clung like black plaster but she smoothed it down anyway. "In a true and awful way, the world is better off without Ted. But I'll love him until my heart's last beat."

"You gave him every chance, Mom."

"I didn't know what to give him."

The clank and groan of the tractor sounded downslope and Patrick turned to see his father guiding the old machine up the road. The frontloader was up and the front tires skittered in the mud but the big heavily treaded rear tires dug in deep and pushed the contraption forward while the diesel clattered and growled and belched smoke into the storm.

"Are you going to be okay, Pat?"

"Soon as we get through this storm."

"Hurricane Harley is nothing." Caroline yanked her hood back over her drenched head, slid the keeper tight and took back her gloves and shovel.

Archie dumped the first load of tractor mud on the bank and tamped it down with the bottom of bucket. Patrick and his mother packed the earth down harder with their shovels but still the new rain washed away the berm almost as fast as they built it. Patrick, panting deeply, saw that the Big Gorge

305

was now only inches from being full and that their wall and their road, and everything below them, would soon be eaten by the deluge. The sky did not lighten and the rain did not lessen.

Patrick watched his father bring another raised bucket load of dripping mud up the road, the front tires of the Ford gliding on the downrush, Archie up like a jockey in a crouch with his face raised. "You can take my son and trees! But you can't beat me down! You don't have the *balls!*"

Suddenly from uphill came a thunderous *crack!* It sounded to Patrick like some huge and violent thing had thrown its shoulders up through the earth. He saw the hillside shudder and break away and start downhill toward them, leaving behind a great crater. The hillside gained speed. Even in combat Patrick had never seen death written so clearly. He looked at his father, still crouching in the tractor, fist raised but speechless in the face of this. Patrick took his mother's arm and pulled her away from Big Gorge, up the slick road. They slipped and fell and struggled up again.

Then Patrick was down without having fallen, swept swiftly away without leaving his feet. He clutched Caroline close and down and down and down on the great escalator of mud they went, and where they had been just seconds ago was far above them now. Patrick realized that they were riding a speeding mountain of mud. He saw the blue tractor spinning downhill, Archie clenching the wheel like a life buoy, his body mid-air, legs bicycling frantically. Then Patrick heard another sharp roar and he watched a second mountain of mud break off and rush down and bury the culvert and the road finally and completely.

Careening downhill, he felt the clench of the mud around his legs and saw that he was waist-deep in it. Caroline's slicker tore away, leaving nothing in his hands but rubber. She lunged and caught his jacket and they continued their

306

rush downhill, locked in mud. They cascaded past avocado trees, black and sharp. Patrick sunk to his chest and his breath was cut to almost nothing. He struggled against the earth. Caroline gasped and flailed and Patrick saw the tree that they would hit. With a wild scream he pulled his arms free and when they crashed into the branches Patrick grabbed a heavy limb with both hands and held on with all the strength he knew. Somehow his mother got her arms around his middle and Patrick felt her weight and told himself yes, I can hold onto this branch forever if I need to, forever not a problem, hold, just hold . . .

Then, as if bored, the earth let go of him. Patrick looked downhill and saw the tractor on its side, moving with heavy, mudbound momentum. It lurched upright and the seat was empty. No one clutched the steering wheel. Patrick's heart dropped and he looked down at his mother, staring at the tractor, shock on her face. The tractor pitched upside-down again, surging away. Then Patrick heard faint tufts of words against the roar of the earth and the rain. Then there was movement in one of the uphill trees and he saw his father splayed awkwardly in the branches, spewing faint curses, one fist shaking.

Patrick looked down and watched the wall of mud, now divided by the stout trunk of the avocado tree, surging past them just a few inches below his dangling boots. Archie clambered higher into the tree. He looked like a bug in a spider web. The wall of mud blundered past beneath him. Patrick scanned the grove for the next earth slide but saw only the rain pounding down on the black windblown trees.

Then movement on the ridge above what had been Big Gorge. Patrick saw headlights, and, to his surprise, two vehicles. One was a passenger car and the other a mini-van, neither suited for this. Patrick watched them swerve and slide, their headlights raking left and right. His first thought was that they were trying to outrun the storm and had gotten very lost. Then he recognized the car as it shimmied to a stop.

The lights went off and Iris Cash jumped out and hustled around to the trunk and threw it open. Natalie and Mary Ann spilled out and they all took shovels from the trunk. Iris slammed it shut and the three women, buried in rain gear and using their shovels as staffs, came sidestepping down the hill toward them. The van picked its way along the high road and stopped well short of Iris's car. Evelyn Anders and her husband clambered out, shovels at the ready, and followed Iris down the slope. "Look," said Caroline.

Patrick said nothing as a white crew-cab pickup came across the ridge from the opposite direction. He recognized the logo on the door. The driver motored along at some speed, keeping the truck flush to the road with smooth corrections of the wheel. A moment later Lew Boardman climbed out and looked down and pulled a shovel from the truck bed. Two more men piled out and they found shovels too. A moment later they were bracing themselves down the slope. "Well," said Caroline. "Archie's God might have totally forgotten us, but our friends and neighbors haven't."

Patrick, in some amazement, watched the little platoon moving toward them. When he dropped to the ground it was solid enough to stand on and when he looked up at Iris he could see her clearly. The rain lessened and he heard the faint cadence of her breathing as she hurried slipping and sliding down the slope toward him.

308

34

Just after sunrise Patrick was readying his boat at the Glorietta Bay launch. *I'd Rather Be* was an aged fourteen-foot aluminum skiff with a dependable Honda engine and an outdated Lowrance fish-finder. His hours were complete, his license issued, his insurance current. He could guide two anglers. Salimony had kicked in five hundred twenty dollars toward the boat and Messina four hundred forty more – self-imposed fines for the rumble in Iris's home. They'd helped him shake her down and rebuild the Honda and now she was sound.

The late-March morning was cold, with wispy white clouds circling in from the northwest. Rain tonight, he thought, and a shiver wavered down his back. He was nervous enough as it was this morning. He checked the radio and the life preservers, the lunches and the electric motor. Checked them again. The seat pads were new and had set him back nearly a hundred dollars, but he'd saved five times that by refinishing the casting decks himself. *I'd Rather Be* reminded Patrick of his older dog, Jack – youth gone but still some good years left ahead. Like Jack, *I'd Rather Be* was optimistic and can-do.

He sat in the captain's chair and strung up the extra rods with fresh leader and flies. Ted was extra present with water, boats and fish. Patrick tried hard to let only the good memories squeeze in, and sometimes this worked. Sometimes he believed that he had done right by Ted. He told himself that he had helped Ted accomplish his one big thing, the thing he would be remembered for, and that Ted had made the world a small fraction better by this final act. And Patrick told himself that helping Ted be remembered for accomplishing it on his own was the best small dignity Patrick could give him. But sometimes he didn't believe any of that at all. Sometimes he felt that he had never known or loved his brother fully. And become his murderer. And let Ted take the blame that Patrick wanted to construe as credit. Thereby acquitting himself. At night his dreams broke him down and in his waking hours Patrick put himself back together.

Sangin still ran through everything he did, just more quietly. He flinched less, saw fewer ghosts, remembered less ugliness. But the only time he was really free of Sangin was when he was fishing or with Iris, or lost in thoughts of his boyhood, which, having ended at age seventeen, now seemed magical and important.

Sangin and Ted. Ted and Sangin.

The difference is Sangin meant nothing to you and Ted meant everything. Family was why you served. Family past and family present and maybe family future. Duty. Freedom. The United States of America. Nine-eleven. And your own small glory: be a man. Get some.

His phone throbbed in his pocket and he braced himself for a last-minute cancellation.

"You're working," said his father. "I trust."

"Yep."

"Rain tomorrow. A piddling half inch."

"I can see it coming. Did you blade that one-track on the north side?"

"Cakewalk. Pat – listen to this. I woke up way before the sun this morning, like I always do. I got coffee, checked the plumbing and the computer news. Soon as there was light I went out to the groves and did the standard drive-through. You will not believe what I found there, Pat. You will not."

310

Patrick checked his watch. "You better tell me soon because my sports just got here."

"*Life*. I saw life in the trees that the good lord and his mud bath left us with. Of course that's only half of the trees I had before the fire, but I'm pleased to still own that half, free and clear. Green on most of them, Pat, budding out and more to come! We can make it through this year cashing out the last of the investments, just barely. Then, we pray for no late frost or high winds in early fall – neither of which would surprise me, given my reputation upstairs. And now the Farm Credit bank will loan against my forty acres of life, believe me. My trees are going to get us through. Your mother, of course, is pleased. Got up early and dressed herself this morning very carefully, like she used to. She's starting to seem like . . . Caroline again. I've won, Patrick. I have *won!*"

And his father was starting to seem like Archie again, too, thought Patrick. The months of darkness were beginning to admit light. "I'm off to work, Pop."

"You and Iris on for dinner Saturday?"

"We'll be there."

"Fresh fish would be nice. Catch a big one for your mother and brother."

The two men came down the dock bedecked in new fly-fishing gear – boots and waders and belts and vests – none of which they would even need on the boat. But what was wrong with that? Patrick guessed each at roughly twice his age. They walked fast, talking and laughing as good friends do. Patrick saw the glimmer of the rods in the new sunlight and identified their high-end makers by color and sheen. The reels were shiny new and the lines were rigged for river trout.

First-timers, he thought. Just like me. Love is what you do. He offered his hand and welcomed aboard the first customer of his life.

311